FOXMAN AND THE CAT BURGLAR

FOXMAN
AND THE
CAT BURGLAR

A NOVEL

DELAS HERAS

DOUBLE SIX BOOKS | NEW YORK

DOUBLE SIX BOOKS
New York, New York

Foxman and the Cat Burglar is a work of fiction.
Names, places, and characters are all products of the author's imagination.
Any resemblance to actual locales, persons, or events, is entirely coincidental.

ISBN 978-1-7353175-3-3 (trade paperback)
ISBN 978-1-7353175-2-6 (ebook)

For Griffin, who changed everything

1. WILFREDO: THE CROCODILE IN THE CLOSET

October 2008

Steeling himself, Wilfredo grabbed hold of the closet's brass doorknob and flung open the door. A cardboard box filled with shiny participation trophies leaped out and did its best to brain him, but he stepped back in time and the trophies clattered harmlessly to the floor. An odor reminiscent of ripe Camembert cheese proved harder to dodge, and he held his breath as he hurried to crack open a window.

Wilfredo armed himself for battle, shoving his hands into thick rubber gloves and priming the heavy-duty cleaning spray. He had made a special trip up from the city just to clean out his old closet, borrowing a friend's car and speeding along winding highways and narrow country roads, until he arrived back at his childhood home in Beacon, New York. Wilfredo wished he could've just kicked the can down the road like he always did, but his mom had recently turned his old bedroom into an art studio for herself, and she needed his closet to store her materials.

Rolling up his sleeves, he took a closer look at the jumbled remnants of his past—old clothes, board games, Nerf guns, and VHS tapes from the eighties. Most of the stuff was garbage and he worked his way through it in unsentimental fashion. When he stumbled across any childhood treasures worth saving, he tossed them into the empty suitcase he had brought with him.

Soon, all that was left was the upper shelf. Standing on a step stool, Wilfredo finally caught a glimpse of the ventriloquist dummy tucked away behind a bin of old cassettes. *Ahh, Captain Pete, is it really you?* Carved out of wood, the puppet had a green crocodile face with gleaming white teeth and a navy blue captain's hat stapled to the top of its head. It had been a birthday present from Uncle Henry, and Wilfredo spent a big chunk of his middle school years perfecting a zany crocodilian voice, writing cringe-worthy jokes, and talking through a frozen smile. As a kid Wilfredo delighted in tugging on the hidden strings that manipulated Captain Pete's clackety jaw and his bulging eyes. But the Captain soon developed a bad habit of saying out loud the things Wilfredo was afraid to say, and of thinking things Wilfredo was afraid to think. He began hearing Captain Pete's sarcastic voice in his head during class, and at dinner, and while watching television, even if the dummy was nowhere near. Worried he was going crazy, young Wilfredo quit ventriloquism and stashed the dummy permanently on the topmost shelf of his bedroom closet. After that he built up a wall of junk between himself and Captain Pete, plugging holes and filling gaps, until one day, when he was twelve, the closet was full to bursting. Wilfredo had simply closed the door and slid his dresser in front of it, deciding that some dark corners of the universe were best sealed off forever.

Almost twenty years had passed since that moment, and Wilfredo was not a scrawny middle schooler anymore. He was a grown man, and a large one at that. Six feet tall, he had shoulder-length sandy brown hair and two days' worth of stubble on his cheeks. He was wearing an unbuttoned flannel shirt over a plain tee, cargo pants, and work boots—practical, manly clothing.

Hesitantly, Wilfredo grabbed hold of the wooden croc and stepped down to examine him in the light of a nearby standing lamp. The dummy had been well preserved in the total darkness of the closet, and Wilfredo felt foolish to have ever been afraid of this lifeless doll. Fond memories of his early days as a budding ventriloquist came flooding back to him.

Pulling off his rubber gloves, he slipped a hand into the dummy while his other hand grabbed hold of the stick that manipulated the crocodile's arm. He faced himself in the mirror that was hanging on the back of the closet door, and Captain Pete's eyes swiveled to look up at him.

"Hey there, big guy. Did you happen to see a pimple-faced kid, about yay high?" The doll's arm hovered about five feet off the ground. *"With a rat's nest of hair and a gap-tooth smile? That brat pulled a Houdini on me a while back."*

"Captain! It's me, Wilfredo. Don't you recognize me?"

"Freddy? 'Zat really you? You look like you need a shave! And why are you dressed like a lumberjack?"

"It's nice to see you too, Captain."

"Well, well. Freddy. Where have you been hiding?" The Captain grinned at him maniacally in the mirror, his fixed expression changed only by the furtiveness of his eyes. *"How old are you now, anyway?"*

"I'm thirty-two."

"*Wait. Are you telling me I've been shut away in there for nearly twenty years?*"

"The good news is you don't look a day older."

"*It's impossible to keep track of time in that closet. I thought maybe a few months had gone by, and then it started feeling like maybe a whole year, but . . . twenty years! I'll never get that time back.*"

"I'm sorry, Captain. I guess ventriloquism just wasn't my bag."

"*Are you kidding? You were a natural! We could've been great. But instead you left me sitting in the dark, fighting off moths determined to turn my hat into their lunch.*"

"I'm sorry, Captain. But I finally got you out. Better late than never, right?"

The Captain glared at him. "*So where are you living these days?*"

"I'm renting a small place in the city with a friend."

"*Sounds perfect. A change of scenery is just what the doctor ordered.*"

"I'd love to bring you back with me, Captain. I really would. But I just don't have the room. My closets in town are jam-packed."

"*Who said anything about closets? Enough with closets already! If I never see the inside of another closet again it will be too soon.*"

Wilfredo pulled at the dummy's strings so that he did an eye roll. He waved around the croc's hand in dramatic fashion. "Well what do you want me to do? Put you on a bookshelf for all the world to see?"

"*Freddy, Freddy, Freddy. You were always ashamed of me.*

Please don't make me beg. I'm a grown croc. Let me hold on to a shred of my dignity. We used to be pals, right? You can't leave me here."

"I wasn't gonna leave you here."

"I knew it!"

"I was gonna shove you in that plastic bag and leave you by the curb."

"Hilarious, Freddy." The dummy did a pretend clapping motion. "You should write that joke down before you forget it. But I know you would never do that to a friend, would you, Freddy?" A wavering note of insecurity had crept into the Captain's voice, and those googly eyes were staring up at him imploringly.

Wilfredo sighed. Captain Pete was exactly the sort of thing he didn't need back in his apartment. Yet, he couldn't bring himself to throw the carved wooden figure in the trash. "Okay. You win this round, Captain." Somehow, the croc managed to look relieved. Wilfredo propped the dummy up on his nearly full suitcase and turned his attention back to the closet.

The smell of warm biscuits drifted up the stairs from the kitchen, where his mother was cooking dinner to the sound of Ray Charles's "Georgia on My Mind." Outside, gusts of wind from the brewing storm whistled through the oak trees surrounding the house, battering the windowpanes with sporadic onslaughts of rain.

It wasn't long before he was knotting up the last trash bag. He could hardly believe it—the closet was bare. The only things he hadn't found were his old yearbooks. Glancing around the room his eyes snagged on his sister's college trunk, shoved in a corner. Wilfredo dragged the faux leather

chest into the light and threw back the lid. Colorful leotards
and frizzy tutus filled the old trunk. He was about to slam it
shut when he glimpsed bright orange fabric poking out from
under a pile of silk and tulle. A spark of recognition flitted
through his brain. Reaching in he fished out the fox costume
he'd worn in high school for a musical adaptation of Pinocchio. The costume was a little faded, but it had kept its thick
wooly texture. He flashed to an image of himself fifteen years
earlier standing onstage in his high school auditorium in this
fuzzy orange-and-white onesie.

Hey, Freddy, why don't you try it on? The Captain's sarcastic voice resonated inside his head, jerking Wilfredo from his
thoughts. *You know you want to.*

Wilfredo looked from the fox costume in his hands
over to Captain Pete, still perched on the suitcase. That stupid croc was not wrong. Stripping down to his gray boxer
briefs, Wilfredo stepped into the woolly paws and shoved
his hands into the sleeves. He zipped up the body of the
costume and pulled the elasticized hood over his head. He
stood there with his hands on his hips and examined his
reflection in the mirror. His bristly cheeks were framed by
the furry hood that obscured the top half of his face. Two
oval cutouts circled his eyes and stiff triangular ears poked
out of the top of his head. He turned sideways and cast a
critical glance at the fluffy orange tail protruding from his
backside. He looked even goofier now than he had back in
high school. Wilfredo patted the bulge around his midsec-
tion and told himself that he really needed to cut down on
his weekly beer count. So much for being magically trans-
ported back in time.

Hey, Freddy, you've lost your girlish figure!

Turning to face the doll, Wilfredo scowled. "I'm starting to remember why I left you in the closet for the past twenty years."

You gotta admit it wouldn't hurt you to hit the gym once in a while. Maybe ease up on the cheesecake?

"No one asked you, Captain."

Suddenly Wilfredo heard his mom's voice coming from the hallway. "Wilfredo! Who are you talking to?" The door creaked open and he turned to see his mother framed in the doorway staring at him, mouth agape. She was a compact woman with an old-fashioned beehive of dyed blond hair, dressed in the purple tracksuit that she always wore around the house. "For heaven's sake! Wilfredo! Why are you wearing that old costume?"

"I was just curious to see if it still fit," he said sheepishly.

"Well I suppose it does, in a way. You fill it out better than you did back then."

"Thanks, Mom."

"I meant it as a compliment. Nobody likes a skinny Santa! Seeing you in that suit really takes me back. You were great up onstage."

"I never had any talent, Mom."

"You just never found the right roles!"

"Because there wasn't a role out there that I couldn't run into the ground."

"Well, it all worked out in the end. I'm so proud of you, Wilfredo. Being a Broadway set designer is a huge accomplishment!"

"For the last time, Mom, I'm not a set designer. I'm part of the team that builds them."

"Just because some fancy-pants swoops in and takes the credit doesn't mean you aren't the real creative force." She took a few halting steps toward the closet and peered into the vacant interior. "I can hardly believe it! After all these years!"

"About that—I'm really sorry, Mom. It shouldn't have taken me this long."

"Forget it, sweetie," she said with a smile. Then she turned and spied Captain Pete. "And would you look at that—you found your old ventriloquist dummy! I bet you forgot all about him." Wilfredo shrugged. "Now take off that silly costume and come downstairs. The mac and cheese is cooling on the counter. Extra breadcrumbs, just how you like it. Are you sure you don't want to spend the night? I don't like the idea of you driving back in this weather."

"No, Mom. I've gotta be at the workshop by eight a.m. to help paint the scenery for the new play we're setting up for."

His mother went back down to her kitchen while Wilfredo changed back into his street clothes. There was just enough room left in his suitcase for him to cram in the fox costume. The Village Halloween parade was coming up and he liked to march in it every year with his theater buddies. This fox outfit was sure to be a hit at this year's celebration.

You taking that stuff down to the car? I'll give you a hand! croaked Captain Pete.

"You just don't want to get left behind. I'm onto you. Let's hope there's room for you in the trunk of the car." Wilfredo was already regretting his decision to bring the dummy back with him.

The trunk? Did I mention I'm claustrophobic? I call shotgun!

2. CASSANDRA: UNFORESEEN ENTANGLEMENTS

Cassandra had kept Gregory waiting outside the movie theater for half an hour last Saturday—in the rain. It wasn't entirely her fault. As an aspiring actress she was at the mercy of casting directors and their scheduling whims. But since then her fiancé had become fixated on her lack of punctuality. "I bet you anything you'll be late to our wedding!" he'd said reproachfully as they walked home after the film. Cassandra rolled her eyes and said nothing. She was pretty sure that brides were supposed to arrive late to their own weddings. It was a thing.

Her day job, the one that paid the bills, was as a sales clerk at the Upper West Side Baylor & Bowman department store. She was currently standing behind the counter in Bags and Accessories, keeping one eye on the manager hovering nearby and the other on the clock. She was meeting Gregory at 6:45 outside of his favorite restaurant—La Fontaine—down in the Village. And no auditions meant no excuses. It irked her that Gregory seemed to view their dinner plans tonight as some sort of a test. Nevertheless, as quitting time approached, she got ready to bolt. With no customers around she touched up her makeup in the tabletop mirror, smoothed the collar of her floral-patterned blouse, and pulled her long brown hair over to one side of her face.

At 6 on the nose she slipped into the employee area of the store, stamped her timesheet, and grabbed her backpack and jacket from her locker. Then she darted down the stairs and ducked out of the service door. She hung a right on Sixty-Sixth Street, heading for the subway entrance. With a little luck she would beat Gregory to the spot.

But moments later she skidded to a halt on the sidewalk. Out of the corner of her eye she'd spotted a tiny bird with greenish gray feathers, hopping pitifully in the gutter. She leaned in closer. The poor thing was clearly hurt. Nearby pedestrians were oblivious to the injured creature, with the exception of a bald man with binoculars hanging from his neck, who approached and peered down at the bird. "That's a hermit warbler!" he said. "He's got those distinctive yellow cheeks and dark beak. Not many of those around here."

"He looks like he needs help."

"Poor fella seems dazed. He might've flown into a window."

"What should we do?"

The man walked over to an overflowing trash can on the corner and plucked a crumpled paper bag from it, smoothing it out with his hands. "Try putting him in here."

Cassandra took the bag from him, then she reached down and gently scooped up the pretty little bird, depositing him gingerly in the empty bag. The bird put up no resistance and immediately tucked his beak under his wing. She tried handing the bag back to the man, but he held up his hands. "He's all yours, lady."

"What am I supposed to do with him?"

"There's a bird sanctuary up on Columbus and

Eighty-Seventh. Try bringing him there. They'll take good care of him."

"But I'm in a rush!"

"You and me both. I gotta pick up my kid from her after-school program and drop her off at my ex-wife's!"

"Eighty-Seventh and Columbus? Are you sure?"

"Thereabouts." He gave her an apologetic smile before walking away.

She poked tiny holes in the brown paper bag with her fingernail, then she headed north, cradling it in her hands. It turned out to be a twenty-minute walk, and by the time she handed off the bag to a kindly old woman at the sanctuary, she was running horribly late. She dashed over to the closest subway, swiped her card, ran down the steps to the platform, and hopped on a downtown B train that had just pulled into the station.

The train she ended up on seemed content to mosey from station to station at a snail's pace. The subway operator appeared entirely unconcerned with getting New Yorkers from point A to point B in a timely fashion. Cassandra swung her backpack off her shoulders and parked herself on a grubby orange bench with a sigh. She glanced down at her lock screen and her green eyes went wide—how was it 6:35 already?

Gregory had already arrived at the restaurant, naturally, and he'd been texting her nonstop. She had sketched out her injured bird story in a series of texts, complete with a photo for proof. But Gregory seemed completely immune to the tiny bird's ordeal. He had pointed out that "It was always something with her." And followed that up closely with an "If it's not one thing it's another."

Cassandra tapped out another quick "Be there soon" text but it failed to send from inside the tunnel. She stared at her reflection in the subway car window and her exasperated thirty-three-year-old self stared right back at her. She still read parts written for twentysomething characters and no one ever suspected a thing. But for how much longer?

The train rocked wildly on a twisting stretch of track and Cassandra latched onto a pole to stop herself from sliding in her seat. The engagement ring on her hand glimmered as it caught the light. Gregory had popped the question at a crowded family barbecue a month ago, catching her completely off guard on the second anniversary of their first date. He'd put her on the spot in front of her future mother-in-law, so of course Cassandra had said yes, ignoring the niggling doubts in the back of her mind.

Doubts that had only grown stronger of late. Something had shifted subtly in their dynamic once they became engaged. It was as if Gregory expected her to be grateful that he'd proposed. He had this pet theory that eligible men in New York were commitment phobes. Players who bounced from girlfriend to girlfriend in a never-ending succession. For all Cassandra knew that might be true, but she didn't see what it had to do with them. And she was getting tired of her fiancé acting like he deserved a medal for yanking her off the shelf before she hit her sell-by date.

As her train approached Thirty-Fourth Street a garbled announcement declared that the train would be making all local stops. Which meant she still had four stops to go before she arrived at West Fourth Street. Her latest "Sorry I'm late. Be there in five" text finally zipped through the ether as she caught a fleeting cell signal. Gregory replied quickly with a snide "As always" and an angry face emoji. Cassandra swiped it away. She was annoyed with *him* now too. He was probably staring at the second hand of his Swiss watch, the one that was synced to the atomic clock somewhere.

At Twenty-Third Street the train stood in the station with the doors wide open for five minutes. Cassandra glanced at her phone again and grimaced. She slid the device into her back pocket mindlessly. She'd get there when she got there.

The doors finally closed and the train began to move. Another stop came and went, and the train picked up speed. West Fourth, her stop, was next. They were so close. The number of passengers had thinned out and Cassandra was now sitting by herself at the very front of the train. She hopped to her feet and put her arms through the loops of her backpack, securing the sternum strap so it was nice and snug. Then she parked herself in front of the doors just as the white-tiled station streaked into view through the windows. The train came to a stop with a final jerk, the doors swished open, and she stepped through them out onto the platform.

Oh crap, where's my phone?

Cassandra stopped short just beyond the doors as she patted down her jacket pockets. Nothing. Her heart began to race. She swiveled around and glanced back at her now-empty seat. Nothing. Her phone was not the latest and greatest, and yes the screen was cracked, but still—her whole world was in that phone. She rechecked her pockets again with the same results, and then she reached around to feel in her back pocket. Oh thank god. How she had managed to shove her phone into her back pocket from a seated position would go down as a mystery for the ages. But the important thing was she hadn't lost it.

Cassandra took a step forward just as the doors slid shut behind her, only to discover she was somehow stuck. *Oh no—what's happening? This is bad.* Peering over her shoulder she saw that a dangling clasp of her backpack had managed to wedge itself in the jaws of the door. Her first thought was to quickly ditch the backpack. *But—my wallet, my credit card, my keys!*

Panic-stricken, she lunged forward, attempting to break free by brute force. But she was yanked to an abrupt stop. The door had clamped onto the buckle of the wayward strap and wasn't letting go.

A man's voice on the platform nearby yelled at her to take off the backpack.

"No . . . I can't!" she gasped.

And she couldn't. It was too late already. Horrifyingly, the train had begun to move. To her left loomed the cavernous entrance to the tunnel. Her mind boggled at her own stupidity as a dismaying thought popped into her head—*this is how I'm going to die.* In her mind's eye she could see Gregory standing at a lectern, pompously doling out her eulogy to a teary-eyed crowd. *This is not happening.* Cassandra strained forward once more, with no better luck than before. She began to crab-walk sideways in a frantic effort to stay on her feet.

3. WILFREDO: AN UNLIKELY HERO

Wilfredo had been holed up in the theater's workshop all day making new legs for a cabinet television from the 1950s that played a big role in the play's staging. In the world of theater, every prop had to be rock-solid so it would withstand the daily rigors of the stage. All he had left was to screw the fourth leg into place and cement it with some industrial-strength adhesive. The hazy sky glimpsed through the workshop's windows was growing dimmer as quitting time approached. He couldn't wait to get home and park himself on the couch with a cold beer.

This old television set reminded Wilfredo of all the Saturday afternoons he'd spent as a kid watching classic westerns with his granddad. Pops was a big fan of the old shoot-'em-ups and every week the two of them would spend a few hours glued to the TV screen. The rough-and-tumble life in the Old West had cast a strong spell on Wilfredo's young imagination. He had idolized the figure of the lone lawman, marching into a saloon and confronting a band of outlaws with nothing but a six-shooter and a badge. Deep down, he saw himself as the same kind of man as those tight-lipped technicolor heroes—honest, fearless, and willing to put his life on the line when it mattered.

Sadly, his own life was notably lacking in heroic moments

as his daily routine presented him with few opportunities for proving his worth. The biggest risk he'd taken today was ordering the black-bean-and-chipotle taquitos from the Mexican deli for lunch.

Face it, Freddy—you're not the hero type! You're more what you might call an average Joe! Captain Pete's mocking voice echoed in his head.

Wilfredo's face clouded over. Bringing that stupid doll back to the city had been a big mistake. "I'm warning you, Captain," he mumbled under his breath. "Any more nonsense from you and I'll chuck you off a bridge."

Leaving the old cabinet upside down so the glue could set overnight, Wilfredo folded up the drop cloth and went to clean his hands in the utility sink. Almost everyone else had left for the day, but one of the few people still kicking about was Toby, his friend and roommate. Toby was a lanky guy with dark curly hair, well-defined sideburns, and round wire-rim glasses. He had a fondness for vintage tees, and today's pick was a yellow Earth Wind & Fire concert shirt, neatly pressed and tucked into his jeans. Toby liked to bounce around the workroom doing ten things at once and popping up when you least expected him. Like he did right now when he appeared directly behind Wilfredo, who was still washing his hands. "All done for the day?" Toby yelled over the running water.

A startled Wilfredo nearly jumped out of his boots. "I thought we'd talked about you not sneaking up on people?"

"Sorry, buddy," Toby said cheerfully. He had one of those wide, disarming smiles that made it hard to hold anything against him. He was a great roommate, except for his habit of binge-watching anime for hours while munching on dry cereal.

Wilfredo wiped his hands on a rag. "Yeah, I'm all done. I'll see you back at the ranch."

Toby shot him a reproachful look. "Don't get too comfortable on my couch."

"For the last time, it's not your couch. Or your television. We went splitsies on both. And come to think of it, I paid for half of that cereal you're gonna eat for dinner."

"Cheapskate!" Toby flashed his electric smile.

"Couch potato!" With this parting jibe Wilfredo grabbed his jacket and made his way out the back. Two flights down he pushed through a creaky metal door and stepped out onto the street. A steady drizzle was coming down, turning the asphalt slick and dark. He set out on foot in the direction of the West Fourth Street subway and soon found himself trudging down the familiar steps to the orange line platform. He got there just in time to see the red taillights of a downtown F train retreating into the tunnel to his right.

The missed train had swept the platform clear, but after a few minutes other passengers began to materialize around him, so Wilfredo wandered down to the far end of the platform, where the arriving train cars were typically less crowded. He snuck along a narrow stretch of the platform until he reached an empty nook behind the stairs.

There was a large poster for a cruise line framed on the tiled wall. The advertisement was staged from the point of view of a young woman sitting on the deck of a cruise ship with a fancy cocktail in her hand. Her bronzed legs stretched out seductively in the foreground while turquoise waters sparkled at her feet and palm trees rose out of white sand in the distance. Staring at this poster Wilfredo wondered if it might be time to use some of those vacation days he had saved up. A little time in the sun with the ocean breeze rippling through his hair might do wonders for his outlook on life.

Who are you trying to kid, Freddy? You could never get a girl like that.

"Seriously. Captain. Stay out of my head."

When was the last time you even went out on a date? Wait, don't tell me, you've been striking out ever since that Nadia chick dumped you three years ago.

"I'll have you know I've been out on several dates since Nadia."

Dead-end dates to Nowhereville. You know what your problem is, Freddy? You're too nice. Haven't you ever heard that nice guys finish last?

Wilfredo wasn't about to argue with that. Nadia had treated him like a doormat. Then she'd dumped him unceremoniously for a flashy, motorcycle-riding insurance salesman named Zack. Five good years flushed down the toilet because of a fifty-thousand-dollar Kawasaki and a distressed leather jacket. If Wilfredo's life were a western movie, then Nadia would play the role of the villainess who had stolen his gun, stripped him of his badge, and left him to wander alone in the wilderness while the buzzards circled overhead.

Wilfredo detected the growing whisper of an approaching train. A minute later it glided into the station and he was disappointed to note that it was a B train. He watched it coast to a stop, the doors parted, and a young woman stepped out.

She came to an abrupt stop and patted her jacket pockets, a look of alarm spreading on her face.

Pickpockets were rampant on the subways and Wilfredo wondered if this pretty chestnut-haired girl was their latest victim. He didn't mean to stare but he was intrigued by the minor drama she was caught up in. Seconds passed, then an expression of relief flooded her face as she dug her phone out from a back pocket—crisis averted.

A beep sounded, the subway doors slid closed behind her, and she continued on her way. Or tried to at least. She was wearing a backpack and from the look of panic that came over her, Wilfredo realized that a loose strap must have gotten stuck in the doors. She threw herself forward, but it wasn't budging.

"Ditch the bag!" he called out, stepping toward her.

"I can't!" She lunged forward again, but the strap still anchored her in place.

Then the train began to move, and she was forced to side-step as it pulled her along the platform toward the tunnel entrance only a few feet away. Time froze, and in some dusty corner of Wilfredo's brain a light began to flash red. This was it. The opportunity he had been waiting for. The world sped up again, and Wilfredo leaped toward her, wrapping his arms around her and pulling back with all his strength.

With their combined weight the strap finally broke free and the two of them toppled away from the train. He tried to keep his balance, but his leg got tangled with one of hers and the next thing he knew he was falling backward. He landed flat on his back on the platform, the jolt taken mostly by his tailbone and elbow, while she fell directly on top of him, knocking the wind out of him. They both lay there stock-still, her face inches away from his own, her green eyes wide and panicked as she sucked in deep breaths of air.

"Are you okay?" he asked quietly. "That was a close call."

"I-I think so," she stammered. "You?"

"Yes, I'm fine," he mumbled. This wasn't quite true, his elbow hurt some, and his tailbone stung even more. He was also lying on a subway platform that was probably caked with decades' worth of human filth. On the other hand, this was the most contact he'd had with a member of the opposite sex in years.

"I thought I was going to die. But I'm okay—thanks to you." It finally dawned on her that she was lying on top of him and her expression changed to one of apologetic horror. She sprang to her feet. Wilfredo stood up as well, moving a little more gingerly than her, rubbing his elbow and brushing off his backside.

She looked around in disbelief. With the staircase blocking them from view their little mishap had passed unnoticed by their fellow passengers. It was just the two of them standing in that little bubble on the platform. She leaned back against the cruise line poster, closed her eyes, and let out a slow whistling breath. "I can't believe that just happened," she said.

Wilfredo decided to ask the question that was bugging him. "Why didn't you just take off your bag right away?"

She opened her eyes. "Because I'm an idiot."

That sounded about right. Wilfredo knew the feeling. "Well, next time maybe don't stop short right by the doors?"

"Don't worry. I'll be taking the bus from now on. Or not leaving my apartment." She pushed off from the wall and turned to face him. "I'm Cassandra by the way."

"Nice to meet you, Cassandra. I'm Wilfredo."

"Here's the thing, Wilfredo. I think you just saved my life."

"Well, let's not get carried away," he replied, even though that corner of his head where the alarm bells had been ringing a minute ago had transformed into a conga line celebration replete with disco balls, popped corks, and noisemakers.

"Seriously. Things could've gotten real ugly if you hadn't grabbed hold of me . . . I mean, I've seen it in the news—stories of passengers getting dragged to their deaths. But I never dreamed it might happen to me."

"I'm glad you're okay."

She noticed him rubbing his elbow. "You *are* hurt!"

"Oh, it's nothing. Banged my elbow a bit." Her piercing eyes burned into his own, and he felt a nervous flutter in his stomach.

She brushed a stray lock of hair out of her eyes. "I feel like I should buy you a drink or something. I have dinner plans, but maybe you'd like to join us?"

"That's okay. I don't want to intrude on your dinner."

"How about we meet up this weekend then and you let me buy you a coffee and a cupcake or something and thank you properly?"

"I'd like that," Wilfredo replied, trying to appear calm, even though his heart was racing again. Had they just made a date?

The loud roar of an approaching train made them both look up. This time the orange circle on the front had an *F*.

"Is that your train?" she asked.

"Yes."

She reached into her bag, pulled out a small notebook and a pen, and quickly scratched out her name and number. Tearing off the sheet, she handed it to him, and he folded it up and tucked it deep into a pocket of his wallet.

"Text me," she said emphatically.

"I will."

She brushed dust from her blouse and pants and flipped her hair back. "Wilfredo, you're a life-saver. Literally." And then she flung herself at him, wrapping her arms around him in a tight hug. For the second time in five minutes, Wilfredo found himself locked in an embrace with this beautiful stranger.

The train came to a stop, the doors parted, and Cassandra let go of him, taking a big step back. Wilfredo turned and hopped reluctantly into the train car.

"Don't forget to text me!" she yelled as the doors slid closed between them.

"I won't," he assured her. "Forget, I mean!" he added quickly. But the doors were already shut. The train rolled away and moments later he was staring out at the blackness of the tunnel.

Freddy, my boy, it looks like Lady Luck has dropped the catch of the day in your lap! Reminds me of the time a six-foot halibut jumped into my boat, landing right at my feet!

The Captain sounded jubilant, but Wilfredo was in too much of a daze to pay him any attention.

4. CASSANDRA: CHIANTI AND DUCK

She spotted Gregory outside La Fontaine as she drew closer, and right away she knew he was in a lousy mood. He was standing stiffly in his herringbone coat, his neatly parted black hair glistening under the lamplight. His chin was lifted high as he scowled at the world through his tortoise-shell glasses. Rattled by her close call, she had spent the short walk from the subway to the restaurant picturing the Cassandra-shaped hole that would have been left in the world if her life was cut short. She wasn't in the right headspace to cope with irate fiancés. Their eyes locked as he caught sight of her in the crosswalk, and moments later, when she came to a halt in front of him he didn't move in to kiss her.

She took a deep breath: "You'll never believe what just happened to me—"

"What, no apology? No, 'sorry I'm so late, honey'? 'Sorry you were left standing outside the restaurant for half an hour—again!' Just because of some stupid bird!"

"I am sorry," she lied. "But let's not argue about the bird. The thing is—I almost died just now."

"What on earth are you talking about?"

"My backpack got stuck in the subway doors five minutes ago and I was nearly dragged off the platform. If it wasn't for the quick action of a stranger who grabbed me and pulled me to safety I wouldn't be standing here right now."

"A stranger? What stranger? I hope this person didn't manhandle you?"

"Of course not! He saved me! He threw his arms around me and helped me break free."

"I don't like the idea of strange men grabbing my fiancée on the subway."

"Focus, Gregory. I almost died."

"Are you sure you're not being overly dramatic? A lot of people get things caught in the subway doors every day without getting themselves killed."

"I was about three steps away from being pulled into a tunnel. I suppose it's possible I might have been just horribly mangled . . ." Was she exaggerating the whole incident? She didn't think so. She could still feel the adrenaline coursing through her.

His expression softened and he closed the gap between them, wrapping his arms around her. "Well, darling, I can see you've had a big scare. I'm glad you're okay." And just like that, as he held her, gently stroking her hair, it was as if her old Gregory was back.

"Come on," he said a minute later, holding her at arm's length and giving her a reassuring look. "Let's go inside and you can tell me all the gory details. A bite of food will do you a world of good. Hopefully they are still holding our table." Cassandra followed him through the restaurant doors. Lit by yellow globe lights, the cozy bistro was a buzzing hive of activity. Patrons sat in the café chairs that flanked the rustic wood tables while staff dressed in white wove gracefully around them. Art Nouveau posters and rows of wine bottles decorated the walls. Ceiling fans twirled overhead. The hostess led them through the restaurant to a small table in the back near the kitchen that Gregory was less than thrilled with. Cassandra proceeded to give him a blow-by-blow account of her subway mishap, and he listened with an arched eyebrow.

"And that's the whole story. I'm a bit shaken up."

He reached out and patted her hand. "Don't give it another thought, honeybun. There's nothing to be gained by dwelling on a near miss."

"I just keep imagining that in some other universe the me who stepped off that train was dashed on the tracks, but in this world I'm walking around as if nothing happened."

"That's because nothing happened. Now how about we take a look at this menu?" His face took on a look of deep concentration as he perused the list of specials. But he was startled when the kitchen door banged open right behind him and a waiter burst through carrying a loaded tray. "Blasted door!" he muttered, shooting the waiter a venomous look. "I don't know why she had to seat us all the way back here."

Cassandra silently appraised her fiancé. Whenever Gregory got mad, he always reminded her of an angry quacking duck. It had something to do with the way he puckered his lips. Gregory glanced up and caught her watching him. "What are you smiling about?"

"Nothing," she said innocently.

"Did you hit your head when you fell?"

"No. I'm afraid my rescuer bore the brunt of the fall. I landed on top of him."

"Of course you did! Let's hope this subway fellow didn't follow you here. You really need to be more vigilant about strangers on the subway."

In the blink of an eye that spiteful Gregory was back in the driver's seat. Cassandra sighed. "That stranger saved my life. And he has a name—Wilfredo."

"You exchanged names?" Gregory looked appalled. "What an odd name too. What did this guy look like? Was he homeless?"

"He looked like a normal guy. He was wearing cargo pants and a flannel shirt. I noticed some paint splatters on his pants, so I'm guessing he may be a house painter. I didn't ask."

"Blue collar. I suppose that's better than homeless. Well, thankfully you'll never run into him again."

"Do you *have* to be so snobbish?"

"I'm not snobbish. I just don't see the value in being ordinary."

Cassandra cleared her throat. "I wouldn't be surprised if I *did* see him again, since I gave him my phone number and offered to take him out for coffee this weekend. You know— to thank him."

The wine menu jumped out of Gregory's hands, landing at the feet of a nearby waiter, who stooped to pick it up. Her fiancé stared at her aghast. "You did *what*?"

"Gave him my number," Cassandra repeated, enunciating the words slowly and looking him right in the eyes. She tore a slice of warm bread from the basket and scraped a dab of butter onto it. As she took a bite she wondered whether the urge to stab your fiancé in the thigh with a butter knife could be considered a red flag. "What did you want me to do, just say thanks very much and hurry off? You can join us for coffee if you like, but you would have to appear grateful."

Her sarcasm was lost on her future husband. "Well, Cassandra, I have to say I'm quite astonished by your actions. It's bad enough that you insist on wandering around the city rescuing stray pigeons, but then I hear you've been rolling around on a subway platform with random men?"

Cassandra glared at him. Surely buying Wilfredo a warm beverage and extending him a sincere thank-you was the bare minimum required of someone in her position. They fell silent for a stretch as they studied the menu. La Fontaine was an upscale bistro with pricey entrees that ran heavy on fish and meat, with barely a token option for vegetarians like herself. Cassandra zeroed in on the ravioli with zucchini and shaved black truffle, a decent pasta dish that she had ordered before. She wasn't a huge zucchini fan, but it would have to do. If it were up to her, they would have gone for cheap Mexican tonight, but Gregory had balked at her suggestion, insisting that they needed to take their gastronomic choices up a notch.

A familiar waitress with stringy blond hair appeared to take their order, digging a notepad out of her apron. Cassandra put in her pasta order, and the woman scribbled it down. Gregory picked out a bottle of Chianti without consulting her, then he hesitated as he eyed the menu. "I'm torn between le coq au vin and the roasted duck special. Which would you recommend?"

The waitress, a large woman with the cautious smile of a veteran server, mulled over his question. "The duck is a popular choice, sir."

Cassandra could've told him that. When she'd worked as a waitress the managers had always instructed them to push the specials. And then it hit her. A mental picture of Gregory poised knife and fork in hand over a steaming roasted duck that was staring back up at him with his own pouting face plastered on it. "Don't forget about the trout, honey?" she said quickly. "You're always raving about it to everyone."

"I'm not in the mood for fish tonight."

"The duck seems like a risky choice to me."

"Nonsense. I'm sure they know how to make a top-notch roast duck." He faced the waitress and said: "I'll have the duck." Cassandra cringed.

The conversation turned to wedding cakes. Gregory had spent the past week researching bakers and he was eager to give her the lowdown. She didn't have strong opinions when it came to cakes. If Gregory wanted a floral pistachio cake with vanilla fondant that was fine with her. She nodded along.

"Great. I'll call the bakers and set up some taste tests. Listen, darling, I wanted to talk to you about inviting the managing directors at my firm to the wedding."

Cassandra frowned. When it came to their wedding the real battle line was the wedding list. Gregory was constantly adding family friends and work colleagues to the list, and the intimate celebration she had envisioned was ballooning out of control. "But I thought we'd agreed—close family and friends only!"

"Yes, honey. But you need to understand that inviting

the partners would be extremely helpful to my career." Cassandra had met these men at the company Christmas party last year. Each of them was more wizened and ancient than the next. She pictured them all sitting in the front row at the ceremony.

"I suppose that would include their wives too?"

"Naturally."

"What about our budget? We can't just keep expanding the guest list. My dad will flip out when he sees how much this is going to cost. And every time a vendor gives us a price list you pick the most extravagant option!"

"Don't worry about your father, darling. I'll have a chat with him. He can pay for your dress and the ceremony, and I'm happy to pick up the rest." Thanks to his position as chief contracts officer for Sullivan, Stanley & Moore, Gregory had been raking in the dough for the past few years.

"My dad won't like that idea."

"Are you kidding? Your father loves me. He will absolutely be fine with it." Cassandra's mouth twisted to one side. It was true, her father approved of Gregory, and he probably wouldn't put up much of a fight if her fiancé insisted on footing the bulk of the bill. In one fell swoop her cost objections to a large wedding were crushed. Gregory smiled smugly. Cassandra realized with horror that she was dealing with a full-blown Groomzilla who had just burst free of his chains.

Gregory dabbed his lips with his napkin, then broke into a wide smile. "You know," he said, "we can always just hire a wedding planner. Let a professional sweat all the organizing headaches!" He beamed and sloshed his wine around in his glass.

Cassandra winced. She couldn't think of anything worse than hiring a stranger to plan their special day. Her eyes narrowed. "We don't need a wedding planner, Gregory," she said firmly. "What would really help is if we took a machete to the wedding list and hacked it to bits. So unless this wedding planner of yours is some sort of machete-wielding virtuoso I'm not interested."

"I knew you wouldn't like my idea."

"Under a hundred guests, remember? That was what we talked about."

"Well plans can change."

"Then why don't we just elope at City Hall like I wanted to do?" Gregory looked as if she had just lobbed a hand grenade into the bread basket. He pushed back his chair and pulled what she'd come to think of as his "incredulous duck" look. Then the quacking began as he went off on a long rant about how much seeing him walk down the aisle meant to his mother and how they would recoup most of their expenses from generous wedding gifts.

Cassandra listened resignedly. He was in full courtroom mode, gesticulating wildly as he made his impassioned plea in favor of a larger wedding. She wouldn't be able to get a word in edgewise until he ran out of steam. When had he become so overbearing? Where was the delightful man she knew and loved? She took a sip of water, her engagement ring clinking against the stem of the glass. Gregory finished his fiery speech and peered at her to see if it had softened her position at all. She gazed back at him coolly.

"Just promise me you'll think about it, okay?"

She shrugged.

Their dinner arrived moments later and Gregory looked relieved, nodding to the server gratefully when she topped off his wineglass. Cassandra poked at her steaming ravioli with her fork half-heartedly while her fiancé carved off a chunk of flesh from the duck breast, speared a carrot, and stuffed the forkful into his mouth. Gregory looked up from his food and noticed her watching him. "You're making a face," he grumbled. "Just pretend it's chicken. You're supposed to be good at pretending right?"

"I *am* good at pretending," she replied. "Sometimes I wonder if maybe I'm a little *too* good at pretending."

5. WILFREDO:
THE BEER RUN FROM HELL

Night had descended on the city by the time Wilfredo emerged from the subway. Lights dotted the dark silhouettes of the buildings around him, while the gray clouds blanketing the sky were lit up by the city's glow. He trudged down the pebbled concrete sidewalk, past the food cart selling empanadas, weaving his way through the handful of oncoming pedestrians. He had a slightly troubled look on his face as a nagging worry took root in his mind. Beer bottles had been vanishing inexplicably from their fridge in recent weeks. When he had accused Toby of drinking bottles on the sly, his friend vehemently denied it. Not wanting to make a fuss, Wilfredo had joked that it must be the work of the "Beer Fairy," even though he didn't consider it a laughing matter. And if he ever got his hands on this thieving Beer Fairy there was going to be hell to pay. But in light of these mysterious fridge disappearances Wilfredo decided that the safest thing would be to stop at the small deli on Rivington and pick up reinforcements. There was no point in leaving this kind of thing to chance.

He continued his eastward march along Delancey, keeping step with a sprinkling of fellow pedestrians, the headlights from cars coming off the Williamsburg Bridge making the shadows dance around him. Taking a left on Suffolk, the street turned bleak and empty around him. Having settled the tricky problem of the beer, his thoughts had drifted back to his encounter with Cassandra. He replayed the whole scene over in his head—seizing hold of her, falling backward, her radiant face suspended right above his own, their friendly chat, and the goodbye hug. Her precious number was tucked safely inside his wallet, but he would wait a day before contacting her so that he didn't come across as overeager.

Don't wait too long, Freddy, the Captain chimed in. *Or you might chicken out! You need to strike while the iron is hot.*

"I know," he replied under his breath. "I'll shoot her a text tomorrow." The thought sent a little jolt of fear coursing through him.

You gotta play it cool, Freddy! None of this sweating bullets nonsense. Just take your best shot. There's no shame in striking out with a bombshell like her.

The thought of making any kind of move on someone so clearly out of his league made him even more flustered. "Coffee is just coffee," he muttered defensively. "I'm not gonna read too much into it. I mean, for all I know she has a boyfriend."

Heck, maybe she's married! Did you do a ring check? Don't tell me you didn't do a ring check!

"Nope."

Well then, you're flying blind, kiddo.

The one thing Wilfredo knew for sure was that he knew absolutely nothing about her except her name. He ran a worried hand through his hair—this whole meeting for coffee thing was a minefield.

He caught sight of the Lucky Deli's yellow awning up ahead. A bedraggled figure of a man was leaning against the brick wall near the door. He had all the telltale signs of a vagrant—untied boots, tattered clothes covered in grime, a scraggly beard, and an army cap. "Spare a dollar?" the man croaked as Wilfredo edged around him.

"Sorry," he mumbled, stepping into the cramped deli. He made a sharp right and headed over to the refrigerated cases that lined the wall in the back of the store. He spotted a white can with a red label—Narragansett. An old favorite. He spun back toward the register clutching a can in each hand.

He placed the beers on the counter and dug out his wallet. The stony-faced guy behind the register gave him a nod and rang him up. Wilfredo was watching the clerk count out change for a twenty when out of nowhere a sharp object was pressed into his lower back. "Don't move a muscle!" a gruff voice growled. Wilfredo froze. "I'll take that, buddy." A tattooed arm reached around him and plucked his wallet right out of his hand. It was gone before he even registered what was happening. The arm returned a second later to snag first one beer and then the next.

The register guy began to hop around furiously. "Johnny, I've told you before many times! Do not rob my customers!" he shouted. "Steal somewhere else! Not in here!"

"But, Lee, you gotta understand, this is the perfect spot to snatch wallets!" His assailant's words were slightly slurred and Wilfredo could smell the alcohol on his breath.

The counter guy was furious. "Don't worry," he said to Wilfredo. "He does not have a knife. Only a pen!"

The object poking him vanished as his assailant took a step back. Wilfredo pivoted to face him.

The bum named Johnny held up a blue ballpoint pen and

double clicked the button. He smiled, revealing a jagged line of yellowed teeth.

Wilfredo stole a sideways look at the counter guy. "You *know* this guy?"

"Yeah. His name is Johnny. Third time this month he robs one of my customers! I am calling the cops!"

"Give me back my wallet!" Wilfredo yelled. His first thought wasn't for his cash, or his credit cards, or even his driver's license. His mind went straight to Cassandra's phone number.

"I don't think so, buddy. I need it more than you." Dirty fingers were thumbing through the cash in the wallet's fold.

"Take the cash. I just need the wallet back."

"Ahh, but I bet I can trade your credit cards and ID to someone for a blunt." The man was swaying gently from side to side, as if caught in a gentle breeze. Then for a moment he seemed to find his balance, and he blinked slowly, a look of mild surprise in his eyes. Then his head dipped. Seconds later he straightened up, his eyes popped open, and he began to wobble once more.

Wilfredo sized up his mugger. This guy was clearly strung out on something. And his weapon of choice was a ballpoint pen. Initial fear gave way to a sudden fury and Wilfredo rushed at the man, grabbing at his coat. But the robber showed surprising nimbleness, stepping to one side in a blur of movement and deflecting Wilfredo's charge with a two-handed shove that sent him sprawling into a shelf full of candy.

"Watch it, buddy," the homeless man slurred. "No point in gettin' hurt over a stupid wallet!" A dazed Wilfredo sat sprawled out on the deli floor surrounded by scattered candy bars and packets of gum. He could hear the store clerk yelling at a 911 operator. Wilfredo scrambled to his feet and set off in pursuit of the ragged figure scampering out the door.

On the street Wilfredo raced after his mugger who was jogging south along the narrow sidewalk. The hobo glanced back over his shoulder, scowled at Wilfredo and quickened his pace.

"You don't give up do you? Here! You want it? Go fetch!" Having picked the wallet clean of valuables the man flung it high into the air, and Wilfredo watched it arc over his head.

The world fell silent, and for an instant it was as if everything was moving in slow motion. Wilfredo wheeled around, arms raised toward the sky as he raced after the wallet. Bouncing off the roof of a parked car it shot toward the gutter, and he watched helplessly as it disappeared through the narrow slots of a sewer grate, into the darkness below. Seconds later Wilfredo was on his hands and knees, grasping at the filthy metal grill and squinting into the inky blackness. The sound of trickling water reached his ears. All he could make out was a tangle of glistening leaves. Then he saw movement and two red eyes peered back up at him. As his pupils adjusted to the darkness Wilfredo recognized the shaggy silhouette of a rat, its thick tail slithering through dead leaves. Clamped inside the rat's mouth was a square leather object. The rodent stared back at him brazenly, then it turned and scampered away.

Tough break, kid. On the plus side you can stop shitting yourself over a stupid coffee date.

6. DETECTIVE MOLINA: THE DONUT STORE DILEMMA

It had been nearly twenty years since Detective Ramon Molina had darkened the door of East Village Donuts. Back then he was just a police cadet with a weakness for fried dough. He'd had a rough time at the police academy. Pegged as a geek, he'd been the target of hazing by his fellow cadets. The donut shop had been his refuge, although it had nearly scuttled his career right from the start when his weight ballooned and he came close to failing the job standards test, which included a six-story stair climb. So after graduation he had sworn off the glazed treats and never looked back.

But here he was once again, standing in the familiar shop, last in a line of donut-loving customers. He was wearing a tailored brown suit paired with a dotted green tie. No one around him had any clue that the bald gentleman with the mustache at the back of the line had a badge clipped to his belt and a 9mm in his hip holster. Detective Molina was grateful to be incognito, as he would hate to be seen as a walking cliché by the people around him.

Detective Molina had picked up his order at one end of the counter, and this second line was just to pay. Grease stains were already spreading on the brown paper bag in his hands. An X-ray machine would have revealed the contents to be half a dozen Boston creams. After his shift today he'd been gripped by a powerful craving for these custard-filled treats, and his feet had led him on the zigzag route back to his old haunt. He wondered if they would taste as good as he remembered. He took a step forward in the line. He was only six customers away from sinking his teeth into one.

It would have been hard to guess from Detective Molina's sober expression that he was a man caught in the throes of a titanic inner struggle. Part of him was insisting that he didn't have to do this. That it was not too late to just walk away. But another part of him scoffed and pointed out that the battle had been lost from the moment the bell above the entrance dinged and the smell of baked yeast hit his nostrils.

He inched his way closer to the cash register. This lapse could be traced back directly to his hellish week at the thirteenth precinct. The stress had caused the bad habits of his youth to bubble up to the surface. "*Omne vetus novatur,*" he murmured—everything old is new again. He'd been fond of Latin phrases ever since his schoolboy days at Saint Francis in Astoria. Reciting the short proclamations helped him to stay calm in moments of stress.

Detective Molina reported to police Lieutenant Kopski, who had recently been assigned to the thirteenth precinct. Kopski was one of the youngest lieutenants on the force, and he was determined to assert his authority by hammering down on any nails that stuck out. He had pegged Detective Molina as a part of an inflexible old guard whose best days were behind them.

"I've been told you're old school," the new lieutenant declared when they first met. Kopski's tight smile suggested that he ate old school types for breakfast. Detective Molina had honed his *modus operandi* over the years and he wasn't about to toss it out the window because some young whippersnapper thought it old fashioned. His record for solved cases was up there with the best detectives on the force.

Three days ago the lieutenant had called him out for falling behind on his entries to the CompStat database. Which was rich considering he had reassigned the administrative aide who usually helped him complete this task. And during Monday's briefing the lieutenant had changed the way cases were assigned, and Molina's caseload now consisted of domestic violence, petty thefts, indecent exposure, and even community outreach.

Then, this morning, the lieutenant had taken yet another whack at the Detective Molina piñata. Kopski had called him into his office and asked him to take Detective Scarlet Garcia under his wing and mentor her. Garcia was a recently appointed third-grade detective who was struggling in her new role. Detective Molina had been watching her crash and burn for the last two months and he wanted nothing to do with her. He explained to the lieutenant, in his most reasonable tone, that he wasn't cut out for mentoring.

"I figured that since you're both Puerto Rican you guys should get along." Kopski regarded him with raised eyebrows.

"Actually, my family arrived in the U.S. from the north of Spain. I've never set foot in Puerto Rico." Lieutenant Kopski appeared momentarily perplexed. Then with a shrug he rephrased his initial request as an order and dismissed him.

Just what he needed—babysitting duty for a newbie who should never have been promoted to detective. How was he supposed to do his job if he was constantly tripping over a hapless rookie? Good detectives drew on a teachable skill set that included gathering evidence, interviewing people, conducting surveillance, and following up on leads. But there were other hallmarks of a good detective that, in Detective Molina's view, could not be taught. You had to be smart, you had to be relentless, and, most importantly, you needed imagination. He doubted Garcia had any of these qualities. The words *nihil ex nihilo* flashed through his mind. Nothing comes from nothing.

Detective Molina had briefly considered asking for a transfer. But he was too old to start over at another precinct. He could always make a living as a private investigator, but that would consist of surveillance jobs for suspicious spouses and landlords, which was hardly an improvement.

The person in line ahead of him pocketed their change and trundled away. Molina stepped up to the register, smiled awkwardly at the cashier, and swiped his credit card. Grabbing his receipt he bolted for the exit—where he collided with a young woman coming in through the door. She had short cropped hair, mischievous eyes, and puffy cheeks. He did a double take as he realized it was none other than Detective Garcia herself.

"Molina! Funny running into you in here." Garcia stepped inside.

"Garcia." Detective Molina acknowledged the junior detective with a curt nod. What were the odds of bumping into her outside the precinct? Then he remembered where he was.

"I thought you hated donuts! You're famous at the thirteenth for never going anywhere near them."

"Well, as you can see, the rumors are false."

"Well I'm glad I bumped into you. Do you have a minute to talk?" Detective Molina nodded reluctantly.

They stepped over to an empty table in a far corner of the shop. Garcia sank into a bucket chair and Detective Molina sat down opposite her. The phrase *persona non grata* bubbled up to the surface in his thoughts. He'd been hoping to avoid this kind of new partner chitchat. Reluctantly, he offered her a Boston cream, and Garcia's eyes lit up as she accepted his offer. Detective Molina held off on grabbing one for himself—he didn't want anyone witnessing his relapse.

"I don't know if you've heard yet, but the lieutenant says we are going to be teaming up," Garcia said in a muffled voice, half the donut already crammed into her mouth.

"So I have been informed." Detective Molina pursed his lips.

"I'm hoping to learn a lot from you."

"Well, Garcia, I won't lie to you. I'm used to working alone, and this arrangement is going to be . . ." Detective Molina groped for the right words. ". . . an adjustment for me."

"I hear ya. But look, you're the veteran, so I'm just going to follow your lead. I've had a difficult start. But I'm hoping to turn things around—with your help."

"Let's see how things go. We are in *terra incognita* at the precinct these days."

"I'm sorry, I don't really speak Spanish. I was born over here, and my aunt and uncle always preferred English at home."

"That wasn't Spanish. It was Latin. *Terra incognita*. It means uncharted waters."

"Okay . . . I didn't realize anyone still spoke Latin."

"Even dead languages have their uses. I am fond of the

occasional Latin phrase. If we are to work together, I suggest that you familiarize yourself with the most common ones."

"Wait, what? You want me to read up on Latin sayings?"

"Have you considered, Detective Garcia, that our system of laws was built on Latin phrases?"

"But I'm no lawyer, and we don't need lawyer-speak to do our jobs."

"Didn't you just ask for my guidance? Well you can consider this my first suggestion for your development as a detective."

"I just can't see how it's gonna help." Her furry caterpillar eyebrows knit together.

"Think of it as a code that only the two of us will know. Good communication between partners is essential."

"I guess it can't hurt." Garcia looked doubtful.

"You may consider it the *sine qua non* for our successful partnership."

"Latin again?"

"Correct. It means precondition."

The two detectives stared at each other. Detective Garcia swallowed the last few crumbs of her Boston cream and wiped her fingers on a napkin. Detective Molina sat there impassively, drumming his fingers on the table. He hoped that their little chat was winding down.

She licked her lips. "Sounds like a *Karate Kid*–type situation. You know—wax on, wax off. I'll play along. I want us to get off on the right foot. I've hit enough bumps in the road already. Homework assignment accepted! Man, these are *amazing*." She eyed the brown bag. "Good old Boston creams. They're my favorite, you know."

"Mine too." Surely she didn't expect a second donut?

"Well, whaddayaknow. We have something in common." She grinned and pointed to the bag containing the remaining five donuts. "Are those all for you?"

Detective Molina gave a noncommittal grunt. It was humiliating, getting caught like this with a bag full of donuts. If she mentioned this at the precinct his reputation would take a serious blow.

"Can I have one more? It's so hard to have just one!"

"Help yourself." Detective Molina groaned inwardly. What was he supposed to say? *Sorry, but I need all of the rest to help me cope with my crippling stress?* She unfolded the top of the bag and selected another of his chocolate-frosted goodies. She made short work of this second donut, finishing it off in three or four bites.

She eyed the bag again and Detective Molina could have sworn she was debating whether to push her luck. But at that moment the radio on her hip crackled to life. She unclipped it from her belt and pressed the push-to-talk button, identifying herself. Detective Molina sighed. Heads turned to watch them inside the shop. So much for not getting noticed as donut-munching cops.

The call turned out to be for a 10-20 at a deli down on the Lower East Side. Garcia informed the dispatcher that she was on her way. She jumped up and looked at him expectantly. "Come on, let's go. I'm parked outside."

Detective Molina stared down at the table. Garcia was a typical rookie—overeager. Sadly, as her new partner, he was obliged to join her.

* * *

When they arrived at the corner of Rivington and Suffolk there was already a squad car with flashing lights blocking the street outside the deli. They were informed by a patrolman that the store holdup had been downgraded to an in-store mugging. The register hadn't been cleaned out, and no real weapon was used. The victim, a thirtyish white male who had been relieved of his wallet, was standing outside the deli looking dejected.

As crimes went this one was barely a blip on the city's radar. If they slipped away quietly there would be no paperwork, no CompStat, and no follow-up report. But naturally Garcia jumped right in to interview the victim. Now they would be required to conduct a cursory investigation and follow up on any leads. Meanwhile, the bag of donuts was sitting on the dashboard of Garcia's Toyota Camry. She had cut the contents down to just three on their ride down, with a glib "one more for the road" excuse. Detective Molina sidled up to his partner, curious about her interviewing skills.

She got straight to the point. "Can you give me a description of the perp?" Detective Molina approved of this opening question. The victim's memory would only grow hazier and it was important to nail the descriptors down right away.

"Like I told the other guys already. He was about my height, maybe in his late thirties, with a beard and a green cap. Definitely homeless."

"Caucasian?"

"Yes. And his name was Johnny."

"How do you know his name?"

"The deli guy recognized him. Said this has happened a few times recently."

"How do you know he was homeless?"

"The stench? The lack of personal grooming? I live in New York—I know a homeless person when I see one."

The questions kept coming. Molina felt a twinge of sympathy for this poor bastard when he heard that his wallet had ended up in the sewer. And he'd had to stifle a laugh when he'd learned that a rat had run off with it.

"Were there any items of value inside your wallet, sir?"

"He took out my cash and cards and put them in his pocket. There was about fifty dollars in there, a credit card, and a driver's license. Probably an old library card too, and a few other cards I can't even remember. And a phone number." Detective Molina's ears perked up.

"A phone number?" Garcia parroted.

"Yeah, this girl gave me her number earlier today. Now it's getting chewed on by a rat and I'll never see her again." He looked down at his feet.

"Where did you meet this young lady?" Garcia inquired.

"On the subway."

"Do you typically meet a lot of women on the subway?"

"No. I don't. Hey, here's an idea—why don't you guys quit asking me questions and comb the neighborhood for this crook? If you find him, I'm pressing charges."

"Did this man assault you?"

"I tried to grab hold of him to get my wallet back. Then he pushed me into a rack of candy."

Detective Garcia waved her pencil back and forth. "It's inadvisable for civilians to confront criminals on their own. Next time just hand over your valuables and call 911."

"Don't worry, this guy won't be winning round two if I

catch up with him. Did I mention that he also stole two cans of beer?"

"Got it. One brown leather wallet. Fifty dollars cash. Two cans of beer," she said. Detective Molina groaned as he watched her write this down. Unbelievable. A thorough investigation for two missing beers and an irretrievably lost wallet? Being partnered with Garcia was going to be a nightmare. She stepped over to her double-parked car and reached through the window. "Here, have a donut." She held out the open bag to the unlucky man. Hesitantly he reached in and took one. Garcia put away her pencil and notebook. "We'll let you know if we make any arrests."

Detective Molina's mouth was agape. Where did she find the gall to give away one of his few remaining donuts? He gave her a sharp look and took the now-almost-empty bag from her. This was the last straw. For a brief moment he had toyed with the idea of turning this neophyte into a real detective, nurturing whatever kernel of talent she had with his expert tutelage. But no longer.

It shouldn't take much to sabotage Garcia's career. She was already on thin ice at the precinct. A nudge in the wrong direction at a critical moment would be enough to get her demoted. Maybe she would end up assigned to traffic duty? That would teach her to mess with other people's donuts. One of his favorite Latin phrases came to mind. *Canis canem edit*—it was a dog-eat-dog world.

7. CASSANDRA:
CAT EARS AND WHISKERS

Cassandra pulled her bedroom drapes closed and flicked on the bedside table lamp. Yellow light bounced off red painted walls sending a warm glow radiating throughout the room. Clothes were scattered all over the place, piled high on her chair and on her dresser, and completely obscuring the quilt on her bed. She sat down on the piano stool in front of her vanity mirror, dressed only in black underwear, and reached for her makeup kit. She used a waterproof eyeliner to give herself a bold lash line with a crisp cat's-eye flick, and then added some freckles to her cheeks. Switching to a black pencil she drew whiskers and a black triangle on the tip of her nose. She tried out a few different expressions in the mirror and smiled.

Cassandra loved dressing up for Halloween. Her closet was filled with vintage thrift shop pieces that were easily adapted to a variety of looks. She also had a few wigs, half a dozen hats, and a bagful of masks. Most years Cassandra would throw a cheap costume together and head over to Sixth Avenue with her friends to watch the Village Parade. She loved standing in a crush of cheering New Yorkers as the procession of colorful characters and floats streamed by.

Unfortunately, her two best friends, who were also her parade buddies, had abandoned her this year. They had jetted off to faraway London for a few months, eager to share their new bundle of joy with proud grandparents. So she was spending the evening with Gregory instead. He had come through—big time—with an invite to a costume party at a friend's apartment, with a prized balcony overlooking the parade.

Cassandra brushed her hair and parted it down the middle. Pulling one side of her hair back she grabbed it by the tip and began to twist it so that it rolled up into a bun, which she pressed flat against the back of her head, fixing it in place with the help of a few bobby pins. She repeated the process on the other side. Then she pulled on the wig cap and tucked any stray hairs into place. With all the preparations made, she reached for the dark coppery wig she had picked out. She loved her natural chestnut hair, but for tonight she wanted something bolder.

Curious yellow eyes watched her intently. Nestled in a jumble of clothes on top of the dresser was her cat Jupiter, a handsome gray tom. Done with her makeup and hair, Cassandra stood up and walked over to him. She meowed playfully, then laughed at the face he made. "Oh, Jupe, you must think I'm crazy!"

She rifled through a pile of clothes until she unearthed the cat ears and tail that she had picked up at the Halloween store for just twelve bucks. It came with a black ribbon collar that had a small silver bell attached. She tied it around her neck with a neat bow and did a little shimmy to the sound of tinkling. Gregory might consider it tacky, but she thought it was a fun touch.

Perching herself on the edge of the bed she tugged on

a pair of gray tights. Next she attached the black tail to her waist with its elastic loop. Then she stepped into her black miniskirt and pulled on a striped jailbird sweater. Finally, she slipped the black mask into place over her eyes, and pushed the furry cat ears headband into her faux red hair. A sexy cat burglar stared back at her in the mirror.

She was counting on tonight to be a reset button of sorts for her and Gregory—to prove that they could still have fun together. Their wedding planning squabbles had escalated over the past few weeks and she was scared that something was seriously wrong with their relationship. They never used to argue this way.

Not so long ago, Gregory had been more of a "your wish is my command" kind of guy. She had reminded him of this the other day by bringing up the time he'd escorted her to that infamous audition callback that had turned into a five-hour grind. When she emerged from the auditorium, exhausted and defeated, she'd been met with an unexpected torrential downpour. And then Gregory had appeared through the rain, holding a giant umbrella in one hand and a bouquet of pink roses in the other.

His response to this story had been dispiriting: "I can't believe I waited for you that whole time." He shook his head disapprovingly. "What was I thinking? I was such a fool back then." She'd searched his eyes for some hint of the old Gregory. Didn't he realize that this was one of her fondest memories of him? That she had fallen in love with that fool?

Cassandra wished someone would explain to her how it was possible to feel this lonely when you were *engaged*. With her closest friends gone, there wasn't anyone she could turn to for advice. But for tonight, the plan was to put all of that aside. She just hoped Gregory would do the same and that he would stop asking her if she had heard from Wilfredo. He was getting on her last nerve with that subject. Tinged with jealousy at first, the question had taken on a more mocking tone of late. He would draw out the name teasingly—Will-fray-doh—chuckling to himself. And each time she was forced to admit that she had not heard a peep from her subway hero. Presumably the stranger with the kind blue eyes and the spattered shirt who had so bravely thrown his arms around her in her moment of need had just crumpled her number up and tossed it in the trash. She knew it was petty of her to resent him for it. He'd only saved her stupid life.

She tossed some extra kibble into Jupiter's bowl and refreshed his water, then she grabbed her bag and headed for the door. The gray cat hopped up on the lowboy to say goodbye and she gave him a big smooch on his furry head. "See ya later, Jupe. Don't wait up!"

Out in the hallway she hung a left, heading for the elevator, and then she stopped in her tracks. A large man with a bulbous nose was standing in the corridor ahead of her. He was facing away from her, busy taping an orange paper to her neighbor's door. Cassandra got a queasy feeling in the pit of her stomach. She'd heard rumors that building management was trying to eject the last few renters so they could transform their units into condos. But it was a shock to witness it happening in real time. The man hadn't noticed her, so she took a step back and hid behind the corner wall, watching him surreptitiously as he held his thumb to her neighbor's buzzer.

Cassandra heard the faint *clink* of the brass plate over

the peephole. Then the locks clicked and her neighbor Mrs. Rosen appeared in the gap of the door. She leaned on her cane and glared up at the man. She was a small woman with peppery gray hair. Red reading glasses dangled from the collar of her turtleneck. Cassandra ran into her mostly in the elevator, when Mrs Rosen would invariably vent about their superintendent's many shortcomings.

"What is the meaning of this?" Mrs. Rosen demanded.

"I'm from the management office," the man replied brusquely. "I'm here to give you this." He shoved a brown envelope at her. "We need you out by the end of November. This place needs to be broom clean if you expect to get any of your deposit back."

Mrs. Rosen opened the envelope and peered at the documents through her glasses, outrage written all over her face. "You can't do this to me!" she sputtered. "I already told that blasted woman on the phone that I *did* pay my rent this month. You cashed my check!"

"You were three hundred dollars short. Rent needs to be paid in full. No exceptions."

"You're going to evict me over three hundred dollars? You raise my rent every year! I'm on a fixed income!" She shook her cane at the man.

"Now, don't you give us any trouble. The law will be happy to enforce our legal rights if it comes to that."

"The law? You ought to be ashamed of yourself. Kicking an old woman out of her home!"

"Just doing my job, lady." With this last remark he turned on his heel and trudged away.

"Heartless bastard!" Mrs. Rosen yelled after him. She

ripped off the taped-on notice and then slammed the door, the loud *bang* reverberating throughout the hallway.

Cassandra counted to twenty before venturing out and walking quietly over to the elevator. She hoped Mrs. Rosen had family or friends who could come to her rescue, because she didn't even want to think about the poor woman ending up on the street. Had this city gone crazy? Booting old ladies out of their homes? Meanwhile, impossibly tall residential skyscrapers were sprouting up all over Manhattan, like mushrooms after the rain. Shiny glass towers built so billionaires would have someplace to park their cash. It made her furious to think about it.

8. WILFREDO:
THE DISGRUNTLED FOX

Some of Wilfredo's fondest childhood memories were of his parents bringing him into the city to see off-Broadway plays. Captivated by the raw energy of the city, he'd always viewed New York as a magical place, and his love for the Big Apple continued unabated to this day. Or, at least it did until a few weeks ago, when the rose-colored glasses were snatched from his face and trampled to bits on the grimy, gum-riddled sidewalk. New York, he'd finally realized, was the kind of town that would throw a priceless pearl in your lap one minute, only to snatch it away cruelly moments later, never to be seen again.

He knew it made no sense for him to be all hung up on her. This Cassandra person was a complete stranger that he'd met for all of five minutes. Yet, he couldn't help feeling that the connection they'd made was somehow important. He'd been wandering around town for the past few weeks scanning faces on the sidewalk, hoping against hope that he might cross paths with a certain green-eyed girl. Day in and day out he kept his eyes peeled, until eventually it sank in that his chances of bumping into her again in a city of this size were one in a gazillion. Having her melt away into the bustling metropolis was a bitter pill to swallow. Not only that, but she was the only witness to the most heroic moment in his life. Without her around to back up his story no one would ever believe it. When he had told Toby about it he'd been met with cheerful skepticism and a raised eyebrow.

I'm your witness, Freddy, declared the Captain. *Don't I count? What am I? Chopped liver? But what you call courage I call having rocks in your head. You don't need a medal for bravery—you need an ounce of common sense!*

Wilfredo muttered something unintelligible under his breath, but the croc had sharp ears.

Verbal abuse won't bother me any, Freddy. I've got thick skin! I once traded insults nonstop with a Macedonian trader during a three-day bender. We ended up best mates!

Wilfredo sighed. This croc was turning into a real problem. But he had no time for that now. It was Halloween, and even though he was in no mood for celebrating this year, he had promised Toby and the guys that he would march in the parade with them. So he stripped down to his skivvies and slipped into the fox costume he had brought back with him from his last visit home. The furry orange costume fit his bulgy torso like a glove. He pulled the hood over his eyes and checked out his reflection in the hallway mirror. He looked utterly ridiculous, but at least no one would recognize him.

And no one else would have a costume like his. Miss Vivian, his high school drama teacher and sewing machine virtuoso, had made the costume herself. The first time he had tried it on backstage, Miss Vivian had tottered on her feet at the sight of him, grabbed him by the shoulders, and fixed him with a piercing stare: "Hold on to this costume, Wilfredo—someday it will draw a kindred spirit your way." Miss Vivian's unexpected clairvoyant moment had weirded him out, but it had also given him hope, because at the time he had been sharing the stage with his high school crush—Ruby Greenwood.

Freshman year Wilfredo had witnessed Ruby rehearsing the dance routine for "You're the One That I Want" in a black tube top. Coppery hair swishing wildly and slim hips moving rhythmically, she had nailed every pout and gesture with an effortless flair that would have made Olivia Newton John proud. That moment had kicked off a one-sided infatuation that had lasted well past graduation. Each year they both signed up for theater, and he was always cast in some minor role while she took the lead. They became friends of sorts, but nothing more, and his fox costume senior year failed to break the pattern. Sadly, Miss Vivian's wild prediction never came true.

Pasted in a family photo album somewhere back home was a picture of Wilfredo with his arm around Ruby, smiling for the camera in front of their school lockers. That was as close as he ever got. At some point after graduation Ruby had moved to Hollywood, where she eventually landed a starring role on a hit TV series. And now she had a Malibu home, legions of fans, and her face plastered on magazine covers from coast to coast. Wilfredo's mom, a big fan of her TV show, brought Ruby up in conversation all the time, asking if he was still in touch, and insisting Ruby had a soft spot for him. When the truth was Ruby had been fond of him the way people were fond of stray dogs. He'd be shocked if she even remembered him anymore.

Wilfredo patted his woolly belly and his stomach gave a loud grumble in response. He would need to scrounge up some grub before heading out. Strolling into the kitchen he peered into the empty white interior of their fridge and was perplexed to see they were out of beer again—that Beer Fairy was getting out of hand. But he managed to scrounge up enough sandwich bread and cheese slices for a grilled cheese, which he set about making in a crusty cast-iron pan.

Toby appeared in the doorway dressed in a shiny store-bought pickle costume. Green leggings and a green long-sleeved T-shirt made his limbs appear like skinny vegetable stalks. A round cutout revealed his cheery face.

"Splendid fox costume, buddy. You look hilarious!"

"This ratty old thing? I feel dumb."

"You gotta play it up!"

Wilfredo shrugged. "I guess."

"Where'd you get it? I've never seen anything like it."

"I found it when I was cleaning out my room back home. It's from an old high school play I was in."

"What a find! Hey, you don't seem that excited this year. I hope you're not still moping about Subway Girl? The mysterious beauty who you rescued from certain death, only to have her slip through your fingers."

"I'm not moping," he replied defensively.

"If you say so. By the way—that stupid crocodile of yours is starting to weird me out. I swear he keeps giving me side-eye when I'm watching television."

"That sounds like Captain Pete. I'll tell him to cut it out."

"I can't tell if you're kidding. But maybe you could just shove him in your closet?"

"That's not gonna work. It's a long story. But don't worry, I'll figure something out."

"So are you ready to go? What's the dill? We're supposed to be at the parade staging area by five thirty. If we don't get there on time we'll be in a real pickle."

Wilfredo winced. Clearly Toby was going to lean heavily on the pickle puns tonight. "I'll be ready in a few. I just gotta make myself a quick grilled cheese."

"We're late, man! And you know I can't sit down once I put on this costume!"

"Well *some of us* didn't spend all afternoon eating cereal on the couch."

"Maybe if you had you wouldn't be getting hit with the munchies at parade time."

"Just go ahead without me. I'll ride my longboard over to make up for lost time."

"In that getup? Do you have a death wish? If you get hit by a bus, you're gonna be flattened into a fox-shaped pancake."

"Don't worry. The costume will cushion my landing if I wipe out."

"You *are* pretty well padded."

"Says the guy in the stuffed pickle suit!"

Toby flashed one of his trademark grins. "All right, I guess I'll head out without you, but make sure you get there before the parade starts."

"Don't worry. I'll be there."

Wilfredo buttered the bread slices and placed them in the pan with two slices of cheese wedged between them and lit the burner. He heard Toby banging about in the hallway followed by the sound of the front door closing.

Freddy, I thought he'd never leave. That palooka is driving me nuts. Sitting on the couch all day eating frosted flakes and watching cartoons? That manboy needs to find himself a real hobby, like knife-throwing, or gambling!

"How about you stop giving poor Toby the evil eye, Captain?"

I'm a doll, Freddy. You know my eyes don't shut unless someone tips me over, right? I have no choice but to stare at his ugly mug all day.

"Keep in mind that he's my best friend."

I'll say this for him, he's right about you sulking like a sad puppy. That brunette wasn't your soul mate, Freddy. Just get her out of your head. This parade is gonna be crawling with chicken dinners in skimpy outfits!

Wilfredo's mouth set in a hard line, but he said nothing. It was impossible to have the last word with that croc around. He pressed the spatula down on his sandwich and gooey yellow cheese oozed out of the sides and sizzled in the pan. After sliding the greasy sandwich onto a paper plate he cut it in half then he plopped himself down at the kitchen table and took a large bite.

9. CASSANDRA:
A MOMENT OF MADNESS

It was an unseasonably warm night as Cassandra walked east along St. Mark's Place on her way to meet Gregory. The sidewalks were crowded with people, many of them in costume and headed toward the parade like herself. Cassandra spotted ghoulish devils, ashen zombies, creepy clowns, sexy fairies, and superheroes with ridiculous foam abs. Parents followed younger kids around as they went from store to store, their bags already bursting with candy.

Cassandra's acting teachers had drummed into her that once you put on a costume you needed to snap into character. So it was not surprising that her thoughts were centered on how best to inhabit the role of Cat Burglar, keeping in mind that she was basically a walking pun. Whacky and unpredictable? Sneaky and mysterious? She wasn't sure.

Her phone dinged in her bag. She fished it out and saw that it was a text from Gregory: *I'm running late. Will you pick up two bottles of wine for the party? Something nice! See you at the Prince Street subway.*

Cassandra grimaced—the cost of two bottles of wine might be chump change for her fiancé, but it would put a big dent in her weekly budget. Begrudgingly, she set course for a liquor store over on the Bowery that was more or less on the way to their meeting spot outside the subway station.

When Cassandra arrived at the liquor store she found it bustling with customers on similar errands to her own. Not being much of a drinker herself, she felt out of her element shopping for booze. Cassandra enjoyed a glass of wine now and then, but as Gregory was fond of pointing out, the good stuff was wasted on her. He favored European wines, but California girl that she was, she zeroed in on the Napa section. Shockingly, she didn't have a favorite grape, but she knew Gregory was partial to Pinot noir, so that narrowed things down some. And now she had arrived at the point where she usually resorted to picking one at random.

A haughty voice startled her. "*Excuse* me! Do you *mind*? You're blocking the aisle." Cassandra straightened up and pulled her tail to one side, letting a middle-aged blond woman in a green wool coat squeeze past her in the narrow space. The lady shot her a disdainful look. "Some people," she heard her mutter under her breath. Cassandra pursed her lips. As a Baylor & Bowman sales clerk she was used to dealing with rude customers. But she wasn't at work now, so she allowed herself an eye roll before turning her attention back to the shelves, and picking out two thirty-dollar bottles based entirely on the label design.

Circling back around to the register she ended up on the tail end of a longish queue. Directly in front of her was the lady in the green coat, cradling a bottle of sweet sherry with a cell phone pressed to her ear. Cassandra studied her, taking in the dyed hair, the Hermes neck scarf, and the expensive leather tote slung over her shoulder.

The woman had an affected accent that reminded Cassandra of how movie stars talked in old black-and-white films. "But, darling, I had to steal Ruben. I needed the car to get the boxes of champagne home. Yes, of course I realize he's *your* driver, but can't you just take a taxi home this once? I don't think you know how much pressure I'm under. Tomorrow night's party needs to be flawless. It's not every day that the mayor accepts a dinner invitation. We need to pull out all the stops."

After a brief pause, she continued: "I realize that. But there are a million details left to take care of. I have an appointment with the florist in the morning. I have to get Marta's uniform dry-cleaned. And the leader of the quartet wants to stop by and rope off a portion of our living room. Yes I *did* have to come all the way downtown! This is the only store that could guarantee me five boxes of Moet. No *kidding* it's a lot of champagne! But we simply *cannot* afford to run out. Whatever is left over we'll just use up over the holidays. I'm not stupid, you know. I've thought everything through carefully. Look, I'm in line to pay." The woman sounded exasperated. "As soon as the boxes are in the trunk I'll shoot uptown and you can have your precious Ruben back. I've already picked up the place cards at the stationery store *and* I stopped at the bank to get cash for the caterer—who *refuses* to take a check—so it's straight home for me after this."

Cassandra's eyes bored a hole in the back of the woman's head. This lady was getting on her last nerve. Her gaze wandered to the woman's leather tote bag, which was unzipped, and she noticed a bright red wallet poking out amid a jumble of eyeglass cases, cosmetics, tissues, and hand sanitizer. This idiot was running around the city with a small fortune in cash and her wallet sticking out of her bag? Must be nice to live in her world. Cassandra scowled—there was probably enough cash in that wallet to pay poor Mrs. Rosen's rent several times over.

And that's when a stray thought popped into Cassandra's head. She'd always been a goody two-shoes her whole life. The closest she'd ever come to breaking the law was that one time she got a parking ticket in San Jose, and it had left her in tears. But at this moment the thought of stealing that red wallet and giving this arrogant woman's cash to her poor neighbor seemed like a fantastic idea. Of course, there was no way she could actually go through with it.

And yet her eye kept getting drawn back to the wallet. She was already wearing a mask and a wig, which made it the perfect moment in her life to break the law. Plus she'd always had dexterous fingers. And it wasn't as if she wanted this lady's money for herself, she just wanted to restore some much-needed karmic balance to the universe.

The woman was still talking loudly into her phone. "You would not believe the number of grown people who are wandering around dressed in ridiculous costumes. It's so juvenile. This one young woman in a cat costume was staring cluelessly at the merlots, looking as if she was going to grab a bottle at random, all while blocking the entire aisle with her stupid tail. No manners whatsoever."

If Cassandra had been wavering until that point, reluctant to embrace an impromptu life of crime, this last comment bumped her right off the fence, and her inner Cat Burglar took over. Delicately, she set down the two bottles of wine she was holding on the nearest rack. Adjusting the mask over her eyes, she wriggled her fingers in her black fingerless gloves. She became suddenly hyperaware of everything going on around her. The neon Guinness sign on the wall over the register was flashing on and off. "Monster Mash" was playing over the speakers. The fruity aroma of an open bottle of white wine filled the air. And the door dinged as a customer exited to the street.

Cassandra glanced around one last time to make sure no one was looking her way. Holding her breath she reached out and grasped the corner of the red wallet between her thumb and forefinger and drew it smoothly from the woman's bag. In a flash, the deed was done. She slipped it discreetly into her own drawstring bag, and pulled it closed. No alarms went off. Nobody yelled. She let out her breath and quietly edged backward, looping around until she had a clear path to the exit, about a dozen steps away. Moments later she had her hand on the door handle. She had actually done it. She was home free.

"Stop! Thief! That girl with the red hair just stole my wallet! The one with the cat ears! Someone stop her!"

Cassandra bolted from the store without looking back. She took off down the sidewalk, running at top speed, turned the corner onto Houston, and sprinted east.

10. WILFREDO:
FOXMAN VERSUS CAT BURGLAR

Wilfredo's mood improved like magic the moment he stepped onto his longboard. Fuzzy feet planted hip length apart, he rolled westward in the bike lane on Stanton, humming to himself as he zigzagged his way up to Houston, easy as you like. He hung a left, hopping up onto the spacious sidewalk, and weaved effortlessly around pedestrians.

His peripheral vision was lousy and this getup made keeping his balance harder. But skateboarding in a fox costume was the bomb. People on the street seemed to think so too, judging by all the attention coming his way. Passersby were getting a big kick out of the orange fox wheeling past them on a skateboard.

"Way to go, bro!"

"Look at that guy!"

"Hey, fox dude, great costume!"

He happily hammed it up for photos, alternating between a big thumbs-up and putting his shaggy arms out on either side like a surfer. With his identity concealed he found that any hint of self-consciousness had evaporated, so he acted as goofy as he liked. This was going to be the best parade ever.

As he passed through the intersection with Chrystie Street he heard some sort of commotion up ahead. Something was going down. He slowed a little, and it was a good thing he did too, because a figure came hurtling along the sidewalk toward him.

"Hey, watch it!" he cried out. A masked girl in a black-and-white sweater pivoted, spinning around him at the last second as she raced past him.

"Stop that girl! She stole my wallet!" A lady farther down the street was yelling at the top of her lungs. "Stop her! She's a pickpocket! Grab her!" The yeller was barreling through bystanders, flapping her arms like a lunatic, her green coat billowing around her like a tent. "Don't let her get away! That girl! The one in the cat costume!"

Wilfredo looked from the woman in the green coat, to the fleeing girl. Still yelling, the blond lady scrambled past him. Wilfredo hesitated for a moment. There was no way this lady was gonna catch up to that human blur in the striped sweater booking it down the street. As someone who had recently had his own wallet stolen, he felt a pang of sympathy for the arm flapper, who was clearly the latest victim of a neighborhood crime wave.

That settled it. Cat costume girl wasn't going to get away with this. Not if he had any say in it. Wilfredo stomped on the end of his longboard with a fat orange paw, popping it up in the air and grabbing hold of the deck. He flipped it around and hopped back on, heading back in the direction he'd just come from. He wondered absently if this hero business might be habit forming.

Picking up speed he soon zipped past the woman in the green coat, who was panting heavily, and had slowed to a desperate, staggering walk. Meanwhile, the costumed delinquent had nearly vanished from sight, but he caught a glimpse of a

black-and-white-striped sweater disappearing into the play-
ground area of the park that ran parallel to Chrystie Street.
He hopped off his board to run up the steps, then threw it
back down and jumped back on without missing a beat.

It was a lot darker inside the park, and it seemed as if the
thief was doing her best to slip away into the shadows. But
she had chosen the wrong outfit for that. Her white stripes
were clearly visible up ahead, even in the dim light. Thanks
to his wheels he was gaining on her slowly but surely. Her
red hair swished around her as she glanced over her shoulder.
Her eyes went wide behind the mask when she saw him, and
she redoubled her pace. He could see her more clearly now,
and it struck him that it wasn't just a cat costume. It was a cat
burglar costume. An appropriate disguise for a pickpocket.
He watched as she vaulted over a park bench to gain herself
a sliver of time.

Wilfredo went around it, and almost rammed into a
delivery guy on a bike. At the last second they veered away
from each other, with Wilfredo nearly losing his balance as
he teetered on the board. Yikes! He had to swerve sharply in
the opposite direction to avoid ending up in the bushes, but
somehow he regained his balance and kept going. It occurred
to him that he hadn't really thought this through. Air was
whooshing past him and it was harder to spot obstacles in
the darkness. This stunt could easily end with a trip to the
hospital for him, but he couldn't bring himself to quit. They
had left the wallet's owner way behind, so it was all up to
him now.

The girl stole another peek over her shoulder and saw
he was closing on her. Wilfredo smirked—he had a big

advantage on this straightaway. She must've had the same thought, because she made a sharp right at the next walkway that cut through the park, and he lost sight of her around a corner. When he got to the turn he leaned heavily to the side and veered right, sweeping through a group of teens who gave him a loud whoop of approval, even though he had almost plowed into them.

He was just in time to see a black boot disappear south on Chrystie. Seconds later he made a hard left onto another bike lane, and spotted her once more, jogging on the sidewalk up ahead. He put his foot on the ground and gave himself three strong push-offs to help close the gap. She heard the sound of his board and shot him a dirty look. They were only about ten feet apart now and Wilfredo's face set with grim determination.

When they reached the next intersection, she pretended to go straight, only to dart left at the last second. Unable to stop in time he rolled right past her, and it took him a few precious seconds to stop and reverse course. She was heading east now, out of the park, a street with intermittent traffic in her path. Wilfredo broke into a sweat under his costume. She was about to dash across the crosswalk when a woman pushing a stroller stepped into her way and she was forced to skid to a halt.

"Time-out!" she yelled and held up a hand in his direction. Time-out? What the heck? This wasn't some game they were playing. But maybe she was right. He didn't want any bystanders to get hurt either. Not over a wallet. Hesitantly he pulled up about six feet away. They stood frozen, abiding by this strange truce, while the woman with two little kids in tow moved into the clear. Cat Burglar Girl was breathing heavily. She looked back at him quizzically.

"Ready to give up?" he asked. "I just need that wallet back. I'm not trying to bring you in or anything."

"Not a chance!" she snapped, and took off running again. Wilfredo pushed off once more. Clearly this was going to end the hard way. Well, he was bigger than her, and well padded, so if it came down to a wrestling match he liked his odds. Thankfully the traffic was stopped as she dashed across the road with him close on her heels. She kept going straight down Rivington and as they passed some road construction she flipped a large plastic traffic barrel into his path.

Wilfredo sucked in his breath and plowed right through it, knocking it to one side. "Cheap shot!" he yelled. At the next cross street they hit more construction as the sidewalk was blocked off from the road with metal barriers. She ran straight up to the metal gates and flipped over one with ease.

Wilfredo veered left in the street, skating on the road parallel to her, with the barriers between them. An oncoming car's headlights lit up the asphalt ahead. She was so close! With a burst of speed he pulled ahead of her, did a running jump off his board, and tried to hop over the metal barrier. But weighed down by his costume he failed to get enough lift and ended up crashing into the metal gate. "Oomph." He felt it in his diaphragm. Somehow he pulled himself over the barricade, landing facedown on the ground, directly in the Cat Burglar's path. Without batting an eye she leaped over him. Rolling onto his back, with the wind knocked out of him, he stared up at the jumping figure silhouetted against the gray sky.

In desperation he reached up at the last second and grabbed hold of her tail, managing to get a firm grip on the furry appendage. He yanked on it and she stopped cold. Judging by the way it stretched it appeared to be attached firmly around her waist with an elastic. He climbed to his feet, still holding her tail.

"Got ya!"

She glared at him indignantly. "Let go of my tail, you creep!"

"Hand over the stolen wallet!"

"I don't know what you're talking about." She reached down into the waist of her skirt, grasped a black elastic, and yanked it apart with both hands, snapping it in half.

"See ya around, Foxy."

"Oh no you don't." He bounded forward just as she was about to bolt and threw his arms around her from behind. This was it—he had her now. Except that a moment later his feet had left the ground and he was flying through the air as she threw him over her shoulder, judo style. He landed on the pavement in front of her with a thud.

Stunned, he stared up at her masked face. His brain was trying to process multiple thoughts at once. The pain of hitting the sidewalk. The surprise of getting his butt kicked by a woman. And a sudden awareness that this Cat Burglar standing over him had lovely eyes. A tiny little bell tinkled on a ribbon around her neck.

She peered down at him with concern. "Are you okay?"

"Yeah," he said in a strangled voice. "I think so."

She smiled, and it was like a balm to his jolted vertebrae. "Better luck next time, Foxy!" She spun around, snatched her cat tail off the ground, and sped away. Wilfredo lay there unmoving, taking long deep breaths.

Hey, Freddy? How's the hero business working out for ya? No broken bones, I hope? Maybe you should ditch the knight-in-shining-armor routine before you get yourself killed!

Sirens blaring on Third Avenue sent Cassandra ducking down a side street. She held her breath as they went past and let it out as they grew increasingly distant. Slowing to a walk, she checked over her shoulder every so often, in case anyone was following her. It occurred to her that she needed to ditch her costume—fast. The dark silhouette of a church loomed across the empty street and its shadowy stairwell struck her as a promising spot for a quick change. She crept down the steps and yanked off her sweater, stuffing it into her bag along with her wig, the mask, and the rest of her accessories. She shook out her long brown hair, then she spit on the palms of her hands and rubbed at her face until her painted-on whiskers were smudged beyond recognition.

She walked the rest of the way home dressed only in a black bra and her miniskirt. Blasé locals barely batted an eye, habituated to all manner of outlandish street wear, doubly so on a night like Halloween. She made it safely back to her apartment, where a surprised Jupiter brushed up against her shins. The curious cat jumped onto the arm of her sofa when she upended her bag on the cushions. The two of them stared at the pile of stuff that included the various pieces of her costume, a makeup kit, and not one but two wallets.

The unfamiliar red wallet proof that the past hour had not been some crazy dream.

With trepidation she picked up the stolen item, slid the gold zipper around the edge, and flipped it open. A white bank envelope was tucked inside and Cassandra gasped when she thumbed through the thick stack of hundred dollar bills it contained, feeling simultaneously exhilarated and horrified. She reminded herself that it wasn't as if she intended to keep a single penny for herself. One way or another she would give it all away.

Even so, this was way too much money to just shove all of it under Mrs. Rosen's door. Dumping that much cash in her neighbor's lap might attract the wrong kind of attention. The smart thing to do would be to split it up. She could think of several places that would appreciate a donation, starting with the black box theater on Seventh Street that was hanging on by a thread. And maybe that used record store on Bleecker that looked like it might close permanently at any moment. Or she could donate a chunk to the community garden on Avenue B. Surely those ladies deserved a reward for their hard work. She would just pop envelopes with cash in the mail, including to her neighbor, along with a friendly note from their benevolent Cat Burglar.

12. DETECTIVE MOLINA:
A POLITICAL HOT POTATO

The doorman stood under the green canopy of 770 Park Avenue, inspecting his little patch of sidewalk with a critical eye. When the two detectives approached his orbit he stepped inside and held open the door, regarding them inquisitively as they stepped into the well-appointed interior.

"Can I help you?" he asked, polite but wary, stationing himself expectantly next to a sign that read ALL VISITORS NEED TO BE ANNOUNCED.

Detective Molina looked him up and down, taking in the gray suit with gold buttons and gold trim. This doorman had an honest face, Molina decided, as he fished his badge from his waistband. "We're here to talk to a Mrs. Wilhelmina Van Gelder. Apartment seventeen." The doorman hastily called up on the intercom and waved them toward the elevators. Visits from the police were surely a rare event at this address. Striding through the lobby Detective Molina gazed admiringly at the beaded chandelier, the fleur-de-lis wallpaper, and the matching antique mirrors. He had always considered these prewar doorman buildings to be the *ne plus ultra* of civilization.

"Pretty swanky, right?" Detective Garcia whispered. "I guess we get to see how the other half lives."

They stepped into the elevator and pressed a shiny brass

button. Detective Molina turned to his partner as the doors closed. "Don't be afraid to ask some tough questions when we get upstairs? I know the lieutenant said the commissioner himself has taken an interest in this case, but that doesn't mean we should pull our punches. If grilling this lady is what it takes to get some leads then that's what we have to do."

Detective Garcia nodded. "Sure thing, partner. I'm the queen of tough questions!" Molina kept a poker face, but inside he was smiling. Being easily suggestible was a terrible quality in a detective, and he knew that pressing too hard on the politically connected woman upstairs could easily land his partner in hot water. Personally he planned to treat her with kid's gloves.

The elevator made its way slowly up to the building's higher echelons. Garcia pulled her phone out of her pocket. "Take a look at this. I came across a viral video earlier—"

Detective Molina's chevron mustache quivered. "I don't want to hear about any viral videos you found on the internet! Keep your mind on the case."

"But—"

"Stay focused, Garcia. Remember—*aquila non capit muscas!* The eagle does not catch flies. Don't let yourself become distracted by trivial matters." With a shrug she put the phone back in her pocket.

Moments later the elevator opened directly into a private apartment. A woman in a maid's uniform was waiting there to greet them. "This way, please. Mrs. Van Gelder will be with you very soon." She led them into a cozy library with floor-to-ceiling bookcases, a colorful Persian rug, and a recessed bar area replete with an assortment of liquor bottles and decanters. The maid waved them toward two leather chairs and then left them alone in the room. The two detectives remained standing, listening to a conversation taking place in the neighboring living room. A disdainful woman was arguing about the room's layout with a vexed-sounding gentleman. The man favored a spot by the window as the best location for his quartet to set up, but the lady refused to block her guest's view of the park. In the end the woman put her foot down and they settled on blocking off a corner by the grand piano. Moments later the double doors to the study were pushed open and a woman in a black-beaded dress swept into the room.

"The doorman said you were with the police? Does this mean you've found my wallet?"

"I am Detective Molina, and this is Detective Garcia. I presume we are speaking with Wilhelmina Van Gelder?"

"Of course I'm Wilhelmina Van Gelder. Who else would I be? Now, answer my question!"

"No, not yet, unfortunately. We are still working on the case, ma'am—"

"Don't call me ma'am," the woman interrupted. "Do I look like an old woman to you?"

"Sorry, er, Mrs. Van Gelder. As I was saying, we are still working the case and we were hoping to ask you a few questions."

"I don't have time to go over all that again. We are throwing a major dinner party tonight!"

"I understand, ma'am." The exasperated woman shot Detective Molina a dark look. "I apologize—Mrs. Van Gelder. I promise we won't keep you long. We just wanted to hear the story straight from your own lips in case any important details got lost. Or you might have remembered something new today?"

"Well I haven't. And I want to remind you that I had just stopped at the bank and I was carrying a boatload of cash! And my wallet was a Gucci special edition. My husband says that makes this a felony."

"Unfortunately, we have no way to verify how much cash anyone has in their wallet. I take it you have canceled all your cards?"

"Of course. I was on the phone for an hour! And I can verify the cash withdrawal with a bank statement!"

"Yes, but we have no way of knowing how much money someone spent between the time the money was withdrawn and the moment a wallet was stolen." Detective Molina was not entirely comfortable with the direction this conversation was taking. He looked to his partner for help. But she just smiled and stayed quiet.

Wilhelmina Van Gelder was turning pink. "That's ridiculous! I didn't spend any of the cash. I always use my credit cards in stores. So if I understand you correctly you're saying that if you catch this hussy all she will get is a slap on the wrist?"

"We will prosecute her to the full extent of the law," Detective Molina said emphatically. "And I promise you that we will leave no stone unturned in our attempts to find her."

Wilhelmina Van Gelder looked far from satisfied with this response. Detective Garcia cleared her throat. "Excuse me, Mrs. Van Gelder" she said sweetly, sneaking a sly look at her partner. "May I show you a video I've uncovered?"

Detective Molina's brow furrowed. What was she talking about? What video? They had gone through a security video from the store and nearby street cams, but that footage had not revealed anything helpful. Oh well, maybe Detective Garcia was about to stir up some trouble for herself with this stupid video she kept harping on about.

His partner tapped on her phone screen a few times, then held it out to the socialite. "I discovered a viral video online of an altercation that was recorded last night and uploaded to the internet by someone on the street. Do any of these individuals look familiar to you?"

Mrs. Van Gelder grabbed the phone from her and hit PLAY on the video. Looking over her shoulder Detective Molina saw two costumed figures on the screen. A man dressed as a fox was gliding along on a skateboard in the street. Then he hopped off and tried to jump a metal barrier. Another costumed character was running on the sidewalk, and she jumped over him as he fell. The person taking the video moved in closer and managed to get a better view of the struggle that followed. Mrs. Van Gelder's mouth fell open. "That's her! That's the thief who stole my wallet! And that fox guy on the skateboard started chasing after her when I was yelling for help. Did he catch her?"

All three of them stared down at the video, transfixed. They watched the tussle and saw the girl dressed as a cat burglar throw the fox guy over her shoulder. They cringed when the fox hit the sidewalk hard, and groaned when the cat burglar took off running.

Mrs. Van Gelder looked furious. "So she got away? That fox guy turned out to be a real wimp! Just my luck. But that's her all right—the pickpocket." She glared at Detective Molina: "I suggest you follow your partner's lead. At least she's working the case and finding clues! That thief has probably spent my money by now, but I want her caught and sent to jail. Now, if you'll excuse me, I have work to do." She yanked open the library doors and stormed off, leaving the two detectives alone once more, exchanging bewildered glances.

"You could have told me about that video!" Detective Molina snapped as they made their way back to the elevator.

13. WILFREDO:
BLAST FROM THE PAST

The prop master at the Cornelius Theater was a notorious crank who had been in the business for fifty years. Most of the stagehands, including Wilfredo, were afraid of her. When someone screwed up she would chew them out in her raspy smoker's voice, using highly unprofessional language. Goldie, as she was called, didn't typically trust any of the stage-hands to find props. But they were way behind schedule with *The Imaginary Knight,* and unable to do it all herself she had reluctantly circled a few missing items on the prop list and sent Wilfredo and Toby off on a rainy Sunday morning to comb the city's flea markets and thrift stores.

Six hours later they were headed back to the theater with their loot from the day strapped in the back of the theater's pink van. Toby was at the wheel, punching the gas at every yellow light and cutting across lanes of traffic for last-minute turns, as usual.

Batten down the hatches, Freddy! Your friend Toby is a loose cannon! Captain Pete sounded terrified as the van made another screeching turn. *Somebody take the helm away from this maniac before we all end up dashed on the rocks!*

Thankfully they made it back in one piece and without putting any fresh dents in the already beat-up van. They dou-ble-parked outside the orange brick facade of the Cornelius and Wilfredo hopped out on the passenger side while Toby climbed out of the driver's seat, the two of them converging at the back of the loaded-up van. Between flea markets, thrift stores, and stoop sales they had found everything on the list, including a beat-up tricycle, an oval floor mirror, and a dress-form mannequin. This last one had been Wilfredo's big find, so he carried it inside himself, while Toby followed with the mirror, and a couple of the guys came out with a wheeled bin to grab the rest.

As they came through the stage door they saw Goldie coming down the stairs. She had wiry gray hair, which she parted down the middle, and was wearing a vest over a white shirt and blue jeans. Wilfredo and Toby exchanged a nervous glance. Her eyes went to the dress form first. She tested the wheels to make sure the castors were working, she spun it around, and poked and prodded at it. This culminated in a satisfied grunt of approval, and Wilfredo breathed a sigh of relief. Unfortunately, Toby wasn't so lucky with his mirror.

"This thing is falling apart! It wouldn't last two days onstage! How many times have I told you that anything you find needs to be built like a brick shithouse? I want a mirror I can push off the stage without worrying it might break. You paid money for this garbage? Toss it and put everything else in the trap room. And don't forget to make labels." Toby hung his head as they headed down to the storage area under the stage.

Let me tell you, Freddy. That's a woman after my own heart! the Captain gushed. That dame runs a tight ship. I would sail my boat under her flag any day of the week!

"Knock it off, Captain," Wilfredo begged him under his breath.

He spent the next hour organizing the storage area with Toby, after which they took advantage of their break time to grab a late lunch. Wilfredo nuked a frozen burrito, while Toby picked up a chicken gyro from the cart on the corner. Then they snuck up to a bench outside the control booth in the very back of the auditorium to chow down. Technically they weren't supposed to eat there, but until rehearsals began no one was around to object.

They had a view of the whole theater, which they had expected to be empty, but while they ate, a cluster of people began to gather around the stage. Smartly dressed, they looked like the usual theater bigwigs: producers, agents, financial types, and maybe some talent. It was clear that some major news about the play was about to drop.

Toby was scrolling through his phone with one hand as he ate, white earbuds snaking up under his hoodie. Suddenly he sat up straight, eyes bulging, his jaw stopping mid-chew.

"Check this out, Wilfredo. I think that's you!" he whispered. "This guy in the fox costume is you!"

"What?"

"You're in a viral video!"

Wilfredo scooched closer to peer over his friend's shoulder, and Toby shared an earbud with him. He was amazed to see a recording of the scene from last week when he'd chased down the costumed pickpocket. "Hey, that *is* me!" Some unnoticed passerby on the street had recorded the encounter on their phone.

"Man, you sure didn't come out on top in that scuffle. That was some landing! It hurts me just watching it."

"Well the padding did cushion the fall some."

"Why didn't you tell me about this?"

"I did, remember? When you got back from the parade."

"Oh yeah. That's right. I thought you were making up some bogus excuse for not showing up."

"Who would make up something like that?"

"Hey, I believe you now! This is awesome! My friend the vigilante!"

"I'm not a vigilante. I'm just someone who objects to pickpockets and muggers."

"Said every superhero ever. Wait until I show this video to the guys. They are gonna flip!"

"Now wait a minute. I don't want to become a public laughingstock. No one but us needs to know that's me."

"Seriously? But this is internet gold!"

"Well I think it makes me look like a chump. So don't tell a soul, got it?"

"Fine, whatever. But look at you, jumping into action to chase down the bad guy—or bad girl, in this case. Dude— they're calling you Foxman in the comments! You got over two million views. Foxman is blowing up! We need to make a follow-up video, pronto. You'll be famous and I'll be your manager, maybe land you a skateboard sponsorship, and your own line of merchandising . . ."

Wilfredo gave his friend a baffled look. "Never gonna happen, buddy. I'm not gonna run around in public in a silly fox costume."

"Er . . . you already did, remember?"

"That was on Halloween. Everyone does stuff like that on Halloween."

Their debate was cut short when a figure strode out onto the stage below. Declan Crumly was a self-possessed young director with prematurely white hair. He liked to wear sunglasses indoors and never passed up on an opportunity to show off his tats. Toby and Wilfredo plucked the earbuds out of their ears and leaned forward to listen.

"Friends, thank you for coming." Declan's nasally voice filled the theater. "I've asked you all here for a special announcement. We have finally cast the lead role of Violet in our production of *The Imaginary Knight*. I couldn't be more excited to introduce an actress we all know and love. Best known for playing Cassidy Prince in *Santa Monica Vibes*—ladies and gents, the incomparable Ruby Greenwood!"

A peppy young redhead in a strapless gold dress strutted out from the wing to stand beside the beaming director.

"Hey." Wilfredo nudged his friend. "I know her."

"Duh. She's famous!" Toby replied in a hushed voice.

"No, I mean I really know her. We went to school together."

"Seriously? You went to school with Ruby Greenwood? How have I never heard about this?" Wilfredo shrugged, and Toby looked indignant. "You didn't think to mention this to your best friend? I feel like I don't even know who you are anymore."

Ruby addressed the gathering, telling them how excited she was to be on Broadway for the first time, punctuating her comments with her dazzling smile. Wilfredo had a hard time focusing on her words because he was flooded with a mix of emotions, foremost among them astonishment. He couldn't believe Ruby Greenwood was standing on the stage at the Cornelius.

"Wait, did you actually talk to her in high school? Or was this a you-saw-her-in-the-hallway-one-time kind of situation?"

"We were in drama together. I was in three school plays with her."

"No way! She probably remembers you then."

"Not a chance."

Done with their lunch they made their way backstage and found it buzzing with talk of the new casting. Everyone was excited that rehearsals could finally get underway. The stage manager sent them to help set up Ruby's dressing room, introducing them to Annie, Ruby's personal assistant, who would oversee the operation. Annie was a nervous young woman with short black hair, who seemed flustered by her new surroundings.

The two largest dressing rooms were next to each other on the third floor. Annie had a list of items Ruby had requested, which included a couch, an armchair, a small coffee table, a standing lamp, and a changing screen. "So basically she wants us to turn her dressing room into a lounge," Toby joked as they searched through old props from past shows, looking for items that matched the list.

As they hauled a purple settee up the stairs, they heard Ruby's silvery voice carrying down the hallway. She was in conversation with her costar Sebastian Estrada, a modern-day Latin heartthrob with some major movie credits to his name.

Sebastian had been cast as the play's titular knight, and his presence backstage had caused a stir among the female crew members.

As they turned the corner into the hallway, Wilfredo caught sight of the two stars. Sebastian towered above Ruby, his broad chest and shoulders straining the threads of his light blue sport jacket. "I will take you to Via Carmina sometime. It is my favorite restaurant in Nueva York. Their pappardelle with wild boar ragu is fabuloso!"

"I would love that." Ruby clapped her hands.

Wilfredo walked backward through the doorway of Ruby's dressing room carrying his end of the love seat, with Annie directing them over to a spot along the wall. After they set it down, they turned around and headed straight back downstairs to grab a wooden coffee table.

When they returned with the table, they found Ruby in her dressing room, testing out the love seat.

"Thanks for your help, guys," Ruby said, turning her high-wattage smile on them.

Wilfredo wiped the sweat from his forehead with his sleeve. "No problem."

"Ruby, meet Toby and Wilfredo," said Annie. "The two best stagehands ever. They've found practically everything you wanted."

Seen up close, Ruby was even more stunning than he remembered from back in high school. And she still had that cute little wedge nose. With a toss of her head, she flipped her coppery hair over to one side as she smiled at them, a dimple appearing in her cheek. "Wilfredo, what an unusual name. Is it Italian?" She looked right at him with her large gray eyes.

"No—Spanish. It was my grandfather's name." Toby nudged him in the ribs, but Wilfredo ignored him. He was not going to remind Ruby of their connection.

"How fascinating." She put her finger to her lips, deep in thought. "Hey, guys, you know what this space needs? A rug to help warm up the room. Do you think you could find something with natural fibers?" Wilfredo nodded, and promised to find her a wool rug. "And Annie, do you remember that Moroccan pouf I circled in that catalog? See if you can get your hands on one in indigo blue, would you? Just pick it up in store, use your credit card." Ruby spread her hands apart to encompass the space around her. "With a little work and imagination, we'll turn this place into an oasis." Toby and Wilfredo went off in search of a rug while Ruby and Annie dove into a discussion about lighting.

Who knew you were so forgettable, Freddy! It's too bad cuz she's a real hot tomato! It's probably for the best. No sense in punching above your weight!

14. RUBY: HER NAME IN LIGHTS

The Cornelius lobby was an ornate affair with marble walls, red carpeting, three beaded chandeliers, and two ticket windows framed with an elaborate gold art-deco pattern. Ruby Greenwood stood alone at the foot of the stairs in the otherwise empty lobby, impatiently tapping her foot. Waiting had never been her strong suit. She'd sent her assistant out to grab coffee about twenty minutes ago, and it was as if the earth had swallowed her up. How hard was it to get coffee? She texted Annie another lone question mark.

There was nowhere to sit, unless she wanted to sit on the dusty steps, and she couldn't sit on the steps without taking off her faux-fur coat. And if she did that she would probably freeze to death. She needed to stay warm so she wouldn't look like a frozen popsicle in the photos.

It had been a taxing day. Broadway might look glamorous from afar, but she'd been surprised that behind the scenes everything felt shabby and rundown. She missed sunny California. She missed her on-set trailer with its private kitchen, bathroom, and full-sized bed. By comparison her new dressing room resembled a broom closet. And shared bathrooms in the hallway? The horror.

Meeting Sebastian Estrada for the first time had been nerve-racking. She'd found the temperamental actor intimidating, although she'd done her best not to show it. She was worried about what their chemistry would be like onstage. Usually she had no trouble winding men around her little finger, but her costar seemed to expect adulation himself, and she refused to play the part of another Sebastian fan girl.

Ruby glanced at her phone. She had hired Annie only three months ago, a fresh-out-of-school communications major, and clearly her assistant had skipped the class on how to reply to your boss's texts in a timely fashion. Ruby had wanted someone young, who she wouldn't feel funny about ordering around. But on days like today she wished she'd opted for someone older, as Annie had appeared out of her depth.

A text from Chad dinged on her phone. Finally, a reply to her three texts, even if it was just a short "I miss you Baby let's talk tonight." Chad was shooting on location down in the Yucatán and had been hard to reach lately. Who knew if he would really have time to chat later, or if a late-running shoot would keep him tied up. So long as it wasn't his sultry, raven-haired costar who was tying him up. Ruby knew all too well that actors got up to all kinds of shenanigans on set. She just had to hope Chad wouldn't ruin everything. Their relationship was still new, but Ruby was convinced they made the perfect power couple—Chuby? Chaduby? The press would figure it out—once Chad's agent gave them the go-ahead to go public!

Ruby let out another sigh and bundled her coat around herself. For the past ten years she had celebrated the holidays in a variety of tropical locations and she'd forgotten how cold it got in New York in the winter. Growing up outside the city her winter memories were of sledding, roaring fireplaces, and Christmas caroling. As a child she'd come into the city once a year to see the Rockettes and the Christmas windows. She'd been expecting the New York from her childhood, but the reality was much darker, colder, and dirtier. To make matters worse she was here by herself, with only Annie for company.

Seeing a familiar face in the theater crew had been a surprise. Poor old Wilfredo from Beacon High. It was heartbreaking to run into people she'd grown up with only to find them leading such ordinary lives. She had pretended not to recognize him, which was surely the kindest thing she could have done in that situation. Having an old classmate as a stagehand was too awkward for words.

Ruby reached into the flowery green duffel bag at her feet and pulled a small point-and-shoot Fuji from an inside zipper. She'd been given this state-of-the-art camera as swag at an award show, and it was coming in really handy. She scrolled through the pictures Annie had taken so far, documenting her personal journey from Hollywood to Broadway. There were some shots of her from the airport, some shots of her walking into the theater, and some shots in front of her dressing room mirror. They were fine, but what she needed now were some photos with uniquely New York backgrounds for social media. Ruby Greenwood strolling through Times Square. Ruby Greenwood eating a hot dog. Ruby Greenwood climbing out of a yellow cab.

Annie jogged into view through the glass doors. Ruby shoved the camera back in the bag and opened the door for her assistant. Breathless, Annie held a paper coffee cup out to her and apologized for the delay, explaining that they had made it all wrong the first time around so she'd had to wait while they remade her order.

"Annie. We've talked about this. I just want simple things done quickly. I can't wait twenty minutes every time I need a latte. And there's no way I'm settling for a cup of that luke-warm sludge we saw in a dirty pot backstage."

Annie smiled timidly.

"Now, I have a few more items for your to-do list."

Annie whipped out her phone and said she was ready.

"*One*. I need some real plants in my dressing room. Find something that will stay alive for a few months and will give my dressing room some leafiness. Splurge on elegant pots. *Two*. Research Sebastian Estrada for me. I need to know what his relationship status is before we start working together. Feel out his publicist discreetly to see if he'd be open to some photos together around town. *Three*. Book me twice a week for an early-morning session at the spa in my hotel."

Ruby took another sip of coffee and felt the life seep back into her veins. Just a few more gulps and she'd be ready for that photoshoot.

"All right, Annie, time to put your photographer hat on!" The actress led the way outside.

Annie put away her phone. "Lots of pictures, from different angles, and your right side is your good side."

"And don't be afraid to get down low on the sidewalk if you need to get that bug's-eye angle. It will make my legs look longer."

"Low on the sidewalk. Got it."

"How do I look?" Ruby let her coat drop open, revealing

a powder white suit underneath. Her high waisted skinny pants were accented with a metallic belt, while her open coat showed off a sheer blouse with a neckline that stretched down to her waist.

"You look like a million bucks!"

Ruby Greenwood grinned and tossed her red hair. Still holding her coffee cup she strode off in the direction of Times Square. Her assistant pulled the tiny camera from the bag and hurried after her boss.

15. CASSANDRA: THE GOLD WATCH

The Lancaster Hotel lived in the shadows of the various sky-scrapers that surrounded it. The burden of easing the gloom within the hotel walls was taken up by a legion of ornate lamps sprinkled around the common areas of the hotel, each one forming a weak bubble of yellow light.

Cassandra was perched on a humpback sofa in the fifth-floor lounge of the staid Vanderbilt Avenue landmark, a spacious room that was broken up into numerous seating areas replete with armchairs, couches, and coffee tables. Stiff-backed waiters crisscrossed the space carrying teapots and teacups on silver trays, a scene that had played out unchanged for over a hundred years.

Cassandra had settled on her favorite little black dress as her outfit for the evening. Sitting there with her legs deco-rously crossed and her hands resting calmly by her sides on velvety cushions, she did her best to project the classic elegance of Audrey Hepburn. She was meeting Gregory's father for the first time, and she was determined to make a good impression.

Her brow furrowed as she worried that she might have overdone it with her crimson lipstick. Perhaps she should blot her lips with a napkin? But she pushed away these nervous thoughts, and did her best to calm her mind.

Gregory was sitting in the armchair next to her, his upper

half obscured by the open newspaper he was holding in out-stretched hands. His father should be joining them at any moment. The renowned Professor Dingle lived in Switzerland, where he taught music history at the University of Geneva. He was in town this week for an academic conference.

Gregory's arms dropped and his face popped up from behind the wall of paper. "Remember that video you showed me the other day?" Gregory asked her.

Boy did she. She'd been amazed and alarmed when she'd seen it on the local news. "The one where the guy in the fox costume gets flipped on the sidewalk?" Cassandra smiled serenely.

"Yes, that's the one. Well, there's a follow-up to the story in the metro section today. Apparently, a community garden down on Avenue B got an anonymous donation for a substantial sum, along with a small note stamped with the image of a black cat and signed by someone calling them-selves the Cat Burglar."

"How bizarre."

"And a used record store in the Village claims it received a thousand dollars in the mail with a similar note." Gregory's voice was rising as was the color to his face. "This article is insinuating that the costumed pickpocket is some sort of modern-day Robin Hood!" He waved the paper about in exasperated fashion.

Cassandra had no idea why Gregory was so outraged. "Well it does seem like she might be the real hero after all."

"Are you kidding? Where does she get off taking people's hard-earned money and giving it away? She's a criminal plain and simple, and a publicity stunt doesn't change that."

Cassandra forced herself to take a deep breath before

speaking. "You can hardly accuse her of acting selfishly if she's giving the money away."

"It's easy to give money away when it's not your own! Her actions are indefensible."

"Can I look at that?" She took the paper from him. Sure enough there was a two-inch-long article where the recipients of her largesse came right out and compared her to Robin Hood. She felt a thrill go through her. Just like that she had transformed herself from bad guy to champion of the down-trodden. And by the same token that annoying Foxman was now cast as a defender of wealthy socialites. She handed the paper back to Gregory and they let the matter drop, which was what worked best for them these days.

At a quarter to six on the dot, Cassandra caught sight of a fastidious-looking older man with a neatly trimmed goatee who was headed their way. He was wearing a paisley cravat and was clutching a shiny black cane. She recognized him immediately from photos and she nudged Gregory with her toe.

As he drew closer, Professor Dingle tugged on a chain in his waistcoat, pulling out a gold pocket watch. Flipping open the cover, his expression took on a satisfied look. Being a stickler for punctuality must run in the family, she thought.

She shook his hand, and with the initial pleasantries out of the way Gregory caught the eye of a waiter and placed their order for a large pot of Ceylon tea and a selection of tea sandwiches. Professor Dingle sat down on the sofa beside her and eyed her appraisingly. He spoke excellent English, with only the occasional misstep, and a slight French accent. He entertained them both with anecdotes about his brushes with European royalty and celebrities in the world of classical music.

The waiter soon returned with a tray, setting down a large silver pot on a trivet and a plate of sandwiches beside it. There were cucumber sandwiches for her, and ham and brie ones for Gregory and his dad, who both seemed to find great humor in teasing her about taking a little bite of the ham. Cassandra smiled thinly and declared herself quite happy to leave those sandwiches for them.

They only had about half an hour allotted for tea, after which Gregory and his dad would be heading over to Carnegie Hall for a benefit concert. There was something a little off-putting about Gregory's dad that she couldn't quite put her finger on. Lurking behind that superficial charm she sensed an uncompromising old-fashioned view of the world. She could spot a male chauvinist when she saw one. But she could easily manage to be fake charming for another twenty minutes or so.

After his second cup of tea, Gregory excused himself to go use the restroom. The professor took this as an opportunity to scooch closer to her, his leg pressed against her own.

"Cassandra, you will have to come and stay with us this summer at the château. We have a swimming pool so make sure to bring your bikini!" He chortled as if he had made a huge joke, then he reached out, put his hand on her bare knee, and gave it a squeeze. Cassandra frowned and edged away from him slightly. She was pretty sure that the more permissive European customs didn't extend to groping your own son's fiancée. Gritting her teeth, she made a show of pouring them both fresh cups of tea, and was grateful when Gregory returned from the bathroom.

Twenty minutes later Professor Dingle fished out his

pocket watch again and declared that they'd better head out if they didn't want to be late. Gregory paid the check, and they all grabbed their coats. When they stepped into the dark elevator Cassandra did her best to keep Gregory between her and his leering father, but at the last minute a family of four squeezed in and she ended up sardined in the back, pressed right up against the professor. It was a short ride down to the ground floor, but Gregory's dad made the most of it, his eyes fixed on her modest cleavage the whole way down. She glared at him, but he just winked at her, smiled impudently, and leaned in just a touch closer.

The elevator ride felt interminable, but a couple minutes later they were outside the hotel saying their goodbyes. Even though Cassandra was fuming, she did her best to pretend everything was fine—for Gregory's sake. "Delighted to finally meet you," she declared, smiling widely, and shaking Professor Dingle's hand. Gregory gave her a peck on the lips, and then the two men walked briskly north, while she turned and strolled in the opposite direction.

On her way to the subway in Grand Central, Cassandra passed by a homeless man sitting on a grate, a scrawled cardboard sign propped up next to a large plastic cup with some singles jammed inside. She bent down as she passed by and dropped a gold pocket watch into his cup.

The homeless man fished it out and looked at it. "Wow, look at this thing. That's real gold! It's not stolen is it?"

"There's a pretty good chance it is."

The panhandler shrugged. "Not a problem. I know just the right pawnshop!"

16. WILFREDO: WALLET SHOPPING SURPRISE

Wilfredo had been clipping his cash together with a small binder clip, but now that his new driver's license and credit card had arrived in the mail, he couldn't put off purchasing a new wallet any longer. He didn't want some bulky whopper of a wallet that would bulge out in his pocket, or something so tiny he couldn't fit anything in it. He needed to find the Goldilocks of wallets. Local stores in the neighborhood had nothing but cheap plastic junk that he knew would fall apart in six months. He wanted genuine leather, and he was willing to pay for it. So on Monday after work he dragged Toby up to the Baylor & Bowman department store to check out their selection.

"Why you want to shop here, man?" Toby complained, as they pushed through the revolving doors. "These prices are jacked up. I know a place in Hell's Kitchen where you can pick up a spiffy wallet for cheap."

"I'm not looking for some shoddy Hell's Kitchen wallet."

"Why so picky? You'll just end up dropping it in a sewer." Toby grinned, and Wilfredo gave his friend a dirty look. "Sorry, too soon?" Toby's smile grew even wider.

Your friend's got a point, Freddy! This store is for fat cats. Back in my day we would make our own wallets out of tanned seal hides and stitch them together with walrus whiskers. Captain Pete began to ramble and Wilfredo shushed him in his mind.

A helpful employee directed them to Bags and Accessories on the second floor and they rode the escalator up. They soon located a long display case filled with men's wallets, and Wilfredo bent down to examine them. Through the distorted glass he saw the legs of a sales clerk appear behind the counter.

"Let me know if you want to look at anything," she said helpfully.

Wilfredo pointed to a blue leather wallet in the back. "Maybe I could see that one if you don't mind." When he looked up at the girl with green eyes standing behind the counter he did a double take.

"You!" he exclaimed.

"You!" she replied, equally astonished.

They stood there dumbstruck for a few seconds.

"You never texted me!" she said finally.

"I know. Because I got mugged right afterward at a bodega and someone stole my wallet that had your number in it."

She looked at him skeptically. "You don't have to make up a story you know."

"Oh my god, is this Subway Girl?" Toby butted in.

"Subway Girl?" her eyebrows knit together.

"This is my friend Toby. Toby, this is *Cassandra*. And I'm—"

"You're Wilfredo, yes, I remember."

"You do?"

Toby's eyes were popping out of his head. "So you're the girl who got her bag stuck in the subway doors?"

"That's me! And I doubt I'd be standing here if your friend Wilfredo hadn't bravely jumped in and pulled me to safety that day." Turning to Wilfredo she said: "Did your wallet *really* get stolen right afterward?"

Wilfredo opened his mouth to respond but Toby jumped in before he could say a word. "It sure did. Some vagrant snatched it from him at a deli and ended up throwing it in a sewer. Wilfredo has been bellyaching about it ever since! That's why we're here, shopping for a new wallet! Hey, dude, show her your money clip."

Wilfredo dug out his wad of cash held together with a binder clip and waved it at her. "I was totally planning to take you up on that coffee."

"Well the offer still stands. You are my savior after all!" Her smile lit up her face.

Wilfredo stood there like a dope. He couldn't believe his luck. The universe had granted him a mulligan with Subway Girl. Toby elbowed him in the ribs to snap him out of his stupor. "G-great. Let's do it," he stammered. "Coffee, I mean."

"*And* you get the friends and family discount on a new wallet, which is fifty percent!"

"Wow, thanks! You don't have to do that."

"Of course I do."

"Of course she does," Toby echoed.

Well this really fries my wig! Captain Pete began to jabber in his head. *What are the odds of you stumbling across this chicken dinner a second time? It's almost like you two lovebirds were meant to be. Now if only she didn't have a giant ROCK on her finger!*

Wilfredo looked down at her hand, and his face fell. It was true. She had a big old diamond ring on her left hand, which meant she was either hitched or about to get hitched. Of course it had been too good to be true. Coffee would be just coffee after all. Following Wilfredo's gaze and reading the disappointment on his face, Toby quickly became clued in as well: "What a lovely ring," he commented. "Are you engaged?"

Cassandra flattened her hand to show off the ring, although her expression seemed less than enthusiastic on the topic. "As a matter of fact I am."

"Have you set a date yet?" asked Toby.

"Not yet," she replied, and filled them in on the trials and tribulations that came with wedding planning.

You'd better step to it, Freddy! There's no time to waste if you're hoping to steal her away from her fella. She hasn't made it to the altar yet, which makes her fair game in my book!

Sunlight filtered in through the glass roof of the sculpture courtyard creating a patchwork of light-filled rectangles on the stone floor. The airy space was bustling with a mixture of tourists and locals, their voices echoing off the museum's walls. Among them was Cassandra, who was gazing up wondrously at the golden Diana statue perched high on a column, her gilded arrow aimed at some indeterminate spot in the distance. Standing at her side was Gregory, his craving for a mid-afternoon coffee prompting him to pull her impatiently toward the nearby café.

He rolled his eyes when she asked him to order her a peanut butter and jelly sandwich and a glass of water. "What are you, five?" Cassandra left him in line and went to snag a free table. Shortly afterward he reappeared, carrying a tray with her sandwich as well as a cappuccino and a raisin danish for himself. He poured a packet of raw sugar into his coffee, mixing it with a coffee stirrer. "Well, we've seen your Greek and Roman art, and that crass photography exhibit you inflicted on us—"

"Which was amazing!" she insisted.

He waved a hand dismissively. "That means that the European paintings galleries are up next."

Cassandra wrinkled her nose. It was the most boring

section of the whole museum, so naturally it was Gregory's favorite. "I guess it's only fair."

As always their conversation drifted back to the all-consuming subject that was their wedding. They urgently needed to reserve a venue and Gregory was pushing for a historic mansion in Cold Spring, with outdoor gardens overlooking the Hudson. Cassandra had her heart set on the Key House in Brooklyn, a boho-style concert space with a laid-back vibe and an epic beer list.

She pleaded her case. "I just don't want our wedding to be this big stuffy affair. Next thing you know you'll be insisting I have to change my name!"

Gregory looked like she had just clocked him on the head with a day-old baguette. "You're not actually thinking of keeping your maiden name?" he groaned.

"Of course I am! Why would I change it?"

"Tradition! My dad will be deeply offended if you don't take our family name."

"I hate to break it to you but I'm not going to factor in your father's opinion on the subject."

"I'm beginning to think you didn't like him. You know, he was very complimentary of you. He said you were a real knockout."

"How flattering," she said dryly.

"Geesh. You need to learn how to take a compliment, Cassandra. But if my dad's opinion means nothing, then think of the kids! You still want kids don't you?"

"Of course I do. But I doubt they will have strong opinions about my last name."

"You're not thinking of hyphenating?" he asked incredulously. "Dingle-Bell? That sounds ridiculous."

"Finally something we agree on. And no, I was thinking that I like being just plain old Cassandra Bell."

"You *do* realize you are marrying into my family?" He looked hurt.

"And *you* are marrying into mine."

"I find your unwillingness to compromise disturbing."

Cassandra's mouth fell open. "But it's *my* name! You want me to compromise on *my* name?"

"The point is that you will be *my* wife." Gregory noticed her eyes narrowing dangerously and he bit his lip. "But let's not argue."

"I wish it were as easy as that."

"It could be, if you just stopped fighting me on every little thing. Have you stopped to think about what our lives could be like a few years from now? If I get that promotion then maybe we can buy a house with a yard up in Rockland County and you can stop worrying about landing roles or selling handbags at Baylor and Bowman."

"So you think I should just give up on my dream of performing on Broadway when we're living in this suburban paradise of yours?"

"Rushing about town, jumping through hoops, facing constant rejection. Why do you put yourself through that?" he said brusquely. "I don't like seeing you bang your head repeatedly against a solid wall."

His words jolted her. She knew better than anyone that the odds for success were stacked against her. But believing in herself was hard enough without having her life partner suggest it might be time to throw in the towel.

He sipped his coffee, looking suddenly defensive. "All I'm saying is that maybe you could come up with a plan B." Cassandra swallowed hard and grasped for her water glass, taking a few big gulps just to give herself a moment to recover. He wasn't done yet: "You've spent the past ten years chasing acting roles in this city, introducing yourself to people as an actress, even though the only place they might realistically recognize you from is a Pepto Bismol commercial. You've chalked up a handful of roles in off-off-Broadway productions, two local insurance commercials, and a leading role in an indie film directed by a grad student that never saw theatrical release and whose biggest selling point is a gratuitous shower scene. Did I miss anything?"

"I thought we agreed never to mention the shower scene."

"I wish I didn't have to," he said snidely.

Her head was spinning. "Well. You know what? I wouldn't trade the past ten years of my life for anything. Shower scene and all."

He ripped off a piece of his danish and took a nibble. "I'm sorry, Cassandra. But it's the people who care about you who have an obligation to be honest sometimes. Do you want to be a sales girl your whole life?"

"There are worse things than working at a department store. I get to meet lots of interesting people. You'll never guess who showed up at my counter yesterday. I completely forgot to tell you about it."

"Someone famous? Gwyneth Paltrow?"

"No nothing like that." Cassandra put her elbows on the

table and balanced her face in her hands. "Do you remember Wilfredo?"

"Wilfredo? Not that subway guy? The one who never called you?" Gregory's face clouded over. "Don't tell me we're back to that again."

"Turns out someone stole his wallet with my number in it. That's why he never texted. So there he was, in my store, shopping for a new wallet. It was so serendipitous."

"Serendipitous, my ass!"

"We have plans to meet for coffee so I can thank him belatedly for, you know—saving my life. You're welcome to tag along if you think you can be civil."

"I have zero desire to meet some random person you bumped into on the subway. And honestly, Cassandra, I'm baffled as to why my fiancée is making dates to meet up with other men."

"It's just a friendly coffee. Don't you think we should still be able to have friends of the opposite sex?"

"No, I don't."

"Well, what about that girl who moved here from Boston. I don't give you a hard time about hanging out with her."

"Penelope? That's different—she's a family friend. I've known her my whole life."

"You don't want me to keep my name. You don't want me to have guy friends. Where does it end? Barefoot and pregnant in the kitchen?"

"Would that be so bad?" He smirked, then seeing her face he quickly reversed course. "I'm kidding!"

Cassandra stared into her fiancé's eyes. If only he *were* kidding. She pictured herself strapped into a minivan driver's seat for the next couple decades and fought back the impulse to yank off her ring and plunk it in his coffee. She probably shouldn't do anything rash, but there was no escaping the fact that she was at a crossroads in her life. She could pick door number one—the life of a blissfully bored suburban housewife. Or door number two—the solitary life of an aging actress waiting for her big break. And then there was the newly minted door number three—the life of a masked bandit living on the wrong side of the law.

18. WILFREDO:
AN ACCIDENTAL ROLE

After a busy day spent decorating the stage backdrops, Toby and Wilfredo were enlisted to help out in wardrobe. The costume department was working frantically to get the recently signed principals fitted for their costumes. Wilfredo was given a bin full of plastic-mold medieval weapons and leather accessories to ferry upstairs.

He rode the elevator up and then pushed the bin down the hallway to Sebastian Estrada's dressing room. The hulking actor was standing in the center of the room dressed in chain mail, a bucket-style helmet on his head. It had thin slits for his eyes and colander-style breathing holes. A team of costume designers around him futzed with his tunic and his armor, pins held between their lips.

Declan was pacing along one side of the room. "Don't forget, we have a preliminary rehearsal scheduled for four o'clock today!"

"We're working as fast as we can!" a costume assistant replied defensively.

"I can't see a thing in this helmet," moaned Sebastian. "And it's hot in here. I can't breathe!"

Declan was unsympathetic. "We had that helmet custom made based on your head measurements. The slits should be right at eye level."

"I don't understand why I can't wear a helmet that sits on top of my head. So my fans can see my face and hear my manly voice!"

"The whole point of your character is that he is supposed to be a faceless knight," the director replied, exasperated.

Wilfredo traipsed back downstairs to wardrobe, missing the rest of their quarrel. He took a perverse pleasure in hearing about the leading man's discomfort. Sebastian Estrada was the kind of star who never bothered to learn anyone's name in the crew. And he had an annoying tendency to barrel through the hallways, expecting everyone in his path to scatter.

Captain Pete whispered in Wilfredo's ear: *You could stand to take a page or two out of that guy's book, Freddy. He walks around like he owns the place and all the girls are swooning in his tracks.*

"I don't want to be anything like him," Wilfredo muttered. "I can't stand all that macho bullshit."

A little macho bullshit would do you a world of good!

"It figures you would take a liking to that jerk."

Wilfredo's next trip upstairs was with a rack of fresh outfits for Ruby, whose loud objections to *her* costumes could be heard from the hallway. It seemed she was taking her fitting cues from her vociferous costar. Her dressing room door was ajar, and Wilfredo knocked perfunctorily as he backed in. He turned around inside and his eyes landed on Ruby, standing six feet away, with her arms out to the side, wearing nothing but a red bra and bikini bottoms. Three costume designers hovered around her with measuring tapes, jotting down numbers in their notebooks. Ruby looked over at him and he made the colossal blunder of making eye contact.

"Why don't you take a picture, it will last longer," she snapped.

Wilfredo cringed and looked away. "Sorry," he mumbled, grabbing the rack loaded up with rejected outfits and flying out of the room as fast as he could manage while staring up at the ceiling. This was just what he needed—to get caught ogling the half-naked lead actress. He knew guys who had been fired for less. There was no denying his gaze had lingered longer than it should have. But that was only because it was Ruby, his old classmate, who he'd had a crush on all those years ago.

Don't be too hard on yourself, Freddy. You're just a regular red-blooded lad. I reckon that peek was worth getting canned. What a swooner she is! I wouldn't mind running aground on her sandbanks! If you catch my drift.

"You're not helping, Captain," Wilfredo grumbled as he pushed the rack down the empty hallway.

I wouldn't kick her out of my cabin for eating sardines!

"Zip it, already."

I'd like to take a stroll down her gangway!

He cursed the Captain under his breath. That croc was getting out of hand. Wilfredo took the elevator back down to the first floor, where he ran into Toby, waiting with a cart full of clothes for secondary cast members. His friend took one look at his face and asked him: "What happened?" Wilfredo filled him in on the red underwear incident, and Toby let out a long whistle. "If you would have just told her the other day that you went to school together you wouldn't be getting all weird around her."

"I don't see the point of bringing it up if she doesn't remember me. That would make it even worse."

"Everybody's just tense because of the schedule. Keep your head down and in five minutes there will be some bigger drama popping up somewhere else. And speaking of drama, isn't tonight your date with Engaged Subway Girl?"

"Yeah, I'm meeting her after work. I keep wondering what her fiancé does to afford that ring."

"He's not pushing clothing racks around an old theater, that's for sure." Toby chuckled as he disappeared into the open elevator.

As the first rehearsal got underway everyone was a little on edge. Toby and Wilfredo were done for the day, but after clocking out they lingered in the auditorium, curious to watch the early stages of production. It took forever for Declan and the lighting designer to set all the lighting cues, and Ruby seemed to be wilting onstage as she moved from mark to mark. She kept asking for bottles of water, and then after taking two sips she would abandon them in random locations.

Sebastian's mood had gone from bad to worse. Declan had insisted the actor needed to wear the helmet, even though it wasn't a dress rehearsal. And the actor kept yanking it off every five minutes and pretending to gasp for air as he clomped about the stage. Once the lights were set, they ran the first scene, where Ruby was introduced, and thankfully it went off without a hitch. Declan had minimal notes.

Scene two was supposed to kick off with a big aside between the knight and the audience. Sebastian strode confidently downstage, followed by a spotlight, but between his helmet obscuring his vision and his giant strides he ended up overshooting his mark by a few feet. His right foot stepped into thin air as he plummeted off the front of the stage, pitching forward into the first row of seats with a frightful wrenching sound that reverberated through the theater. The actor let out a drawn-out "Argh!" followed closely by a cry of "Ay Dios!" Everyone froze for a split second and then they all rushed to help him at the same time.

"Sebastian, are you okay?" yelled Declan hysterically.

"Does it sound like I'm okay, *idiota*? I've busted my leg! I think it's broken!"

One of the sound assistants happened to be in nursing school, and she took one look at him and agreed that it looked broken. This was confirmed with a string of Spanish curses the moment Sebastian tried to move. The actor pulled off his helmet and flung it angrily onto the stage.

Emergency responders arrived within minutes and carried the still-cursing Sebastian out of the theater on a stretcher. As the sound of sirens faded in the distance, Declan sat on the edge of the stage, holding his head in his hands. "We've got under a month to turn this hot mess into a well-oiled machine, and one of our lead actors just broke his leg. What's the recovery time on broken legs, anybody?"

"Six to eight weeks for a straightforward fracture," stated the nursing student timidly.

"I guess we'll just have to rehearse with the stand-in and hope Sebastian can make up for lost ground when he gets back on his feet." Declan let out a heavy sigh. "Remind me who his understudy is?"

All eyes turned to Declan's assistant, Prisha. She was the person who single-handedly managed to keep everyone organized and on task. She flipped through her clipboard, her expression grim. "Declan, if you recall, his only understudy quit two days ago when he got offered a starring role in a music video."

"Isn't he under contract?" Declan yelled, hopping to his feet and pacing back and forth on the stage.

"He said we could sue him if we wanted, but he was taking the job. We've just begun looking for his replacement. I can have someone signed in two or three days."

"I don't have two or three days," Declan thundered. He clutched at the air around him with clawed fingers. "I need someone by tomorrow morning. I don't care who it is so long as they wear the helmet, stand where I need them to stand, and read the lines, so I can work the kinks out of this damn play. I'll grab someone off the street if I have to!" This pronouncement was followed by dead silence. And that's when Toby began to wave his arm about wildly. "Hey, Declan, Wilfredo here went to acting school for a few years. He's been in a few productions, haven't you, Wilfredo? I bet he could stand in as the knight in a pinch!"

Now everyone was staring at Wilfredo, who couldn't believe Toby had just put him on the spot like that. He squirmed uncomfortably in his seat. "Well, actually—" he began to say.

"Wilfredo! Get over here!" Declan boomed. Wilfredo shot up and hurried down the aisle and up onto the stage, coming to a stop next to the white-haired director. "Is that true?" Declan asked. "You've done some acting?"

"Just high school and college. Until I dropped out. I wasn't any good."

"Beggars can't be choosers." Declan picked up Sebastian's discarded helmet, and lowered it into place over Wilfredo's head. He walked around him, scrutinizing him thoughtfully. "You know what they say—if the shoe fits! I'm going to give you a copy of the script. Learn your lines for the first four scenes by tomorrow morning. Got it? It will just be for a few days, a week tops."

Wilfredo nodded. "Sure thing. I'll give it a whirl."

"And, Wilfredo?"

"Yes?"

"Don't fall off the stage."

19. GREGORY: TACOS FOR THREE

Gregory stared at his clean-shaven face in the bathroom mirror. A bottle of spirit gum sat open on the marble countertop in front of him. He dipped a paintbrush and applied the glue gently to his upper lip. He waited patiently for a few minutes, then dabbed at his skin with his index finger to make sure it felt tacky. He placed the fake mustache carefully, pressing down the mesh backing until it became invisible against his skin. He took half a step back and inspected the results. The bristly lampshade mustache under his nose looked convincingly real. He was especially pleased that the color matched his dark brown hair perfectly.

Out in the living room he put on his tortoiseshell sunglasses and his new tweed cap, tucking his hair carefully under it. Another mirror check, this time in the hallway, brought a smile to his face. Even his own mother wouldn't recognize him.

As he went out the door, he threw his Burberry trench coat over one arm. It might be a bit conspicuous—Cassandra had seen him wear it on occasion—but he wanted to stay dry, and he reasoned that many people had tan coats just like it.

Climbing into a cab, he told the driver to drop him on the corner of Mott Street and Houston, about a block away from where Cassandra was supposedly meeting her new friend.

Every time he thought about Cassandra's plans he quivered with rage. Apparently, spending ten grand on an engagement ring wasn't enough to make her think twice about going on a date with another man. He had yet to set eyes on this Wilfredo person, and he was itching to get a look at him. The plan was to keep a close watch on the two of them tonight—from a safe distance.

He had purchased a micro wireless earpiece set, and last night at dinner he had surreptitiously tucked one of the two earpieces into the side flap of Cassandra's purse, with the microphone dot placed close to the top. He had tested it by asking her to order for him and pretending to slip away to the bathroom. Her voice had come through loud and clear. The only drawback was that he had to be within fifty feet for it to work.

Slamming the cab door, he slunk down Mott Street, heading toward the cupcake shop. He was about ten minutes early, which, knowing his fiancée, would leave him plenty of time to stake out a good spot. When the bakery came into view Gregory noticed a large man standing outside, his hands shoved into the pockets of a barn jacket. He was a little ragged looking, his longish hair hanging down from a cuffed beanie, and his unbuttoned blue flannel shirt revealing a stained T-shirt underneath. The man's head was bobbing from side to side, as if he were moving to music, although he didn't appear to be wearing headphones. If this was Wilfredo, Gregory was unimpressed.

There was a small bookstore just around the corner from the bakery with a slatted wooden bench out front, and Gregory stationed himself there, tugging down the brim of his cap and pretending to look at his phone, while keeping one eye on the cupcake shop stranger. Sure enough, Cassandra showed up ten minutes late. She greeted the flannel shirt guy with a lingering hug and Gregory resisted the urge to spring up off the bench and pry them apart. His earpiece cackled with static but the conversation it picked up was garbled and broken—he was too far away. Judging by her gestures Cassandra seemed to be apologizing for her tardiness, but Wilfredo waved his hand dismissively and was all smiles. *Easy enough to be gracious the first time, chum,* Gregory fumed. He watched them peer dubiously into the bakery window, exchange some words, and then turn and walk west together.

It would seem that the coffee and cupcake plan had been scrapped. With growing suspicions Gregory stood up and followed them, careful not to get too close. The pair made a left on Elizabeth Street, so he made a left on Elizabeth Street. About halfway up the block they stopped in front of what looked like a small taqueria, and this Wilfredo person held the door open for Cassandra. Gregory wanted to run up and punch him in the nose, but he restrained himself.

Gregory lingered outside for a few minutes, making sure they didn't come right back out again, then he made his way over to the restaurant. Outside, a painted sign read BAJA TACOS. There was no way to see into the interior as the windows were blocked with colorful curtains. He tapped his upper lip to make sure the mustache was still holding firm, and walked in. It was an unassuming taqueria with colorful metal tables and chairs and white-tiled walls. It was packed with mostly young people hanging out after work, their tables sprinkled with shot glasses. A young hostess greeted him and he asked for a table for one. She tried to seat him near the door, but Gregory demurred as he had spotted Cassandra and Wilfredo seated farther inside. Instead he pointed over to a small table along the back wall that was the right distance and ensured Cassandra would be facing away from him.

As he walked past their table Gregory looked the other way. His earpiece crackled to life and he heard a little snippet of their conversation faintly in his right ear. Maybe he'd missed his calling. Maybe he should've been a spy. At his table he took the menu from the hostess, hopped up onto a square stool, and turned up the volume on his earpiece so that two voices came to him clearly above the din of the crowded restaurant.

He had an excellent view of their table. Cassandra was already sipping a pink beverage and Wilfredo had a beer bottle in front of him—no glass. Gregory inadvertently let out an indignant snort. Suddenly worried that Cassandra might turn and look his way, he held the small menu in front of his face. Peeking over the edge moments later he saw that a smiling waiter had appeared at his table and was looking at him expectantly. Gregory glanced quickly at the paper menu and ordered the tacos al pastor, a side of guacamole, and a sparkling water. He had never warmed to tacos, considering them messy street food, so he wasn't expecting much from his dinner tonight.

The waiter went straight from his table to Cassandra's. Gregory saw Wilfredo's large hands nervously twirling the mini pencil used to mark their dinner selections. They were beaming at each other, having just discovered that they were both vegetarians. Gregory cursed under his breath. Just his luck that this guy would turn out to be another veg-head bozo.

"I can vouch for the mushroom tacos," Wilfredo remarked. "And the fried avocado tacos are amazing too."

"I would kill for a mushroom taco," replied Cassandra excitedly, her voice tinny in his ear. They ordered two tacos each and a side of street corn to split, and the waiter collected their menus. Gregory felt that he already had Wilfredo's number. This guy's schtick was to pretend to be friendly and easygoing until she let her guard down, at which point he would no doubt move in for the kill.

The waiter brought Gregory his sparkling water and said the guacamole would be right out. Gregory nodded and waved him away. With his hand cupped over his ear he listened in on the conversation taking place a short distance away:

"Thank god you were standing on that subway platform that day. I was terrified when that train started moving."

"Anyone else would have done the same. I just happened to be close by."

"Oh please, don't be modest. It was so brave of you to jump in the way you did. Most people would have just watched in horror. You realize we barely broke free in time?"

The fathead had the gall to act embarrassed, and Gregory heard him change the subject, asking Cassandra where she was from. She filled him in on how she'd grown up in the Bay Area, but had lived in New York for the past ten years. He volunteered that he was from a small town upstate on the Hudson, and had moved to the city right around the same time as her.

Finally, she mentioned her fiancé. It had only taken fifteen minutes for her to bring him up. Not that he was keeping track or anything. Gregory waited expectantly for Wilfredo's reaction.

"Have you picked a wedding venue yet?" Wilfredo asked.

Cassandra sighed. "We're still working on it."

Gregory's view of their table was suddenly blocked by the waiter, who had popped up with his guacamole, clearing some room on the tiny table before putting it down. "I hope you like it. It's freshly made!" The waiter's smile was grating, and Gregory glared at him until he wandered off.

Gregory hated waiters, he hated Mexican restaurants, and he hated tacos. But most of all he hated the breezy conversation that was being piped into his right eardrum. These two were having a grand time, and not even talk of her engagement seemed to have dampened their fun. Gregory tensed as he was struck by an alarming thought. Maybe this guy targeted married women? Wilfredo might specialize in spotting ring-toting women to yank from in front of buses and trains, using the whole heroism angle to lure them back to his apartment?

The smiling waiter appeared once more with Gregory's pork tacos. Plates of food had arrived at Cassandra's table as well, and she was already biting into the vaunted mushroom taco. "Oh man! This is *so* good. I've been craving Mexican."

"Amazing, right?" Wilfredo beamed. Gregory's eyes bulged as he watched Wilfredo dump an ocean of hot sauce onto his two tacos.

"Er, Wilfredo?" said a concerned Cassandra. "You do realize that's ghost pepper hot sauce?"

"Yeah. Don't worry. I always do this."

"I guess you're just one of those guys who likes living on the edge."

Cassandra was sampling her fried avocado taco. "Oh my god, this one's even better. I can't believe I haven't been here before. My fiancé isn't a fan of Mexican food, so I've been a bit taco deprived lately."

"Well he doesn't know what he's missing." Wilfredo clinked his raised beer bottle with her pink agua fresca. "To tacos."

"To tacos," she repeated. "The best food in the whole universe."

Gregory looked down at his pork tacos. "The best food in the whole universe," he muttered mockingly under his breath. With some trepidation he scooped a bit of guacamole up with a tortilla chip and took a tentative bite. His eyebrows shot up. Not bad. He took a bite of his pork tacos, and chewed thoughtfully. It was delicious, he couldn't deny it. But boy were they messy, and it wasn't long before guacamole found its way onto his fake mustache. He wiped at it, and then panicked that the darn thing had shifted.

The voices continued unabated in his ear. "How about you, Wilfredo? Which box do you check? Single or taken?"

"I'm single."

"Not seeing anyone special?"

"Nope. I've been unattached for the last five years."

"That's a long time."

"No kidding. I mean I go out on the occasional date, but nothing seems to stick."

"But you used to have a girlfriend?"

"Yep. Nadia. We dated for four years, and lived together for one."

"What happened?"

"She rode off into the sunset on the back of a motorcycle belonging to this guy she met in a bar."

A momentary pang of sympathy hit Gregory, but he choked it down.

"Sounds rough," said Cassandra sympathetically.

"Well. It's just how things worked out. I'm over it. But it's not easy meeting new people. Everyone's doing online dating these days, and I just recently got my first smartphone."

"So you're a bit of a Luddite then."

Wilfredo nodded hesitantly and Gregory harrumphed, sure that the man had no idea what that word meant. "I'm sorry," Wilfredo said, "but I have to point out that there's this strange guy with a mustache sitting alone at a table by the wall who keeps giving me strange looks. It's been weirding me out since we sat down."

Gregory, who was taking a sip from his sparkling water, nearly spit it out in surprise.

"Really? I'm going to sneak a look at him," Cassandra said. Gregory hunched down, turning his face to the wall. "I can't see his face," her voice said in his ear. "But I wouldn't worry. He's probably just one of those harmless oddballs New York seems to have in spades."

"You're probably right. And it seems like he has finally lost interest in me, thankfully."

"Tell me Wilfredo, how do you keep busy in this crazy city of ours?"

"I work as a stagehand and workshop guy at the Cornelius Theater."

"No way! You mean you work backstage on Broadway? Making the magic happen?"

"That's me, toiling away behind the scenes so everything goes smoothly on opening night."

"That sounds like an amazing job."

"It has its moments. Like today, when I walked in on our lead actress in her underwear during a fitting." Gregory's mouth fell open as he listened to Wilfredo explain about how he'd gone to school with the actress, and how he'd been taken aback to see her standing there in silky red undergarments, and how she didn't even remember him from back in the day. "So she looks right at me and says: 'Take a picture, it'll last longer!' I was mortified. I thought for sure I was going to get canned. And I mean I wasn't gawking at her, I was just caught by surprise. Luckily, she doesn't seem to have complained to anyone."

Cassandra had been cracking up throughout the whole story, her rolling laugh ringing in Gregory's ear. He loved her laugh. It was one of the things that had drawn him to her. And he realized only now that it had been ages since he'd last heard it. Yet here she was chortling away with this stranger.

"Oh my god, that's the funniest thing I've heard in weeks." Cassandra took a deep breath trying to bring her laughter under control. "I'm an actress myself, you know. Still waiting for my big break. Getting to Broadway is my dream." Cassandra sketched out her acting experiences for him, and Wilfredo listened intently.

"I was a theater major too," he confessed. "Before I dropped out."

"What made you quit?"

"I wasn't any good."

"That can't be true."

"I had terrible stage fright. Standing onstage looking out at the audience all my lines would fly out of my head. But weirdly enough it looks like I'm going to have to dust off my acting skills. We had some major drama during rehearsal today. The lead actor fell off the stage and broke his leg."

"What? Is he all right? Who is the actor?"

"He'll be fine. You've probably heard of him. Sebastian Estrada? Latin heartthrob extraordinaire."

"Wow. He's a big deal! Sounds like a real setback for the play. But I guess it's the understudy's lucky day."

"You'd think. But it turns out his understudy got a role in a music video and abandoned us for Tinseltown about a week ago."

"Ouch."

"So get this. The director was suddenly desperate for a warm body onstage, and Toby goes and talks up my acting experience. And the next thing you know the director grabs me and tells me to fill in at rehearsal tomorrow! So after our little dinner I have to rush home and learn the co-lead's lines for the first four scenes."

"That's incredible! How exciting! This could be your big break!" She paused, and then her voice took on a note of concern. "I hope I'm not keeping you from memorizing the script?"

"Don't worry, he doesn't have a lot of lines early on. He's more of the strong silent type. And I didn't want to postpone our little meetup."

I'll bet you didn't, Gregory thought furiously.

"Hey, do you need someone to run lines with? I'd be happy to help if I can."

Gregory's hands tightened into fists.

"Do you mean it?" Wilfredo asked. "Are you free tonight? It would be a *huge* help. My friend Toby—you remember Toby—said he'd give it a go. But he's got basketball tickets, and won't be home until late."

"Hey, it's not like I owe you a favor or anything," she joked. "You know, in some cultures saving someone's life means they become your slave forever."

"I'll settle for a rehearsal partner."

"Are you freaking out about tomorrow?"

"I've been doing a great job distracting myself."

"Well, let's get out of here and get to work. And don't even think about reaching for the check, mister."

"Hey, your fiancé won't mind, will he? You coming over, I mean. I don't want to cause any issues for you."

"Oh, don't worry about Gregory. I'm sure he will understand when I explain the situation."

No I won't bloody understand, Gregory fumed. Here she was having dinner with this nimrod, and now they were headed off to his apartment? Unbelievable! He gripped the edge of the table with white knuckles, willing himself not to look their way. He needed to ditch his disguise and find a way to intercept her. It was time to nip this in the bud before it got completely out of hand. He was clenching his jaw so hard that the earpiece suddenly popped out, and fell into his sparkling water. *Oh crap!* He looked up and saw Wilfredo speaking, but now he had no idea what he was saying. He watched him flag down the waiter.

Gregory reached into his water glass with a fork and fished out the dripping earpiece. Drying it with his napkin he pressed it back into his ear. It was cold, and wet, and made no sound whatsoever.

He glanced over again in time to see Cassandra and Wilfredo dump some cash on the table and head for the exit. Gregory waved his credit card madly at the waiter, who wandered over with that moronic smile still plastered on his face. Taking the credit card, the waiter strolled off, stopping along the way to take an order at a crowded table. Gregory drummed his fingers on the metal tabletop. Maybe he should just bolt out of here without his card? But no, the waiter was finally approaching with his receipt.

"I hope you enjoyed your meal, sir."

"Yes, yes, it was delicious. Where is the pen? I need a pen." The waiter fished a white ballpoint from his apron. Gregory wrote in a seven-dollar tip, signed his name, and leaped off his stool.

"Don't forget your card, sir!"

Gregory backtracked for his card and then dashed out of the restaurant. But once he got outside, Cassandra and Wilfredo were nowhere to be seen.

20. WILFREDO:
A NEW REHEARSAL PARTNER

They walked east together along the narrow sidewalk, past the popular hotspots on Orchard and Ludlow, after which the streets began to empty out and the city turned colder and darker. They wrapped their coats a little tighter around themselves and kept up a brisk pace as he told her all about the play, interrupted repeatedly by Cassandra's dinging phone, until she finally muted it.

Wilfredo hit her with a raised eyebrow. "Call me crazy, but I get the feeling your fiancé is trying to get ahold of you."

"He is, but I don't really want to talk to him right now. He can get a tad possessive sometimes, but there's no way I'm going to let him stop me from helping out a new friend. If he can't deal with it, then he can go soak his head in a bucket."

Wilfredo plodded along on the sidewalk beside her, wondering what exactly he was getting himself into.

Don't worry about that bucket-head, Freddy. Their romance is clearly on the rocks! This is where you swoop in and steal her out from under him. If you have the apricots!

Wilfredo's brow darkened as he willed the troublesome Captain out of his head. Cassandra had said it herself—they were just friends. An unexpected friendship born of unlikely circumstances and nurtured by a mutual love of tacos.

Gimme a break, Freddy. You don't really expect to be pals

with a dish like her? Look at you—you're like jelly around her. Every time she looks at you with those green eyes of hers it's like you've just been clocked in the back of the head with a brick.

Wilfredo snuck a glance at Cassandra's profile. She was astonishingly pretty. And the Captain was right—it made things confusing. When he was around her he had a constant flutter of nerves in the pit of his stomach. Was it possible she felt something similar for him? Or was that just wishful thinking?

Ah, Freddy, you're making a tactical error. You should never try to get inside a woman's mind. It's a fool's errand is what it is. It's a sure way to drive yourself mad!

Wilfredo was forced to admit that he didn't have a clue what was going through her head. Superficial emotions would flicker transparently over her face, but it was as if all her deeper feelings were tucked safely behind an impenetrable wall.

They made a right on Clinton Street and were soon standing in front of the red brick building Wilfredo called home. "This is it. Fifth floor. No elevator I'm afraid."

"I live just ten blocks from here. We're practically neighbors!"

They headed upstairs, where Wilfredo fumbled nervously with his keys before unlocking the door. The first thing Cassandra noticed when she walked in was Captain Pete, propped up on the shelf near the entrance. "Whoa! Is that a ventriloquist dummy?"

"That's Captain Pete, sea croc, and relic of my days as a seventh-grade dork."

"It's like his eyes follow you around the room!"

"Tell me about it." He made a lip-zipping gesture at the dummy behind Cassandra's back. Wilfredo dug two copies of the script from the inside pocket of his coat and handed one of them to Cassandra. "Would you like some tea while you read? Chai? Chamomile? Rooibos?"

"Chamomile sounds perfect, thanks. I'm going to dive right into this script!" She perched herself on the edge of the couch in the living room and flipped over the title page. Wilfredo filled the kettle and placed it on the burner. It wasn't long before he had two steaming cups of tea. Cassandra took the mug from him and warmed her hands with it.

"Hey, Wilfredo, maybe you should improvise a costume? The knight's armor feels important to the role."

"Why didn't I think of that? A paper bag might work for a helmet. I mean, I might look a little goofy."

"Go for it. Don't worry about being goofy."

Wilfredo trimmed down a paper grocery bag to fit over his head. Then he cut eye slits in the right spots, and poked breathing holes in it with a pencil. The result bore a surprising resemblance to the actual helmet. He grabbed an old mop handle from the closet to use as a pretend sword and turned the lid of a storage bin into a makeshift shield with some duct-tape straps. He was finished just as she looked up from her reading.

"Wow, Wilfredo, you really *are* playing one of the leads!"

"I'm the last-minute stand-in for the runaway understudy for rehearsal tomorrow. I doubt my acting gig will last for more than a day. For all I know they may have lined up someone more experienced than me already."

"Or. Maybe you will astonish them with your performance

and earn a spot in the cast." She gave him a pointed look. "A lot of people would kill for an opportunity like this."

"I'd be happy just to not make a fool of myself."

"You won't. Not if I have a say in it." She took the paper helmet from him, plopped it on his head and grinned. Wilfredo stuck the mop handle through a belt loop in his pants and grabbed his fake shield. With Toby gone, they had the run of the living room, so they pushed the coffee table and the armchair out of the way to make full use of the small space. They started out with scripts in hand, but after just a few readings Cassandra somehow managed to memorize her lines. Wilfredo was shocked to discover her interpretation of Violet was more layered than Ruby's.

They ran through the scenes over and over until he had all his lines down cold. Thankfully the knight—despite being the titular character—did most of his talking in two extended monologues. Wilfredo's acting skills were rusty, but Cassandra's helped him work out that the best way to play the character was with exaggerated gestures and head movements that straddled the line between the dramatic and the comical. At other times Cassandra encouraged Wilfredo to sit and stand like a lifeless statue, playing up the question of whether he was nothing more than a figment of Violet's fervid imagination.

It was nearing eleven o'clock when she took her last sip of tea and glanced at her phone. "Well. I think you're ready, Wilfredo. Which means it's time for me to head out."

"Thanks, Cassandra. Without your help I would've been a complete disaster tomorrow."

"Text me after rehearsal. I'll be curious to hear how it went."

"You betcha!"

"And remember—don't pull your punches. Use their low expectations to your advantage."

"Will do."

"I had an absolute blast. And I'm happy to do it all over again tomorrow night if you need me."

"I don't think I could ask you to do that."

"Of course you can. Don't forget about—you know—the subway train! But, I mean you only have to take me up on it if you want my help."

"Honestly, I don't think I could do this without you. I'll keep you posted about tomorrow then." Wilfredo carried their mugs over to the sink. He watched Cassandra put on her coat and her gloves. "I hope your fiancé isn't too annoyed with you."

She rolled her eyes. "He has no reason to be mad."

He walked her to the door and they hugged goodbye. She gave him a smile and a wave as she headed down the hallway, and he waited until she had disappeared down the stairwell before closing the door. When he turned around, Captain Pete fixed him with a piercing stare.

You can't fool me with this just friends business, Freddy. I know that glazed look in your eyes. I've seen it in many a shipmate caught in the lure of the sirens' song. Take it from me, pal, your best bet is to plug your ears and tie yourself to the mast!

21. CASSANDRA:
SHOWDOWN IN TUDOR CITY

She had been avoiding Gregory's texts and calls since they'd left the restaurant, even though her phone was blowing up. Apparently, Gregory was having a bit of a meltdown. As she walked east toward First Avenue Cassandra steeled herself and looked at her screen. There were thirty-five increasingly deranged messages from Gregory, and a bunch of missed phone calls. She read through them, gritting her teeth.

When she was done, she just typed: *Sorry, my phone was on mute. Just got these*

Gregory replied: *What do you mean your phone was on mute!!!*

Cassandra: *It's a little switch near the top*

Gregory: **triple angry face emoji**

Cassandra: *You know, not answering phone messages right away isn't actually against the law*

Gregory: *Where are you? We need to talk*

Cassandra sighed. If some sort of showdown was inevitable then she might as well get it over with. And if she met him at his place that might make him think twice about yelling at her, since he was always worried about disturbing his neighbors.

Cassandra: *I'm downtown. I can hop on a bus up first ave if you're home*

Gregory: *Take a cab. I'll reimburse you*

When she arrived, he was standing in his apartment doorway, a dark look on his face. Right away he demanded to know where she'd been all this time. She pushed through into his apartment and poured herself a glass of water at the kitchen sink. "We went out to dinner, and then I went to Wilfredo's apartment to help him run lines. It turns out he's an actor too."

"I thought you said he was a stagehand."

"He is. It's a long story."

"This is unacceptable, Cassandra. I won't put up with my fiancée going over to strange men's apartments."

"He's not a strange man. He's my new friend Wilfredo. And *I* won't put up with *you* telling me who I can and can't be friends with."

"I didn't sign up for this garbage."

"Neither did I. The man who asked me to marry him was sweet, caring, and considerate. The man I've been engaged to this past month is jealous, controlling, and unsupportive."

"What are you saying?"

Cassandra slid the engagement ring off her finger. "Here, I think you should take this." She held it out to him.

Gregory looked genuinely shocked. But he didn't reach out to take the ring from her. "Let's not do this, Cassandra. Breaking off our engagement is not what I want. We can get through this. You're right, I shouldn't have gotten myself all worked up over nothing tonight. I'm sorry. I haven't been myself lately. I'm under a lot of pressure at work, and I've let the wedding planning get to me. I'm sorry I lost my temper. Let me take you to dinner Friday night and make it up to you."

She stared at him doubtfully.

"Please, Cassandra—anywhere you want to go."

"Even . . . tacos?"

"Of course."

"Fine. I'll meet you for dinner. But I'm worried about us, Gregory. I think we're in very different places in life."

He stepped forward. Taking her hand and the ring he slipped it back on her finger. "It's my fault. I see that now. I've ruined everything. But I swear, we can get through this together."

"It's my fault too. I always knew you were straitlaced, but I figured I'd get you to loosen up—eventually. We both made the same mistake."

"And now that we know where we went wrong, we can fix it. You know what they say—opposites attract."

Cassandra wasn't so sure. But she knew she hadn't really been honest with Gregory in a long time. She felt like a hypocrite. If he really knew the kind of person she was he would've been quick to take back the ring. A void had opened up between them recently and she had no clue how to close the gap. But a good place to start would be to put the whole Cat Burglar business behind her. Because ever since she'd stolen that wallet on Halloween, her life had been spinning out of control.

22. WILFREDO: FOXMAN
PATROLLING THE CITY

Wilfredo lay sprawled on the living room floor staring up at the ceiling, three empty beer bottles lined up beside him, when he heard keys rattle and the sound of the lock turning. Toby walked in, letting the door slam shut behind him. He stopped short when he caught sight of Wilfredo and pushed his headphones back onto his neck.

"Having a one-man party?" Toby asked with a raised eyebrow.

"Toby! I'm so glad you're home. I think I'm in love with Engaged Subway Girl."

"I thought we already knew that?"

"What do I do?"

"Don't worry too much about it. She's way too good for your sorry ass anyway. I mean you're like a five-and-a-half on a good day."

"We ate dinner at Baja Tacos and then she came over to help me rehearse for tomorrow."

"I see. The two of you all alone in this apartment . . ."

"It wasn't like that. We just ran lines."

"Great! I'm glad to hear you don't need my help rehearsing after all. Because there's something else we need to do."

Wilfredo groaned. He didn't like the sound of this.

Toby plopped himself down on the couch. "I've been keeping tabs on the stats for that viral video of yours. The numbers are through the roof! It's all over the web, dude. We've gotta make a follow-up while this thing is still hot!"

"Not a chance. I'm wiped"

"Oh c'mon. I don't ask for much. Just put on that costume and we'll go outside for five minutes and I'll shoot some video of you on your longboard. Then I'll upload it to the web and sit back and watch the view count spin!"

"Not gonna happen. I've got a big day tomorrow, remember? I need my rest."

"You know, Wilfredo, I bet you wouldn't want me hanging around the living room next time Cassandra comes over to help you rehearse. It would be a real shame if your roommate was up in your grill the whole time." Wilfredo stared coldly at his friend, who gave him a shameless smile. "My camcorder is all charged up. I'm ready when you are. Just five minutes."

A short while later Wilfredo found himself outside on the street in his Foxman costume. Luckily it was late and the street was basically deserted. Toby took footage from various angles, throwing himself on the ground, and then climbing onto a planter and holding his camcorder over his head. Wilfredo struck various action poses with his arms on his hips and his chest puffed out.

At Toby's direction Wilfredo skated east toward Norfolk, with his roommate jogging backward ahead of him. And that's when Wilfredo noticed a guy in a Mets cap stepping out of the ATM booth belonging to the bank on the corner. The man was shoving some fresh bills in his wallet and didn't notice the figure looming behind him until it was too late. A different man, this one dressed in a tattered coat, leaped out of the shadows, grabbed the guy's wallet, and shoved the poor man against the parked cars. Then the thief took off running, heading right in their direction. Wilfredo would have recognized this mugger anywhere. He was wearing the same army hat and had the same loping run. It was Johnny, the vagrant who had stolen his own wallet many weeks ago.

Without even thinking Wilfredo swerved to intercept him. Johnny was glancing back to see if the guy he'd just mugged was going to chase him. Wilfredo lowered his shoulder and popped the thief right in the solar plexus. The street bum flew backward, landing flat on his back. The wallet he was holding popped up into the air, and this time Wilfredo stuck out a hand and caught it as it fell. He stared down at the dazed criminal.

"Not this time, jackass!"

The victim ran over and Wilfredo handed him back his wallet. "I believe this is yours, sir."

The vagrant had recovered enough to scramble to his feet and pick up his hat which had fallen on the ground. Then he took off running down the street, slower than before and with a little hitch in his step. The man in the baseball cap waved his arms frantically: "He's getting away!"

"He can run but he can't hide!" Toby exclaimed. "I got the whole thing on tape. Including a close-up of his face. Now the cops will have some solid evidence to arrest him."

The Mets fan turned back to Wilfredo. "That was amazing

what you did. Aren't you the guy from that video? Foxman! I can't believe Foxman just recovered my wallet and decked the creep who stole it. Here, take fifty bucks as a reward." The man held out some cash to him.

"That won't be necessary, sir. Justice is its own reward," Wilfredo replied solemnly, staring into Toby's still-rolling camera.

23. CASSANDRA:
CRIMES OF OPPORTUNITY

Cassandra spun out through the revolving door at Baylor & Bowman into the chill winter air, tucking her nose under her scarf when she was met with a gust of wind. The short-lived winter sun had long since dipped behind the skyline, bestowing an early nightfall on the city. She needed to run over to the pet store on Columbus before heading home, as she had used up the last can of cat food that morning. With a little luck they would have Jupiter's favorite sardine flavor, otherwise he would be in a real funk come dinner time.

It was a four-and-a-half-block walk north along the quiet avenue. Most shops were already closed and restaurants were slowly emptying out. By the time she got to the pet store the chill had begun to work its way into her extremities. Nearing the shop, Cassandra saw an older woman in a fur-lined coat walking a French bulldog who had just finished doing its business on the sidewalk. The woman blatantly ignored her duties as a dog owner, leaving the steaming deposit in the path of her fellow New Yorkers. She took no notice of the nasty look Cassandra gave her either.

Cassandra pushed into the narrow store, its messy aisles crammed floor to ceiling with pet-related paraphernalia. She paused on her way to the back of the store to greet a store cat who wandered down the aisle. Then she located Jupiter's beloved sardine cutlets and tossed twelve cans into her basket. When she got to the counter she was annoyed to see the woman with the French bulldog standing at the register. "Please send four cases around to my building first thing in the morning." She had a silvery pixie-cut hairdo and arched painted eyebrows. "The doorman will take the delivery. I need to stock up for little Duke." She dug a platinum card out of her purse. Cassandra waited patiently as the woman struggled to swipe her card and click the right buttons. It didn't help that her eyesight was terrible. As she waited, holding her basket, Cassandra gazed down at the bored French bulldog at the end of the leash. He was wearing a functional mesh harness as well as a glitzy diamond-studded collar with a large blue teardrop gem dangling in front. Cassandra's brow furrowed. These things had to be cheap rhinestones, right?

Curious, she whipped out her phone and searched for diamond dog collars. After clicking on a few links she found it. The exact collar this pooch was wearing, down to the sapphire pendant. Her eyes locked onto the price tag and she almost dropped her phone. Three hundred grand? This crazy woman had spent three hundred grand on a dog collar?

Cassandra sighed. The odd thing about becoming a thief, she realized, was that you became attuned to the myriad opportunities daily life presented for swiping other people's valuables.

The machine finally processed the woman's payment and she went on her way, dragging the French bulldog toward the exit. "Come on, Duke. You know those cheap doggy biscuits are full of fillers." Cassandra quickly paid cash for her cat food and was out the door soon after. She spied the old woman and her dog down the block and turned to follow them. When they made a right onto a side street, she made that same right. Cassandra tucked her long hair under her knit hat, and wrapped the white scarf a little more tightly around her face. Picking up her pace she scooted by the woman and the dog on the narrow sidewalk. It was a quiet block, illuminated by street lamps casting patches of yellow light on the terracotta brownstone stoops.

Cassandra could hear the woman's heels clicking on the cement behind her. Just then, Cassandra's toe snagged on a crack in the sidewalk and she tumbled forward, scattering cat food cans on the ground. She crouched down to pick them up as the old woman and her dog drew near.

"Excuse me, you are in our way!" grumbled the old woman impatiently.

"I'm so sorry. I'll just need to pick up these cans. Aww, who is this little guy?" The French bulldog was yapping at her nonstop.

"I should warn you that he doesn't take to strangers."

But Cassandra had pocketed a free doggy treat at the pet food store counter, which she now had palmed in her hand. Feisty Duke ceased his yapping once he caught a whiff. *There's a good boy.* All that was needed now was a little misdirection. "Ooh, watch out for that mean-looking pit bull!" Cassandra pointed behind the old woman. The old lady swiveled around. "Where? Where? He'd better not come anywhere near my Duke!"

Cassandra fed the treat to the dog surreptitiously as she deftly slid the jeweled collar from his neck and slipped it into the grocery bag along with the cat food. "Oh, never mind. I think they ducked into an entranceway." Cassandra finished scooping up the fallen cans, hopped to her feet, and hurried on her way, crossing the street mid-block and then doubling back in the other direction. A last glance over her shoulder showed the silhouette of the old lady disappearing in the distance.

Her pulse was pounding as she hurried toward the subway. She had succumbed yet again to this thieving madness, and now she was holding a fortune in jewels in a paper bag along with her cat food. An alarming thought hit her: What if the stones were actually fake? Spying an empty liquor bottle discarded on a stoop she reached down and picked it up. Pulling the collar out of the bag she discreetly scraped the point of one of the stones across the glass. It left a deep scratch in its wake.

Cassandra breathed a little easier as she made her way down the subway steps. As soon as she got home, she would pry the jewels loose and put them in a Ziploc bag with one of her calling cards. Then she would pack them up in a jiffy bag and drop them into a mailbox addressed to the animal shelter on Twenty-Third Street. This score would be the perfect capstone to her brief career as a thief.

24. DETECTIVE MOLINA: THE LIEUTENANT BLOWS HIS TOP

The steam radiators were cranked up full blast inside the bustling thirteenth precinct, turning the large main room into a veritable sauna. Industrial metal desks were spread a few feet apart, laid out from wall to wall under hanging fluorescent lights. At one such desk sat a sweltering Detective Molina, his jacket spread on the back of his chair and his shirtsleeves rolled up to his elbows. He was staring woefully at a video on his computer monitor. That unsolved pickpocket case should've dropped off the radar by now, but with both individuals from the original video back in the media, this case wasn't going away anytime soon.

"Cheer up, partner. We'll track down this nut," said Garcia, who was parked at the adjoining desk, busy making enhanced still frames from the fox guy's new vigilante video. "Here, have a donut." She slid a box of chocolate glazed donuts across her desk in his direction.

Hesitantly, Detective Molina grabbed one and took a large bite of the sugary treat. "I just hope the lieutenant doesn't get wind of this video."

"I'm sure he has bigger fish to fry," replied Detective Garcia, a touch of nervousness in her voice.

"*Laborare est orare,*" Detective Molina recited.

"What does that mean?"

"To work is to pray."

"Well amen to that!"

But their prayers proved futile, as Lieutenant Kopski's booming voice soon rattled the windows of the precinct room. "Molina! Garcia! In my office! Now!" Their colleagues' heads swiveled in their direction, twitching lips betraying their poorly concealed glee.

The burly lieutenant was pacing in the space between his desk and a row of filing cabinets. His face was flushed, and his large hands were swatting at the air around him. "Can either of you two clowns explain to me," he yelled, "why I'm watching a news clip of some costumed vigilante in our sector tackling a mugger and recovering a victim's wallet? He's making us look like fools! He's doing *our* job, dressed in a ridiculous costume!"

"Don't worry, Lieutenant," said Garcia. "We're following up on some leads, and we're going to find that vigilante and throw the book at him."

"You have been searching for this guy for weeks without results!" The lieutenant stabbed a beefy index finger in their direction, his face twisted into a scowl. "And that Cat Burglar woman is getting press that makes her out to be a champion for the poor because she donated a quarter of a million dollars' worth of stolen diamonds to an animal shelter? Are you kidding me? Where did she get those damn jewels?" Lieutenant Kopski pounded his desk with a sledgehammer-like fist that sent his pens and paper clips leaping into the air.

"We're working on that, sir. We've had the gems examined by an expert. We think they came from a dog collar?"

"A dog collar? Are you telling me there are people walking

around this crazy city with a quarter of a million in jewels tied around their dog's neck?"

"It would seem so, sir."

"Tell me the diamonds are in the safe in the evidence room."

"The shelter has retained possession for now. They aren't considered stolen property until someone reports them stolen, and we think the owner may be hesitant to report the theft in view of likely negative media attention."

"I can't take any more of this bullshit! Get out there and crack this case! I want both of these costumed punks collared—today!" Kopski had worked his voice up to ear-drum-shattering decibel levels. A mortified Detective Molina followed his younger partner out the door, and they walked back to their desks with their heads bowed, turning a blind eye to their snickering colleagues.

25. WILFREDO:
A CURE FOR AMNESIA

When act one ended there was a brief moment of blackout before the house lights came on. Wilfredo turned his head from side to side as he looked around, the world around him reduced to what he could glimpse through the helmet's narrow eye slits. Scattered applause and a few whoops of encouragement from the crew brought smiles to the cast's faces. It was Wednesday, Wilfredo's fourth day playing the knight, and he was becoming increasingly comfortable onstage. Cassandra had generously returned each evening to help him run through the scenes and give him tips for injecting some real flair into the role.

The actors streamed off into the wings, while the crew worked to reset the stage. Toby's voice rang out from somewhere overhead: "Wilfredo! Way to go!" Wilfredo looked around for his friend, but couldn't spot him. Lifting off the helmet he took a deep gulp of fresh air, and mopped his forehead with his sleeve. Now that he had to wear this metal bucket on his head for hours on end he had a lot more sympathy for Sebastian, although Wilfredo was determined to endure the discomfort stoically. Two stagehands wheeled the couch offstage, and Wilfredo stepped back out of their way, bumping into Ruby who had somehow materialized directly behind him.

"I'm sorry. I didn't see you there!"

"You were great today, Wilfredo," she said, beaming at him. "You're really throwing yourself into the role, and it's helping me out big time." She leaned closer and whispered: "I don't feel like I'm all alone onstage anymore."

"Glad to hear it. I'm just learning as I go, this is all very new to me."

"That's the thing, you don't seem like a bumbling rookie. Far from it. Who did you study with again?"

"I did two years as a theater major at the New School, here in New York. And a few plays back in high school, of course."

"That's all your theater training? Wow." Her lips formed a perfect *O*. "Where did you go to high school?"

Thoughts raced through Wilfredo's head. In an instant, Ruby had stumbled over a tripwire and he had no choice but to level with her. What he wanted to say was, *I went to the same high school as you, dumbass!* But instead he just said, "I went to Beacon High School, up in Dutchess County."

She took in a sharp breath. "Beacon? In Dutchess? But, that's where I went to school!" She stared at him in disbelief. "Wait a minute. Wait a minute. I remember you now! Wilfredo! Of course, you played the Tin Man freshman year. I was Dorothy!"

"Yes, I know. My mom has a photo of the two of us from opening night."

"Wait, you mean, you've known we went to school together all along and you didn't say anything?"

He nodded.

"Why?"

"Well, I figured you just didn't remember me and I didn't want it to be awkward. You're a big star now."

"Oh my god, I can't believe you didn't say anything. And I can't believe we are sharing a stage together again after all this time. Crazy!"

"It sure is!"

"Hey do you remember—" She snapped her fingers repeatedly. "What's her name? Our drama teacher?"

"Miss Vivian."

"Miss Vivian! She was so wonderful. The way she made all the costumes was just incredible."

"She was a legend. I think she finally retired like ten years ago."

"This is so perfect! I feel like I have a friend in the cast now. Hey, we should grab lunch sometime and chat about the old days."

"Sure. Great idea."

"Splendid! I'll have my assistant set it up." She gave his arm a squeeze, flashed a smile, and skipped away.

Wilfredo stood rooted to the spot. Ruby the star he could cope with. She moved in a world far removed from his own. But Ruby the suddenly buddy-buddy old high school friend he had no idea how to handle. Why did he get the feeling his life was about to become even more complicated?

"Wilfredo," yelled Declan, yanking him out of his thoughts. "A word, please?" The director, his assistant, Prisha, and one of the producers were huddled together in row seven.

With his helmet tucked under his arm, Wilfredo clomped down the stairs and came to a stop in front of them. They either had notes for him, or they had signed a proper actor, and this marked the end of his little acting spree. That was probably it. Thanksgiving break was coming up—they had the long weekend off—and the new person would probably start Monday.

"So, Wilfredo," said Declan. "We've auditioned half a dozen understudies for the knight in the past two days—"

"Gotcha. Will the new guy be starting on Monday?"

"Wilfredo."

"Yes?"

"Don't interrupt me when I'm speaking."

"Sorry." Wilfredo looked down at his feet.

"What I was about to say is that none of them come close to breathing life into the role the way you have." Wilfredo's mouth fell open as he stared at the director. "So the understudy job is yours for the foreseeable future. You will continue as the lead in rehearsals until Sebastian gets back on his feet. Just keep doing what you're doing."

Declan's assistant spoke up. "I've drawn up a new understudy contract for you to sign. And we need to write a short bio for you, for the playbill. Can you remind me what's on your acting résumé?"

"Er . . . I did two years as a drama student at the New School."

"How odd." Declan looked at him curiously. "You're bringing a lot of presence to the stage. What's your secret?"

Wilfredo gathered his thoughts. His secret was Cassandra. Without her he would have screwed this up right out of the gate. He was pretty sure that technically speaking he shouldn't have shared the script with her, but at the same time he didn't want to keep her help a secret. "I asked this actor friend of mine to run lines with me, and she's been incredible. Basically my whole approach to the role and all the little flourishes were her idea."

"I see. It's a little irregular. But considering the circumstances I get it. Do me a favor, bring her around so we can meet her. We'll need her to sign a non-disclosure agreement, and we can offer her a small coaching honorarium so she can keep working with you. Prisha, would you take care of that?" His assistant nodded. "Perfect. We'll see you Monday, Wilfredo. Get act two under your belt."

Wilfredo walked up the stairs to the dressing rooms in a daze—he couldn't wait to tell Cassandra the news. It was hard to believe how quickly his humdrum life had been turned upside down. What would his mom say when he told her about his acting gig?

Don't hoist the mainsail till you're out of the harbor, Freddy! The Captain barged in on his thoughts. *Right now it's clear sailing, but when you least expect it a typhoon can pop up on the horizon!*

26. CASSANDRA:
TWO MEN AND A CAT

The phone rang just as she was dropping the ramen noodles in the boiling water. Gregory's timing was lousy. He was calling to remind her she'd promised to help him cook Thanksgiving dinner for his work friends on Thursday morning. He wanted her to bring her A game in the kitchen, since he was determined to impress with their holiday spread. She assured him she'd be there, even though turkey day was her least favorite holiday.

"So, what are you up to tonight?" he asked her.

"Cooking dinner. And I think the noodles are done, so I'd better run."

"You're not going over to Wilfredo's?"

"No, not tonight."

"Good."

"He's coming here."

"What?"

"Yeah, his roommate wants to watch the game on television, so we're relocating to my place."

"You don't say."

"I thought we agreed this wasn't going to be a problem?"

"I know. I know. Hey, maybe I'll stop by and meet good old Wilfredo."

"We're gonna be kind of busy rehearsing."

"What time do you think you'll be done?"

"Maybe by nine thirty or so."

"Perfect. I have some things to finish up here at the office, and then I'll pop in around then."

"Fine. But promise me you'll be civil. No, wait—*friendly*."

"My manners are impeccable, Cassandra. And do me a favor . . ."

"Yes?"

"Lock that fleabag cat of yours in the bedroom. I don't need him attacking me again."

"He has a name. And I'm not going to put him in kitty jail. Just give him some space and I'm sure he'll warm up to you." Hanging up the phone Cassandra ran over to the stove and turned off the burners. She poured the broth into a ceramic bowl, dropped in the noodles, and scraped the shiitake mushrooms and edamame toppings out of a cast-iron pan with a metal spatula. Spearing a forkful, she gave it a taste test. It was delicious—except for the soggy noodles. Cassandra sighed. Gregory seemed determined to make a nuisance of himself tonight.

She was having the time of her life playing Violet in their informal rehearsal sessions. It made her feel like she was actually connected to Broadway. Wilfredo had texted her earlier that he had some big news to share, and she hoped that didn't mean his time onstage was coming to an end. It wasn't just the acting she would miss either. She never felt any pressure to be anyone but herself around Wilfredo, which was a refreshing change.

Done with dinner, she pulled her ponytail loose and combed out her chocolate brown hair in the bedroom mirror.

She was touching up her makeup when the downstairs buzzer sounded. Wilfredo announced himself over the intercom—either he was early, or she was running late.

She hurried to clear a week's worth of junk off her wooden coffee table—catalogs, magazines, a cereal box, and dirty mugs. She lit some candles on the bookshelves, admonishing Jupiter not to go near them, and ran a dustcloth over the Moroccan mirror in the living room and the bronze Ganesh statue in the entryway. When she heard approaching footsteps she put her eye up to the peephole and spied her new friend's sturdy outline.

Cassandra hung his coat on a hook in the closet and gave him a quick tour of her place. Jupiter got up and stretched, then leaped down from his perch atop the bookshelf, and wandered over to inspect this newcomer. Cassandra bit back a warning as Wilfredo crouched down to say hello. To her surprise Jupiter let himself be scratched behind the ears.

"He likes you!"

"Of course he does. He's a sweet boy. I love your apartment by the way. It's huge!"

"Thanks. My great aunt used to live here and she left it to my dad. Of course I pay him rent every month."

"I can tell your place has some family history to it."

"So what's this big news you were hinting at?" Cassandra shot him a quizzical look.

"Declan, the director, officially offered me the understudy role, over a bunch of other candidates."

"Wow! That's incredible news! So you're like a cast member now?"

"Looks like it. And when he asked me what my secret was I told him it was you."

"Me? I thought our little rehearsals were a strictly hush-hush operation?"

"It didn't seem fair not to give you the credit you deserve, so I came clean about how you've been coaching me every night, and now he wants to meet you. They want to bring you on board and pay you to be my acting coach."

"Acting coach? Are you serious?"

"Or drama coach. Whatever you want to call yourself."

Cassandra stood stock-still in the middle of the dining room, staring at Wilfredo. "Hold on. You're telling me they want to *pay me* to run lines with you and give you pointers?"

"Yep. And we'll have access to the theater. Declan's assistant said you should try and work out how many hours you've already put in."

Cassandra felt giddy. She threw her arms around a surprised Wilfredo and hugged him tightly. "I can't believe this!"

"Keep in mind that they can yank the rug out from under us at any time."

"I know, I know. But even so. This feels monumental for me. For us." She punched him in the arm. "Well, as your acting coach I say it's time we got to work!"

They lifted the coffee table out of the way, Wilfredo put on his grocery bag–inspired costume, and they ran through the next few scenes of *The Imaginary Knight*, going over the material repeatedly until his delivery was perfect. Cassandra made sure Wilfredo took his time with his lines and didn't rush through them. "It's like music, Wilfredo—the spaces between the notes are just as important as the notes themselves. Find the rhythm in the dialogue."

They were finally getting close to the end of the play. Cassandra glanced at the clock in the kitchen and saw that it was 9:20. Gregory would be here soon. They had just enough time to go through the big finale once. But Wilfredo confessed he was worried about the ending. "I'm going to have to take off my helmet for the big reveal, when Violet and the audience discover that I'm the boy next door."

"Well, it's a helmet, not a security blanket."

"But without the helmet everyone's going to see that I'm actually a terrible actor."

"I hope you're not saying I'm bad at my job."

"No, of course I'm not saying that."

"Because as your coach I should be able to help you get past this obstacle. Right?"

"You're not a miracle worker."

"Says who?"

"I just don't see myself stomping around the stage like Sebastian Estrada."

"Let's think about this. The knight spends most of the play hiding behind a mask, pretending to be someone he isn't. Does that remind you of anyone?"

Wilfredo scratched his chin. "Me?"

"Yeppers. It seems to me that the knight is actually a timid person deep down. So forget about Sebastian and how he would play the character. Let's just take all your fears and transfer them to the role. Use your own vulnerability to show how the knight feels when he reveals his true self to the girl he loves. Which is *scared*."

"So I should just be myself?"

"Bingo."

"I might be able to do that. I'm beginning to think you are a coaching genius."

They went through the big climactic scene together. Cassandra played Violet to the hilt, striding about her apartment, swooning dramatically on the couch. Throwing a cushion at him in anger. Wilfredo lifted off his paper bag helmet and was playing the final scene unencumbered. She reached out a hand and turned his head so he was facing her. They stared longingly into each other's eyes, inching closer together. They both knew what came next. He took her in his arms, and as he moved in she closed her eyes—but then, before their lips could touch, the buzzer rang.

She opened her eyes again, and looked straight into Wilfredo's startled blue eyes. They both froze before letting go of each other a bit awkwardly. Wilfredo cleared his throat. "Expecting someone?"

She gave him a rueful look. "Actually, it's Gregory. He called earlier and I told him you were coming over. He wants to meet you."

"I see. Well, it will be great to finally meet *him*."

Cassandra buzzed her fiancé in and peered at her flushed face in the entranceway mirror. She had to hand it to Wilfredo, he was a much better actor than he let on. She'd really let herself get swept up in the play and the buildup to the impending kiss.

She opened the door for Gregory and made the introductions in the dining room area. The two men shook hands. "I have some amazing news!" Cassandra declared, and brought her fiancé up to date on Wilfredo's big break and her own new gig in the theater.

"Congratulations, honey. What a stroke of luck. For the both of you!"

"Just when I felt as if I was getting pushed out, I get pulled back in."

"How perfect," Gregory said, but his tone had a note of insincerity to it. "So, Wilfredo, you're Sebastian Estrada's understudy?"

"Yep. Officially, as of this morning."

"And who is playing opposite you?"

"Well the lead is being played by Ruby Greenwood. You may have heard of her?"

"Cassidy Prince from *Santa Monica Vibes*? *She's* in your play?"

"Yes."

"So this *is* a real Broadway play then?"

Cassandra found his question aggravating. "Gregory, I've been telling you that all week!"

"Sorry, darling. I guess I should've listened to you." Gregory reached out and put a proprietary arm around her waist, pulling her closer. He was not usually a fan of public displays of affection, but apparently he was making an exception tonight. But just as he leaned in for a smooch, Cassandra glimpsed a gray blur out of the corner of her eye. Jupiter launched himself at Gregory, leaping from the table onto her fiancé's shoulders. "Ahh! Get this damn cat off me!" Gregory yelled. Cassandra quickly grabbed Jupiter off his back, his claws clinging to Gregory's suit. "Bad boy, Jupiter! Bad kitty!"

She tossed her cat in the bedroom and closed the door.

Inspecting Gregory's shoulders, Cassandra saw that Jupiter had drawn blood.

"Great, blood stains on my favorite shirt. That's perfect. I told you to lock him up!"

"I'm *so* sorry, Gregory. I swear Jupiter has never done anything like this before. I don't know what got into him!"

Wilfredo shuffled his feet awkwardly. "I guess I'd better head out! It was nice meeting you, Gregory." He packed up his stuff and pulled on his boots. Cassandra waved a quick goodbye, as she led her incensed fiancé to the bathroom to apply witch hazel to the bright red claw marks.

27. WILFREDO:
THE MAIL TRUCK JOYRIDE

A perplexed Wilfredo sat in the passenger seat of the pink theater van as they cruised east on Forty-Ninth Street, with Toby behind the wheel. Wilfredo was wearing his costume under his coat, with the masked hood pulled back off his face. He was trying to work out how he'd let himself get talked into doing yet another Foxman video. It wasn't as if he didn't have enough excitement in his life. True, the wallet snatcher video had made a huge splash on the web. But what were the odds of stumbling on another minor crime?

Turning to Toby he said: "I don't think you've thought this through. Nobody wants a video of me skateboarding down the sidewalk. It's going to look like a letdown."

"Don't worry. I'm way ahead of you." When they were stopped at the next light Toby pulled a strange-looking radio out from under his seat, switching it on and placing it on the armrest between them. The radio crackled to life with the sound of a police dispatcher calling in a 10-53 on the corner of Ninth Avenue and Forty-Eighth Street.

"A police radio scanner? That's your big plan? Are you nuts?"

"What! It's perfect! We learn about crimes at the same time as the cops do."

"And then what? You want me to insert myself into a

dicey situation? You must have me confused with a comic book superhero!"

"We just need to listen for a ten thirty-two, that's a larceny in progress code. Could be some punk stealing mouthwash from a pharmacy. And all I'm looking for is a chase shot. If I get it from the right angle you don't even need to get close to the perp."

"What if the guy has a knife or a gun?"

"That's a different code. We're on the lookout for run-of-the-mill shoplifters. The grab-and-go types."

Wilfredo let out a heavy sigh. "Just so we're clear, I'm not gonna tussle with any petty criminals."

"Roger that." Toby drummed his fingers happily on the steering wheel. "Man, I'm totally stoked! Even if we get a fraction of the views as the last one that's still, like, a million eyeballs. I feel like Spielberg directing his first indie." Wilfredo followed up his sigh with a low groan.

Quit your bellyaching, Freddy. We both know the real reason you went along with this boneheaded scheme is that deep down you like the attention! Just try and remember you're not a hero, you're just some dope in a fox costume!

Captain Pete had a point. A small part of him was enjoying the notoriety that came with being Foxman. And if they didn't make new videos it would all just fade away.

Traffic thinned out as they drove farther west. They passed a large high school that was letting students out for the day, and a stream of youngsters ran out into the road, heedless of traffic. The van came to a standstill, surrounded by the rowdy kids, with some of the larger boys knocking on the side of the van as they stormed by. Wilfredo noticed a poor mailman caught in the melee. Kids were snatching letters from his pushcart and throwing them up in the air.

"Bunch of troublemakers," grumbled Wilfredo.

Toby nodded. "That's the spirit. Try to build up some outrage so you can tap into it for the scene."

After a few minutes the street cleared out and they were on the move again. Toby pulled the van over on a quiet corner near Tenth Avenue, next to a warehouse. This remote part of Hell's Kitchen consisted mostly of car dealerships and generic office buildings.

Toby turned up the volume on the scanner. "Now we just wait for someone to report a crime nearby. And then we do our best to get you in the foreground of the scene. Get ready to jump into action! Pick up some speed, and if you can manage a hop or a jump that would be perfect." Wilfredo gave Toby a skeptical stare. This business could go wrong in so many ways.

Numerous calls came in over the radio scanner. It was remarkable how many minor emergencies were plaguing the city at any given time. Finally Toby's ears perked when he heard a 10-32V for the corner of Forty-Eighth and Ninth Avenue. "That's only a couple blocks away. Let's check it out!" Toby switched on his Flip pocket camcorder. "All charged up and ready to go! Skate down Tenth Avenue and hang your first left!"

Wilfredo ditched his coat and pulled the hood up over his head. He checked the side-view mirror to make sure no one was nearby, then he hopped out with his longboard under his arm. Skating over to the corner he made a left onto the avenue, dropping into the street. He gave the longboard a few extra pushes going into the downhill, zipping along next to a lane of parked cars. He was vaguely aware of Toby jogging along the sidewalk behind him. As he skated south a small detail snagged in his mind. The code the dispatcher had called out was 10-32V. What did the *V* stand for?

When he turned the corner onto Forty-Eighth Street he heard a loud crash up ahead. A white mail truck had just smashed into a lamppost mid-block. The truck's engine was steaming, and the lamppost was leaning away at an awkward angle. Vehicle. The *V* stood for *vehicle*. That's just great. Toby had him chasing a stolen truck!

A teenager leaped out of the driver's seat and darted across the road, looking fearfully over his shoulder at a mailman and a cop running in his direction. Wilfredo realized instantly that this teenager must be one of those dumb school kids they'd seen earlier, who had foolishly got it in his head to take a mail truck for a joy ride.

The teen was running right toward him, and Wilfredo had no intention of getting tangled up in this mess, so he swerved to avoid him. But the teen had caught sight of him that same instant, and he dodged in the same direction that Wilfredo swerved. They collided heavily, and both of them fell to the ground. Dazed, it took Wilfredo a moment to climb to his feet. By then the cop and the mailman had caught up with them, and they seized the teenager with rough hands. Wilfredo took a few unsure steps back. This was exactly what he'd been hoping to avoid. Ending up right in the middle of a crime scene. Stepping onto his longboard he gave a slight push, letting the board roll slowly backward.

That's when he heard a loud wrenching sound above him.

Looking up he saw that the damaged lamppost was teetering on the verge of collapse. A handful of onlookers who had stopped to gawk at the scene were standing in its direct path. Hearing the sound several of them scattered, but a few others with less sharp hearing seemed oblivious to the imminent danger. Wilfredo pushed off forcefully, his eyes locked on the falling lamppost. He waved his arms and yelled, "Watch out! Get out of the way!" The remaining bystanders didn't need to be told twice, scrambling to safety. The lamppost landed with an earth-shattering *crash* directly behind them, partly on the sidewalk and partly on a shiny new Toyota, shattering its windshield. Phew. That was close.

Wilfredo was suddenly conscious of being the center of attention of a small crowd, standing a safe distance away.

"Way to go, Foxman!"

"He's a real-life hero!"

The sound of sirens grew louder by the second, and Wilfredo knew that cops and firemen were converging on that spot. The lone policeman on the scene had finished cuffing the truck-stealing teen and was looking over in their direction as he talked on his radio. Wilfredo pushed off with a modest wave to the gathered onlookers, picking up speed as he raced around the corner and up Ninth Avenue, circling around to the parked van. He checked to make sure nobody was looking his way before hopping in the back to change, stuffing his costume into his backpack. Minutes later he was sitting in the passenger seat in his regular clothes, breathing a big sigh of relief.

Toby finally showed up a few moments later, climbing back behind the wheel. "That was unbelievable, Wilfredo!

I told you this would work out. You took down the dumbass who stole the mail truck and you saved some bystanders from getting crushed. I'd call that a good day's work for any super-hero. And, I got it all on tape!" Grinning, he tapped his mini camcorder. "Wait until the world sees this!"

28. CASSANDRA:
THE TECHNICALITIES OF KISSING

It was after hours at the Cornelius and Cassandra was sitting on the edge of the stage next to Wilfredo, eating Thai food takeout. They had the space to themselves, except for a cleaning woman pushing a noisy vacuum around the auditorium. Cassandra scooped some more pineapple fried rice onto her plate, picked out a fried dumpling with her bamboo chopsticks, dunked it into the dipping sauce, and popped it into her mouth. The delicious flavor of ginger and garlic flooded her senses.

The stage behind them was bare except for two folding chairs. But the background scenery was still up. It showed a basement interior with wood-paneled walls covered in thumbtacked rock posters and metal shelves cluttered with vintage objects from the 1970s.

Things had been going well since Cassandra began coming into the theater regularly. She'd been determined to be noticed, going through her beauty routine religiously each morning to ensure that she ended up with glowing skin, putting in the time to achieve that wavy retro do that you could only get by resorting to old-fashioned curlers, and reaching deep into her wardrobe for her most eye-catching vintage dresses from the sixties and seventies. Today she had mixed things up with a thrifted denim jumpsuit, paired with a canary yellow wide-brimmed hat that had earned her a compliment from Declan earlier. By this point in the day she had long since hung up her hat and loosened the topmost buttons on the jumpsuit.

"I still feel like pinching myself sometimes," said Cassandra, looking around. "Here I am on a Broadway stage!"

"Eating fried rice."

"It's not *exactly* how I'd pictured it. But I'll take it." Cassandra took a sip from a can of orange soda. "Hey, have you seen the viral video of that Foxman guy? Everyone is talking about it."

Wilfredo coughed as he almost choked on a chunk of pineapple.

"You okay?"

"I'm fine. It just went down the wrong pipe." He drank some water. "You mean the video with the mail truck, right? Yeah, I've seen it. That guy is pretty amazing."

"Really? Don't you think he looks ridiculous skateboarding around in that fuzzy orange costume?"

"Well, he did save those people from getting flattened by that falling lamppost."

"To me he comes across as this self-righteous busybody, skating around the city making citizen arrests."

"I guess you're not big on the whole law and order thing? You must be more of a fan of that Cat Burglar gal then."

"Now *she's* amazing! Did you hear she donated nearly half a million dollars' worth of jewels to an animal shelter?"

"The word you're missing in that sentence is *stolen*! She's a thief!"

"You sound just like Gregory." She stuck her tongue out at him.

Wilfredo shoveled the last bit of food on his plate into his mouth with a plastic fork. "You can have the last dumpling if you like," gesturing at the plastic container sitting between them.

"Are you sure? I don't want you to accuse me of stealing it."

"Well, it could be a trap. I might arrest you for grand theft dumpling."

"I'm gonna risk it." Cassandra scooped up the last dumpling. Wilfredo stood up and gathered together the dirty plates and empty containers, taking them over to the cleaning woman, who held open a garbage bag expectantly.

Back up on the stage Cassandra clapped her hands together. "Right. Time to get back to work! Let's tackle that closing scene."

"About that . . ."

"Yes?"

Wilfredo stared down at his feet. "I've never actually kissed anyone onstage before."

Cassandra took in a deep breath. "I keep forgetting how new all of this is to you. Let me give you the basics. First of all, always brush your teeth and use mouthwash beforehand. You don't want to be *that* guy. Secondly, there's various ways to fake a kiss. There's the cheek, or chin kiss. There's the sneak-your-thumb-onto-her-lips-and-kiss-your-thumb technique. That one takes some practice to get right. There's also the get-real-close-but-your-lips-don't-actually-touch method. Then there's lip on lip. And finally we have open-mouthed kissing. With that last one it's still advisable to refrain from sticking your tongue down your partner's throat, but a little tongue action can help it look real."

Wilfredo was pacing nervously back and forth across the stage. "So how do I know which one to pick?" he demanded.

"That's simple. You talk to Ruby beforehand and work it out. Maybe sneak in a practice kiss or two."

Wilfredo's brow furrowed. "Which one do you think she'll prefer?"

"She's a Hollywood actress. She's done nude scenes on camera. You do the math." Wilfredo's eyes got large and Cassandra grinned. "I bet you never thought you'd be kissing Ruby Greenwood onstage. It's your high school dream come true!"

"Only I'm not in high school anymore."

"Nope. This is Broadway, baby!" Cassandra grinned. "Ready to get to work?"

"Hold on. So are you and me going to kiss in this scene?"

"Technically speaking, kissing you is part of my job description tonight." She gave him a deadpan look.

"So which option on the kissing menu do we try?"

"I think we should go for an open-mouth kiss, as that will likely be Ruby's pick. Luckily we both have ginger scallion breath, so I think we just cancel each other out on that front."

Hesitantly, Wilfredo pulled on his helmet and they ran the scene. As she went through her lines Cassandra couldn't help wondering what it would feel like to kiss him. In spite of her blasé front, she was nervous about it too. How would it compare to kissing Gregory? Although her fiancé's go-to kiss these days was the perfunctory peck on the lips, and that wouldn't be hard to beat.

They went through the buildup to the scene. About five minutes in, Wilfredo hit his mark in the middle of the stage. "If your wish is to see my face, Violet, then I can hide it from you no longer." He pulled off his helmet, facing away from her. She reached out and put a hand on his rough cheek, slowly pulling him around to face her.

"You *are* real. You *are* flesh and blood. Why, you look just like Alexander, my neighbor!"

"I am Alexander, your neighbor, Violet. I have always been your neighbor."

"And yet, you are also my knight."

"I will *always* be your knight," he repeated softly, his face an inch away from her own. She could feel his warm breath on her face. She held his gaze, his clear blue eyes full of unanswered questions. Her breath hitched in her lungs as he closed the sliver of space between them.

Their lips had barely brushed when Wilfredo took a step back. "I can't do this," he said, breaking character.

Cassandra put her hands on her hips. "Seriously, Wilfredo? It's just acting!"

He avoided her gaze. "I'm sorry. It just doesn't feel right."

"Is this because of Gregory? You realize he isn't going to jump out of the wings!"

"No. It's just that you're engaged. Which means you're off-limits."

"Can't you just let *me* worry about being engaged?"

"I just don't think I can pretend to kiss you. I wish I

could explain it better. But I can't. Why don't we try it again with the close-but-not-touching method?"

"Sure, I guess. If that's what you want." It was a disconcerted Cassandra who went through the scene one more time. This time their lips stopped millimeters away from each other, in a weird pantomime of a kiss that felt frustratingly wrong. Apparently there was a worse kiss than the routine peck on the lips.

When they were done Cassandra felt subdued. "Listen, how about we knock off early tonight? We can tackle things fresh tomorrow."

"You read my mind."

Cassandra cringed inwardly as they packed up their stuff and tidied up the stage. His words echoed in her head. *I just don't think I can pretend to kiss you.* What on earth had he meant by that? Try as she might she couldn't put a positive spin on him shying away at the last second. She didn't get it. What was he so hung up about?

29. WILFREDO:
LUNCH AT THE PARROT BAR

Wilfredo had never heard of the Parrot Bar, but apparently it was an exclusive hotel restaurant in Midtown, and Ruby ate lunch there all the time. When they pushed through the revolving door Wilfredo immediately felt underdressed in his cargo pants and flannel shirt. Power lunchers whispered to each other and heads swiveled to catch a glimpse of Ruby, but no one accosted her for a photo or an autograph as the hostess escorted them to a secluded table in the back. Wilfredo did a double take when he saw the prices on the menu, but Ruby, noticing his expression, told him not to worry, that it was her treat.

Leaning in, she whispered conspiratorially: "You're doing me a favor by having lunch with me, otherwise I'd be stuck eating with Annie. *Again.*" She rolled her eyes and mimed a yawn.

Wilfredo's gaze landed on the nineteen-dollar price tag for a grilled cheese. It seemed almost criminal. The cheapest beer was an eight-dollar Spanish import. He should probably just stick with water.

Oh c'mon, Freddy, knock back some giggle juice. It'll help loosen you up. You're as stiff as a stuffed eel. Here's a crazy idea! You're out for a free lunch with a beautiful girl. Maybe try to enjoy it?

Wilfredo willed the Captain to silence. But when the server materialized he took the croc's advice and put in an order for a cold one. Declan had unexpectedly given the whole cast the afternoon off, saying that he was meeting with investors. So a couple early beers shouldn't do any harm.

The drinks showed up almost instantly, and the waitress poured his golden lager into a tall sloping glass. That was celebrity life for you— snap your fingers and things happened right away.

Ruby held up her glass. "To afternoons off."

He clinked his beer with her mojito glass. "And reconnecting with old friends." He took a sip through the foam, smacking his lips approvingly.

They reminisced about the old days while they waited for their food, chuckling about funny stories and embarrassing moments they remembered from high school. Their table was small and every time their knees bumped Ruby would giggle and flash him her one-hundred-watt smile. With every toss of her head her reddish-brown hair whipped and bounced with a life of its own. And when she found anything remotely puzzling she would scrunch up her little wedge nose adorably. Wilfredo was surprised to discover that spending time with her one-on-one was proving very enjoyable.

Still, a remote corner of his mind was flashing caution signs. For one thing, he remembered all too well how painful it had been to be smitten with the unattainable Ruby Greenwood in high school. And still fresh in his mind was how she had looked right through him for weeks when he was just a lowly stagehand. Maybe she was one of those people who could easily turn their charm on and off, like flicking a light switch? The female crew members seemed to think so, as he had overheard them complaining that Ruby was a total diva. Still, sitting this close to her, with her V-neck blouse dipping dangerously low, he found himself falling slowly under her spell.

The arrival of his grilled cheese gave him somewhere else to look. He bit into it and smoky cheese oozed out from between crusty golden bread. It was so good that he wanted to leap out of his chair, barge into the kitchen, and shake the chef's hand. He took another sip of beer. Now this was living. Their conversation drifted to the theater, and he entertained Ruby with numerous funny stories of things he'd witnessed over the years backstage at the Cornelius. Her reaction alternated between bursts of high-pitched laughter and feigned shock.

"And now you can add the story of how you walked in on Ruby Greenwood standing in her dressing room in red underwear to your little treasure trove of anecdotes." She held his gaze with her piercing gray eyes.

Wilfredo flushed and began to stammer. "Look, Ruby, that was an accident. I-I didn't mean to—"

"Relax! I'm just messing with you! Although, I hope you liked what you saw." She twirled the tips of her coppery hair with a cherry-tipped finger and batted her thick eyelashes at him.

Crumbling cannonballs, Freddy, I think this swooner has locked her sights on you! I wonder if she's had her eyes checked recently? My guess is the poor girl is blind as a bat! Such a tragedy, losing her vision at such a young age.

Wilfredo reached for his beer and drained what was left of it. When he put his glass down he found Ruby eyeing his fingernails disapprovingly.

"Wilfredo, how about we take advantage of our afternoon off and go get mani-pedis together at my hotel spa?"

Suddenly self-conscious of his ragged fingers—an unavoidable consequence of working with his hands—he did his best to deflect her invitation gracefully. "I'm not sure that's really my scene, Ruby."

"Nonsense. Have you ever had a facial? I'll sign you up for one of those too. You'll feel like a million bucks when we're done."

Hey, Freddy. Ask her to drop that back into low and run it by one more time, because I'm not catching her drift. What in the name of a dead albatross is a facial? It's not that thing where they put cucumbers over your eyes, is it?

Ruby wasn't done yet. "Come to think of it. Where do you get your hair cut? Or do you cut it yourself in the bathroom mirror with your eyes closed?"

"I go to a barber down on Astor Place," Wilfredo replied, starting to feel offended. "He's first rate!"

"Is he really? And how much does this barber of yours charge?"

"Fifteen bucks, plus tip."

Ruby let out a gasp. She reached for her phone and connected with a receptionist at her hair salon. Putting her hand over the receiver she asked him: "Wilfredo, are you free today at five?" He nodded glumly. And that was it—he'd been booked. She hung up. "And in between getting our nails done and your hair appointment we can go shopping for some new outfits for you at Saks. What do you think, Wilfredo? Will you put yourself in my expert hands for a little makeover?"

"Well the thing is, I know I can be a little scruffy sometimes, but that's kind of my look."

Scruffy, you say, Freddy? Most days you look like a drowned scarecrow that washed ashore covered in seaweed! I've seen wharf rats that looked spiffier than you!

Ruby tilted her head to one side sympathetically. "I get it, you definitely have a ruggedly handsome thing going on. But there are brilliant designers out there who specialize in that frumpy everyman look. You're a professional actor now, Wilfredo, and you need to dress the part! Beauty and style matter a lot in show business. Which reminds me, we need to get your teeth whitened. After that's done I'll hook you up with a photographer friend of mine—he's a genius—and get you some killer headshots."

"Ruby, even if I wanted to I couldn't possibly afford any of this."

"Okay. I'm gonna level with you, Wilfredo. Declan took me aside and asked me to clean you up and get you some pictures."

Wilfredo stiffened. "You're joking."

"Nope. I assured him he had picked the right person for the job. He gave me the theater's corporate card and a budget of two grand—but I plan to treat that as a jumping-off point!" She put her hand on his and turned her saucer-like eyes up to full power. "Just think of looking sharp as part of the job."

His head was spinning—celebrity lunches, teeth whitening, headshots. He felt like he was getting sucked into a giant entertainment machine that would leach out all his personality and grit. It was all too much. His stomach knotted as he thought about standing in the spotlight onstage, about what would happen if he let everyone down, and about how he would soon be kissing those coral-colored lips directly across from him.

You're swimming with the sharks now, Freddy! I'm not a gambling man, but I wouldn't throw down any doubloons on you coming out of this in one piece! But don't worry, I know a guy who can fit you for a peg leg or a steel hook for a fair price!

Just then a flash of light hit them—once, twice, three times. Wilfredo blinked in confusion. Turning his head he saw a photographer crouched nearby snapping their photo. The hostess and a busboy rushed over and chased him away, then the restaurant manager appeared looking stricken.

"I'm so very sorry. He must have slipped in through the hotel entrance. It won't happen again, Miss Greenwood, I assure you. We will be comping your meal today, naturally."

Ruby was unfazed. "Oh, don't worry. I'm used to it. We'll see what juicy headlines the gossip mags come up with this time!" Still apologizing, the manager retreated.

Wilfredo raked his fingers through his hair. "Well, I wasn't expecting that."

Ruby laughed. "Your first brush with the paparazzi. How does it feel?"

"Pretty surreal. Do you really think that photo is going to be published somewhere?"

"For sure!" She spread her hands out in front of her. "Starlet Dines with Mystery Man at NYC Hotspot. This type of thing is exactly why we need you looking your best." She pushed her chair back. "Let's get out of here. We've got a busy afternoon ahead of us."

30. GREGORY:
THE HIDDEN CAMERA

Gregory's inner demons had been duking it out with his better angels for weeks. After the success of the Mexican taqueria operation he was sorely tempted to take his surveillance tactics to the next level. But another part of him was worried that planting a hidden camera in his fiancée's apartment might be crossing a line. This tug-of-war was won decidedly by the spy camp once Cassandra began to spend a lot of time alone with Wilfredo. Gregory quieted his conscience by assuring himself that he didn't have salacious motives for spying on her. All he really wanted was a little peace of mind.

The guy at the spy gear shop recommended a tiny oval-shaped camera. It cost a bundle, but Gregory whipped out his credit card and paid for it without hesitation. He had settled on Cassandra's living room as the best spot. She spent a lot of time there, and having eyes and ears in that room should provide him with valuable intel. He found a good opportunity to place the camera one Friday evening when he stopped by to pick her up for a movie. Cassandra and her dad were big science fiction geeks, and she had a collection of science fiction memorabilia on the top shelf of the living room bookshelf. So when she stepped into the bathroom, he stuck the camera onto the dark face of a red toy robot, and it blended in perfectly. The camera was already connected to Cassandra's

Wi-Fi, and the motion-activated battery was good for about two hundred hours. He turned the robot slightly so that it would capture a corner of the kitchen and the hallway leading to the bedroom.

His first good opportunity to test the device came a few days later. He'd been offered two free tickets to the ballet that were up for grabs at his office, so naturally he asked Cassandra if she wanted to go. But his fiancée, who would normally have jumped at an opportunity like this, said she wasn't up for it. That it was just one of those nights where she just needed to go home and recharge. He volunteered to join her and rent a movie, but she shot that idea down too. Suspicious, he rushed home early from work, sat down at the mahogany writing table by the window, opened his laptop, and logged in on the remote capture website. His mouse pointer hovered above the CONNECT button on the camera.

Once again he couldn't shake the feeling that he was about to do something reprehensible. He would be looking into her apartment in high definition, with sound. He wavered, unsure. That camera had cost a lot of money and he had already set it up. On the other hand, if he did this, he would have to live with the secret forever.

In the end it was his conviction that Cassandra was hiding something that tipped him over the edge. For the past few months there had been something off about her behavior. He couldn't quite put his finger on it, but there was one way to find out for sure. He clicked the button. A window popped up on his screen, and there she was walking around her apartment, turning on lights and pulling the curtains closed.

Spying on her turned out to be quite dull. Cassandra

disappeared into her bedroom for ten minutes, and when she reappeared she was wearing a white terry cloth robe. Then she vanished from view again, and he guessed she must be taking a shower. He took advantage of the downtime to clean his glasses and clip his nails. After waiting a good long while for her to reappear he wondered if she had decided to take a bath instead. Bored and hungry he dialed the sushi place on Lex and ordered a delivery. Ten minutes later the doorman rang to say his food was downstairs, so he slipped on his loafers, took the elevator down, and grabbed the bag from the delivery guy. When he got back to his computer, Cassandra was in her living room, standing by the bookshelf with a thick towel wrapped around her head, wearing only a white cropped cami and black bikini briefs. Suddenly music blasted through the laptop as Cassandra hit PLAY on some pop music on her end. His fiancée began to dance around her living room to the music, her movements becoming freer as she waved her arms over her head and twisted her body this way and that. Gregory's face flushed with embarrassment. This was exactly what he had been afraid of. That she would start prancing around her apartment half naked. Common decency demanded that he respect her privacy and turn off the camera. But for some reason he couldn't tear himself away. He sat there googly eyed, mesmerized by her gyrations. At this point he felt that he had already committed the offense, so he might as well sit tight and enjoy the show. But just as he began to bring his guilt under control, her dancing was interrupted by the sound of her phone ringing. She muted the music and picked up her cell phone.

"Zara! Ollie! Oh my god! I was just thinking of you guys.

I miss you both so much! What time is it over there? It must be so late!" Gregory scowled at his screen. Cassandra's two best friends were over in England somewhere, introducing their new baby to Zara's grandparents. The truth was he'd never really clicked with these friends of hers and had been pleased when they left town for an extended trip.

Cassandra threw herself on the couch and fired off questions about their two kids. She was the godmother to both of them. Gregory had no idea what their responses were, but he took it that things were going well because Cassandra was all smiles. Then they must have asked about him because she said: "Oh Gregory's doing fine. I mean we don't always see eye to eye about the wedding, so things *have* gotten a little strained in that area lately." Cassandra flipped her hair over as she switched the phone to her other ear. "Oh don't worry, we'll work through it. He can be a pain sometimes, but deep down he's a great guy, and I know he cares about me." Gregory frowned, not sure what to make of this backhanded compliment.

"My new job? It's amazing! I love it there and I feel like I'm part of something meaningful. Wilfredo? Oh he's improved so much. We're doing our private sessions at the theater most nights. Which is a blast. Although, we've reached the big romantic finale of the play, and for some reason he refuses to kiss me during our rehearsals. It's very odd, and it's giving me a bit of a complex. No, of course I haven't told Gregory about this. Are you kidding? I keep him on a strictly need-to-know basis. This kind of thing would freak him out!" She burst out laughing. Gregory watched her, his face dark with anger. So Wilfredo refused to kiss her? Had he heard that right?

Which meant that she had been happy to kiss *him*. And on top of that she felt free to joke about it with her pals? It was humiliating.

He watched her for a few more minutes, his blood still boiling. He was tempted to call her, or even to storm over there, but he realized there would be some awkward questions to answer about how he'd found out. The smart move was to bide his time, and use the information he'd gathered to his advantage at some key moment. Maybe catch her in a lie. For now he would have to rely on the common decency of his unexpected ally—in the person of Wilfredo himself. Obviously he had misjudged the poor man. Hopefully he would stand firm, even if Cassandra persisted in throwing herself at him.

After she hung up with her friends Cassandra turned on the television and hit play on some TV show that he couldn't see. From the dialogue he gathered that it was some kind of sophomoric show about a bunch of video game players. Walking over to the kitchen, she plucked a pint of mint chip from her freezer, and grabbed a large spoon. Returning to the comfort of her couch she sat down and crossed her legs. That horrible cat of hers jumped up and stretched out beside her. Slowly Gregory lowered the laptop's screen. He'd seen enough. That spy camera had been money well spent. He had been right about her all along.

31. WILFREDO:
THE DRESSING ROOM RENDEZVOUS

Wilfredo and Toby exited the subway at Forty-Second Street and crossed the busy intersection to make their way up through Times Square, threading their way through hordes of tourists. Above them, LED signs flickered nonstop on shiny skyscrapers, while at street level the din of the city was punctuated by the shouts of people hawking tickets, store entrances blasting music, and impatient drivers leaning on their horns.

Wilfredo walked with his head down, listening to Toby babble about the daily hits the Foxman video was raking in. "Dude, you're internet famous! Everyone in New York has heard of you! And I'm the one who captured your big moment on tape. Did I tell you a reporter tracked me down and has been calling me, thinking maybe I know who Foxman is." Wilfredo shot his friend a worried look. "Relax, buddy, your secret is safe with me. I've been playing dumb! I told them I just happened to be in the right place at the right time."

"Then how do you explain the other video you posted? Pretty big coincidence, don't you think? You should have used an anonymous account or something."

"Chill out. They can't make me talk!"

Wilfredo shook his head and plodded along. He'd slept badly, waking up early with a nightmare about running from the police on a skateboard. Cassandra had appeared in his dream, pulling him into a closet to hide, and he'd woken up with his heart racing.

Wilfredo dodged a costumed cookie monster character coming toward him in a crosswalk and barely even turned his head when they walked past a semi-naked cowgirl posing for pictures with passersby.

Toby noticed his friend's glum expression. "Why the hangdog face? Shouldn't you be dancing in the streets!"

"I wish you hadn't told my mom about the whole understudy thing over Thanksgiving."

"But she's so proud of you."

"Yes, and when I told her the first full rehearsal was today she said she was well aware and was planning to pop into town to watch."

"That's great! Just let her enjoy the big moment!"

"It's not just my mom showing up. It's that I'm under a lot of pressure. I wish none of this had happened and I was still working in the shop with you guys."

"Seriously? Dude, you're our champion! The rest of us are just living vicariously through you."

"Only problem is I'm a fraud. I don't have the acting chops for this role. I shouldn't be on the same stage with the other actors."

"Hey, I've watched you in rehearsals, man. You've been phenomenal! There's no way Declan would have kept you up there if you weren't blowing this thing out of the water."

"But we're just getting to the hard stuff. I've got to play Ruby's love interest in the final scenes and I'm freaking out."

"Ooh, I see. So you're gonna kiss Ruby onstage today.

Yowza! Yeah, I get why you're freaking out now. Just try and roll with it!"

"How can I roll with it when I'm just some schlub whose main skills in life involve a paintbrush and a hammer?"

"That's just your backstory now. You're an ordinary Joe who hit the big time. Who cares if you don't have movie star good looks, or that you've got the whole dad bod thing going on."

"Dad bod? Thanks, Toby. That makes me feel a lot better."

"You know what I mean, Wilfredo. I've known you for a long time. Long enough to know that what's really bugging you is a bad case of girl trouble. You've been nuts for Cassandra from day one."

"I hope it's not *that* obvious," Wilfredo grumbled.

"If I were you, I would forget about her and make a play for Ruby. She's single. And you've already got first base locked up!" he chortled at his own joke.

"I have no idea what I would do without your help," Wilfredo said flatly. "And I won't forget that you were the one who volunteered me for all this."

Toby slapped him on the back. "What are friends for!"

They slipped into the theater through the stage door and fist-bumped the security guy sitting on his stool. Wilfredo signed in. Call time was at noon today, and he had arrived early, but he noticed that Ruby's signature was already on the login sheet. That meant she was upstairs somewhere. He took the elevator up to the third floor, a privilege reserved for cast members, and made his way to the dressing room he shared with the actor who played Violet's dad, tossing his backpack on the counter. He unzipped it and pulled out a manila envelope. Prints of his headshot had been delivered yesterday, and they were the perfect excuse to go talk to Ruby.

He stopped outside her dressing room and put his ear to the door. He heard the sound of a blow dryer coming from within. This might be a bad time. Oh god, what if she was standing there in her underwear again?

Get ahold of yourself, Freddy. You're wound up tighter than an eight-day clock! Stop behaving like a scared minnow and start acting like a big barracuda! Show some panache, you lily-livered powder monkey!

Wilfredo shook his head, trying to free himself from the Captain's intrusive thoughts. He steeled himself and knocked on Ruby's door, softly at first, and then after not receiving an answer a little more forcefully. She yelled "Come in!" and he pushed the door open. She was sitting on her stool in jeans and a silk blouse, getting her hair blown out by a stylist. When she saw the envelope in his hand she let out a squeal. "Hand them over. Let's see what we got. I've known Sergio for years, and he's the best headshot photographer on the East Coast." She pulled out an eight by ten. "Wow! You sure do clean up good! Who knew there was a total hunk lurking under there!"

Wilfredo blushed. "Thanks for your help, Ruby. Declan took a look at them and he's really pleased."

"It was my pleasure!"

"Sorry, I didn't mean to interrupt you while you were getting ready."

"Don't worry, we've just finished." She shooed away the stylist, and closed the door behind her. When she was alone with him, she took his hand and guided him over to her little love seat area. Wilfredo sat down hesitantly, fighting back the inexplicable urge to bolt from the room.

"It's a good thing you came by. I could use your fresh eye on some of these outfits they're thinking of putting me in. Will you give me your honest opinion?"

"Sure, but I don't really know much about fashion."

"Perfect. I'm up to my ears in fashionistas with strong opinions. What I'm looking for is the unvarnished opinion of the man on the street."

Ruby grabbed some clothes off the nearby rack and ducked behind the folding screen to change. Seconds later she threw her blouse and her jeans over the top. Wilfredo's eyebrows shot up. Why was it that every time he was around Ruby he didn't know where to look? Moments later she popped out dressed in a pale yellow jumpsuit.

"This is outfit numero uno," she declared.

"Looks great!" he said diplomatically.

"Can you elaborate? What do you like about it? Be specific." She did a twirl.

"It's bright and summery, and it shows off your legs."

"Perfect! I knew you were the right man to ask." She disappeared behind the screen once more. Wilfredo caught a glimpse of a bare thigh, and some black underwear. He stared up at the ceiling.

Her voice came from behind the screen. "I hear you've been burning the midnight oil with that pretty acting coach of yours . . . what's her name?"

"Cassandra. Yeah, she's been incredible."

"Do I sense a little behind-the-scenes romance brewing?"

"Oh no! It's nothing like that," Wilfredo said quickly.

"We are strictly professional. As a matter of fact—Cassandra is engaged."

"I see. How fascinating."

Wilfredo wasn't sure what was so fascinating about it.

She stepped out from behind her screen again, this time wearing nothing but a bright green bikini and a flowy white cover up. "They are thinking about this look for my sunbathing scene. What do you think?"

What Wilfredo thought was that she must have been standing stark naked behind that screen just moments earlier. "Um. Wow." He struggled to find actual words. "Stunning. You look stunning." She spun around showing him the high cut in the back. His mouth opened again but no actual words came out.

"You're speechless! Once again, just the reaction I was looking for." She scooted behind the relative privacy of the folding screen. "Okay, just one more!"

Wilfredo closed his eyes, doing his best not to picture her naked. He was a professional actor, and he needed to behave like a professional.

Once again her voice rang out from behind the screen. "Oh, and another thing. You have to come to this art gallery party my friend Mari is throwing tomorrow afternoon. They're launching a new artist. It's a large space, and she's terrified it's going to look empty. Mari told me to invite all my friends, and I told her I don't know anyone in New York! So I've asked Declan to come and to bring some of his producer pals. Are you interested?"

"Sure, I'm up for that."

"Do you think that acting coach of yours will give you the night off?"

"I hope so."

"Bring her along too if you like. And anyone else you can think of. Spread the word! I suspect there's going to be free booze—while supplies last! I'll text you the address. It's down in SoHo."

She reemerged. Much to Wilfredo's relief she was wearing a multicolored striped dress and a stylish brimmed hat.

"This is a more glamorous throwback look. For when Violet decides to play dress-up."

"I love it."

"But is it flattering?"

"Yes. It suits you extremely well. You look super elegant."

"Aren't you darling? You're such a big help!"

Wilfredo saw his window of opportunity. It was now or never. "Listen, Ruby, I wanted to talk to you about the whole kissing scene."

She threw off the hat and sat down next to him on the settee. "Oooh. I'd nearly forgotten about that! We should figure out the kiss offstage so it isn't awkward in front of everyone. We can work out the timing, the angles, and what to do with our hands."

"That would be a big help. I've never done a stage kiss before."

"Aren't you just mister adorable? Well, there's a first time for everything."

She held his gaze and Wilfredo was unsettled by the intensity he saw there. "Do you think we should fake it?" he asked.

She arched an eyebrow at him. "We're both single, Wilfredo. That's usually the critical issue in my experience. So why not give the audience their money's worth? Here, let's practice a few different takes." She stood up.

"Er . . . you mean right now?" Wilfredo hesitantly got to his feet. He was a full head taller than her, standing there in her stockings. He was suddenly intensely conscious of the soft curves of her figure in the satin dress.

"Declan will want to get through the end of the play today. So it's now or never. But before we get down to business. I want to ask you a question."

"Shoot."

Ruby tucked a strand of her glossy hair behind a perfectly shaped ear and gave him an odd look. "I need to know. Did you, by any chance, have a crush on me back in high school?"

Caught off guard, Wilfredo had no idea how to respond. It was years ago, so what did it matter now? "Um. As a matter of fact I think I did," he mumbled.

"You think you did?"

"Yes, I had a monster crush on you back in high school."

"So it *wasn't* just my imagination."

"*But,* so did every other straight guy at Beacon High."

"Oh, give me a break. That can't possibly be true." She waved her hands dismissively. "Now that we've got that cleared up, let's get this kiss worked out. Here, you need a helmet!" She grabbed her empty wastebasket and handed it to him.

Wilfredo was confused. "Am I supposed to put this on my head?"

She laughed, a frilly girlish giggle that reminded him of her television show. "No, you silly man. Tuck it under your arm. We'll start from when you've just pulled off your helmet. Let's take it from 'You will always be my knight.'"

"Sounds good. Cassandra says it will have more impact if I have my back to you when I take off the helmet. And then you can reach out and turn me around to face you."

"I love it. Your coach has great instincts. Okay, let's pretend the settee is the couch, so the audience would be over by the vanity wall." They positioned themselves accordingly.

"If your wish is to see my face, Violet, then I can hide it from you no longer." He stood with the waste bin under his arm, facing away from her. She reached out with both hands and spun him around to face her.

"You *are* real. You *are* flesh and blood. Why, you look just like Alexander, my neighbor!"

"I am Alexander, your neighbor, Violet. I have always been your neighbor."

"And yet, you are also my knight. You will *always* be my knight."

"I will *always* be your knight." Her hypnotic gray eyes were inches away, her pink lips were parted. It was just like the other night with Cassandra. In his imagination he pictured Cassandra standing here in front of him, and not Ruby. Clasping her face in his hands he pulled her into him, closing the gap between them until his lips found hers. He kissed her like he had never kissed anyone before. Closing his eyes and pouring his entire soul out through his lips. Her dainty hands tightened around his shoulders, her fingernails digging into his skin.

When they came apart moments later, he felt a great sense of relief. Good or bad, it was over. Ruby's face was flushed, and she seemed bewildered.

"Did I do that wrong?" he asked. "I kind of forgot that I was supposed to be acting. I'm so sorry!"

She took a deep breath in. "Relax, Wilfredo. That was perfect. It's safe to say we nailed it on the first try. Just hit me with that same intensity onstage later." She took a step back and regarded him thoughtfully with her head cocked to one side. "You're full of surprises, Wilfredo."

At that moment someone knocked at the door. Declan's voice rang out. "Ruby, are you free? There's someone I'd like you to meet!"

Ruby looked at Wilfredo who felt as if he'd just been caught with his hand in the cookie jar. "Oh, you look a frightful mess," she whispered. "You've got my lipstick all over you. Quick, duck behind here. We don't need any gossip." She shoved him behind her folding screen.

"Come in!"

The door opened. "Oh you're alone. I thought I heard voices. Can you come down to the theater for a minute? There's a backer I need you to charm. I know I keep leaning on you for this stuff, but with Sebastian out we have only one star to call on."

"Of course, it's no trouble." Through the narrow sliver between the panels Wilfredo watched as she followed Declan out the door. He would just wait for a minute then sneak away. At least he had done what he came here to do. Ruby had declared the kiss to be perfect, and she would know. Apparently the trick to the whole stage kiss business was to pretend he was kissing Cassandra.

32. CASSANDRA: WITNESSING A KISS

Cassandra sat in the mezzanine looking down on the darkened theater. On the stage the actors were getting ready to tackle the last few scenes. Declan liked taking the play in chunks, as it allowed him to pause when necessary and give notes to the actors, fix the lighting, and even tweak the script if need be.

The theater's plush red seats were mostly empty, except for a smattering of producers, agents, show-runners, and their assistants. Declan sat in the fifth row with Prisha hovering at his elbow as always. He had taken a liking to Cassandra, and regularly asked for her opinion on thorny staging issues. Years of pricey acting classes were finally paying off.

She spotted Sebastian sitting at stage left, his crutches poking out into the aisle, and his face brooding. Wilfredo was scared of him, and she could understand why. Her instincts told her that Sebastian was a bad fit for the role to begin with, and it would be fascinating to see what happened once he lost the crutches.

Cassandra sat, as always, with her notebook in her lap, ready to jot down any ideas that struck her during the performance. She usually sat by herself, but today Wilfredo's mother, Matilda, was in the seat to her right. Wilfredo had been terribly embarrassed when his mom showed up. After introducing them he had pulled Cassandra aside and begged her to keep a close eye on his mom and make sure she didn't do anything like take surreptitious photos, which was strictly forbidden. Cassandra had assured him she would be glued to his mother's side.

Cassandra had taken an instant liking to this sweet lady, who clearly just wanted to sit quietly and watch her only son performing up on a Broadway stage. They hadn't even begun and Matilda was already staring up at the stage in rapturous wonder.

Cassandra leaned closer to her. "I'm so proud of Wilfredo. He has done a remarkable job these past few weeks."

"He's always been talented. But I could never get him to really believe in himself."

"The flip side of that is that his vulnerability can be an exceptionally useful quality onstage."

"You are such a dear, Cassandra. You must come up to the house with Wilfredo sometime. Get out of the city for a few days. Then I can thank you properly for everything you've done."

"That would be lovely."

"Wilfredo mentioned you are engaged. Have you and your fiancé set a date?"

"We haven't settled on a date yet. I've been so busy recently that I've had to move the wedding planning to the back burner."

"Deary me, I hope that hasn't upset your fiancé?"

"Well, he's not happy about it." Cassandra gave Matilda a wry smile.

"Did you know Wilfredo went to school with Ruby?"

"Yes he mentioned that. Small world."

"Is it ever! I can't believe they are onstage together again, after all this time. Just between us, he had a real thing for her back in high school."

"Really?"

Their conversation was cut short when the house lights went dark. Moments later the stage lights came on, illuminating a lone figure sitting on a sofa in front of a television.

Dressed in hot pants and a tank top, Violet appeared woeful and disoriented. Cassandra considered Ruby to be a competent actor, perfectly capable of playing the ingenue in a way that won over the audience. But there was something superficial about her take on Violet, a character who had some darkness to her.

The play progressed and Cassandra felt her lips moving to echo every word of Ruby's lines. Wilfredo was doing her proud, hitting his marks, and delivering his most quotable lines with zest. Cassandra's gaze wandered over to Sebastian, sitting in the audience, his profile dimly lit by the glow of the stage lights. Cassandra nearly gasped when she saw the menacing look on his face. He clearly wasn't enjoying his understudy's success.

The play lurched toward its dramatic conclusion as Wilfredo pulled off his helmet, facing away from Violet, just as Cassandra had suggested. It was perfect. Violet pulled his face toward her own and their eyes met. Cassandra leaned forward in her seat, remembering how it had felt the other night to be in Ruby's place, her own face inches away from Wilfredo's, his gentle blue eyes staring into her own. His face onstage radiated that same passionate intensity that she'd felt up close herself. Of course his lips had never touched hers, as Wilfredo had shied away from her like a horse starting from a gunshot.

Cassandra held her breath as Wilfredo grasped Ruby's face in his large hands, and Ruby's delicate fingers crept around his back, digging into him as he pressed his lips to hers. Cassandra counted slowly to ten before the couple onstage finally came up for air. Professionally she had to admit that it had been a striking kiss. There had been nothing tentative or fake about it. The audience had been able to feel the burning passion radiating from the couple onstage.

Cassandra tried her best to feel proud of his work. After all, he had done everything just right. But as she watched the final coda of the play unfold, she found herself filled with an inexplicable sense of indignation. Why had he treated her as if she were radioactive in that same exact scenario? Did she find her hideous? And why had he pretended to be a rank amateur in the kissing department when he was capable of faking that kind of passion? A simple answer popped into her furious mind: perhaps Wilfredo had not needed to fake anything at all.

33. WILFREDO: THE LONG BATH

Wilfredo used his toes to twiddle the faucet, causing a narrow stream of hot water to pour into the tub, which was in danger of becoming lukewarm. Then he leaned back, disappearing into the thick layer of soapy bubbles coating the surface of the water. His elbow knocked a yellow washcloth into the bath, and he fished it out, wringing it dry. A narrow beam of light stole through the frosted glass of the window, casting a dull glow in the bathroom that revealed a pedestal sink, a small toilet, and a shaggy blue bath mat on the black-and-white-tiled floor.

Lost in his thoughts, Wilfredo was startled by a knock at the door. "Hey, buddy, you still in there?"

"Where else would I be?"

"You know it's been nearly an hour?"

"I haven't been keeping track of time."

"What's going on with you today?"

"I'm good," he replied dismissively, wishing Toby would buzz off.

"C'mon, we both know you head straight for the tub when you get in a funk about something. What is it this time?"

"None of your damn business. That's what it is," Wilfredo said vehemently.

"Look, I can't stand here all day needling it out of you. We have that art gallery party to get to. So just spit it out!"

Wilfredo let out another sigh and toggled the faucet off with his toes. "Cassandra is mad at me."

"Why is she mad at you?"

"I have no clue. One second we were fine, and then the next time I see her she's sore about something." When he had come offstage after rehearsal yesterday he knew instantly that she was furious with him.

"Well you must have done something to upset her."

"Yes, but I don't know what."

"Did you ask her what was bothering her?"

"I did. She said everything was just fine."

"Just fine? That's bad."

"Yeah."

"So you've decided to sit in our tub all day and hide from the world."

"Pretty much."

"Look, Wilfredo, you have to end this nonsense once and for all. You need to bite the bullet and tell her."

Wilfredo looked sharply at the closed white door. "Tell her *what*, exactly?"

"You know. Tell her that you're in love with her."

"Are you forgetting she's engaged? I can't go up to an engaged person and tell them that I'm madly in love with them."

"Why not? Think about it. She's not married yet. That Gregory dude hasn't actually sealed the deal. It's now or never."

"Never then. Cassandra isn't about to ditch a guy like Gregory for a bonehead like me."

"Probably not. But at least you would know. So get out

of that tub, get dressed, and let's go to that party!" Wilfredo scooped some bubbles in his hands and puffed at them, scattering bubbles in all directions.

Batten down the hatches and ready the harpoons! There's an enormous whale off the starboard bow. Wait a minute, false alarm! It's just good old Freddy, splashing about in a bucket of his own filth. A pitiable sight if ever I saw one!

"Do me a favor, Captain, and don't kick a man when he's down," mumbled Wilfredo.

But that's when they are right at boot level! Look, pal, I agree with you. There's no way that cupcake is gonna trade in her moneybags boyfriend for a penniless nickel rat like you. But your dumb roommate has a point too. You can't waste your life blubbering about it in a tub!

Toby knocked on the door again. "Wilfredo? Did you say something? Can you still hear me?"

"I can hear you. Clearly a man can't take a bath in peace in this house! Look, if it means so much to you, I'll cut my bath short and we can go to this stupid party!"

"That's all I wanted to hear. Can you be ready in ten? I'm gonna go pull the van around!"

Wilfredo reached for the chain of the plug with his toes and yanked it out. With a gurgle the water began to drain from the tub.

34. CASSANDRA:
THE ART GALLERY RELAPSE

The night went wrong from the very start when she got into a ridiculous fight with Gregory in the cab on their way to the gallery. They argued about the hordes of Santas invading the city streets, celebrating SantaCon. Gregory took a dim view of the boisterous figures in red-and-white plush costumes, referring to them as scumball Santas and likening their bar crawl to a plague descending on the city. Cassandra jumped to their defense, declaring them both harmless and hilarious. She wasn't sure why she felt compelled to take their side. Possibly she'd felt a strange kinship with the unruly band of costumed Santas and their green-hatted elven friends. Gregory had hammered home his point relentlessly: "These boozers are going to leave a trail of debauchery in their path. In a few hours' time they will be puking on the sidewalk and getting into drunken brawls." Cassandra just crossed her arms and said nothing.

When the cab pulled up in front of the gallery Cassandra hopped out while Gregory paid. By the time he was done she was freezing, as she'd opted to leave her coat at home, not wanting to be burdened with it at the art show. She was wearing a textured burgundy dress with only a white cashmere scarf to help fend off the cold. They hurried inside.

Cassandra intended to track down Wilfredo right away

and apologize for being so rude to him yesterday after rehearsal. But Gregory, of all people, soon derailed her plan. Cassandra had stopped to say a quick hello to Prisha, and when she turned back around she was alarmed to see her fiancé chatting with Wilfredo across the room. She could hardly believe it when the two of them made a beeline for the bar up in the mezzanine. She'd asked Toby, who had been standing nearby, what the heck was going on. Toby explained that her fiancé had apologized for getting off on the wrong foot and insisted on buying Wilfredo a beer. "You know Wilfredo, he's not going to turn down a free beer!" Toby chuckled.

"Yeah, Gregory really stumbled on the magic word." Dumbfounded, she roamed through the crowded gallery on her own, feeling abandoned. The colorful lowbrow paintings on the walls featured demonesque figures and raccoon-eyed girls with big heads. She found them strangely captivating, but half an hour later she was bored, and the two drinking buddies had yet to emerge from their watering hole. This party was seeming like a total bust. She stared absently at a particularly droll painting hanging on the back wall of the gallery as she debated taking off. That was when a stranger intruded on her thoughts.

"What do you think of this piece? It's utterly juvenile, isn't it?"

Cassandra turned to see a large woman in a gaudy zebra pattern dress, neon green heels, and a red cape. "I actually quite like it," Cassandra admitted, turning back to the painting. The canvas depicted a cartoonish devil prodding a girl in a white dress with his trident. Both figures had giant heads on small plump bodies. "It's irreverent, and unpretentious. You can tell the artist doesn't take himself too seriously."

"Yes, I thought you might say something like that," the woman replied snidely. "Clearly it appeals to a certain demographic, with, shall we say—less than mature tastes?"

Cassandra never would've guessed that she might run into someone more pompous than Gregory at the art showing. She stood there, mouth agape, trying to think of a suitable reply, but before she could get her wits about her the woman moseyed away.

Toby tapped her on the shoulder. "Do you know who you were talking to?"

"The rudest person on the planet?"

"That's Ayesha Randolph, bestselling author of the Inspector Fig series. I'm working up the courage to ask her to sign this napkin. I've read all her books."

"That vile woman is the famous suspense writer?"

"Yep. She knocks out three books a year and they all hit number one!"

"She must have a team of ghostwriters chained in her basement."

"Whatever she's doing, it's working. She has a private jet and a huge mansion upstate. I overheard someone say she's purchased three of this guy's paintings so far tonight."

"That can't be true. She was just telling me how much she despises them, and she's not about to drop six figures on some artwork she hates."

"I wouldn't be so sure about that. It's probably just a business investment for her. She'll probably flip them in a few years and make a killing."

And that was the moment Cassandra got it in her head to start following the flamboyant Ayesha Randolph around the gallery. She had only just met her, but she detested the woman. Cassandra kept a safe distance from her as they both wandered amidst the nattily dressed crowd. When Randolph stopped to stare at a painting, Cassandra would stop in front of a different painting, sneaking glances at the writer out of the corner of her eye. Crisscrossing the gallery, she stayed close to the heavyset woman in the zebra dress.

For the past few weeks Cassandra had successfully managed to suppress her larcenous impulses. It had not been easy. The city was crawling with rich fools flaunting their high-priced baubles and gadgets. But Cassandra couldn't escape the feeling that a relapse was imminent.

Randolph was wearing a chunky jade necklace around her neck and amber rings on her fingers. Her large leather purse was embellished with mother of pearl, and she had an ornate silk scarf tied around the handle. Cassandra couldn't help herself, she took out her phone and googled "Ayesha Randolph net worth." Her eyes popped out of her head. Was it even possible to make that much money writing books? Cassandra's eyes were drawn again to the woman's purse. It gave off an impregnable quality, with a zipper covered by a flap securing its contents. Then her eyes went to the silk scarf knotted loosely on her bag, which had a distinctive giraffe pattern to it. This time Cassandra searched for "Hermes scarf giraffe" and had an instant hit. She let out a low whistle. A rare collector's item, this exact scarf would fetch upward of twenty grand at auction—pocket change for someone like Randolph. The glimmer of a plan began forming in her mind.

Maybe if she waited for Randolph to go to the ladies room she might leave her bag unguarded?

But a short while later Cassandra got an assist from an unlikely source when a familiar voice loudly exclaimed: "Oh, I feel faint!" Cassandra turned to see Ruby, of all people, standing in the center of the room, the back of her hand pressed to her forehead. The actress tottered backward and then her knees gave out. She was caught neatly by a young man standing nearby. Cassandra rolled her eyes. She knew a stage faint when she saw one. This was purely manufactured drama, probably with the aim of generating some free publicity for the gallery. Sure enough, people had their phones out and aimed in her direction. Partygoers circled around Ruby, murmuring with concern. Half a minute later she opened her eyes and sat up, seeming dazed. Someone pressed a glass of water into her hand.

A familiar zebra fabric caught Cassandra's eye, and she saw that standing right next to her was Ayesha Randolph herself, craning her neck to gawk at the lightheaded actress. Pressed up side by side amid the jostling throng it was as if Cassandra's fingers had a mind of their own. Undoing the knotted scarf with one hand was child's play. She scrunched up the scarf and it disappeared into her fist, which she then discreetly slid into her own purse. Just as quickly she pulled out a Cat Burglar card from her wallet and tucked it into the side pocket of Randolph's purse. The whole thing was over and done within seconds. Cassandra drifted away from the crush of people and less than a minute later she walked nonchalantly out the gallery exit. Her favorite thrift store in Chelsea would welcome the scarf as a donation. Even if it ended up back in the hands of its owner, there would no doubt be a reward and publicity involved.

Cassandra was just outside the propped-open door when she heard a loud voice cry out: "My scarf! Help! I've been robbed!" Cassandra quickened her step and hurried north on West Broadway, which was crowded with groups of roving Santas. She ducked left onto the first side street, adrenaline coursing through her. The narrow street was quiet, except for a pair of costumed revelers who were standing on the metal steps leading up to an apartment building. These two strays from the Santa herd seemed well on their way to fulfilling their pledge of public lewdness. Gregory had been right about these liquored-up bar hoppers. The girl Santa removed her cumbersome jacket and threw it over the railing, pulling off the guy's Santa hat and chucking it on top.

The two lovebirds failed to notice when Cassandra plucked the hat and jacket from the banister without breaking stride. She quickly pulled them on as she walked, tucking her brown hair under the hat, and shoving her arms into the red jacket. She felt warmer already, and they matched her white scarf, which was wrapped snugly around her face.

Cassandra kept moving at a steady pace. Her mind beset with questions as to why she had pulled a stupid stunt like that in such a crowded room. Was it because Gregory had pissed her off? Or was it just because she'd let that awful woman get under her skin? Or maybe she was just a weird klepto adrenaline junkie? Cassandra cast a nervous glance over her shoulder as she hurried down the street.

35. WILFREDO:
STOP THAT SANTA

Word that Ruby Greenwood had fainted spread through the gallery like wildfire. Wilfredo rushed down to the main gallery in time to see a crowd of people circling her, helping her to her feet, and putting a chair under her. Thankfully she seemed okay.

Toby appeared at his elbow. "Don't worry, buddy. I saw the whole thing. He leaned in and whispered: "It looked totally staged to me. I think she's trying to get the art gallery some buzz."

Wilfredo relaxed, only to be startled by a loud yell nearby: "My scarf! Help! I've been robbed!" A plus-sized woman in a loud zebra dress was clutching her purse. "My Hermes giraffe scarf! It's gone!"

"Now *that* sounds real," Toby commented dryly. "Who knew art shows could be so exciting? Do you know who that is? That's Ayesha Randolph, the thriller writer!"

The woman was rifling through her purse. She pulled out a white business card tucked in a flap and peered at it closely. "The Cat Burglar!" she gasped. Realizing she'd been upstaged, Ruby hopped out of her chair, seemingly fully recovered, and offered her newly vacated seat to the now swooning writer.

"The Cat Burglar?" said Toby. "In here? Looks like your nemesis pulled a job right under your nose!"

Wilfredo was stone-faced. "Hey, Toby, are my backpack and my board still in the back of the van?"

"Right where you left them."

"I'm going to sneak out and skate around for a bit. I know what this Cat Burglar looks like, maybe I can catch up with her."

"Go do your hero thing if you've got the bug. I'd go with you but I left my Flip camera at home. I guess I'll stick around here and see what these celebs have planned for an encore."

Wilfredo scooted out the door and jogged over to where they had parked the van. He unlocked the back doors and climbed in. A minute later he poked his costumed head out to make sure the coast was clear.

He skated up past the gallery and decided to follow his instincts as to where the thief might have gone. He headed north, in the direction of the closest side street, and turned left. He skated down the street past a pair of partygoers making out on a stoop, keeping his eyes peeled for long red hair. What were the chances he was on the right trail?

"Hey, someone stole your Santa hat and my jacket!" a voice yelled. Wilfredo swiveled his head to see the girl on the stoop glaring up and down the street angrily. Maybe he was on the right track after all.

On a hunch Wilfredo made the next right, heading north again, toward the Village. He crossed Houston Street, leaving SoHo behind, and kept going straight, glancing down every cross street he passed for any sign of a lone girl in a Santa costume.

Hey, Freddy, I see you're back to your old tricks! Why are you busting your conk chasing this scarf-snatcher? The trail's gone cold! You should head back to the gallery and check up on that hot tomato Ruby!

Maybe the Captain was right. This was looking like a fool's errand. But just as he was about to pop up his board and flip it around, he glimpsed a shapely figure in a red Santa costume in the distance. He was still some ways away when he saw her stop by a lamppost and pull something out of her purse. Standing with her back to him, she held it up to the lamplight, before folding it carefully and tucking it back in her purse. He had closed the gap between them enough to make out yellow giraffes on the silky fabric. Wilfredo's masked face took on a determined look. There was no way he was gonna lose round two.

He was about twenty feet behind her when she first heard the skateboard rolling along in the street and glanced back. She wasn't wearing a mask this time, but her face was hidden behind a white scarf, and the Santa hat was pulled down to her eyes, leaving only a sliver for her to see through. Her eyes locked on him, and she immediately took off sprinting down the street.

"Here we go again!" Wilfredo muttered, pushing off a few times to pick up speed. A car was stopped at the intersection ahead, facing him, and Wilfredo skated past it, his costume brushing up against parked cars on his right. Man she was fast. He was barely gaining on her. But at this pace she would tire herself out soon. He zipped past familiar restaurants and stores on MacDougal. Up ahead he saw her jog into the south west entrance to Washington Square Park. Close behind, he hopped the curb and wove his way past pedestrians into the park.

She was starting to breathe heavily, but he was happy to let her tire herself out some more before closing in for a tussle. They raced past chess players and tourists gathered around concrete tables. The pathway took them diagonally toward the center of the park. Bit by bit he closed the gap between them. When they emerged in the center they were met with the unexpected sight of a large gathering of rowdy Santas around the deactivated fountain. The Cat Burglar sprinted into their midst and hopped the short sill into the dry fountain area. Wilfredo skated to the right, determined to cut her off when she emerged on the other side, taking a wide route around the throng of Santas. He needed to make sure he didn't lose her in the crowd.

But she had stopped cold in the middle of the fountain, panting heavily. He could sense her desperation as he circled around. For now she was trapped within the ring of the fountain, trying to get her wind back. He thought about yelling "Stop that thief," but it didn't feel particularly heroic. He had a reputation to uphold.

Unfortunately, she had struck on a plan of her own: "Hey, look, everyone, it's Foxman!" she yelled, pointing at him, her voice muffled by the scarf. He had been attracting a few curious glances, but the second she spoke up dozens of Santa heads swiveled in his direction.

"Three cheers for Foxman!" yelled the exhausted thief. "New York's true hero!" Almost instantly Wilfredo found himself mobbed by red-suited Santas. They cheered for him and reached out to give him high fives and clap him on the back. One Santa, with an unglued beard and breath that reeked of tequila, offered him a drink from a bottle concealed in a brown paper bag. Wilfredo tried to roll past them toward the fountain, but there were too many Santas blocking his way. He picked up his skateboard determined to push through on foot, but just then he felt strong arms grabbing hold of his legs, and before he even knew what was happening he'd been lifted up into the air by two beefy Santas. They carried him around the park on their shoulders, chanting "Foxman! Foxman! Foxman!" Wilfredo held on for dear life, no longer in control of his own movements. The Cat Burglar gave him a taunting wave before darting away in the opposite direction.

Captain Pete was not impressed: *Hey, Freddy! By my count that's Cat Burglar two, Foxman nil. She outsmarted you this time! But I guess it doesn't take a criminal mastermind to do that. Let's hope this rowdy crew doesn't drop you on your head!*

Detective Molina slid behind the wheel of the gray Dodge Charger, his belly brushing up against the steering wheel. That was odd. His seat was in the same position as always. Then it dawned on him. He'd had the same problem with the belt of his pants the other morning—his waist was expanding. It was all on account of those accursed donuts. Detective Garcia—damn her—would show up at the precinct with them almost daily.

The two detectives drove over to the art gallery and circled the block a few times before finding a parking spot nearby. They strolled toward the West Broadway address in leisurely fashion. Detective Molina hitched up his trousers as he walked. "So you really think there might be something to this theory of yours?"

Detective Garcia was walking two paces ahead of him. "Yeah, I'm telling you, I think that actress must be involved in some way."

"Seems like a bit of a stretch to me."

"C'mon, Molina. Every pickpocket gang in the city uses the same trick. A carefully orchestrated distraction that gives the thief an opportunity to do their dirty work."

"That is typically how they operate. So you're suggesting Ruby Greenwood may be in cahoots with the Cat Burglar?"

"In cahoots? Who says 'in cahoots' these days?"

"I do."

"Don't be such a dinosaur. You mean to say—do I think she was in on it!"

Detective Molina sniffed. "Just answer the question."

"Yeah, I think she was *in cahoots* with the Cat Burglar. In fact, did you get a good look at her? She's got the same exact hair and build as the Cat Burglar woman."

"She's a professional actress. She doesn't exactly fit the criminal profile."

"Yeah, but this isn't your typical criminal. Think about it, the Cat Burglar isn't keeping any of the loot. What kind of thief gives away the whole take?"

"A rich thief?"

"Exactly."

"Still, she has a lot to lose by turning to a life of crime."

"Tell that to Wynona Ryder."

"Well, it doesn't hurt to look into it. *De omnibus dubitandum*—be suspicious of everything. That's what I always say." His face adopted a thoughtful expression. When it came to celebrities he knew it was better to tread carefully, if at all. This theory of hers was as likely to blow up in her face as not. He would have to make sure to carefully distance himself if that happened, but in the meantime he would give her some rope.

"Imagine if we prove it's her?" said Detective Garcia. "We'd make the papers!"

"Don't worry. Lieutenant Kopski will jump in and take all the credit."

A neatly dressed young blonde was sitting behind the front desk at the gallery when the two detectives arrived. She gave a start when he flashed his badge. Picking up the phone she whispered into the receiver and seconds later an older woman with guarded features came out of the back to greet them. Dressed in a navy skirt, she had chunky eyeglasses and asymmetrically styled black hair. She led them to a small office attached to the gallery, waved them into two free chairs, and then turned the screen on her desk so they could all see it. Using a remote she selected a file on a DVR device.

"I have the files from the showing Saturday all cued up. Sorry I couldn't send you the footage, but there's no way to get them off this stupid machine."

Detective Garcia smiled agreeably. "We understand. We see a lot of these older contraptions in our line of work."

The woman hit PLAY and ran through the silent scene viewed from the ceiling-level camera. Detective Molina sighed. The resolution wasn't great, and with so many people crowded into the room it was impossible to pinpoint when the scarf got stolen. They played the scene over and over without spotting any clues. Then Detective Garcia asked the gallery manager to rewind a little further to when Ruby Greenwood had fainted.

The stern-faced woman obliged them. "It's a good thing that young gentleman caught her. If she'd hit the floor we could've had a much bigger problem on our hands than a stolen scarf."

"Yes, it was quick thinking on his part," Detective Garcia agreed, her eyes narrowed as she peered at the fainting scene reenacted on the screen. With the actress standing conspicuously in the middle of the room the camera had caught a much better view. After watching for a few minutes Garcia said: "Well, I think that's all we need. Thanks for your time. Here's my card. Don't hesitate to call us if you think of anything that may help."

The woman took the card. "Certainly. But didn't I read in the paper that Ms. Randolph has already recovered her scarf from a thrift store?"

Garcia nodded. "That's true, the scarf turned up pretty fast. But this theft is part of a larger criminal investigation we are looking into."

Back outside, the two detectives walked slowly back to their car. "What do you think, Molina? Don't tell me that faint didn't look completely staged! Like something she might have done on screen a million times."

"You're right," the bald detective admitted. "People don't fall backward like that when they faint in real life."

"And did you notice how quickly she popped up when the attention wasn't on her anymore."

"I saw that too. I have to say the videotape lends some credence to your theory."

"My gut tells me that Ruby Greenwood is at the center of this shady Cat Burglar business," insisted the junior detective.

Arriving at their vehicle Detective Molina squeezed behind the wheel. Scowling, he reached down under his seat, pulled up on the lever, and eased his seat back an inch until he heard a *click*. "Maybe we should have ourselves a little chat with this actress?" he said gruffly.

"My thoughts exactly!" Detective Garcia beamed. "I'll find out where she's staying. Hey, what do you say we swing by the donut shop on the way back to the precinct? Pick up a box of Boston creams?"

The backstage area of the Cornelius Theater was buzzing like a beehive that had been whacked with a two-by-four. Cassandra wound her way up the stairs past frenzied stagehands, ducking into a stairwell when she glimpsed Sebastian Estrada hobbling in her direction. He'd taken to roaming the halls like an angry pirate patrolling the deck of his ship, ranting and raving about his slow to mend leg. Sebastian had been furious when Declan announced they were going forward with a soft opening before the holidays for the press, as well as friends and family. A performance where Wilfredo would play the role of the knight. Cassandra knew there was only one reason Declan would gamble on a performance for the media without one of his two stars, and that was because Wilfredo was a hit as the knight. He brought a much-needed comic counterpoint to all of Violet's drama and routinely drew guffaws from the crew during rehearsals. Declan's plan was to forgo the marquee name and try his luck with a fresh face for the reviewers.

Wilfredo, who always approached each rehearsal as if it were his last, had been equally shocked by this announcement. For a hot minute Cassandra was worried he might implode under the pressure. She'd hit him with her best pep talk, reminding him he had nothing to lose. Then they got to work to fine-tune his performance.

She'd had to balance her time between Wilfredo and her new client. Declan had asked her to work with Ruby's understudy, Evelyn, helping her get up to speed. Evelyn was a talented young performer with a pixie haircut, who was a little taller than Cassandra, a little prettier than her, and five years younger. She was exactly the kind of actor who kept edging out Cassandra for roles at auditions.

But that was all in the past. Cassandra poured her insights for the role of Violet into her, and a grateful Evelyn absorbed them like a sponge. And it was nice to have a new girlfriend on set.

Cassandra made her way toward the dressing rooms, where all the actors were ensconced, putting the final touches on their hair and makeup. She found Evelyn sitting in front of her mirror, getting her hair teased by a stylist brandishing a curling iron. Cassandra pulled a small blue card out of her purse. "Check it out! I have business cards!" Cassandra held it out to the younger actress, who took it and read it out loud:

"Cassandra Bell. Acting Coach." She hugged the card to her chest. "Oh wow, Cassandra, this is fantastic. Is this one for me? Here, give me a few more so I can hand them out to my friends! You are so official!"

"I know, I can hardly believe it. I almost cried when these arrived in the mail yesterday."

Evelyn jumped up out of her chair and gave her a hug. "Hey, where were you earlier? Me and Ruby went to that sushi place around the corner for lunch and we wanted you to join us, but I couldn't find you anywhere!"

"I popped out to go give my notice at Baylor and Bowman."

"There's no going back for you!"

"I'm all in. And thanks for thinking of me, but I'm a vegetarian, remember?"

"Oh yeah! I keep forgetting."

"I will let you finish getting your hair done, and I'm gonna go find Wilfredo to show him my new business cards. I'll see you later?"

"Yeah. Let's sit together for the show."

"Sure! My fiancé is coming tonight so you'll get to meet him. And I promised Wilfredo I'd sit with his mom too."

"No worries. I can't wait to meet Gregory!"

As the lead actor for the night, Wilfredo had been moved into Sebastian's dressing room, much to the hobbled star's chagrin. Cassandra found her friend pacing the room in the linen undergarments he wore beneath his armor. The makeup person hovering nearby was shaking his head, as if getting him to sit still was a hopeless endeavor.

Wilfredo lit up when he saw her. "Cassandra! Where have you been? I'm freaking out!"

"Relax, Wilfredo. It's perfectly normal to have butterflies in your stomach before a show!"

"Butterflies? More like elephants stomping around on my chest!"

She reached out and took his hand. "Don't worry, you're going to be great."

"I don't know if I can do this, Cassandra. I want to just grab the keys to the van, drive to Alaska, and spend the rest of my life holed up in a log cabin in the woods."

"Get a grip, Wilfredo. I know you can do this." She stared

into his blue eyes, doing her best to soothe the nerves she saw
there. "Here. Take a look at this." She handed him her new
business card.

With an effort he focused on the small blue card. "Yowza,
this is like a whole new career for you!"

"Yep. I quit my department store job today and
everything."

"You did?"

"And how do you think it's going to look if my very first
client bails to become a hermit right before the show? Don't
you think that will reflect poorly on me as your acting coach?"

"I didn't think of that," he admitted. "I guess you're right.
I don't really have a choice. I have to do this. I can't let you
down."

"Oh Wilfredo," she exclaimed. "You say the sweetest
things sometimes. I could kiss you!" His eyebrows shot up.
"But I won't!" she added hastily.

Just then the dressing room door flew open. A breathless Prisha stood there panting, her eyes wide as saucers. Her
words came in between short gasps for air. "Ruby. Sick. Big
problem."

"Holy shit," said Cassandra. "What is it? Spit it out,
woman!"

Prisha took a deep breath. "Ruby has taken ill. She can't
go on. Declan needs you *now* in Evelyn's dressing room. She
is going to play Violet tonight."

"What? Oh my god! What happened to Ruby?"

"Some sort of stomach bug. She's been holed up in the
bathroom for the last twenty minutes. I went in to talk to
her. Let's just say—it wasn't pretty!" Prisha grimaced. "There

is no way she can go onstage in half an hour. Declan is going out of his mind!"

"Is it too late to postpone the opening?"

"The critics are already arriving at the theater. We have butts in chairs! If the curtain doesn't go up in twenty minutes the play will be DOA."

Cassandra dashed out the door with Prisha close behind. When they got to Evelyn's dressing room they found Declan pacing outside and a half dozen stylists and makeup artists working on the understudy inside. Evelyn looked pale and scared.

"You can do this, Evie! You are so ready!" Cassandra assured her.

"I know I can," Evelyn replied unsurely. "It's just that . . ."

"What is it?"

"My stomach doesn't feel so good."

"It's just nerves."

"I'm not so sure. I'm worried that maybe it's—the sushi!" With a yelp Evelyn tore herself away from the stylists, and raced down the hallway half dressed, heading in the direction of the bathroom, with a stupefied Prisha in tow.

Everyone left in the room went silent. Declan stood in the doorway. "The sushi? Did she just say the sushi? Someone tell me my star and her understudy didn't both eat raw fish for lunch together?"

Prisha returned five minutes later, ashen faced. Declan looked at her searchingly. She shook her head. "Neither of them is coming out of there anytime soon. The doctor is in there with them and he says it looks like a bad case of food poisoning. Ruby is dehydrated and running a fever, and

Evelyn is puking her guts out and headed the same way as Ruby."

Declan closed his eyes. In a despondent voice he said, "Prisha. Tell me our Violet standby is in the theater."

Prisha bit her lip and looked down at her clipboard. "The standby called twenty minutes ago to say she's stuck in Lincoln Tunnel traffic, which has been at a standstill for the past three hours."

Declan let out an anguished cry, like a wounded beast. "It's over!" A crowd of cast and crew had gathered in the hallway, and they all bore the look of horrified spectators witnessing a train wreck. Among them was Sebastian. "I knew it!" he bellowed. "This play was cursed from day one!" He waved his crutch around madly.

There was a drawn-out silence after that, and then another voice spoke up. Wilfredo's voice. "Why can't Cassandra play the role? She knows it inside and out."

Thirty faces turned to stare at her, including Declan from where he had slunk to the floor. "Do you think you could do it?" he asked quietly.

Cassandra nodded. "I know the part as well as anyone."

Declan climbed to his feet and went and took hold of Cassandra's two hands. "Yes, you know the part. But do you think you can do it?"

"Absolutely. I've been preparing for this moment for the past ten years."

Declan whirled around and faced everyone. "Move, people! Get Cassandra to costume and makeup! Now!"

She was whisked down the hall toward Ruby's dressing room, where she immediately became the center of a whirlwind of activity. Hair, makeup, and costume people all swirled around her working their magic. Prisha crammed a pen in her hand and made her sign ten different forms and a contract.

Before the reality of what was happening could even sink in she found herself sitting on a purple sofa on a darkened stage. The inky blackness was obliterated moments later by a bright light that felt warm on her skin.

38. GREGORY: THE LAST STRAW

Gregory stared out the window of the nearly motionless cab. When the light turned green the cab driver inched forward, one hand on the wheel, the other holding the cell phone he was talking into in some foreign language. But they barely moved six feet before the traffic light turned red again. The cars around them all leaned on their horns. Gregory pushed a twenty through the gap in the partition and hopped out—they were already at Forty-Seventh Street and it would be quicker and cheaper to walk the last few blocks.

He soon found himself traversing Times Square, its glass towers blanketed in flashing lights, tourists still roving around in packs taking pictures. It was a part of the city he did his best to avoid. Glancing at the watch on his wrist he quickened his pace. He was admittedly curious to see this play that had so consumed Cassandra for the past two months, leaving her with little time for her fiancé.

When he arrived at the theater he gave his name at the ticket window. They scratched it off a list and handed him a ticket. At the entrance to the auditorium he accepted a playbill from an elderly man in a bow tie who walked him down to row twenty and said: "Curtain goes up in five minutes." Gregory squeezed awkwardly past already seated strangers until he found his seat number. He would have liked to be closer, but he knew the better seats were reserved for the critics. There was no one sitting on either side of him, but one seat over he saw an elderly lady looking closely at the playbill through her reading glasses. She smiled at him.

"My son is in the production," she volunteered. "He's playing the knight. It's the lead. He's the understudy, but the main actor got injured." Gregory nodded noncommittally and buried his nose in his own playbill. From her words he guessed this woman must be Wilfredo's mother.

The auditorium was filling up and the audience was buzzing with excitement, but the seat to his left was still empty. He checked the time—it was already eight. The play would be starting any minute. Where could his fiancée be? He checked his texts—nothing. This was classic Cassandra, leaving him stranded at her own event.

Gregory flipped through the playbill, which seemed to be the object of much comment and attention from the people around him. No doubt this chatter was regarding the injured Sebastian Estrada, and the unknown who had taken over his part. A quick glance at the insert confirmed his hunch. And then he did a double take. There was a second line on the white sheet of paper: *The part of Violet will be played by Cassandra Bell.*

What the hell? That had to be a mistake.

Gregory pricked his ears to listen in on a loud conversation taking place two rows behind him: "Yeah, it's crazy! The lead and her understudy both had food poisoning so the part fell into Cassandra's lap. She hasn't done a single rehearsal! Strap in! We could be in for an epic crash and burn."

He just couldn't wrap his mind around it. Cassandra

was playing a lead role onstage? And yet, it would explain why she was nowhere to be seen. Could the show really open with a promoted stagehand and an untested acting coach carrying the play? It seemed like a surefire recipe for disaster. But it would seem Cassandra was getting tossed in the deep end. If things went badly—a distinct possibility—it might be enough to cure her of the acting bug for good. His mild curiosity about the play from a moment ago was suddenly transformed into eager anticipation.

The lights overhead flickered and a hush fell over the theater. Two minutes later the lights faded to black as the velvety curtains slid open. A spotlight appeared on the stage illuminating his missing fiancée, seated on a purple sofa, her elbows resting on her knees and her chin resting on her hands. She looked different, her wavy brown locks thicker and fuller, her eyes accentuated with dramatic blue eyeshadow. She broke the silence, her voice a mournful lament to loneliness and isolation. Gregory leaned forward in his seat.

If Cassandra had started out strong, she only got stronger as she went along. She captivated the audience with her every word, movement, and gesture. The knight appeared in scene two, a comical presence at first, yet poignant in his silences, as he fashioned a singular relationship with the manic girl.

Gregory's initial consternation that she wasn't embarrassing herself gave way to grudging admiration, and finally to outright wonder. He'd always known she was a sensitive soul, but he'd never suspected her of having such hidden depths. During a particularly heartrending moment his eyes welled with tears, and it was only by dabbing them with his pocket square that he avoided an embarrassing personal moment.

He was struck by a discomfiting thought: She had a remarkable talent, and he had been wholly wrong to dissuade her from pursuing her passion. How had he been so dense?

By the start of act three it was a repentant Gregory watching the play unfold. His beautiful fiancée, putting on the performance of a lifetime, held the audience in the palm of her hand. The knight managed to sustain his end of the bargain, and it became like watching an intricately choreographed dance between two perfectly in-sync performers.

Gregory was spellbound when the knight finally removed his helmet, revealing that he was a real person, her neighbor no less, a guy who had been secretly in love with Violet for months, playing along with her delusional fantasies. She reached out a hand and touched his cheek, turning him to face her. Their beating hearts inches away from one another as they stared into each other's eyes. Leaning in, her hands inched up his back as their lips finally met.

For Gregory the kiss felt like getting doused with a bucket of ice water. He snapped out of the trance he'd fallen into, and watched in disbelief as his fiancée gave this bozo an open-mouthed kiss in front of the whole theater. It was an intensely passionate moment where her heels slowly rose up off the stage and her arms floated out to the side, as Wilfredo cupped her face in his hands. Gregory felt his face flush with heat, and he clenched and unclenched his fists repeatedly. Clearly he had been right about Wilfredo the first time around. And about this acting nonsense. He already had to live with that shower scene of hers, and now he had to watch her swap spit with Wilfredo? Where did it all end? What if her next role called for a full-on sex scene, would he be expected to grin and bear it? As he saw it, acting was a degenerate profession reserved for perverts and libertines, people devoid of any common decency.

The play's coda went by in a blur as an enraged Gregory stared wrathfully out at the stage. When the curtain closed, the theater broke out into thundering applause. People climbed to their feet as they cheered the small cast, who came out to take a bow, hand in hand, wide smiles plastered on their faces. A minute passed and the intensity of the applause showed no sign of letting up. Only two figures in the audience sat unmoving. One was an old woman clutching a playbill, tears streaming down her face. And sitting close by, a young man in a blue suit, with slicked-back hair, whose face bore a dour expression.

39. WILFREDO: DISSECTING THE KISS

Wilfredo removed his tunic and chain mail in Sebastian's dressing room, handing them off to the two costume assistants. Then he chased them out, pulled off his leggings and undershirt and changed into his street clothes—cargo pants and a yellow-and-blue flannel shirt. Seating himself on the leather stool in front of the mirror he used a wipe to clean the makeup off his face.

He'd made it through the whole play with flying colors. Even if this turned out to be his one and only performance it was something to be proud of. Nevertheless his mood was downcast as his thoughts kept returning to that moment when he'd held Cassandra in his arms. Their kiss had unleashed powerful, pent-up emotions inside him. He wanted nothing more than to find her and kiss her again. But they were back in the real world now, the one where she was engaged to be married. And Wilfredo knew he wasn't ever likely to share the stage with her again.

Bad news, Freddy. You've been devoured by that green-eyed swooner! A similar thing happened to my pal Jonah when he got swallowed by a whale. He got sucked into the belly of the beast and they sank down to the ocean's depths, never to be seen again. I expect your own fate will be much the same.

"Spare me your gibberish, Captain," Wilfredo mumbled bitterly.

The sound of approaching footsteps in the hallway were followed by a knock at the door. Cassandra's face appeared in the doorway, and his heart leaped. "We did it!" she exclaimed excitedly.

"We sure did."

"I can't believe it!"

"Me neither. It hasn't really sunk in."

"I'm exhausted yet pumped up at the same time." She dragged another stool over from a corner and came to sit close by. Peering at him curiously she said: "That was some kiss, Wilfredo. You really caught me off guard."

"Sorry. We didn't get a chance to chat beforehand, then I lost myself in the character and I ended up doing the kiss the way I'd rehearsed it with Ruby. I hope that's all right?"

A barely noticeable look of disappointment flashed across her face. "The kiss was perfect, Wilfredo," she said quietly. "Not your typical stage kiss, granted. But that's probably why it works so well. I can't believe you were worried about it."

"I know Gregory was in the audience tonight. I hope that won't cause any problems for you. I know how he gets."

"Let me worry about Gregory. You should just enjoy this moment. You've earned it with your hard work, and the way you faced your fears."

"But you were the real star onstage today." He lowered his voice to a whisper. "You're ten times the actor Ruby is."

They were interrupted by another knock at the door, and this time it was Declan who stepped into the room. "Just the two people I was looking for! Well done, both of you. That went better than I could have dreamed! Wilfredo, you nailed it. And Cassandra—I'm speechless. Where did you get that interpretation of Violet from?"

"Yeah, sorry about that. I'd been playing her differently when I ran lines with Wilfredo, and it kind of stuck."

"No, no, no! What I mean is that your Violet was better. She had more of an edge to her. It's like you flipped the character inside out. I always thought the key to understanding Violet was that she conjures up a fictitious knight. But now I see that what her character really hinges on is her ability to pretend that the guy sitting next to her on the couch is imaginary. It's a subtle difference but it means everything. You played her perfectly. I'm counting on you to help Ruby give her that same spin for our January shows."

Cassandra had a wide smile on her face. "Absolutely, whatever I can do to help."

"Fabulous! I feel like you're the only other person around here who understands staging." Declan clapped them both on the back, then his phone buzzed in his pocket, and he ran off to take a call. He was immediately replaced by Toby and a bunch of the crew who had been hovering outside. "Wilfredo! Cassandra! You guys rock! The betting odds had the two of you going down in flames. Not me though! I knew you guys could do it because I've seen you rehearse in our living room. Are you ready to celebrate? We're heading over to Greystones Pub and you two are drinking for free!"

Wilfredo rubbed his chin. "I feel like we should wait for any reviews to come in before we get carried away."

"You're missing the point," exclaimed an equally excited Prisha. "The two of you were amazing up onstage together!"

Toby pumped a fist in the air. "It's like the backup quarterback throwing a Hail Mary pass and winning the game as the clock runs out."

"More like the water boy," joked one of the stagehands, to much laughter.

But the room fell silent as a familiar *click-clack* sound in the hall drew closer. Nervous glances were exchanged. There were about ten people jammed into the small room, and every face turned to look at the door, which was promptly darkened by the glowering figure of Sebastian. "What are you all doing in *my* dressing room?" He shook his crutch at them furiously. "Get out of here! The lot of you!"

His outburst was met with grumbles and scowls as people looked to Wilfredo for guidance. As tonight's lead actor, this was rightfully his dressing room for the night. Wilfredo calmly stood up and grabbed his coat off the hook. "Actually, we were just leaving."

"Greystones, here we come!" yelled Toby. The group's good cheer returned as they piled out of the room. Wilfredo grinned at his friend. A couple pints were a fair reward after what he'd just been through.

But Cassandra lingered behind. Wilfredo gave her a questioning look. "You coming?"

She shook her head. "You guys go ahead. I have to go find Gregory." For some reason she wouldn't meet his eyes. Wilfredo wanted to ask her if anything was wrong, but he was whisked down the hall by his boisterous companions.

40. CASSANDRA:
THE FOUNTAIN

Cassandra wrapped her scarf around her neck and pushed out through the stage door. She found Gregory standing stiffly outside the theater on an empty sidewalk, the collar of his wool coat turned up, and his hands shoved deep in his pockets. Hearing the door he whipped around. "Well, well. Look who it is. I was just about to give up and head home." Wispy puffs of vapor formed in the air with his every breath.

"Gregory. I'm really sorry."

"Sorry about what? Making me wait out here in the cold? French-kissing another man? Being a lousy fiancée?" His voice was thick with sarcasm.

"About everything," she said, and she meant it.

His forehead creased and he seemed momentarily puzzled by the sincerity of her apology. Clearly he'd expected her to put up a fight. Sucking in his breath he rallied his outrage. "Don't think for one second that a simple apology is going to magically make everything all right."

"Let's walk, Gregory." She took his arm and guided him away from the theater. A recent downpour had left the city streets slick and glistening with inky puddles that reflected the red taillights of passing cars. They strolled down toward Forty-Second Street in silence. Cassandra was at a loss for where to begin. The kiss with Wilfredo had been an electrifying moment for her. She wasn't blind to the feelings that had been brewing inside her for some time, but she'd been caught off guard by the intense connection she'd felt onstage with him. If she'd been wondering whether kissing Wilfredo would feel different from kissing Gregory she now had her answer, and it was as plain and unambiguous as she could have wished for.

"People seemed to enjoy the play," Gregory conceded grudgingly as they made a left and began to walk east along the south side of Forty-Second Street with no particular destination in mind.

"Did *you* enjoy it?"

"I did. Very much so. Up until the end, that is. I'm guessing you guys practiced it many times?"

"No. Tonight was the first kiss. It was completely unrehearsed, unless you count the times Wilfredo rehearsed it with Ruby Greenwood."

"That Wilfredo guy is a piece of work. He acts all dopey, and then the next thing you know he's putting the moves on every gorgeous woman in a ten-mile radius."

Cassandra sighed, but didn't bother to defend Wilfredo. She had no strength left in her to argue with Gregory. Instead, she listened without responding as Gregory vented all his anger and frustration. By the time he was done fulminating they had arrived at the corner of Bryant Park. Cassandra steered them up the steps and into the shadowy gardens. They proceeded quietly along the gravel path, under a rustling canopy of trees. When they drew near to the granite fountain they stopped to gaze at the mass of icicles that had formed on the upper rim, hanging down into the pool of water in the basin below. A lively group of young girls were taking selfies by the fountain but they soon wandered off.

With no one nearby, Cassandra decided this was as good a moment as any to take the plunge. "So where does this leave us, Gregory?"

"I've been giving it a lot of thought, and I just don't know how we can move forward with the wedding this way, and I'm not sure that ring really belongs on your hand anymore."

"You're right, Gregory. It's awful to hear you say it out loud, but there's no denying things have gone way offtrack. And maybe I do deserve the bulk of the blame for that. Here. Take it." She slipped the engagement ring off her finger and held it out to him.

He looked astonished. "Wait a minute. Aren't you even going to fight for us?"

"What's the point? All we do is argue. This engagement isn't working out, you just said so yourself." She grabbed his hand and tried to press the ring into it, but he pulled his hand away and balled it into a fist.

"This is very easy for you, Cassandra, isn't it? Just hand back the ring and walk away, is that it?"

"No, it's not easy for me. Not in the least. But it's clear to me now that there's no way we can get married." She was becoming exasperated.

"I thought perhaps you might beg me not to do anything drastic!"

"Oh, Gregory. Sometimes I think you never really understood me at all. Please—just take back the ring."

"Why are you so eager to get rid of it? Is it because you're in love with Wilfredo?"

"If I'm being honest, I think I do have feelings for him. I admit it. You were right all along. But the thing is, I didn't fully realize it myself until he kissed me tonight." She held the ring out to him once more.

He kept his arms stiffly pressed to his sides. "I bet you're planning to run into his arms the second we call it quits."

"No. The crazy thing is, that kiss tonight wasn't meant for me. I was just a stand-in for Ruby. He gave *me* Ruby's kiss. He told me as much himself. It was a stolen kiss, really."

"What are you saying? You think Wilfredo is after Ruby? Then why would you end our engagement? It doesn't add up."

"His kiss made me realize what I'm missing. I might never be lucky enough to get those fireworks for myself, but knowing that kind of passion is out there makes it hard to settle for anything less."

"Well, I'm not taking back the ring. We've both said some horrible things tonight, but at the end of the day I still care for you, Cassandra. We have passion. At least we used to. You mean everything to me, and my guess is this little infatuation of yours will peter out and not amount to anything in the long run. We just need to be patient."

"It's over, Gregory," she said gently. "It's been over for a while. We've been in denial. And you should know better than to ask for the ring back unless you mean it."

"How on earth can you choose being alone over marrying me?" His tone had grown sharp again. "You're thirty-three, Cassandra. Do you really want to throw away what might be your last shot at getting married and having kids?"

Cassandra set her jaw. She wasn't going to miss this mean streak of his. "Take the ring."

"I won't."

Cassandra's gaze narrowed, and her eyes were drawn to the gurgling marble fountain. Taking aim she threw the ring into the air, and it traveled in a high arc before plunking into the water.

"Oh my god. I can't believe you just did that! That ring cost me nearly ten grand. You are so irresponsible. Now we have to fish it out!"

"Goodbye, Gregory." She turned and walked away, not caring what direction she went, blotting her eyes with her scarf.

"Cassandra! Stop! Cassandra!"

She looked back just once, with blurry vision, and saw that he had pulled off his socks and shoes, rolled up his trousers, and was climbing into the icy fountain. He looked completely ridiculous. What a way for their engagement to end. She didn't know whether to laugh or cry.

41. WILFREDO:
A HERO STANDS ABOVE

Toby and Wilfredo were sitting in a red-leather booth at Greystones Pub. The crowd in the two-story bar was beginning to thin, and one by one their friends called it a night. Finally, it was just the two of them, and that's when Toby began to pester him about the declining views on the Foxman videos. "You know what we gotta do, buddy? We gotta make another video. Keep Foxman in the public eye! You haven't been seen in public in your costume since the whole SantaCon debacle."

"I'm not going out on the street dressed as Foxman after what happened last time. Getting mobbed by dozens of drunk Santas isn't my idea of a good time."

"Dude, that was a one-time thing! Do you see any Santas around?"

"I think Foxman has had his day. We had our fun with it. Now it's over."

Toby looked miffed. "Hey, if you want to retire from superhero duty, I guess that's your business."

"The only way I'd get back in the suit is if that Cat Burglar pops up again."

"So you're happy to keep your little vendetta going, but you can't be bothered with petty criminals?"

"That's right. I gotta save my strength for my arch nemesis."

Toby cracked a smile. "Arch nemesis! That's a good one. I'm gonna work that into the script."

Wilfredo glared at his friend. "There is no script."

"Well, what if you didn't have to be in public. What if we did a rooftop video? Foxman keeping a watchful eye on the city—that sort of thing."

"If we shoot a video on the roof of our six-story apartment building people are going to figure out who Foxman is real quick."

"Ah, but I know where they keep the key to the roof at the Cornelius."

"Are you trying to get us both fired?"

"There's no one around at this hour! We go up, we make a quick video, and then we're done. Piece of cake."

The Captain piped up in his head. *This rooftop scheme of his is pure gold, Freddy. It's the sort of tomfoolery me and the lads used to get up to back in the day after hitting the old rum jug!*

Wilfredo resisted until Toby volunteered to take on all the housekeeping duties for the week. Then they settled the tab and rolled out of the bar in the direction of the theater. Doubts lingered in Wilfredo's mind. "Who knows if we'll even be able to get into the theater at this hour."

"Just tell Carl you left something in the dressing room. Don't forget—you're talent now."

They stopped to grab Wilfredo's longboard and his backpack from the van, which was still parked just down the block from the theater. Carl, the late-shift security guard waved them through with an unconcerned smile. "Great show, man. I managed to catch a few minutes on my break!"

"Thanks, Carl!"

The two of them climbed up the gloomy stairwell. It was weird being in the theater at this hour. They were surprised to see a crack of light coming from under Sebastian's dressing room door. Tiptoeing closer they heard his drunken voice singing a song in Spanish.

"Sounds like someone is drinking alone," Toby whispered, his eyes flickering with amusement.

"What's he still doing here? Doesn't he have a hotel room?"

Toby shrugged. Then he ducked into the nearby maintenance closet and came out grinning, holding a gleaming key up to the light.

Wilfredo lifted an eyebrow. "Let's just hope there isn't a roof alarm."

"You worry too much, pal."

They headed back over to the stairwell, not daring to take the elevator in case someone saw what floor they got off on. It was seven more flights of stairs before they arrived at the door of the roof. The key turned smoothly and moments later they stepped out onto the theater's shadowy roof. Gray clouds churned overhead. A silhouetted water tower gave the rooftop an atmosphere of menace and gloom, as did the metal funnel chimneys on the neighboring building.

They walked around the roof, scoping out the space. Air conditioning equipment took up a big chunk of real estate. A short wall went around the perimeter of the building, and stepping over to it they were met with a view of Times Square's lights flickering to the east. Sticking their necks over the side they saw a tiny yellow cab the size of a matchbox car make a left at a light. Ant-like pedestrians trudged down Forty-Eighth Street.

Toby's face lit up. "This is going to be epic!"

Wilfredo quickly stripped to his underwear and stepped into the suit, pulling the mask over his face. In the meantime Toby walked around the roof framing his view through L-shaped fingers.

"Hey, Spielberg, hurry it up will you? You promised to make this quick."

"Okay, so you need to hop on your board over here," Toby gestured to a corner of the roof that was lost in dark shadows, "Then skate across the roof in an arc, hop off at this spot right here, and jump up on the ledge. Then put your hands on your hips and say the line just as we sketched it out. Do your best to sound badass!"

"Err. I must be hearing things because I could swear you said 'jump up on the ledge'?"

"C'mon, Wilfredo, if you can balance on a skateboard then surely you can balance on a two-foot-wide ledge!"

"I think you're forgetting that I'd rather not fall a hundred feet to my death in a drunken rooftop stunt."

Don't knock it till you've tried it, Freddy. I remember the last time I drunkenly fell off a roof. What a rush! The trick is to land on something soft, like a mattress, or a pile of hay!

Wilfredo sighed. He'd come to recognize the mindless prattle that set in when the Captain was tipsy. Any booze Wilfredo drank seemed to go straight to the dummy's head. It was hard enough thinking straight without having the Captain's alcohol-addled musings added to the mix.

Toby paced back and forth on the roof, peering over the

edge. "Okay, okay, if it makes you feel better, you can skate to this spot instead. Then you're standing over the fire escape."

Wilfredo looked down. "That's still a ten-foot drop, but I guess I can live with that."

Wilfredo zoomed across the roof in his costume, jumped off the board, and climbed carefully onto the ledge. He faced the video recorder, pointed a finger directly at the lens, and said in his best gravelly voice: "This is a message for the Cat Burglar. You'd better mend your ways! We don't need thieves like you in our city!"

"And . . . cut! Wow, that was perfect. You know, buddy, you really are a decent actor. I don't know what you've been doing painting scenery all these years. This video is gonna blow up, no question!"

Wilfredo was already stripping off the costume. He had to admit the view was pretty cool up here, but it had been an exhausting day, and all he wanted to do now was to go home, take a hot shower, and climb into bed.

The Captain objected to the idea of hitting the hay: *The night is young, you poltroonish buffoons! In my day you couldn't call it a proper bender unless you woke up on a strange boat, on your way to some faraway land, pressed into service while you were sleeping by some enterprising first mate in need of deckhands!*

42. RUBY:
A MORNING AT THE SPA

Ruby rolled out of her king-sized hotel bed and poked her feet into fuzzy pink slippers. She'd had a fitful night's rest but was still feeling a little queasy. Sitting down at a small table she took a sip of room-temperature still water. Then she braved a couple spoonfuls of the steel-cut oatmeal with berries that had just been delivered to her room. What a disaster yesterday had been. It was the worst case of food poisoning she'd suffered in her whole life, and she'd once spent a whole weekend in a Tijuana motel bathroom.

Every time she had called Chad it had gone straight to voice mail. So she'd texted him instead to tell him about her troubles, and he had replied with a puking emoji and a "feel better" with an exclamation point. And that was the last she'd heard of him. Here she was all alone at one of her life's low points, and her supposed boyfriend couldn't care less. After their quarrel earlier this week she had a sinking feeling their relationship was on the rocks. It went back to the tabloid photos Annie had shown her of Chad embracing the voluptuous Gabriella on a Mexican beach. The article mentioned a close confidant who had confirmed that the two costars were romantically linked. She had left Chad a furious voice mail demanding an explanation, and he had texted back that it was just the tabloids making stuff up as usual. But she had *eyes* didn't she? That intimate clinch with Gabriella spoke for itself. But Chad had the audacity to try to pass it off as an innocent hug. And he'd had the nerve to bring up her recent paparazzi photos at the Parrot Bar, holding hands with Wilfredo. As if touching someone's hand and giving a bikini-clad Gabriella a full-body embrace were remotely equivalent! Either way it was clear that her attempt to make Chad jealous by orchestrating the Parrot Bar pics had backfired.

Ruby still couldn't believe that because of the fiasco with the sushi Declan had let that opportunistic hussy play her part in the debut. If this had been a TV show they would've just wrapped early and started over the next day. But no, everybody in the theater insisted that the show must go on. Would it really be so terrible to cancel a performance every now and then due to unforeseen circumstances?

Gazing over at her bed Ruby felt the urge to crawl back under the crisp linen sheets. But she needed to find her way back to the land of the living, and for that she would rely on the hotel's famed Emerald Spa. Ruby considered herself something of a spa aficionado, and this spa was right up there with the best. So she pulled on her sweats, hid her puffy eyes behind sunglasses, and rode the elevator down to the S1 level, where she quickly signed herself up for the three-hour-long "ultimate extravagance" package.

Her body was blasted from all sides in the spa's full-body shower. This was followed by a thirty-minute body scrub, then a one-hour massage by Bekka, a certified massage genius. The grand finale was a half hour cucumber and ginger ultra facial, guaranteed to make wrinkles wish they'd never been born. All of this was delivered in a bamboo-walled room that was misted with a mix of lavender and eucalyptus oil and surrounded by the calming sounds of ocean waves.

When the session drew to a close, Bekka escorted her to the private cabana that doubled as her changing room. It was situated next to the glistening aquamarine waters of the hotel's indoor pool. Ruby laid back on a wooden lounge chair, wearing a knee-length terry cloth robe. Under the plush robe her pampered body was still au naturel. Bekka told her she could lie here and enjoy her post-massage bliss for as long as she liked. Then this spa angel brought her a white ceramic cup filled with chamomile tea that tasted so pure and sweet that Ruby finally managed to eke out a smile, her troubles soothed, if not forgotten. After sitting there for who knows how long, thoughts of lunch drifted into her brain and she was pleased to note that they didn't make her the least bit nauseous.

There was a sharp knock at her cabana door. She opened her eyes and saw Bekka standing in the doorway, a deeply apologetic look in her eyes. "Sorry, Miss Ruby, there are some people here who need to speak with you."

Ruby frowned, wondering if she had somehow managed to miss an important meeting. But she didn't recognize the two individuals who came into her cabana, a tubby, balding man and a younger brunette woman, both of them dressed in depressingly austere outfits. They certainly weren't show biz people.

The man introduced himself as Detective Molina and indicated that his companion was Detective Garcia. He flashed a badge. "My apologies for disturbing you here, Miss Greenwood. I did not realize you would be . . . um . . . we will step outside and give you a few minutes to get dressed."

"Never mind that," Ruby snapped. "Why are you here?"

The female detective stepped forward: "We have some questions about the gallery robbery that we were hoping you could help us with."

"How on earth would I be of any help with that?"

"Well, you were there at the time of the robbery, correct?" asked the bald man.

"Yes. Me and about two hundred other people."

"We are aware it was crowded. Excuse me, but I really would prefer to continue this conversation once you are appropriately attired."

Ruby could tell that by sitting here in her robe she was making him ill at ease. Obviously he was the prudish type, but perhaps that was just as well. "I assure you I am quite comfortable. Now please explain to me how you think I might contribute to your investigation? Didn't Ayesha Randolph get her scarf back? I could swear I read that somewhere."

The female detective smiled agreeably. "Yes, I am happy to report that the scarf is back in her hands, but this robbery is part of a broader investigation." She handed Ruby a printed photograph. "Do you recognize the man in this photo?"

"It's the Foxman guy people are buzzing about. The hero!"

"Do you happen to know his real identity?"

"I don't have a clue. How would I know? I've never seen him in my life."

"And what about this person?" The detective gave her another photo.

"That's the Cat Burglar woman. The one who supposedly stole the scarf."

"Do you have any idea who she might be?" The two detectives peered at her intently.

"No idea. I'm puzzled as to why you think I might know anything about this."

The bald man cleared his throat. "We noticed you happened to faint right before the robbery took place."

"That's right."

"Did you really pass out, or were you just pretending?"

"I was acting. I'm an actress. I was trying to drum up some free publicity for my friend, the gallery owner."

The female detective's eyes squinted at her. "So you admit you faked your swoon?"

"I have only ever fake-swooned. Is pretending to faint in public a crime? What are we talking about here?"

The two detectives exchanged a glance. The older detective gave the faintest shake of his head. "We are just interviewing witnesses. There have been a series of robberies and various incidents with this thief and vigilante, so we are just doing our best to leave no stone unturned."

Ruby took a moment to gather her thoughts. Through the open doorway she noticed an older lady swimming breaststroke in the pool, the woman's head suspended elegantly above the water. Ruby refocused her gaze on the two detectives. "I can't believe New York City police have nothing better to do than *harass* a television actress at her hotel spa. I have a good mind to call the mayor's office." She got to her feet and pretended not to notice when her loosely tied robe fell open, exposing her left breast to the detectives' view. The older cop's eyes darted to her chest momentarily and his eyes took on a look of panic. Ruby hurriedly "caught her mistake," and knotted her robe up securely.

"We're awfully sorry to bother you, Miss Greenwood," said the female detective with an amused smile. "Please take my card and be sure to call us if you think of anything that might be useful to our investigation."

Ruby took the card that was being held out to her, ripped it in two, and dropped the pieces onto the floor. The older detective dabbed at his forehead with a handkerchief, then he turned and walked out of the cabana without a word. The younger cop gave her a pointed look before following her partner out the door.

Ruby sat back down on the slatted lounge chair. Everyone always said New York was a crazy town where anything could happen, and apparently it was true. But she was stumped as to why these police detectives had decided to question her. What could it possibly mean?

She decided to try Chad again, but her call went straight to voice mail, as she knew it would. She didn't leave a message this time. What good was having a boyfriend if you couldn't call him in an emergency? Or if he spent his time hanging around with voluptuous brunettes in bikinis?

Next, she called her agent. Artie was privy to all the dirty details of her life, functioning as part lawyer, part publicist, and part confessor when necessary. And he always picked up when she rang him.

Artie sounded delighted to hear from her, which was also his job. She could picture him sitting at his desk on Ventura Boulevard, looking out through the wall of glass behind him. She'd sat in his office a thousand times. She gave him the rundown on the social call the two detectives had just paid her. "They seem to think my fainting at the gallery was fishy."

"They may have suspected you of causing a diversion, giving the thief a chance to strike."

"Or maybe they decided to hassle me because I look a bit like this Cat Burglar girl?"

"I've seen that Cat Burglar video online and they're not wrong. You look a lot like her."

"Yes. But I had absolutely nothing to do with it!"

"You know you can trust me with the truth, Ruby. If you have gotten yourself in a mess, I need to know."

"And I would tell you in a heartbeat, Artie. I haven't forgotten how you came through for me with that disorderly conduct mess at that nightclub. But in this case I'm blameless. I swear!"

"Then you have absolutely nothing to worry about. Sounds like they are just chasing their tails. But you know, Ruby, it's funny you should call me up about this Cat Burglar business because I just got off the phone with Chariot Pictures this morning, and they've cooked up a movie script for this whole Foxman versus Cat Burglar story. It's a news item, so nobody owns it, and they are moving fast on it because they don't want anyone to beat them to the punch. I've already lined up a writer for them. And get this, they asked me if I knew any actors who might work for the roles, and my first thought was—oh, this would be perfect for Ruby! And then I remembered that you've dragged yourself off to New York to do *theater*."

"I did do that, didn't I? I'm beginning to think it wasn't my smartest move ever."

"I warned you that the theater is more grueling than glamorous. And the audience is tiny compared to television. Not to mention, no royalties."

"I should've listened to you, Artie."

"I take it the play isn't going gangbusters?"

"We've hit a couple snags. As you know, I had to sit out the big debut yesterday with food poisoning, and then this nobody of an understudy goes and hits it out of the park."

"Tough break. Do you want me to try and get you out of your contract? Just say the word."

"Do you think they would go for it?"

"In my experience, when an actress is unhappy, then the play's producers are just as unhappy. I bet I can persuade them that minting a new star is going to help the play more than a big name who is a poor fit."

"Oh my god, if you could get me out of this stupid play and set me up for that Cat Burglar role, I would die!"

"You're sure about this?"

"Yes. Yes. A million times yes!"

"Okay. I will put things in motion immediately and make some inquiries. Be prepared to audition for the Cat Burglar part at a moment's notice. It's gonna go fast."

Ruby had a huge grin on her face when she hung up. This was big. Filled with a sudden sense of urgency she dropped her sunglasses into place, and not bothering to change out of her robe she strode briskly toward the elevators, her flip flops slapping against the tiled floor.

43. CASSANDRA:
A MESSAGE IN AN ALLEY

It was Christmas Eve day, and Cassandra was all alone in the city. The holidays were usually her favorite time of the year in New York, but with her best friends overseas, her family in California, and her engagement called off, she was spending the holidays at home with her cat.

In the afternoon, in an attempt to get into the spirit of the season, she went to look at the department store window displays and the Rockefeller Center Christmas tree. She stood for a while afterward watching the ice skaters circling in the ice rink below to the tune of upbeat holiday classics, but it did little to improve her mood. Last December she and Gregory had been two of the smiling people gliding around on the ice. She missed him, and surprisingly, she didn't feel any bitterness toward him. The only reason she was ignoring his calls and texts was because she didn't want to encourage him into believing they would patch things up.

Tired and cold, Cassandra walked all the way home. The sun vanished slowly behind Midtown skyscrapers and the city lights winked on around her. When she got back to her apartment she took a shower, ordered Chinese takeout, and settled in for the night. Then she sat on the couch and ate her dinner while watching *Die Hard*, with Jupiter curled up contentedly beside her.

"It's just me and you, Jupe. I picked up some of that fresh

salmon you like so much. You can have a special lunchtime treat tomorrow." At the mention of his favorite fish, the gray cat picked up his head. The living room radiator began to hiss and let out a banging sound as the steam heat surged through the building. Cassandra nudged the volume up on the TV.

She had not told anyone about her breakup yet. If she shared the news with her friends, it would only make them feel guilty for being away when she needed them most. If she told her *dad* he would drop everything to fly out, and she had no intention of ruining his holiday plans. And if she'd told her newest friend, Wilfredo, he would have invited her up to his mom's place for a holiday meal, and she didn't want a pity invite. Nor did she feel up to pretending to be cheerful for an extended period of time. For all she knew Wilfredo could have made plans with Ruby. Cassandra scrunched up her face. She still couldn't get the memory of that stage kiss out of her head—the Ruby special, she had dubbed it. It really bugged her that Wilfredo was stuck on Ruby, and she didn't see the two of them working out. Not that it was any of her business. And considering her own personal life was such a train wreck, she wasn't about to go around handing out relationship advice.

When the movie was over Cassandra surrendered to the guilty pleasures of eating mint chip ice cream right out of the container while mindlessly surfing the internet on her laptop. It wasn't long before she stumbled across Foxman's latest video. She watched it over and over with increasing aggravation. She couldn't believe he called her out in the clip. The nerve of that guy! He had another thing coming if he thought she was going to take this challenge from him lying down. Cassandra's mouth set in a hard line.

Thirty minutes later she was back out on the bitterly cold street. Alleyways were rare in Manhattan, but Cassandra knew of one graffiti-tagged alley down on Rivington that she was convinced would make the perfect backdrop for the Cat Burglar video she had planned. She needed a special location if she hoped to compete with Foxman's rooftop clip.

It was 11:30 already, and powerful gusts of wind were rattling street signs and setting the traffic lights swaying. A thick flurry of snow began falling from the sky, light and feathery flakes that melted the second they hit the ground. Cassandra made her way south on Chrystie, accumulating a thin layer of white powder on her black coat. She passed many lively bars and it seemed as if the whole world was out at a party except for her. But she was a woman on a mission. The hood of her coat shielded her painted whiskers, cat ears, and cat eyes from view, while the body of the coat hid her tail.

She made a right when she got to Rivington and a short ways down the block she found the entrance to the narrow alley she remembered. For a city that had taken a hard pass on alleys, this Rivington alley was weirdly archetypal. Its walls were covered in street art and hundreds of colorful stickers. Garbage cans sat outside mysterious locked doors that led to who knows where. And the farther she wandered down the dark alleyway, the more a prickling sense of danger crept up her spine.

In short—it was just what she was looking for, a gritty urban scene that would lend her some street cred for the response she had planned. Maybe she was being petty by stooping down to his level, but it beat sitting at home feeling sorry for herself while shoveling ice cream into her piehole.

Cassandra drifted deeper down the grimy passage, feeling

more and more uneasy with every step. This might not be her brightest move ever, but there was no turning back now. She was wearing her striped black-and-white sweater under her coat, and her black mask was in her pocket. Digging it out she snapped it into place over her eyes. Glancing left and right to make sure she was alone, she yanked off her coat and tossed it on top of an empty crate, hoping that would be enough to keep it out of the path of the rodents she had seen scampering about. She shook out her hair, pulling the red tresses of her wig forward over her shoulders. Propping her phone up on a brick-sealed window ledge, she hit the VIDEO RECORD button, and took two steps back.

"Every corner of this city is being carved up by plutocrats who think they're gods among men. Billionaires who try to buy our admiration by donating a rounding error of their treasure hoards to charitable causes. I'm doing my part to stand up to the greedy fat cats in this town. You're welcome to try and stop me, Foxman, but I'll remind you that I've beaten you twice already, and I'm happy to do it again if you're a sucker for punishment!" With a snarl and a big raking sweep of her gloved hand she spun out of the frame.

Cassandra quickly cropped the ends off the video in edit mode, and played back final results, listening carefully to make sure that her voice, which she had dropped into a lower register, wouldn't give her away. The graffitied bricks behind her and the streaks of light and shadow lent the video the edgy sensibility she'd been after, juxtaposed with the falling snow. Cassandra signed into social media using the throwaway email account and fake profile she'd set up. With a few more taps on her phone screen, she posted the clip.

44. GREGORY:
A SECRET REVEALED

In Gregory's mind there was no call for Cassandra to start chucking engagement rings into fountains. It was true that he'd asked her for it back, but he was just trying to scare her straight. Gregory had watched the diamond ring twirl through the air with his heart in his mouth. It had dropped into the water with a tiny *plop* that would haunt his dreams forever.

Since that moment his life had been thrown into disarray. He was sleeping poorly, he had lost his appetite, he was having a hard time concentrating on everyday tasks, and his personal grooming habits had taken a turn for the worse. Sporadic showers meant that his hair was often clumped and poking out in all directions. And with his razor lying untouched in the medicine cabinet his face had gone from clean shaven, to a patchy castaway-style beard.

His friends were avoiding him too. Gregory suspected they were put off by his literal and metaphorical funk. To make matters worse, his boss had insisted he take a leave of absence until he sorted out his personal issues. Which might take forever, since Cassandra was completely ignoring his texts and calls.

The spy cam Gregory had installed in Cassandra's living room was his last tenuous connection to the woman he loved. In the evenings when she walked through her front door, he was glued to his laptop screen as he scrutinized her moods and eavesdropped on her phone calls, on the lookout for those moments when she was feeling most vulnerable, to once again dial her number.

Unfortunately, that snugly cat of hers and her addiction to ice cream appeared to be helping her through the low points. It was comforting to see that she was having a hard time, except that she seemed committed to not looking back. Why couldn't she understand that calling off the engagement had been a horrible mistake? Tugging open a small drawer in his desk, Gregory stared down at the diamond ring, glinting against the dark wood. He'd nearly lost a few toes to frostbite, but he had recovered it in the end, and he was determined to return it to its rightful place on Cassandra's hand.

Each evening Gregory's routine was the same, as he allowed himself to become consumed by his voyeuristic fixation with his ex-fiancée. He watched her eating General Tso's tofu on her couch. He watched her sprawled on the rug brushing Jupiter to his heart's content. And he watched her, with a diminishing sense of guilt, as she traipsed about her apartment in various states of undress. He was even watching her on Christmas Eve, when Cassandra unexpectedly peeled off her black jeans and her slinky red top, tossing them on the back of a chair. His eyebrows shot up, but she disappeared into her bedroom for what felt like forever.

When she finally reappeared, Gregory was astonished to see she had undergone a transformation. She was now wearing a striped black-and-white sweater and had concealed her chestnut brown hair under a dark red wig. Perplexingly, her face was painted with a cat nose and whiskers. She had cat ears on her head, and a long, curved tail protruded from her backside. She stopped to appraise herself in the hallway mirror and Gregory stared googly eyed at Cassandra's peculiar getup. The wheels turned slowly in his mind as he attempted to reconcile everything he knew about his ex-fiancée with what he was seeing on the screen. It wasn't possible. Except the proof was right there in front of him in high def. Pulling on her ankle boots she looked ready to step out and perpetrate some Cat Burglar–style mayhem.

It just goes to show, thought Gregory, you never really know who anyone is deep down. But the more he'd thought about it, the more it all made sense. He remembered asking her to stop and buy the wine on Halloween. She must have been dressed as a Cat Burglar and gotten herself into some kind of trouble at the liquor store. And the whole thing had spiraled from there. It was just like her to donate the loot to charities, all of which, come to think of it, happened to be things she cared about.

Finding out she was the Cat Burglar made it easier to understand why she had ended their engagement. He was an upstanding lawyer, and she was basically a criminal. The gulf between them was as vast as the Grand Canyon. Taking a moment to search his feelings Gregory was surprised to discover that this revelation didn't change how he felt about her. His only thought was whether this intel could somehow help him win her back.

Still watching his screen he saw her put on her black coat, pulling the hood up over her head to conceal herself from prying eyes. As she grabbed her keys his video feed went suddenly black. A "charge camera battery" error message popped up on his screen. Gregory sat there dumbstruck. The dead camera effectively erased Cassandra from his life. He felt a sense of panic rising up within him. He needed to break into her place and fix this. Why had he never asked her for a key? She always double-locked her door, and when you factored in the security cameras in the lobby and the lack of fire escapes, her apartment might as well be Fort Knox.

Gregory turned the problem over in his mind until finally he had a brainstorm—the next best thing to monitoring Cassandra would be to have a camera in Wilfredo's apartment. She talked to him on the phone regularly, and he was sure she went over to his place now and then. A spy cam at Wilfredo's would let him see if that louse was putting the moves on her, and maybe even turn up some useful dirt on his rival. If he had learned one thing tonight it was that you never knew what you could glean from a little surveillance. Know thine enemy, wasn't that what Sun Tzu advised? Gregory allowed himself a thin smile.

45. WILFREDO:
LIFE IS A SERIES OF BRIDGES

It was nearly nine o'clock, and they were headed over to Long Island City, where Declan had organized an impromptu New Year's Eve bash for the cast and crew. Toby turned the key in the ignition and checked his mirrors as a grumpy Wilfredo climbed into the passenger side of the pink cargo van and slammed the door. As they pulled into traffic the darkened winter city swept by in a blur of glowing shop signs. Toby glanced over at him. "Hey, did you text Cassandra so she can be ready when we swing by?"

"Yeah. She says she'll be outside."

"Good. We'll pick her up and head straight to the party. With a little luck we won't hit too much bridge traffic!" Toby hit the breaks as the van swerved around a giant pothole. "I see you've busted out some fancy new threads for tonight?

Wilfredo was wearing a rugged tan blazer over a gray button-down shirt with a square black tie and suede loafers. "Yeah, Ruby called me last night, seconds after the invite landed in my inbox, and told me I needed to look sharp in case there's any press there."

"Good advice, you look spiffy. And you can't be showing up to a party in cargo pants and a flannel shirt!" Wilfredo grunted in reply. He considered his everyday look to be beyond reproach, even for a party, whereas he felt like a total poser in these clothes.

The Captain smelled his chance for a cheap shot: *You're not fooling anyone with that jacket and tie look, Freddy. You're a phony, a fraud, a sham, an impostor. You remind me of this jellyfish I used to keep as a pet, cuz just like him people are gonna see right through you!*

Wilfredo willed the Captain to be silent. He really hoped the stupid croc wasn't right about this. The problem was, he didn't feel like a legit actor. And he had no idea what would happen when this brief Broadway stint came to a screeching halt. Would he audition for other parts? Or would he slip back into his old life at the workshop?

Toby made a left onto East Fifth Street, and when they pulled up in front of Cassandra's building they saw her standing by the curb. Wilfredo climbed out of the van and gave her a hug. She looked him up and down appraisingly. "You look great. Love the jacket!"

"And you look absolutely spectacular," he replied, eyeing her chic dress as she slipped off her coat and did a twirl for him. Emerald green, with a wide collar and buttons down the front, it brought out the color in her eyes. He chucked their coats over the back of the seat as he climbed into the van after her. The passenger side had a small double seat that could be shared by two people in a pinch, but was more suitable for one person. He settled awkwardly beside her, hyperaware of her figure pressed up against him. He felt himself begin to sweat. She's engaged, he reminded himself, for the millionth time. "Sorry, it's going to be a tight squeeze."

"I don't mind. I'm glad you guys could give me a ride."

Toby put the van back in drive and hit the gas. "Hey, Cass, did you get a load of Wilfredo's photo in *Chatter Magazine*?"

Cassandra grinned. "You mean the snapshot of Ruby Greenwood's new mystery man grabbing lunch at a New York City hotspot? How could I miss it!"

Toby's belly laughs filled the van. "Me and the guys at the workshop were in stitches!"

Wilfredo was not amused.

"All joking aside," said Cassandra, "a photo like that is great publicity. I wouldn't be surprised if you got a few calls from some talent agents."

"I doubt it," grumbled Wilfredo, turning to look out the window.

Cassandra's face took on a thoughtful look. "Speaking of publicity, I wonder if there are any reviews out yet? I have a feeling Declan wouldn't have spent the money on a party if he didn't have some good news to share."

"That's what Ruby said too," Wilfredo replied.

Toby slammed on the brakes to avoid rear-ending a taxicab, and Wilfredo braced himself on the dash with one arm, throwing the other out in front of Cassandra. Luckily the van managed to stop in time, and they were soon rolling along again. "Never a moment's rest for my guardian angel," joked Cassandra, giving Wilfredo's arm a hug. "But you do realize we're wearing seat belts, right?" Wilfredo felt his face grow warm.

"He has a bit of a hero complex!" chuckled Toby. Wilfredo shot him a warning look.

Just then the Captain's voice blared loudly in his head: *Look alive, Freddy! All hands on deck! Man the cannons! This is not a drill!*

What the heck was the Captain babbling about now? He needed to get this dummy's voice out of his head.

Her hand, Freddy. Look at her hand! It's as naked as a jaybird! Wilfredo looked down at Cassandra's left hand. Sure enough she wasn't wearing any rings. Most notably the usual polished boulder was absent from her ring finger.

"Er, Cassandra?" he asked nonchalantly. "Is your engagement ring at the jewelers getting resized?"

She held out her bare hand and studied it. "Nope. It isn't. You know, Wilfredo, I didn't have you pegged as the observant type."

"So where is it?" demanded Toby, as he turned left onto the on-ramp for the Queensboro Bridge, tires screeching.

"As a matter of fact—I returned it to Gregory the other night. Well, to be specific, I threw it into a fountain. The last I saw he was wading up to his knees trying to fish it out."

There was a brief silence in the van, as both men turned over her words in their heads, examining them carefully from all angles. Finally Wilfredo decided to repeat back what she had said, just to make sure he had heard clearly: "You threw your engagement ring into a fountain?"

"Yes."

There was only one possible interpretation for this. And while Wilfredo didn't dare speak it out loud, his heart leaped. Toby had no such qualms. "Oh man!" he yelled. "You called it off with Gregory! I can't believe it! You called it off with Gregory!"

"Yes, we called it quits," she said softly.

Wilfredo's inward joy took two steps back, as he realized

the poor girl sitting beside him sounded utterly heartbroken. His suspicions were quickly confirmed by a loud sniff.

His arm crept around her and he pulled her in for a side hug. "Cassandra, why didn't you tell us right away? What happened?"

"Now you've done it. I'm going to ruin my makeup." She sniffed again, and he saw a tear roll down her cheek. "It just wasn't working out. That's all." Wilfredo drew her in until her head was pressed into his shoulder.

"You poor thing. It wasn't Gregory who broke things off, was it?" He had a sickening notion that their onstage kiss the other night could explain this latest development.

"No. It was both of us. But I'd rather not rehash it. If that's all right with you."

"Of course. I understand." He hugged her tightly, and his heart wrenched when he realized she was starting to sob. They were on the bridge now and metal trusses were flickering past as the van sped along in the right-hand lane. Glittering views of the Manhattan skyline opened up to their right. Wilfredo's jaw set firmly. Her engagement had been wrecked, and it was probably his fault.

This is your big chance to make your move, you nimrod! hissed the Captain. *She'll be easy pickings if you catch her on the rebound!*

Wilfredo scowled. No way was he going to take any advice from that scheming croc.

They parked the van on a side street around the corner from the venue. Cassandra flipped down the visor, examined her reflection in the mirror, and cringed. She blotted at her smeared eye makeup with a tissue, before following them out of the van into the crisp December air. Wilfredo helped her put on her coat.

"I'm sorry, guys," she said. "I don't know what came over me."

"There's no need to apologize," said Wilfredo.

Toby slammed the van door and locked it. "You're better off without him!"

Cassandra made a sad attempt at a smile. "We're better off without each other I think."

The three of them strode down the quiet sidewalk, their breath coming out in wispy clouds of vapor. The blocks in this part of Queens consisted of short brick buildings, none of them tall enough to hide an expansive horizon of city lights that they were unaccustomed to seeing in Manhattan. Four-way stop signs punctuated the intersections and a span of the bridge they'd just driven over was silhouetted up ahead.

Cassandra wrapped her arms around herself. "I haven't exactly put us in a party mood."

"You know we don't have to go if you don't want to," Wilfredo assured her.

"Oh we're going," said Toby firmly. "All three of us are going. I didn't drive you guys all the way here to turn around on the doorstep. We're gonna go to this party and we're gonna have a fantastic time."

Listen to your pal, Freddy, chimed in the Captain. *He has his head screwed on straight! And give the beer a miss this time, you witless landlubber! Ask the barkeep for some proper rum and we'll be three sheets to the wind before you can say "Land Ho!"*

46. CASSANDRA:
A SLAP IN THE FACE

She was in no mood for a party. All she had wanted to do this weekend was snuggle up with Jupiter on her couch, watch TV, and dig a large spoon into a pint of ice cream. But here she was, standing like a wallflower on the sidelines of a large room, crowded with theater people. The cavernous brick-walled space was adorned with leafy plants, wall vines, and a few small trees. Drinks and finger food were being walked around by attractive wait staff dressed in striped aprons and bowler hats.

Standing next to her was Wilfredo, and as if by magic a beer had already appeared in his hand. Bowie's "Ashes to Ashes" was playing on overhead speakers and Wilfredo was bopping his head to the music. He smiled at her, cupped a hand to his mouth, and leaned in: "I hear there's a rooftop garden in this place with skyline views."

"Someplace to go hide when we get tired of schmoozing?" she shouted back.

"You read my mind!"

At that moment the music cut out and a beaming Declan climbed onto a chair, pulling papers from his jacket pocket. Cassandra's heart began to race as she realized the white-haired director was about to read early reviews of their performance out loud in front of the whole room. She glanced anxiously at Wilfredo, but he seemed more concerned with snagging a spring roll from a nearby tray. She elbowed him in the ribs.

The first review, from the paper of record, was enthusiastic: "This show reminded me of why I fell in love with the theater. . . Bravura performances by two unheralded actors." Cassandra was stunned. The second review was even more glowing: "Cassandra Bell, understudy for the sidelined Ruby Greenwood, played the role of Violet with the wild abandon of a modern-day Ophelia." And Wilfredo got called out as well for a "gift for pantomime that was perfectly suited for the secretive knight."

Huge applause broke out in the room when Declan stepped down from his chair, with a few hoots and whistles thrown in from the likes of Toby. Cassandra's breath caught in her throat—she couldn't believe this was really happening. Wilfredo looked equally dumbfounded. "Hey, you did it! You pulled it off!" he yelled, giving her arm a squeeze.

"*We* pulled it off!" She corrected him.

And then people started coming over to congratulate them. Prisha appeared, grabbed her hands, and spun her around in a circle. Close behind her was a gracious Evelyn, who seemed genuinely happy for her, even though only rotten luck had kept her from being the understudy that night. They were followed by a swarm of people gathering around to toast their success, some of whom had never spoken more than two words to her before. Wilfredo, surrounded by jubilant stagehands, was being pulled farther and farther away from her.

Two rave write-ups for her Broadway debut? Not in her wildest dreams could she have imagined this. She couldn't wait to call her dad and share the news. Her second thought was of Gregory. She wanted to shove these reviews in his face.

Ten minutes later, feeling dazed, she escaped to the women's restroom. It was an open-ceilinged space with three raised basin sinks on a brass countertop that glowed in the soft light of the wall sconces. She stared into the oval mirror on the wall, and a wide-eyed girl in a belted green dress stared back. She gave her hair a toss and struck a confident pose with her hands on her hips. *Cassandra Bell, acclaimed Broadway actress.* Nope. It just didn't seem real.

The restroom door swung open and in strode Ruby, dressed in a black-and-gold cocktail dress. "Cassandra! The woman of the hour, why on earth are you hiding out in here?"

"Just catching my breath. It's all a bit overwhelming."

Ruby walked over to stand next to her, setting a champagne flute down on the vanity. They made eye contact in the mirror. "Nonsense. You should be out there enjoying your fifteen minutes of fame while it lasts."

Standing side by side, Cassandra had to admit that they really did look a lot alike. Everybody said so. They were about the same height, with a similar build. Ruby's hair was more reddish, but other than that they could easily be mistaken for sisters. Ruby would be the prettier one of course, with those jutting cheekbones and that dainty little nose of hers.

Her twin dug a lipstick out of her purse and leaned into the mirror. "You know, Cassandra, you played Violet exactly how I wanted to play her. I only wish Declan had given *me* free rein. Hopefully he will listen to my ideas now." Cassandra stiffened. Was it her imagination or did Ruby sound resentful?

Ruby prattled on without waiting for a response. "It's that time of the year, one party after another. The Tribeca awards ceremony is this weekend, and I have a fabulous gown picked out. I'm being loaned a sapphire necklace by Winston Brown. Hey! They are always looking for presentable seat warmers. If you are interested, let me know. It's an easy gig and I could put in a good word."

Cassandra hated when girls did this pretend-to-be-nice thing when their tone said they wanted to scratch your eyes out. It was obvious that the positive reviews had rattled Ruby, even though it was hard to believe that a famous television actress could feel threatened by her. *It's not my fault you ate bad sushi,* Cassandra wanted to scream. But she needed to remain professional and not let herself get baited. Thankfully Ruby was done touching up her makeup and she disappeared into a stall, the lock clicking into place, so Cassandra made a break for it.

Back at the party there was no sign of Wilfredo anywhere. She checked the time on her phone and saw that midnight was fast approaching. Wilfredo better not have abandoned her at this party by herself. She decided to go check the rooftop terrace, in case he had made good on his promise to hide out up there. But when she got to the roof she found it deserted except for a lonely photographer, who was lurking about with a heavy camera dangling from his shoulder. He did a double take when he saw her, raising the camera, and then lowering it, probably confusing Cassandra with her doppelgänger. She veered away, but kept one eye on him and saw him duck down behind a hedge near the rooftop entrance. *That was odd. Maybe he's sneaking a cigarette?*

The roof was illuminated prettily with strings of patio lights hung from wooden beams that crisscrossed the space. Cassandra found a wooden bench tucked away behind a row of planters. A nice quiet spot where she could gather her thoughts. But after a few minutes she began to get chilly, so she got up to head back downstairs. Just then, she heard footsteps crunching in the gravel, and a familiar voice said: "Isn't the skyline just gorgeous from up here? Although, the wind chill is no joke . . . Oh! Thanks, Wilfredo, you're such a gentleman."

Cassandra peeked out and saw Ruby and Wilfredo walking over to the rooftop edge together. Ruby was wearing his jacket over her shoulders. As they wandered farther away their voices grew indistinct. Cassandra couldn't help herself, and she followed them quietly. Now that she knew how spiteful Ruby could be, she didn't like the idea of a nice guy like Wilfredo getting sucked into her orbit.

Cassandra crept along a parallel garden row heading in their same direction, carefully placing her feet on paving stones to avoid the noisy gravel. Much to her consternation the photographer she had spotted earlier seemed to be stalking Ruby and Wilfredo as well, but from the opposite side. He must be a paparazzi! He glared at her from a distance, and she glared right back. Neither one of them made a move to back off, so they both kept closing in on their target from opposing ends.

Wilfredo and Ruby came to a stop by a leafy trellis, their elbows propped up on the rooftop's ledge. Cassandra was closer now, and she could make out their silhouettes by peering through the leaves of a boxwood hedge. She was alarmed to see Ruby take hold of Wilfredo's hand, pulling him around to face her. Then the starlet stepped closer to him, her face turned up toward his. In a faltering voice Ruby said: "It's almost midnight, Wilfredo. I'm happy it's just the two of us up here together." When he didn't reply she went on: "Have you ever wondered if you and I might ever be a thing? Because I've been thinking about it ever since that first time you kissed me in the dressing room a few weeks ago."

"Honestly, Ruby, it's never crossed my mind. I mean, you're a famous actress and I'm a nobody. It would never work." Cassandra couldn't see his face, but Wilfredo sounded distinctly uncomfortable.

"You don't know that. You need to dream big, Wilfredo. If people thought we were an item your career might take off overnight! That one restaurant pic of us got a ton of play."

"Yeah, that was crazy."

"Here's the thing. I wasn't born yesterday. I know what a stage kiss feels like, and that's no stage kiss you keep planting on me."

"I told you I don't know how to stage kiss. I've never done it before!"

"What I mean is—there is some real passion there. That you weren't just acting."

Wilfredo rubbed his chin with his gloved hand. "I'm pretty sure it's called method acting?"

"Oh, Wilfredo—you're so adorable. The whole point of method acting is that you're basing your performance on genuine feelings."

"That's what I mean." Wilfredo kicked the ground with

his loafers. "When I was kissing you, I put the feelings I have for someone else into my kiss."

Ruby took a step back and stared at him in disbelief. "Are you saying that every time you kissed me you were thinking of another girl?"

"Bingo."

Cassandra let out a soft gasp when Ruby slapped Wilfredo. The poor guy never saw it coming. But the photographer, who was a professional, and had a lot more experience with these kinds of moments, had spotted the windup from a mile away. Judging from his grin a slap was probably better than a kiss when it came to selling magazines. The photographer popped up from the hedge he was crouched behind and fired off a barrage of clicks and flashes at the critical moment, with the pretty city skyline framed in the background.

Cassandra gawked through the leaves at the scene she was witnessing. Her mind was reeling. If Wilfredo wasn't in love with Ruby, then who was he in love with? She had no idea who it could be. And then the penny dropped, and it was as if the whole world tilted on its axis, and everything that was down was suddenly up. She remembered the way he had kissed *her* the other night. She put a hand over her mouth as she took in a sharp breath. Her lower lip trembled.

On the other side of the hedge Wilfredo was standing there stunned, his arms hanging down by his sides. Ruby cursed the photographer, then she cursed Wilfredo, threw his jacket at him, and whirled around. Cassandra realized with alarm that the furious actress was stomping in her direction. Ashamed to be caught spying on them she dove into the bushes, worming her way into the middle of a thick hedge, heedless of the branches snagging on her dress. Seconds later, Ruby stormed right by her. The two men were slower to leave, but Cassandra eventually heard the crunch of their footsteps on the gravel as they retreated. Cautiously, she poked her face out of the hedge and looked around. She was alone on the roof. She extricated herself from the shrubbery with a little more care than she'd shown on the way in. Stepping over to the edge of the roof she looked out at the shimmering Manhattan skyline. She couldn't believe it. First the reviews and now this. To think she'd almost been a no-show at this party.

When she got downstairs, she was shivering. With midnight come and gone the party was breaking up. There was no sign of Wilfredo anywhere. Prisha and Evelyn grabbed hold of her. "Where have you been hiding?" they exclaimed. "We've all been looking for you! We thought you must've gone home already."

They dragged her outside to a waiting car. "Declan's treat. He's paying for car service for everyone," said Evelyn. Cassandra dug her phone out of her purse and saw that she had missed about a dozen texts from various people. Whoops. She replied to Wilfredo first and told him she was fine and was heading home in a car with the girls. He sent back a "Happy New Year!! Let's talk tomorrow!" and a champagne popping emoji.

47. DETECTIVE MOLINA:
A NEW SUSPECT

It was midday, and a gray Dodge Charger sat parked on the corner of Stanton and Clinton. Inside the car, Detective Molina drummed his fingers restlessly on the vinyl steering wheel. Sitting beside him in the passenger seat was Detective Garcia, a can of ginger ale in her hand. Wishing he had more willpower than he did, Detective Molina lifted the lid of the donut box on the armrest and helped himself to another Boston cream.

Garcia gave him a sidelong glance. "You might want to pace yourself." He found her smile hugely irritating.

At least they were finally making progress on this frustrating case. They had followed Foxman's path on a chain of security camera videos from the scene of the mail truck crash, until they hit on a grainy sidewalk recording that showed the orange figure climbing into a pink van a couple blocks away. With some technical enhancement the van's plates had been rendered legible. To no one's surprise, the vehicle turned out to belong to the Cornelius Theater.

"What do you think the chances are that this Toby guy turns out to be our Foxman?" Detective Garcia asked.

"Don't you think he seems kind of skinny?"

"That's true, the Foxman has a paunch."

Detective Molina used a napkin to wipe icing crumbs from his thick mustache. "It could just be padding. And let's not forget that some of the videos were posted from this Toby guy's account."

"Or maybe Toby is just the wingman and the vigilante is a friend of his."

"You know, we aren't far from where the video of Foxman stopping the ATM mugger was taken."

"Yeah, I think that was right down the block." Detective Garcia's eyes took on a faraway look. "Once we bust Foxman I bet he gives up the whole operation, and Ruby Greenwood turns out to be our thief."

"After talking to her I had my doubts. But now we know she's up for the part in a Cat Burglar movie, that publicity theory of yours is looking solid. She put on a pretty good act in that spa."

"She's a professional actress. You can't believe a single word out of her mouth. I'm telling ya, these Hollywood types have no shame. They will stop at nothing to drum up attention for their little projects."

"The most dangerous criminals are the ones who can pass as upstanding citizens. *Nulla fides fronti!* Appearances are deceiving."

Just then Detective Garcia sat up a little straighter and pointed to a man who was loitering near the entrance of the building. "What do you think that bozo is up to?"

They saw him try a buzzer without success. Then he stood nearby, clearly waiting to sneak in after someone else. Detective Molina squinted at the man, who had a somewhat disheveled appearance. "My guess is he's up to no good."

Detective Garcia put her soda down in the cup holder. "Should we go ask him some questions?"

"Let's wait and see if he finds his way in. What floor does our friend Toby live on?"

"The fifth floor in the front of the building, over to the right. Do you think this guy could be an associate?"

"In my experience criminals attract other criminals like magnets."

"Well if this jackass breaks in we have our excuse to go in and search the place."

Sure enough the sketchy man snuck in behind a woman walking her dog. The two detectives stepped out of the car and positioned themselves under a small tree where they could get a good view of the building. It wasn't long before the suspicious character popped up on the roof of all places. They watched him climb down to the fifth-floor fire escape where he quickly yanked a window screen out of a window and disappeared into the dim building interior.

Garcia jogged toward the building entrance. "That was 5C, as we suspected. Let's go!" They pressed the buzzer labeled SUPER, identified themselves as police, and were immediately buzzed in. A middle-aged female superintendent met them in the lobby. She was wearing a matching mint green sweatshirt and pants, and her hair was wrapped in a towel. Her breath smelled vaguely of liquor, and Molina pegged her as a morning drinker. They showed their badges and told her they needed quick access to apartment 5C in order to stop a robbery in progress. The woman ducked back into her ground-floor apartment and grabbed a set of keys from a cabinet by the door. Then she led them back to the stairs, and Detective Molina groaned when he realized this was a walk-up.

He started up the steps at a steady pace, with Garcia and the super close behind him. But by the third floor he began to pant heavily and had to stop to catch his breath. "Hold on. I just need a minute." Those damn donuts. He felt like he was back at the academy taking the fitness test all over again, only this time he was going to fail. Detective Garcia and the super both brushed past him and kept going.

48. GREGORY: THE BREAK-IN

Gregory checked the intercom outside the building and saw Wilfredo's name next to the buzzer marked 5C. He pressed it, and there was no answer. He hung around the entrance until a woman walking a dog fished out her key, then he followed her through the open doors with a grateful smile that said *of course I live here*. As if he would ever rent a place in an old rundown building like this. They didn't even have an elevator.

Gregory hiked up five floors and walked down the hallway until he was standing in front of apartment 5C. He jiggled the handle, but the door was locked. He rang the doorbell and then ran and ducked into the stairwell. He waited, listening intently, but no one came to answer the door. Clearly no one was home in the middle of the day.

Gregory stared at the door, frustrated. He didn't know the first thing about picking locks, so he would need to find a different way in. On a hunch he climbed up one more flight to the roof entrance. He gave the door a push and it swung open without any alarms going off. Out on the rooftop he found what he was looking for in the shape of a black ladder bolted to the side of the building that led down to the fire escape on the fifth floor. Seconds later he was standing outside Wilfredo's living room window, which had been left cracked. Gregory yanked on the window screen, tearing it out. Digging his nails under the window he raised it up as far as it would go, and ducked into the apartment.

Climbing across rooftops, breaking into buildings, planting spy cameras—Gregory couldn't remember the last time he'd felt this alive. He could almost understand how easy it had been for Cassandra to fall into a life of crime.

Looking around Gregory saw he was standing in a dilapidated living room. It had a pitifully small television, a beat-up couch, and a small wooden coffee table on a threadbare rug. This was where Cassandra had been spending her time? He strolled over to the entryway and came to a stop by the front door. Peering through the peephole he saw the empty hallway—this would be his easiest way out. Now he just needed to take a quick look around and find a good spot to hide the tiny camera.

Turning away from the door his gaze fell on a strange crocodile doll sitting up on a shelf. Was that a ventriloquist dummy? The creature's eyes were staring at him accusingly and seemed to follow him as he moved around the room. Gregory shuddered. Doing his best to ignore the dummy, he began to rummage through drawers, closets, and cabinets, thinking maybe he would uncover drugs or a weapon. But all he found was junk. It was hard to believe that two grown men shared this cramped apartment with only one bathroom? What a joke.

He was about to go nose around in Wilfredo's bedroom when he heard a key turning in the front door. Gregory paled. In a panic he ran toward the living room window that had been his way in, but when he got there he saw a figure looming outside, blocking his escape. He skidded to a halt, his heart pounding in his chest. By then the front door was thrown open and a portly bald man in a brown suit stood in the doorway holding a black handgun.

"Police! Freeze! Let me see those hands!"

Trembling, Gregory raised his arms up in the air. The figure in the window turned out to be another cop, a tough-looking policewoman in plain clothes, who climbed in the same way he had. She flashed her badge. "Turn around and put your hands on your head!" she shouted. Gregory followed her directions and moments later felt a cold metal handcuff close around one of his wrists. She guided first one arm and then the other down behind his back and cuffed him. "In case you were wondering, you are under arrest." She patted him down and soon found the spy camera shoved in his pocket. "Looks like we got ourselves a real double oh seven here! Wow, this thing is high tech. It must've cost a pretty penny. You're not KGB, are you?" Both cops laughed and Gregory felt his heart beating madly. This little escapade had not ended well. They asked him for his name and address, and he gave it to them. After that he stayed quiet and refused to answer any more questions. The less he said the better, he remembered that much from law school.

The female cop turned to her partner and said brightly: "Climbing down from the roof was a great idea. He had nowhere to run!"

"He was trapped all right," the bald cop agreed. Then he addressed a second woman wearing sweats who was lurking behind him. "Do you know this man?"

The woman, who Gregory pegged as the building superintendent, shook her head and twirled a key ring on her finger. "I have never seen him before. He does not live here. He is well-dressed for a thief, no?"

The female cop regarded Gregory critically. "That's true. Those are some fancy-looking loafers. A bit scruffy though. He seems to have clammed up, but we'll get his story out of him down at the station. Bet it's a good one, we caught him—what is that expression you like to use?"

The bald cop adopted a supercilious look. "*In flagrante delicto.*"

"That's the one!" For Gregory's benefit she added: "It means red-handed, in case you were wondering."

Gregory rolled his eyes.

The two detectives took a witness statement from the super and asked her to notify the tenant about the break in, while Gregory hung his head in shame. He couldn't believe he was being taken down to the precinct to be booked for breaking and entering. If word got back to the office he might be out of a job. The firm was extremely sensitive about its reputation. And if Cassandra found out that he'd broken into Wilfredo's apartment with a spy camera she'd never speak to him again.

The female cop read him his rights and hustled him toward the door. On his way out, Gregory caught sight of the super poking around furtively in Wilfredo's kitchen. He saw her grab two beer bottles out of Wilfredo's fridge and tuck them into her pockets. Feeling Gregory's eyes on her she looked up and gave him a conspiratorial wink behind the cops' backs. Gregory shook his head in disbelief—only in New York.

49. WILFREDO:
AN INVITATION YOU CAN'T REFUSE

Toby yanked on the steering wheel and the van veered over two lanes. Wilfredo held onto the handle above the door for dear life. Toby was in rare form, and he was being treated to a white-knuckle ride, but it still beat taking the subway, provided he arrived in one piece. It was Friday night and Toby had agreed to drop him off at Astor Billiards, where Wilfredo was meeting Cassandra to shoot some pool. The traffic light they were approaching turned yellow and Toby punched the gas. Wilfredo tightened his grip on the door handle as they sped past braking cars. Thankfully they hit the next red light and the van screeched to a halt. Wilfredo let out a long breath.

The van inched forward as the crosswalk timer counted down. "I've noticed you and Cassandra have been spending a lot of time together lately. You better be careful, Wilfredo. You don't want to be the rebound guy!"

"Would that be so bad? I've been thinking I need to come clean and tell her I'm crazy about her."

"Don't do it, man. It's too soon!"

"But if I wait she might rebound into someone else."

"Give her some time! Her life has just been turned upside down."

Wilfredo scowled and grabbed hold of the handle again as the light turned green.

Toby punched the gas. "You sure do have a lot of girl problems these days. The whole theater was buzzing today about that slap photo online!"

"You saw that?"

"Me and everyone else! What on earth did you say to Ruby that she felt the need to smack you upside the head?"

"Honestly, it was nothing. She apologized afterward and we had a good laugh about it." His phone rang in his pocket. He pulled it out and saw Ruby's name on his lock screen. "Speak of the devil!" He hit the button and put the phone to his ear. "Hey there."

"Wilfredo! I just hung up with Declan. They're letting me out of the play. I'm free!"

"Wait, so you're not going to play Violet anymore?"

"Nope. I got offered a role in a movie, and shooting starts in two weeks! My last day at the theater was yesterday. They've agreed to be nice about it and not sue me for breach of contract. But keep it under your hat until it's announced."

"Gotcha. So who's going to play Violet?"

"They're giving the lead to your friend Cassandra! Boy did she luck out! All because of some bad sushi. Go figure."

"She's a very talented actor."

"I suppose she has a knack for this kind of moody psychological drama," Ruby admitted grudgingly. "Thankfully, my new movie is nothing like that. It's a lighthearted crime caper based on this whole Cat Burglar versus Foxman thing."

"You're kidding?"

"Nope. They're cashing in on the popular news story and turning it into a romantic comedy."

"You just blew my mind." Wilfredo held his breath as

the van sped past a bus on the wrong side. "Congrats, Ruby! Does this mean you're moving back to Hollywood?"

"No, silly! We're shooting in New York! No cheap back-lot shoots for this feature!"

"So who's playing the Foxman?"

"I'm not allowed to say. But, if you come to the casting announcement tomorrow afternoon you can find out. It's a private party but the details have already been leaked to the press. Never hurts to get a little early buzz going! And we want the news rags to help us stake a claim to the story, in case any other production companies have the same idea."

"Where is this party?"

"It's at the chic rooftop bar at my hotel—the Horatio. Please say you'll come. Having a friendly face around would mean the world to me. It's a costume party, so everyone is encouraged to dress up as their best Cat Burglar or Foxman. Both me and my costar are going to be in our official costumes. And Tiffany is loaning me a Tahitian black pearl necklace worth ten grand because we told them there'd be photographers."

"Don't you get nervous wearing jewelry like that?"

"Are you kidding? It's my favorite part of the job. So are you in? What am I saying, of course you're in. You can't possibly say no to a rooftop party, right? We just need to find you a costume! I'll get Annie to help you with it. You're gonna make an amazing Foxman—you have just the right build! Annie will text you the deets. Gotta run! Another call coming in! Oh, and try to get your hands on a skateboard."

She hung up. Wilfredo was confused as to whether he had actually agreed to anything. But he hadn't said no, and that seemed to be enough for Ruby. Was he supposed to go dressed as Foxman? With other people there dressed as Foxman too? His mind was spinning.

He filled Toby in on his conversation. "Man, that's crazy!" Toby grinned. "You should totally go! You'll get to hang out with a bunch of Foxmans and no one will know you're the real deal!"

"I'm not sure I can handle a situation like that."

"You're an actor now, Wilfredo. You can't pass up on opportunities like this. Ruby will probably introduce you to a bunch of industry honchos."

Wilfredo hated to admit it, but Toby had a point.

Captain Pete seemed to think so too: *You should listen to cheese breath over here, Freddy. You gotta go schmooze with the bigwigs, maybe get your name in the gossip rags. And don't forget the party is at Ruby's hotel! Time to get wise about her, you dumb palooka.*

Toby pulled the van over to the curb on Broadway and Twelfth Street. "You can hoof it from here. Make sure you grab your backpack and longboard from the back. You're gonna need your gear tomorrow night!"

"I'm on it." Wilfredo gave his grinning friend a fist bump and thanked him for the ride.

I swear that pink van is a death trap, complained the Captain. *Every time you step into it I feel like we are gambling with our lives. It always reminds me of the time I rounded Cape Horn in a dinghy during a tropical squall. Only instead of being surrounded by sharks we are being circled by angry yellow cabs!*

50. CASSANDRA: EIGHT BALL
IN THE CORNER POCKET

Cassandra stood on the sidewalk in the freezing cold, waiting for Wilfredo to show up. Arriving early was clearly not all it was cracked up to be. She'd be a human popsicle by the time he rolled around. The red neon sign for Astor Billiards and Bar glowed on the brick wall behind her. Her only company out here was a crazy-eyed guy in a purple hoodie who was smoking a joint on the nearby corner.

She was looking forward to shooting pool with Wilfredo. Things had been so busy lately with rehearsals starting up again in the new year that they'd barely seen each other outside the theater. And after the news Declan had shared with her today Cassandra knew her life was about to become even more frenzied. She was debating whether to confide in Wilfredo. Technically what Declan had told her was top secret for now.

When purple hoodie guy began to walk around in tiny inexplicable circles, Cassandra decided that maybe it would be better to wait inside at the bar. She would happily trade the risk of strangers testing out their pick-up lines on her for a little warmth in her extremities. But just then she spotted a familiar silhouette in the distance. Was she imagining things, or was Wilfredo riding some sort of skateboard? Sweeping along the sidewalk he quickly closed the gap between them and skidded to a stop.

"Hey there! I had no idea you were a skater boy at heart."

"There's a lot you don't know about me," he replied in a mock mysterious tone.

"Well, mister badass skateboard guy, you're late! I've been freezing my buns off out here for ten minutes."

"Sorry, I didn't think you would be so punctual."

Cassandra opened her mouth to reply, and then closed it again when she realized she had no idea what to say to that.

They went up to the reception counter near the entrance. Standing behind it was a man in an oversized yellow polo who nodded to Wilfredo with a look of recognition, handing him a tray of balls with a couple chalk cubes thrown on top. Then he pointed them to table thirty-five over in the far corner.

The dimly lit pool hall gave off an old-school vibe. It was a large space, with red wall-to-wall carpeting, wooden fixtures, and an antique tin ceiling. The decor managed to make the large space feel intimate. The bar along the inside wall was already crowded with men staring up at a television screen while the pool tables all around them were beginning to fill up with boisterous young people, along with a sprinkling of steely-eyed pool league types with their custom cue sticks.

At table thirty-five the overhead light cast a nice even glow on the green felt below. Wilfredo emptied the balls onto the table and tossed the empty tray onto a nearby chair, chucking his backpack on top. He propped up his longboard carefully against a column. Cassandra picked out a decent cue stick from a wall rack for them to share and Wilfredo began raking up the balls in a wooden triangle.

"Do you know how to play Nine Ball?" he asked her.

"I grew up with a pool table in my basement," she replied. "Nine Ball is practically my middle name. All me and my friends did on Friday nights was shoot pool."

"Uh-oh. I don't like the sound of that. Am I gonna be walking out of here without my shirt?"

"Not if you know when to cut your losses."

He let out a laugh. She loved Wilfredo's laugh. Tilting her head to one side she peered at him curiously, wondering if this man, who had always done his best to keep her at arm's length, was secretly in love with her. After what she had overheard him say on New Year's Eve, it was the only explanation that made any sense.

Wilfredo arranged the balls into a diamond shape, with the one ball in the front, the nine ball in the middle, and the two ball in the back. Cassandra broke first, with a sharp *crack*, followed by a diminishing clatter of balls knocking into one another. The seven ball dropped.

Wilfredo looked worried. "Oh boy, what did I get myself into?"

She chalked her cue and lined up her next shot. The one ball landed in a side pocket with a *thunk*. The two, three, and the four balls quickly followed.

"Am I going to get a turn?"

"Don't hold your breath." But on her next shot the five ball rattled around in the corner and refused to fall. "There, are you happy? You jinxed me!"

"It so happens jinxing is at the core of my pool playing strategy." Wilfredo took the cue stick from her.

She watched him go through a seemingly complex set

of calculations before he successfully potted the five ball. But he'd left himself without a good line on the six, and his attempt to bank the cue ball failed to make contact with the target ball.

"That's ball in hand for me," she said, beaming. Lining up her shot she easily sank the six ball, set herself up perfectly for the eight, and sank that one too. With only the nine ball left she buried it in a corner pocket. "One nothing."

"That was quick."

She smiled. "Loser racks 'em up!" She helped dig the balls out of the far pockets and sent them rolling his way. He was looking very handsome tonight in a red-and-black flannel shirt and tan corduroy pants. He had trimmed his sandy hair so that it was off his shoulders, looking more like a wild lion's mane. She wanted to ask him how he really felt about her, but she was plagued by her usual second thoughts. Should she really be rushing into something new so soon after her breakup? Wouldn't she just be proving Gregory right? But it was becoming increasingly difficult for her to deny that she had been falling for Wilfredo since day one. What was the point of fighting it?

The second game went the same way as the first. For someone who was a regular here, Wilfredo wasn't particularly good. She was beginning to feel bad about beating him. As if sensing her thoughts he said: "Don't worry, I'm just getting warmed up!"

"I'm hoping you'll put up more of a fight!" They racked the balls again. "How about you break this time?"

"Sure." He made a show of rolling up his sleeves.

"So how's life as an understudy going?" With Sebastian

Estrada's leg healed, Wilfredo had been relegated to watching rehearsals from the wings.

"Oh I don't really miss the spotlight. But I won't lie, it's been pretty fun to see Sebastian struggling with the role."

"You are a much better knight. Everyone knows it. He's only the lead because the star is always the box office draw."

"Not always," Wilfredo said guardedly. "Sometimes the better actor wins the part." He gave her a funny look.

"Okay, out with it, mister. What have you heard?"

Wilfredo looked suddenly guilty. "Who me? Nothing."

He was definitely hiding something. She looked around to make sure no one was within earshot, then she took a step closer to him. "Declan and I had a little chat today. He had some big news for me."

"Secret news? Ruby related, maybe?" Wilfredo's eyebrows shot up questioningly.

"So you *do* know about Ruby pulling out of the play!" Cassandra was astonished. "Who did you hear it from? Does everybody know?"

"I told Toby already, so I imagine he's spreading the word as we speak. No one can keep a secret in the theater. I heard it from Ruby herself. Apparently she got offered a role in a movie, and she said yes."

"And do you also happen to know who's going to play Violet now that she's leaving?"

"You are! I didn't want to say anything until it was official."

"Thank god we can talk about it, because I'm freaking out. It just doesn't seem real!"

"Relax. You've got the role down pat and you're only

going to get better. I'm so happy for you, Cassandra. You're a Broadway actress now for real, and nobody deserves it more than you." He wrapped her up in a hug, lifting her off her feet and twirling her around. When he put her down his face was a mere few inches away from hers. Their eyes locked, and she leaned slightly toward him. But an obnoxious guy on the neighboring table ruined the moment by sticking the butt of his cue between them as he bent over to take his shot. They stepped awkwardly away from each other.

Cassandra ran her fingers through her hair. "I'm still pinching myself. I don't think it will sink in until I see my name on the dressing room door. This has been my dream for so long, and I came very close to giving up." She gave him a quizzical look. "Wait, did you say Ruby got cast in a movie?"

"Yep. They're making a film about the whole Foxman versus Cat Burglar thing."

"No way!" She gawked at him. "Are you serious?"

"Yeah, it's really happening."

She was dumbfounded. Were her criminal adventures really about to be glamorized on the big screen? And with Ruby, of all people, playing her? It blew her mind. Wilfredo told her about the casting party tomorrow that he'd been roped into. "They're pulling out all the stops. There's going to be champagne, free food, and a well-known DJ."

"So you're going then?"

Wilfredo stopped chalking the cue stick and stared at her. "Now that I'm an actor I pretty much have to go to these things."

"True," she admitted. "But don't let Ruby boss you around. Be your own man, Wilfredo."

"She can be hard to say no to sometimes."

"Ya think?" Cassandra nodded vigorously. "And you'll have to scare up a costume. It's not a lot of notice."

"I'll manage something."

"I'm guessing the party will be crawling with photographers. Maybe you guys can reenact the infamous slap from New Year's Eve for the paparazzi? I can already see the head-line—Mystery Man Turns the Other Cheek!"

"Hilarious. I'm never going to live down that photo. But forget about Ruby and the party. We need to celebrate your big news! I'll go scare up a couple drinks at the bar."

"Good idea. White wine for me, please."

"You got it. I'll be right back."

Cassandra perched herself on an empty armchair, leaning on the cue stick with her knees pressed together and her heels pushed out to the side Her foot accidentally nudged Wilfredo's longboard, knocking it over. When she stooped down to pick it up she noticed a sticker on the back, one of those generic alien heads with the big black eyes. Why did this board look so familiar? Had she seen it at his apartment? She didn't think so. And then a fuzzy memory took shape in her mind, coming slowly into focus. Didn't Foxman's board have an alien sticker just like it? She could swear she'd seen it in one of the photos from Washington Square, when Foxman was being carried around by the Santas with his board tucked under his arm. She took her phone out and in two seconds a search popped up the photo she remembered. Zooming in on it with a pinch of her fingers she saw the alien face staring back at her. The sticker was identical and in the same spot.

Her breath caught in her throat and she nearly fell out of her chair. Could it really be the same board? Was it possible that Wilfredo was Foxman? This thought nearly short-circuited her brain. They *were* about the same height and size. And yes, she remembered looking into Foxman's baby blue eyes that very first night. Wilfredo's eyes were that same exact shade.

The pool hall seemed to suddenly spin around her. The voices, the music, the sound of balls breaking, the laughter in the room, all echoed in her head. Then her eyes shifted to Wilfredo's plump, overstuffed backpack, sitting on the chair next to hers. What secrets might it conceal? She glanced over at the bar. Wilfredo was one of a dozen people crowded around it. He had a twenty in his fist and was waving it frantically in a bid to attract the bartender's attention.

Her heart racing, she reached over and grabbed his backpack. Undoing the zipper she peaked inside. There she saw a bunched-up fuzzy orange costume that was all too familiar. Zipping up the bag she put it back on the chair and sat there stunned. Sweet, down-to-earth Wilfredo, who seemed as genuine and guileless as they came, was actually the masked vigilante who had been taunting her online. It was unbelievable.

Wilfredo eventually made it back with the drinks. She thanked him for the wine and took a sip. Then she appraised him coolly with fresh eyes as he took a turn breaking. The balls bounced around wildly and the five ball rolled into a side pocket. Apparently this uncomplicated guy persona of his was just a front for his exciting secret life, where he skated around the city in a ridiculous costume, rescuing people, and chasing crooks. It was beyond absurd. But of course, she was one to talk.

But one thing was for sure, the Wilfredo she knew was

just a mirage. He had evaporated into thin air, replaced with this enigmatic stranger. She couldn't help wondering what he would think if he knew he was shooting pool with the infamous Cat Burglar.

"You've gone awfully quiet," he said, catching her eye. "Is something the matter?"

"Have you ever wondered if it's really possible to see into someone else's heart? Or do you think we just fool ourselves into thinking we know the people around us."

Wilfredo regarded her quizzically. "Where did that come from? You got awfully metaphysical real fast."

Cassandra smiled. "Sorry. My mind just wandered down a crazy rabbit hole."

"I know *that* feeling. But you'd better get your head back in the game. In case you haven't noticed, I've got a streak going." It was true. He'd just managed to pot four balls in a row. But on his last shot the cue ball had rolled right up against the rail. He took his time trying to figure out the best way to attack it, but ended up missing his shot. Cassandra took the cue stick from him and studied the table. She sunk the next two shots, leaving only the solitary nine ball in the middle of the table. With calm precision she kissed the cue off the outer edge of the nine ball, sending it spinning slowly into the side pocket. Game over.

51. GREGORY: THE LIE DETECTOR

Getting arrested turned out to be the most humiliating experience of Gregory's life. During the booking process they confiscated his things, snapped his photo, conducted a full-body search, and fingerprinted him, all before letting him make a phone call. Finally, they stuck him in a holding cell with a bunch of lowlifes. The squalor, the indignities, the bullying street toughs—it all inflicted a heavy toll on him in the six hours it took for a law school friend of his to post his bail.

On the plus side, what had seemed like an open-and-shut case had soon become muddied. Gregory quickly hired a young female attorney at a boutique firm to represent him. Her good looks belied her attack dog disposition. After a long talk with the two detectives she brought him the good news: Technically they hadn't caught him stealing anything, so they would have a hard time prosecuting him for felony burglary. Breaking and entering on its own was a simple misdemeanor. So, if he agreed to answer questions relating to a wider investigation, the authorities were willing to expunge his record. Eager to put the whole debacle behind him, Gregory took the deal.

"Just make sure not to incriminate yourself in any way," his lawyer advised him.

"Got it. What do they want to know?"

"They seem to think you are tied in some way to the whole Cat Burglar business that's been in the news lately."

"How odd."

"You're not, are you? You should tell me if you are."

"Of course I'm not," he lied.

"My guess is that you may have some personal connection you are unaware of to a suspect in that investigation. Or they are just grasping at straws. Either way, it's going to work to your advantage."

So here he was at the precinct, sitting at a metal table in a cramped and windowless interview room. His lawyer, dressed in a black skirt suit, was in a chair to his right. The two detectives who had arrested him sat across the table from them.

Molina, the bald detective, shuffled some papers in his hands. "Mr. Dingle. Thanks for coming back in to chat with us. We greatly appreciate your cooperation in this matter. Before we get started with our questions, we hope you don't mind if we hook you up to a polygraph machine."

Gregory's lawyer leaped to her feet. "Now wait a minute! You guys didn't say anything about a lie detector!" She glared at them furiously. "Let's get out of here, Mr. Dingle. We're done!"

"Hold on," said Gregory. "Shouldn't we at least think about this if it will help get the charges dismissed?"

"I don't like them springing a surprise like this on us."

The brown-haired female detective adopted a soothing tone of voice and said: "The machine just gives us an added degree of confidence that his answers are truthful. You know how it is with these question-and-answer sessions. Everybody has something to hide. The only reason we didn't mention it beforehand is because forewarning the interviewee has been known to affect the reliability of the results. And I'm afraid that if you don't agree to it, we will have to reinstate the charges and prosecute Mr. Dingle to the full extent of the law."

"Fine. Hook me up to your stupid machine. I don't care." Gregory gave his lawyer a reassuring nod and she sat back down with her arms crossed and her lips pursed.

The younger detective opened the door and beckoned to an older-looking guy standing outside who proceeded to wheel a polygraph machine into the room. This man asked Gregory to roll up his shirt sleeve and put a cuff on his arm, attaching sensors to two of his fingertips. Next the gray-haired man wrapped two straps around Gregory's chest, securing them tightly. The wires all led back to the ancient-looking machine.

"I'm going to ask you a series of questions," the man said. "This machine is ninety-five percent accurate at detecting false statements. Please confine your responses to either yes or no." He led off with basic questions about his identity, where he lived, and where he'd gone to school.

"Now I need you to deliberately lie in response to the next two questions. This is solely for the purpose of calibrating the machine, rest assured that your answers will not be held against you."

He asked Gregory if he had ever been out of the country, and if he'd ever driven a car. Gregory answered no to both questions, and he suspected the needle must've jumped madly on the graph. The technician marked out spots with a pen on the paper chart, and seemed satisfied. Then the real questions began.

"Are you familiar with the individual known as Foxman, a local vigilante?"

"Yes, I've read about him."

"Please stick to yes or no answers."

"Sorry."

"Are you familiar with the individual known as Foxman, a local vigilante?"

"Yes."

"Does he dress in a wolf costume?"

"No."

"Does he dress in a fox costume?"

"Yes."

"Do you have any idea as to Foxman's identity?"

"No."

"Are you Foxman?" Gregory's eyebrows shot up in surprise. Why on earth would they suspect him of being this Foxman character? It must have something to do with his having been engaged to Cassandra.

"No. Absolutely not."

"Please stick to—"

"Yes or no answers. Sorry."

"Are you Foxman?"

"No." Did they really think he would dress up in a furry orange costume and skateboard around town tackling muggers? Boy were they out in left field. It began to dawn on him that these two cops didn't have a clue.

"Are you familiar with the criminal known popularly as the Cat Burglar?"

"Yes."

The two detectives exchanged meaningful glances. Gregory had been expecting this moment. He figured that the police must be onto Cassandra. It was foolish of her to think she could get away with a string of high-profile thefts.

The examiner fixed a stern gaze on him. "Do you know the real identity of the Cat Burglar?"

Gregory took a slow breath and thought calming thoughts. Back in law school he'd written a paper on the reliability of lie detectors as evidence. He knew these devices were not that hard to fool. They couldn't read your mind, they just measured how anxious or nervous a particular answer made you. The trick was to control your breath, and not let any of the questions make you tense.

"No," he answered, blinking slowly.

The investigator paused and glanced over at his charts. Gregory kept his focus on calming his senses and relaxing his fingers and toes. He might never win Cassandra back, but he would still rather go to jail himself than betray her secret.

"Are you familiar with the actress Ruby Greenwood?"

"Yes."

"Do you have any reason to believe that Ruby Greenwood is the Cat Burglar?"

"No." Well that was another surprising turn. Maybe they weren't hot on Cassandra's trail after all.

Two minutes later the examiner switched off the machine, and glancing at the two detectives, the gray-haired man gave a subtle shake of his head from side to side. Gregory was sure he had sailed through the interrogation with flying colors. These old-fashioned lie detector gizmos were worthless. Meeting his lawyer's eyes he could tell she was pleased. The bald detective glowered at him, and he smiled back innocently. He had played their little game, and now they had no choice but to uphold their end of the bargain.

52. WILFREDO: LAUNDRY DAY

A yawning Wilfredo yanked up the window blinds, letting the morning sun spill into his small bedroom. He stood staring out the window, blinking slowly, as he let the details of the day drop into place in his mind. Yes, that was it, Ruby's movie launch party was this afternoon.

His backpack was on the floor leaning against the chest of drawers. Frowning, Wilfredo pulled his Foxman costume out and examined it in the weak winter sunlight. It had been stuffed in his bag for weeks. Before that it had been pawed at by a pack of drunk Santas. And before *that* he had rolled around on a dirty city sidewalk in it. All of which explained why it was looking far from pristine. He put his nose up to it and gave it a sniff.

Holy Moses, Freddy. Your costume reeks! Have you heard of a little thing called deodorant? You might want to try it sometime. I'm not sure if you're better off washing that fur bag or setting it on fire!

"I'm gonna clean it," grumbled Wilfredo. "Now get out of my head, Captain. I haven't even had my first cup of coffee yet." Wilfredo shoved the costume in the bottom of his nylon laundry bag and piled a bunch of his other dirty laundry on top. They didn't have a laundry room in the building, so about once a week he would cart his dirty clothes to the laundromat across the street. Pulling a coat on over his sweats and ignoring his bedhead hair, he dragged the stuffed bag toward the front door. Toby, who was sitting on the couch watching TV, eating his first cereal bowl of the day, looked up as Wilfredo walked past. "Laundry day?"

"It's like you have psychic powers!" Wilfredo joked.

Five minutes later he squeezed past the doorway of the laundry place. It was just a narrow room with a row of stacked washers and dryers along one wall. It was early, so there were only a few tatted-up hipsters milling about, as well as a young mother with a kid putting clothes in a dryer. Wilfredo drifted toward the back and found a free washer. The machines were huge so he managed to cram everything into one load. Discreetly, he shoved the costume in last, and banged the door shut. He added a scoop of powdered detergent to the drawer, turned the dial to hot, and swiped his laundry card. The machine hissed as it began to fill up with water.

He headed over to the bagel shop next door and got himself an egg-and-cheese sandwich and a cup of coffee. Back in the laundromat he picked out a spot in a row of bucket seats facing the machines, and sat down to eat his breakfast. He felt the need to keep an eye on his laundry this morning, as he didn't want some stranger stumbling across his costume.

Sitting nearby, the young child was happily scrawling on a drawing pad with some colored crayons. The boy lifted up his drawing and showed it off proudly. Wilfredo smiled and said: "Cool bear, little guy. I love it." The kid's weary looking mother glanced over, seemed to peg Wilfredo as harmless, and resumed folding clothes at a nearby table.

The boy seemed delighted to have made a new friend and began showing Wilfredo every little thing he drew. Wilfredo ate his sandwich and oohed and aahed over the kid's art work. When a green crayon rolled onto the floor unnoticed, Wilfredo bent down to pick it up. Using the brown bag from the bagel store as his canvas, Wilfredo drew a green crocodile face on the front side. Borrowing a blue crayon he gave the toothy reptile a captain's hat. By this time he had the young boy's full attention. With a flourish, Wilfredo stuck his hand in the bag and turned it to face the boy.

"Ahoy there, matey," he said in his best sailor drawl, his own lips pressed tightly together, while he pretended to talk with the bag itself.

His little friend clapped his hands with excitement at the unexpected puppet show.

"Shiver me timbers. It's time to hoist the mainsail and go search for buried treasure!"

That's hilarious, Freddy. Are you seriously going to turn me into some two-bit pirate show? I'm a respectable sea captain! I don't deserve to be mocked!

"Don't mock me! I'm a respectable sea captain!"

Have some respect for the uniform. My rank might not mean much in this laundromat, but out on the open waters I am the lord of the sea!

"I'm Captain of the Laundromat! I'll sail through an ocean of dirty clothes! Oh no, is that a fearsome kraken down in the water?" With his free hand Wilfredo wriggled his fingers about like tentacles.

We've talked about this, Freddy. You know I draw the line at joking about the kraken. If you'd seen what I've seen you wouldn't make light of a giant squid that could rip your boat in half with the flick of a tentacle.

"Oh no, the kraken has got hold of me!" Wilfredo waved around his tentacle fingers and suddenly grabbed the brown paper bag, pulling it off and scrunching it up while making loud munching and slurping sounds.

"The Captain was eaten by a sea monster!" yelled the boy, a huge smile on his face.

"The poor Captain is fish food," Wilfredo agreed.

He was contemplating reviving the brown-bag Captain for an encore, but the boy's mother called to him and he ran and followed her out the door with a wave. Wilfredo finished off the dregs of his coffee, and checked the timer he'd set on his phone. As he was staring at the seconds counting down Cassandra's name appeared on his lock screen and his phone buzzed. He tapped the green circle and said hello.

"Hey, mister. What are you up to?"

"Oh, just sitting in a laundromat losing my grip on reality."

"So, just a regular Saturday morning for you?"

"Pretty much."

"How's the costume for the party coming along?"

"Geesh! Everyone's worried about my costume! Annie has texted me five times about it already. I'll tell you what I told her—I've got it covered!"

"It just doesn't seem like an easy thing to throw together. But hey, I didn't mean to bug you about it. The real reason I'm calling is to apologize for zoning out at the pool hall last night."

"It did seem like you were there one minute and gone the next."

"I had a lot on my mind."

"Anything in particular?"

"Maybe," she said. "But if I spill my deepest darkest secrets you'll run screaming from the room."

"Hey, we all have secrets."

"Even you?"

"You'd be amazed," Wilfredo replied.

"We should meet up later and swap stories. Put all our cards faceup on the table."

"Even the ones up our sleeves?"

"Especially those."

"I'm game if you are," he said. "What time are you free?"

"I have to go sign some contracts over at my agent's office, and they want to take me out to lunch afterward to celebrate, but maybe in the early afternoon?"

"Look at you, the busy working actress meeting her agent! The thing is Ruby wants me to get to the party before it starts, at like three o'clock. And I have no idea what time it's going to end."

"I see. Let's just make a date for tomorrow, then."

"Sounds good."

"And in the meantime, make sure not to get caught up in any of Ruby's schemes."

"Schemes? You make her sound so devious. She's not a bad person, you know. She's always been straight with me."

"Has she? Did you know she's linked romantically to Chad Evans? The movie star? I was talking to Annie yesterday when she was packing up Ruby's dressing room, and she hinted that Chad Evans and Ruby are secretly an item.

Apparently, Ruby's upset because good old Chad is cavorting with his costar on his tropical movie set."

Out on the street a motorbike roared past with loud staccato bangs from its tail pipe. Wilfredo plugged his other ear with his finger. "So you think Ruby might try and use me to even the score?"

"If the shoe fits."

"Is it so hard to believe she might actually be interested in me? Or am I just not in the same league as a movie star?"

"I didn't mean it like that. It's just that someone like Ruby sees everyone around her as a means to an end. Whether it's you or Chad Evans, or whoever else gets pulled into her world."

"She doesn't let much stand in her way. I'll give you that."

"That's all I'm saying. But listen, I gotta run. I'll see you tomorrow!" She hung up and Wilfredo pocketed his phone. Maybe he should've mentioned he wasn't the least bit interested in Ruby. It felt like the kind of thing Cassandra ought to know. He stared dead ahead at the washing machines, spinning endlessly, round and round.

Don't listen to her, Freddy. She's just stirring the pot! And what's with all the mystery? My guess is she's back with moneybags. On again off again, that's how those things go. If you're dumb enough to put your heart in her hands she's just gonna feed it to the seagulls!

53. RUBY:
CONCOCTING A SEDUCTION

Ruby started her morning at the spa, where Bekka showed herself to be as talented a waxer as she was a masseuse. Then she'd hopped in a cab to her hair salon up on Fifth Avenue in Midtown. Having recently turned thirty-three, gray hairs were starting to show up with disturbing frequency. But the salon made short work of them, dying her hair expertly with a single process deep reddish-brown that was slightly darker than her natural ginger. Perfect for her new role.

Dyed and washed, it was time for Billy, her hair stylist, to do his thing. He waved her into his chair, and spun her around to face the mirror. He slapped a diffuser on the end of his hair dryer, flipped the switch to low, and began blowing out her hair, fussing and teasing it into cascading waves. They were working from a few video stills showing the pixelated outlines of the Cat Burglar's hair. Ruby's hair was already the right length and thickness, so she wouldn't need extensions. But her usual center part needed to be swept to the side.

People didn't realize how much work went into looking glamorous, especially as you got older. She would often look back wistfully at photos of herself in her early twenties, when she had first moved to California. Back then she'd radiated a youthful beauty that felt truly effortless, while her eyes had sparkled with a self-assurance that came only from believing yourself immortal. Those days were long gone.

After this she would get a manicure, but her makeup could wait until closer to the party, since it involved getting her face painted. She stared absently into the mirror, the drone of the hair dryer in her ears. Her thoughts turned to Wilfredo. She was delighted he'd agreed to come tonight. He would finally see her in her element, not in some shabby run-down theater.

It had really stung when he'd rejected her on the rooftop. She had practically thrown herself at him, and he'd confessed that he was head over heels in love with someone else. She knew it had to be Cassandra, that newbie actress who had undermined Ruby's stature at the Cornelius. That girl had poor Wilfredo under her spell. Well, it was time to up the ante. In her experience, men were simple creatures. Under the right conditions the blood flow to their brains could easily be short-circuited. She'd already caught his eye once in her red underwear, and she was betting she could do it again. Of course she couldn't just throw herself at him this time, she would have to be more artful.

Billy cranked the heat up on the hair dryer. "Let me know if it gets too hot!"

Ruby flashed her smile. "It's fine." She liked watching this professional work his magic. He knew how to tame each lock of hair so that it fell in perfect harmony with every other lock of hair around her face. "You're doing a great job matching the photo, Billy. That Cat Burglar sure has a nice head of hair."

"Does she? Hard to say. She's wearing a wig in those photos."

"Really? Are you sure?"

"Oh, I'm sure."

This surprised Ruby. No one else she had talked to seemed to have noticed. But she supposed that Billy, of all people, would know. She was about to press him on the subject when the phone in her hand dinged. Pulling it out from under the cape she saw it was another over-the-top apologetic text from Chad. She wondered if he was writing them himself, or whether his PA had been tasked with sending them out at half-hour intervals. He had finally admitted on the phone the other day to hooking up with Gabriella. She'd been outraged, even though deep down she'd known it had been all but inevitable the moment the casting was set. He'd sworn it meant nothing, and filled Ruby's hotel room with red tulips, her favorites. She'd forgive him eventually, of course—he was Chad Evans after all—but it would be a lot easier to forgive him after she had evened the score. If he was going to have his on-the-side fun, then she was too. But to do that she needed to find a lover she could trust not to blab about it. And the only person she knew in New York who fit that bill was good old Wilfredo from Beacon High, who used to follow her around school like a lost puppy. He didn't know it yet, but she was gonna rock his world.

Cassandra stood in the shadows of a darkened doorway in the Meatpacking District, her face painted with whiskers, pointy ears poking out from her faux red hair, black leather gloves on her hands, and a thin tail swinging freely behind her. Her eyes were glued to the entrance of the Horatio Hotel across the street, a neighborhood hotspot for the chic crowd who frequented the nearby bistros and fashion boutiques. It was just like Ruby to pick this place as her New York base.

In the past few minutes she had watched several people dressed as foxes and cat burglars go into the hotel. She checked her watch: 3:30 pm. The party must be well underway by now. She waited until another group in costume were headed into the hotel, then she hustled across the cobblestone street and walked in right behind them. The doorman waved them all over to the elevator bank, where a frazzled woman with a clipboard was busy scratching names off a list. "We're with Chariot Pictures Ad Promo," said a blond-haired cat burglar in the group.

Clipboard woman made a note on her list. "Go ahead. Take this elevator here up to the roof."

They all piled in: Three orange-suited foxes, including one girl fox. Two cat burglar girls, including Cassandra. And one cat burglar dude. During the short elevator ride the skinny fox who was jammed in next to her looked Cassandra up and down and exclaimed: "Outstanding costume. You look just like her!"

"Who knows, maybe I'm the *real* Cat Burglar?"

This comment drew amused chuckles around her. "And maybe I'm actually Foxman!" joked the skinny fox in his store-bought orange fleece onesie.

Moments later the elevator doors let them out right onto the roof. Smartly dressed media types were milling about, along with a number of more bohemian souls who had embraced the costume party's theme. A DJ was cranking out dance tunes and people were literally shaking their tails on the tiled patio.

It was a perfect afternoon for an outdoor party. The sky was bright and cloudless, and the air was unseasonably warm. Cassandra snagged a glass of champagne from the open bar and drifted through the crowd until she found a quiet spot by the railing that provided a good vantage point. The swanky rooftop was furnished with low-slung sofas and weathered coffee tables, with two central fire pits. There was a small plat-form in the corner, functioning as a makeshift stage, and a banner hanging over it that read FOXMAN VS. CAT BURGLAR. Looking northeast there was a distant view of the Empire State Building poking up above a jagged skyline. To the west stretched the gray Hudson river, crisscrossed by tug boats and ferries, a helicopter flitting through the air.

Cassandra spotted a Foxman at the opposite end of the roof deck with a familiar silhouette and a distinct two-toned orange costume. She knew instantly that it was Wilfredo, aka the real Foxman. He was standing by himself, his skateboard clutched in one hand and a green beer bottle in the other. His suit looked cleaner than she remembered, and she guessed that he must have been washing it when she'd talked to him on the phone earlier. The shock of discovering that her nemesis was actually her close friend had subsided. In its place had come an acceptance that her bond with Wilfredo was much stronger than the manufactured enmity she had with Foxman, and a sense that the whole situation was ridiculous. Her only worry now was whether Wilfredo, law-abiding citizen and moral scold that he was, would be as accepting if he found out *her* secret.

It was quite nervy of him to show up here in costume. She'd figured that if he was going to come to this shindig then it was only fitting that she should be here too. Although she had to admit that keeping an eye on Ruby, who she suspected was still trying to ensnare Wilfredo, was another great reason for crashing the party.

Before long, a woman with a pixie haircut made her way up onto the stage and tapped the microphone. She introduced herself as the director of publicity for Chariot Pictures. She kept her speech short and quickly cut to the chase: "Ladies and gentlemen, I present to you the two stars of the movie, Ruby Greenwood and Noah Brogans!" The two actors popped out from behind the backdrop and hopped up onto the stage together, both of them dressed in full costume. A bunch of confetti cannons popped, and there was a lot of cheering as the DJ blasted some horn sounds. A small huddle of photographers materialized and snapped photos like crazy as the two stars went through a series of comic poses: Back to back, pretend fighting, him

lifting her in his arms, and a pretend chase pose with Foxman on a longboard.

Noah Brogans's costume was similar to Wilfredo's but
with a thicker woolly texture and a more reddish color. Ruby
looked like a Cassandra clone, except for her fake black nails,
glued-on whiskers, and the stunning black pearl necklace
around her neck. Cassandra's eyes went large when she saw
it. Wilfredo had mentioned the necklace, hinting that it was
worth twenty grand. Too bad it would be all but impossible
to swipe it off Ruby's neck.

Both actors said a few words about how honored they
were to be involved in this project, and then the two stars
split up to do mini-interviews with members of the press.
With the official business wrapped up, the DJ cranked up
the volume and the dancing resumed with renewed enthu-
siasm. Cassandra watched the costumed chaos on the dance
floor with amusement, took sips of her champagne, and did
her best to keep an eye on Wilfredo from a safe distance.
She didn't want to get too close, as she was worried he might
recognize her.

As it turned out, his eyes were a lot sharper than she
thought. When she glanced over at him she was alarmed to
see him staring intently in her direction. Then he put down
his beer on a table and set off in her direction, a determined
look on his face. Cassandra ducked into a crowd of dancing
cat burglars, and did her best to shake him off her tail.

Finding her way to a distant spot on the roof she ducked
behind a group of men in suits, and breathed a sigh of relief,
thinking she was safe for now. But just then a random photographer popped up out of nowhere and fired off a burst of

photos in her direction. She put her hands on her hips and gave him a stern look.

"Ruby Greenwood?" he asked tentatively.

"I'm afraid not," Cassandra replied in a heavy southern accent that she had perfected playing Blanche DuBois in college.

"Oh, sorry. You're a ringer for Ruby." The press ID dangling from his neck read HOLLYWOOD BULLETIN.

"If *only* I had her cheekbones. *And* her paycheck."

He laughed. "Are you enjoying the party?"

"Very *much* so," she drawled. "I'm having a *blast*."

"What's your name?"

"*Actually*, I'm the real Cat Burglar. So my name is *confidential*." The photographer grinned. She made a pretend clawing pose. "If you give me away, I'll have to scratch your eyes out."

"Your secret is safe with me. But my boss wants photos of Ruby, so I'd better go find her. I got here late, so I'm playing catch-up."

"Well you're in luck, because that's her coming this way. She's the one with the black pearl necklace." Cassandra jerked her head in the direction that Ruby and Wilfredo were fast approaching from. It was pretty clear Wilfredo intended to track her down.

But the photographer seemed happy to run interference. "Miss Greenwood? A quick photo?" he called out, running up to them. Ruby stopped short. After a moment's hesitation she set her purse down on a nearby table, and struck a three-quarter pose, flashing her best Hollywood smile.

"Here, take one of me with my friend too," she requested.

"Noah Brogans?" the photographer inquired.

Wilfredo shook his head. "Nope, Noah's at the bar. He's the Foxman with the bushy beard."

"Thanks! I'll get him next. A few more solo shots, Miss Greenwood!" begged the photographer. "Let's get the city view in the background." Ruby obligingly moved over to the railing. The impromptu little photo shoot had drawn a few curious spectators, which helped Cassandra put a few warm bodies between herself and Wilfredo. She needed to get out of there fast.

She was about to edge back into a group of fellow cat burglars when her eyes landed on Ruby's purse, sitting on the table nearby. Poking up out of a side flap was a plastic card with the hotel's double *H* logo. Walking over to it Cassandra set her champagne flute down right next to the purse and in the same smooth motion plucked the key card out of the flap, palming it. Half expecting to feel Wilfredo's firm hand on her shoulder, she turned away and melted into the crowd.

55. WILFREDO:
A FOX AMONG CLONES

Wilfredo could hardly believe it when Ruby waved him over to meet funny man Noah Brogans, one of his idols. She introduced Wilfredo as an up-and-coming Broadway actor and the three of them, all dressed in costume, sat at the bar for a friendly drink. It turned out Noah—who insisted Wilfredo call him Noah—was just as funny and clever off camera as he was on the screen. Wilfredo could hardly believe they had cast him in the role of Foxman.

Unsurprisingly, Noah's fox costume was incredible. It had a thick furry quality about it, and it hugged his body and stretched when he moved. Wilfredo's own costume was a little shabbier by comparison. It also felt a bit tight in spots, as it had both shrunk and faded in the wash.

A bunch of other Foxmans began to filter in, most of them wearing cheap orange fleece jumpsuits with pointy ears and glued-on eyes. These fox men and fox women were significantly outnumbered by cat burglars, who were suddenly everywhere.

Wilfredo needn't have worried that people would suspect he was the actual Foxman. His fellow partygoers merely assumed he was a cosplay genius and congratulated him on his handiwork. One guy even gave him a fist bump for the alien head sticker on his board, impressed by Wilfredo's attention to detail. Ruby was convinced that a helpful costume designer at the Cornelius was the real mastermind behind Wilfredo's improbable costume-making prowess.

At first he'd been concerned that seeing him in costume might jog Ruby's memory of his fox costume from their high school Pinocchio play. But fortunately, she didn't make the connection to whatever blurry memories she had from long ago.

Before the casting announcements, Noah and Ruby were whisked off to the VIP area behind the stage by their agents, and Wilfredo was left on his own. He got up from the bar and wandered over to the short wall in the back of the roof, where he leaned against a black ladder and looked out at the mix of old and modern buildings surrounding the hotel. A solitary wooden water tower jutted up into the sky from a nearby rooftop.

The big casting reveal soon got underway, and the two stars of the movie were called up onstage. Wilfredo cheered loudly for Ruby, and was impressed with how she handled herself in front of the audience. She played up her costume for the photographers who took a gazillion shots of her and Noah. Wilfredo had spent so much time with her recently he'd almost forgotten she was this big star.

But if Wilfredo was having a grand time, Captain Pete was out of sorts: *It's like the world's gone crazy, Freddy! Everywhere I look there's foxes and cat burglars jangling about like lunatics. First there's two of you, and now there's ten of you! And what's with the weird pounding music? In my day musicians played a fiddle or just whistled a tune!*

"Relax, Captain. Get a grip," Wilfredo muttered, his words drowned out as the DJ blasted his mixes across the rooftop. Wilfredo nursed his beer and leaned against the railing while he waited for Ruby to be done with her publicity commitments. His eye was drawn to the highly entertaining dancing cat burglars. Some were blond, some had straight black hair, some were short, some were tall and skinny. Ruby, of course, was their designated queen, in her tailored miniskirt, diamond-studded belt, and a clingy striped sweater that showed off her figure.

But there was one other Cat Burglar who really stood out from the crowd. Wilfredo noticed her hanging around on the fringes of the party. Her costume looked the most authentic out of anyone's. Her hair, her cat ears, and her makeup, were all dead-on. He found her resemblance to the actual Cat Burglar uncanny. Clearly everyone else just assumed she was a dedicated cosplayer. But that's what they thought about him too. Could it be that the real Cat Burglar had shown up at the party too?

That's definitely her, Freddy. I'd recognize that sly mug anywhere. She's probably casing the joint. You'd better hope she's not in cahoots with any of these other costumed freaks. Otherwise there's a major rooftop stickup in the works.

This mysterious cat burglar was on the opposite side of the deck from him. Intrigued, he set down his empty bottle and took off in her direction. But by the time he got to where she'd been standing she was gone. His suspicions intensified. He caught sight of a red-haired cat burglar on the dance floor, but when he snuck up around her she turned out to be a completely different girl.

Not to be dissuaded, he followed the perimeter of the rooftop around, keeping his eyes peeled for redheaded cat burglars. His persistence paid off when he spotted her hunched behind a group of men in suits. He would soon clear this up. He set out toward her taking a more circuitous route that would not reveal his approach. He was just about to close in when Ruby popped up in front of him, all done with her press obligations. She began babbling about something or other, but he cut her off. "Wanna hear something crazy?" he yelled in her ear, over the din of the music. "I think that cat burglar over there might be the real Cat Burglar!"

"Wait. Are you kidding?" Ruby's eyebrows stitched together. She swiveled her head in the direction he was indicating and stared at the pretty red-haired young woman, who was chatting with a photographer. "You know, you're right! She looks just like the girl in the videos. I'd recognize that hair anywhere. Come on, let's go talk to her!"

"Exactly what I was thinking. Can you imagine if we caught the actual Cat Burglar at your launch party? That would get you some amazing press!"

"Wilfredo, you do realize everyone sees her as one of the good guys, right?"

"Well they shouldn't—she's a criminal."

Ruby rolled her eyes. "Don't let your costume go to your head, buddy. Let's just have a friendly conversation. This could be a one-time opportunity for me to pick her brain."

They crept across the rooftop, weaving their way between guests and waitstaff, as they approached her from the side. But just as they were getting close the photographer she was talking to turned around and jumped into their path, demanding a photo of Ruby. Torn between their mission and her promotional instincts, Ruby hesitated. Her love for publicity won the day and she posed for the photo, while Wilfredo stepped to the side. Should he push on without her? But then Ruby pulled *him* in for a shot. He tried to keep an eye on the Cat Burglar, but there were too many people in the way. When the photographer cajoled Ruby over to the railing for some shots with the skyline Wilfredo detached himself and tried to locate the mystery Cat Burglar. There she was, a short distance away. He saw her set her glass down on a table then pivot and walk briskly in the opposite direction from him. Wilfredo quickened his pursuit.

Over his shoulder Ruby called out to him. "Wilfredo, wait up!" He turned to see her hurrying after him. And when he looked back again the mystery Cat Burglar had disappeared into the crowd once again.

Ruby read the confusion on his face. "Don't tell me you lost track of her! Didn't you see where she went?"

Wilfredo pointed to where he'd last seen her. "She went that way! Let's go."

But after walking around the roof twice they found no sign of her anywhere. She had vanished, and Ruby was annoyed. "This is hopeless. She's gone."

Wilfredo looked sheepish. "She must be around here somewhere."

"Forget it. We'll never find her now. And I need a drink, let's just head over to the VIP area."

Wilfredo kept his eyes peeled as they made their way over to the roped-off corner of the roof, but Ruby was right, the trail had gone cold. He took a seat next to Ruby on a love seat that had a little place card with her name written on it. Annie was hovering nearby, looking adorable in a petite cat burglar costume. Ruby waved her over. "Hey, would you mind getting me a glass of Pinot noir?"

"Sure, right away." Annie smiled. "Wilfredo? Can I get you anything?"

"A beer would be amazing, thanks! Any kind of lager will do."

Two minutes later Annie returned, carrying the two drinks. She handed Wilfredo a frosty mug of golden beer. Then she went to hand Ruby *her* drink, but somehow she tripped on the deck. She managed to catch herself, but not before the entire contents of the wineglass splashed right in Ruby's lap.

"My costume! I'm soaked!" A dark red stain was spreading fast on the white striped portions of her sweater. A horrified Annie rushed off to find paper towels, and when she returned she went to work blotting Ruby's dripping sweater. Annie apologized profusely, and Wilfredo was a little surprised that Ruby wasn't berating her. "Accidents happen, sweetie. Don't beat yourself up. But I'd better go change out of this sweater, pronto. Luckily, I have a spare hanging in my closet. I hope I can make it down to my room without running into any photographers, the last thing I need is for the paparazzi to get a picture of me like this. Annie, you stay here, and if anyone needs me tell them I'll be back soon. Wilfredo, would you be a dear and help whisk me out of here discreetly? The stairs are thataway, and my room is just one floor down."

"Sure. Anything I can do to help."

You hear that, Freddy? She needs you to help her out of those wet clothes. Man your battle stations, you chicken-livered castaways! Let fly the skull and bones! Ready the grappling hooks and get ready for boarding!

56. CASSANDRA:
THE CAT BURGLAR STRIKES BACK

Cassandra walked down one flight of stairs from the roof and found herself in a long carpeted hallway with closed doors on either side. Wilfredo had mentioned Ruby was staying in a penthouse loft so she guessed one of these rooms had to be hers. Cassandra remembered seeing a photo Ruby had posted online, taken from the terrace of her room with the Empire State Building in the background, which would put it on the left-hand side of the corridor. But that still left three different doors to choose from.

Her pulse quickened when one of those three doors opened, and a middle-aged hotel housekeeper in a gray uniform appeared. Cassandra stopped short in the corridor and pretended to be reading something important on her phone screen as the housekeeper walked down the hallway in her direction pushing a cart stacked with baked cookies and bottles of water. Cassandra looked up as the woman went by.

"Good afternoon, Miss Ruby. I just left two cookies on your coffee table, just how you like."

Cassandra stole a quick look at her name tag. "Thank you, Aurora," she replied in her best Ruby imitation, surmising that the housekeeper must have seen Ruby in her costume earlier. The still-smiling woman kept going and disappeared into the next room down. Cassandra hurried over to the door the housekeeper had come out of. She inserted and removed the key card. The light turned green, and she pushed open the door.

Must be nice, thought Cassandra, taking in the palatial loft. Gold-patterned wallpaper and robin's egg lampshades lent the room a boho downtown vibe. There was a little seating area, a desk, an exposed clawfoot tub in a corner by the windows, and a California king with a tufted headboard. On the far wall diaphanous white drapes framed French doors and the terrace beyond. Cassandra poked her head into a spacious marble bathroom with a rainforest shower.

Tugging open the wide folding doors of an expansive closet Cassandra zeroed in on the room safe. Pressing numbers with her knuckles she gambled on *one, two, three, four*. No luck. A quick web search revealed Ruby's birthday, but no combination of those dates worked either. Giving up on the safe she began to rifle through the drawers in the closet. She found plenty of scarves, underwear, workout clothes, and a disturbing number of shoes, but nothing worth stealing.

Next she checked the desk drawers and the bedside tables. There were a pair of earrings and a watch lying about, but both struck her as cheap fashion accessories. Baffled, she stood in the center of the room and surveyed her surroundings. This little venture was feeling like a bust. It was time to cut her losses and get out.

Just as she was reaching for the door handle she recognized a silvery voice in the hallway: "It's right down here. They call it the Empire loft, because of the view. Where the heck has my key card gone off to? Not to worry, I have another one in my bag somewhere. I'm always losing them, so I make the front desk give me plenty of extras."

Cassandra looked around in a panic. At a glance her options for hiding were the bathroom, the closet, or the terrace. She chose the closet, hopping up onto the built-in chest of drawers and pushing herself to the back, behind a thick row of shirts and sweaters hanging from a pole, reaching through the clothes to pull the closet doors shut. Then she hugged her knees to her chest and did her best to quiet her racing heart, wondering if this was the moment her citywide crime spree finally caught up with her.

"Oh you have to come in and check out the view from my private terrace. And I bet there are some chocolate chip cookies on my coffee table. They seem to appear in my room as if by magic. I think the housekeeper is doing her darnedest to sabotage my career. If you eat them you'll be doing me a huge favor! It will only take me a minute to change my sweater."

Cassandra could hear them now inside the room, on the other side of the closet door, shuffling around. She couldn't believe her bad luck. Why would they leave the party so soon?

"I hope this stain comes out. Otherwise my sweater is ruined. Good thing I have a spare. That Annie is such a klutz!"

"Yeah, she really nailed you with that wineglass."

Inside the closet a lightbulb went off in Cassandra's head. This must be a ploy by Ruby to lure Wilfredo down to her room, just as she had predicted. The closet doors were suddenly thrown open and Cassandra tensed. A delicate hand reached out and yanked a hanger off the pole with a black and white sweater on it. Suddenly there was a gap and Cassandra could see into the room. She nudged a clothes hanger over a smidgen so as to conceal herself better, but left a little sliver of space to peek through. She really hoped Wilfredo wasn't going to fall for Ruby's orchestrated seduction attempt.

He was standing a few feet away munching on a cookie, his hood pulled back to reveal his face. Ruby stood facing him with her back to the closet. She reached up to unclasp the necklace from behind her neck, then stepped out of sight momentarily. There was a delicate clattering sound that suggested the pearls had landed on the glass-covered desk.

"I'd better get out of this wet sweater!" Without warning Ruby crossed her arms, pulled the striped sweater off over her head, tossing it haphazardly in the direction of the bathroom. Cassandra's mouth fell open, shocked at how brazen Ruby could be. Wilfredo's eyes went wide in surprise as he took in the sight of Ruby, still wearing her cat ears and tail, standing there in a miniskirt and a red bra. "Nothing you haven't seen before, right?" She held her arms up in a ta-da gesture. "I'm so glad you came today, Wilfredo. You've been such a great friend to me in New York." Ruby took a step in his direction, and Wilfredo swallowed hard.

Cassandra, sitting in her little nook, found that she was digging her nails into her legs. For some reason she wanted to leap out and put Ruby in a headlock. She took a long slow breath, reminding herself that betraying her presence would put her in a highly problematic situation.

Fortunately, Wilfredo didn't seem eager to take the bait. "Maybe I'll check out that terrace view while you get dressed?"

Ruby stomped her foot on the rug. "Seriously, Wilfredo? Are you really so hung up on Cassandra that you're going to run out on the terrace to get away from me?"

Cassandra's jaw dropped once again. She leaned a little closer to the gap between the hangers. Wilfredo was staring at Ruby with a puzzled look. "Who said I'm hung up on Cassandra?"

"Well you are aren't you?"

Wilfredo rubbed his chin and didn't immediately reply. Finally he said: "Yeah. I am crazy about her. But don't tell anyone. I don't want her to find out before I figure out how to tell her myself." Hearing this Cassandra's heart leaped. Why couldn't he have just mustered up his courage and let her know how he felt? If she hadn't been hiding in this closet she would probably have been the last person to find out. Then again, she reminded herself—he might feel very differently about her once he found out she was the Cat Burglar.

In the seconds it took for these thoughts to run through her head, the drama on the other side of the wall of clothes continued uninterrupted. Ruby wasn't so easily dissuaded. Curling a manicured finger through a lock of red hair she shot him a smoldering look. "If anything were to happen between us it would be our little secret. You get that, right?"

Wilfredo looked at her earnestly. "I just think that would ruin everything."

"Do you even have a shot with Cassandra? I mean she just broke it off with her fiancé. Not exactly good timing, is it?"

"It's terrible timing. And she's way out of my league. But I need to take the chance and tell her, or I'll always regret it."

Ruby shook her head disappointed. "Well I hope she doesn't break your heart. There's something shady about her. I always get a feeling like she's hiding something."

"Aren't we all?"

"What's that supposed to mean?"

"There's a rumor going around that you and Chad Evans are an item."

"I can't believe you've heard about that. No one's supposed to know! Someone's been a real blabbermouth. It's true, but Chad's been cheating on me with his costar Gabriella on the set of his movie. So things are a bit shaky between us at the moment."

"Oh. That sucks. I'm really sorry, Ruby. So are you just looking to even the score?"

"How else am I supposed to forgive him?"

"What if you don't forgive him? What if you put him in the rearview mirror and find someone new?"

"I'm not sure I can do that," Ruby said softly.

"Because you're in love with him?"

Ruby let out a heavy sigh. "You have no idea the kind of dating pressure that comes with being a Hollywood star. I don't have a lot of options."

"Are you kidding? A gorgeous girl like you could get any man she wanted."

"Apparently not."

"Hey, do I need to remind you that back in high school you treated me like I was invisible for years?"

Ruby seemed chagrined. "I guess that's true." She slipped on the clean sweater and went to stand in front of the mirror. "There, are you happy now? Or do I need to put a bag over my head?"

"Was this whole wine incident just for my benefit?"

Ruby looked down at her feet. "I told Annie to do it. And now I feel like an idiot."

"It's pretty funny if you think about it. What do you say we head back upstairs?"

"If we go upstairs now Annie's going to figure out the whole plan was a big fail."

"I see. Then how about we grab a couple drinks from your mini fridge, and sit out on the terrace for a few minutes. Then, when we go back upstairs in twenty minutes, Annie can let her imagination run wild."

Ruby sniffed. "You would do that for me?"

"Of course."

"Friends?"

"Always."

Cassandra heard the sound of a fridge being opened, followed by glass bottles knocking against each other. "Do you really think I could find a new boyfriend? Because I think maybe you're right about Chad."

"We're gonna find you an incredible guy."

Ruby walked over to the terrace door and slid it open, and their voices faded as they walked outside. Cassandra counted to ten, then she risked poking out her head. She saw an orange arm resting on a railing, but otherwise they were blocked from view by the fluttering curtain. Cassandra slid her legs around and hopped down. Her eyes were drawn to the pearl necklace, sitting ten feet away on the desk, the iridescent strands giving off an alluring glow. Treading softly, she closed the distance in a few steps, lifted the gems carefully off the desk, and dropped them into her drawstring bag. She left a Cat Burglar card in their place, then she darted toward the exit. She did her best to close the heavy hotel door softly behind her, but it shut with a loud clunk. Cassandra groaned inwardly. Could they have heard that from out on the terrace? She hurried away down the hallway.

57. WILFREDO: ON THE HUNT IN THE HORATIO HOTEL

To Wilfredo's great relief they were back outdoors and Ruby was fully clothed. She had thrown him for a loop when she whisked off her sweater and gazed at him alluringly. He should've seen it coming, especially after Cassandra had warned him. Put in an awkward position he'd been forced to turn down his high school crush *again*, but at least she hadn't slapped him this time.

The Captain was baffled: *Do you need your eyes checked, Freddy? She was standing right there in her unmentionables, begging for a bit of canoodling, and you made her walk the plank! Do you have a screw loose? We could book you some couch time with one of them headshrinkers if you think it'd help!*

Wilfredo willed the Captain to silence. He didn't need a shrink. What was he even talking about?

They don't literally shrink your head, you know. They just talk to you and give you pills. I learned that the hard way!

He tuned out Captain Pete's ramble and focused on Ruby. It was obvious she had just intended to use him to get back at her two-timing boyfriend. Wilfredo was struck by the fact that even celebrities were sometimes lonely, and he was convinced that what Ruby really needed right now was a friend.

With her Chad Evans troubles out in the open it was like

the floodgates had opened up, and a torrent of words were pouring out of her: "And you know what else really pisses me off? Chad is convinced that if he keeps sending bouquets of flowers to my room I'll eventually come around. He thinks tulips are some sort of get out of jail free card! Well I'm tired of—" But a loud *click* coming from inside the hotel room stopped her cold, mid-sentence. Ruby's eyebrows furrowed.

"What was that?" Wilfredo asked. "Do you think it's housekeeping?"

"Beats me!" They hurried back inside.

Alarmed, Ruby ran to where she'd left the pearl necklace and let out a shriek. She pressed her hands to her face. "Oh my god! It's gone! How can it be gone? It was sitting right there on the desk when we walked out a minute ago!"

Wilfredo pointed to the white card resting on the desk in its place. "I have a bad feeling about this."

Ruby snatched it up and stared at the little cat face stamp. "It's the Cat Burglar's calling card! This is crazy! Do you think she was hiding in here the whole time? Maybe that's why my other key card was missing!"

"I bet she grabbed it when you put your bag down to pose for those photos! We were right about her. She *was* the real Cat Burglar! I'm going after her, she can't have gone far!"

Ruby reached for the hotel phone. "I'll tell the front desk to stop anyone in a cat burglar costume from exiting. And to call the police! I am so dead if we don't get this necklace back. I had to sign all sorts of paperwork promising to keep it safe. Hello? Front desk? This is Ruby Greenwood in the Empire loft! I've been robbed! My pearl necklace worth twenty grand has been stolen!" Wilfredo pulled his hood over his eyes, grabbed his longboard, and was on his way out the door as Ruby sketched out the details for the front desk person.

The hallway was empty. He ran down to the elevator area and found it equally deserted. She must have hopped on a down elevator already. With any luck hotel security would stop her before she got out. He jabbed a finger repeatedly on the elevator down buttons on facing walls, wondering if he was better off hustling down the nine flights of stairs.

You gotta hand it to that Cat Burglar gal, Freddy. She is full of surprises. She stole that necklace right out from under your nose. Made you look like a fool!

"Well she won't get away this time," Wilfredo muttered darkly.

I had a feeling someone was eavesdropping on us! I could sense a presence in the room. You know that feeling, Freddy?

"Boy do I," he muttered.

Wilfredo was still waiting impatiently for the elevator when Ruby showed up, out of breath. "I need to go up to the roof and find Artie, my agent. He is going to kill me when he hears the news, but I'd better tell him right away and he's not picking up his cell. There's so much press around that they're bound to get wind of this, and then all hell is going to break loose! Cat Burglar actress gets cat burgled! I'm going to be a laughingstock!"

"Maybe you can spin it so that it turns into publicity for the movie?"

Ruby looked at him with amazement. "You know, Wilfredo, you're starting to sound like an industry pro."

He poked both elevator buttons repeatedly and stared at the red numbers lighting up above the four doors. One of them was up on the roof and didn't seem to be moving at all. Two others were lingering at lower levels, and the fourth elevator was slowly working its way up. "Let's hope that hotel security locked things down before she got out."

"I told them to look out for a young woman in a Cat Burglar costume with dark, reddish-brown hair. They said they would stop and search any young women matching that description, and that a couple police detectives already happened to be in the building."

"That's lucky. That Cat Burglar is wily though. She may sneak out a back door. I'll head down to the lobby in case they need help identifying her."

"They already used their walkie talkie thingies to alert security at the service entrance. Just let them do their job, you're not the real Foxman, Wilfredo. Look at you with your hood back on and your silly skateboard. I swear that suit is going right to your head!"

"No it isn't." He protested.

"Typical actor. Put you in a costume and you start playing the part."

"I'm just trying to help you get your necklace back," Wilfredo grumbled. "What do you want me to do? Sit upstairs and drink a beer?"

"There's only two ways out of this building. So unless that woman grows wings I think she's gonna have a hard time getting away."

"Don't underestimate her."

Ruby placed a finger on her lips as her face suddenly clouded. "Wait a second. Isn't there a ladder up on the roof, over in the back near the VIP area?"

"There sure is, I remember seeing it earlier. It leads down to a neighboring rooftop."

"You don't think she wouldn't try and escape that way, do you?"

"She's the Cat Burglar," replied Wilfredo. "Using ladders to get away is probably second nature to her."

Finally, an empty elevator opened before them and a green arrow lit up with a ding. Ruby hopped inside as Wilfredo hesitated. Then he stuck out a hand, blocked the closing door, and stepped in beside her. "Someone needs to cut off that rooftop escape route."

"Boys. Always playing the hero! Just promise me you won't do anything stupid." Wilfredo shot her a pained look as the doors slid closed and the elevator set in motion. He was sorely tempted to just tell Ruby that he was the real Foxman. That would put an end to her snide comments. But instead he just bit his tongue for the short ride up.

58. DETECTIVE MOLINA: SIFTING FOR CLUES

Detective Molina stood next to a mirrored column in the lobby of the Horatio Hotel, staring at his reflection. A creeping sense of personal shame overtook him and he wondered if this moment represented a low point in his policing career. Garcia was to blame, he decided, she had talked him into it, insisting that the best way to go undercover at a costume party was to dress in costume. Thus, he had been transformed into a portly, bald, mustachioed cat burglar, with the requisite black-and-white sweater, black pants, and face mask. The overall effect in his case was decidedly comical, a fact that was inescapably driven home by passersby in the lobby who were taking one look at him and sniggering behind their hands.

Detective Garcia, done chatting with hotel security, strolled over to him, an irritating smirk on her face. "Cheer up, Molina! You're gonna be the life of the party. I can't wait to see you out on the dance floor!"

"*Fiat justitia ruat caelum*," he muttered sullenly.

"You lost me on that one. You're gonna have to run it through the translator."

"Let justice be done though the heavens fall to ruin."

"Good one! Well, we'd better head upstairs, guests are starting to arrive."

Detective Molina reluctantly followed his partner over to the elevators. She was also dressed as a cat burglar, and while she was no skinny mini either, with her large bust and wide hips, the costume looked perfectly fine on her. His brown suit and pressed white shirt were hanging in the dressing room behind the front desk that the staff used to change into their uniforms. He wanted to run there and change back into regular clothes, but he knew he couldn't risk being recognized by Ruby Greenwood up on the rooftop. There was no turning back.

They were very much under the gun, with Lieutenant Kopski breathing down their necks, demanding that they wrap up this case once and for all. They had placed all their chips on staking out this casting announcement party. Garcia was convinced that the party's press presence meant that the evening was ripe for another publicity-motivated theft. Especially since Ruby was wearing a high-end pearl necklace, the perfect target for a phony robbery.

Their plan was simple, not to let Ruby Greenwood or her necklace out of their sight. And if the supposed Cat Burglar struck again they would jump in and make an arrest. With any luck the whole charade would then unravel and they would be able to prove that everything had been orchestrated by Ruby Greenwood and her cohorts at the movie production company, with the sole purpose of drumming up interest in their stupid movie. Then the full weight of the law would fall on their shoulders. Misuse of police time and filing false reports were no small matters.

The detectives had taken the precaution of placing a bug in a lamp in Miss Greenwood's bedroom and in the backstage

VIP area. That way they could easily listen in on conversations taking place in both locations, and hopefully anticipate any unforeseen developments.

Up on the roof the party proved tortuous for Detective Molina. People kept chuckling and snapping photos of him, even when he glowered at them menacingly. If his picture ended up on social media he didn't think he could bear the humiliation. Taking a deep breath, he reminded himself that it was best to remain stoic in the face of adversity. He kept his eyes open for anyone suspicious, but it seemed to him that the whole rooftop was crawling with shady characters. A smiling Detective Garcia, covering the opposite corner of the roof, gave him a cheerful thumbs-up every time she looked his way.

Detective Molina was carefully studying the crowd when he noticed a particular cat burglar standing over to the side. Unlike most of the costumed attendees her resemblance to the actual Cat Burglar was remarkable. He pressed the TALK button on his radio. "Garcia, check out the Cat Burglar standing on the edge of the crowd on my left."

"Wow, if I didn't know better I'd say that was Ruby. They're like clones! No necklace though."

"It's pretty odd if you ask me. We'd better keep an eye on her. It's possible they brought in a double, since Ruby can't realistically steal her own jewels."

"So you think this new girl is part of the whole setup?"

Detective Molina smoothed his mustache with his fingers. "Very likely."

Other than the Cat Burglar stand-in, everything seemed to be unfolding more or less as they expected. That is until the moment Miss Greenwood had wine spilled on her by her clumsy assistant. They listened to the exchange on their earpieces, and then watched the actress sneak over to the stairs, heading back down to her room to change. That Foxman friend of hers was in tow, and he too was wearing a suspiciously authentic-looking costume.

Molina's radio crackled and Garcia's voice came through. "Do you think we should follow them?"

Molina hunched over by the wall so he wouldn't be overheard. "We would get made in an empty hotel corridor. Let's just tune into the listening device in her room and use audio to monitor the situation."

"Roger that," Garcia replied. "She will probably be back up in a few minutes."

"Provided those two don't take advantage of their getaway for a little hotel room hanky-panky."

"Hanky-panky? Do you mean screwing around? Oh my god—do you think they would keep their costumes on?" Garcia's voice rippled with excitement at this prospect.

"Let's hope it doesn't come to that."

"Are you kidding? It's moments like this that drew me to police work in the first place."

Detective Molina sighed. The problem with the younger generation was that their moral fiber was frayed beyond repair. He adjusted the input on his earpiece and was soon listening to the voices of Miss Greenwood and her Foxman friend from inside the hotel room. For a moment it seemed to Molina that their encounter was heading in an all too predictable direction, but then the young man in the Foxman costume surprised them all by rejecting Miss Greenwood's advances. A narrow miss it seemed. Unfortunately, the two subject's voices cut out when they stepped out on the terrace. Molina and his partner exchanged a look of alarm. They were suddenly disconnected, having lost both eyes and ears on their target. Garcia hurried over to his corner of the roof so they could confer in a hushed whisper.

But they didn't have long to wait, as a couple minutes later a piercing shriek from Miss Greenwood blasted in his ear, followed by her loud announcement that the gems had been stolen. Garcia, hearing the same development, nudged him in the ribs. "Told you so! The necklace *was* the target of the robbery, and Ruby is already playing her role of victim to the hilt!"

Both detectives rushed over to the dedicated rooftop elevator. They needed to ensure the hotel was locked down, so no one could escape the premises with the necklace. It was crucial they reach the lobby before anyone could make off with the jewels. After that was taken care of they could then interview Ruby Greenwood and try to resolve this case once and for all. On their way down to the lobby they listened to Miss Greenwood's melodramatic phone call with the front desk, and Molina exchanged a skeptical glance with his partner.

Thankfully the dedicated elevator zipped them straight to the ground floor in no time at all, and they immediately checked in with the hotel security liaison to make sure checkpoints were being set up at both exits to the hotel. Detective Garcia called the robbery into the precinct and requested two squad cars be sent over for backup. Molina knew it was quite possible that Lieutenant Kopski himself would show up at this point. This operation had better end with at least one arrest—both of their careers depended on it.

Finding the exits well covered, Detective Molina jogged to the back room where his brown suit was hanging. With a great sense of relief he tore off the striped sweater, stepped out of the black pants, and hurriedly changed into his shirt and suit, knowing it wouldn't be long before other personnel from the thirteenth precinct joined them on the scene. When he emerged he found Garcia waiting for him, and she too had changed into her usual dark jeans and navy sports jacket.

"Well, the lobby is secure," said Molina, "and there's no sign of a thief down here."

"Time to head back upstairs and have a little chat with Ruby Greenwood."

"Exactly," agreed Molina. "We can't let her stash the necklace somewhere and dodge responsibility for the theft. We need to locate those pearls immediately!"

59. CASSANDRA:
NO REST FOR THE WICKED

Cassandra jogged down the hallway to the elevator bank, punched the down button, and stood there staring at the numbers above the elevator doors. The elevators seemed to be moving one floor at a time, as if mischievous children had pressed every button. She had her face turned away from the video camera she had spotted up on the wall. If it weren't for that camera she would have been able to do a quick switcheroo, ditching her costume and makeup, and pulling on the black rain slicker she had in her bag. But it felt too risky until she found a more private spot. For now she just needed to put as much distance as she could between herself and the scene of the crime.

The drawstring bag felt heavier with the necklace in it. Cassandra grinned as she pictured Ruby's face when she realized her precious pearls were missing. This was the perfect payback for all those petty put-downs Ruby liked to dish out, and being a wealthy TV star she could easily afford the loss.

Eavesdropping on them in the closet, Cassandra's views on her lookalike had softened slightly. She now realized that the snotty actress was just a scared young woman with her own set of troubles. Not that she planned on forgiving Ruby anytime soon for her shameless attempt to ensnare poor Wilfredo, who had thankfully passed that test with flying colors.

Not only that, but he had even confessed to being crazy about Cassandra herself. A notion that had yet to fully sink in. It's true she had suspected this for a while, but she'd never let herself believe it. Since her own feelings echoed his, that meant she needed to figure out quickly if she was ready to dive into something new.

Cassandra was brought back to the urgency of the moment by a loud screech coming from down the hallway. It was safe to assume that meant the theft had been discovered. That stupid door click must have given her away after all. She was about to bolt for the stairs at the end of the hallway, but just then the elevator doors finally opened, so Cassandra hopped in. There was one other person in the elevator, the housekeeper she had bumped into earlier. The woman greeted her politely once again.

"Thanks for the cookies, Aurora," Cassandra said, trying to ease the tension in the confined space.

The lady smiled, but her smile did not quite reach her eyes. "You're very welcome, Miss Ruby. Where's that pretty pearl necklace you had on earlier?" There was a note of suspicion in her voice.

"Oh, I have it here in my bag. Thanks for reminding me. I should be wearing it for the photographers" Cassandra fished out the necklace. "Would you mind helping me put it on?"

This time the woman's smile lit up her face. "Of course, Miss Ruby. I'm happy to help. You know, it's funny, for a second there I wasn't quite sure if it was really you behind that mask."

Cassandra slouched, turning her neck toward the woman and pulling her hair out of the way. The housekeeper's nimble fingers made quick work of the clasp. "That's the whole point of masks, Aurora. They keep people from recognizing you."

"Ain't that the truth," the woman chuckled, her hands fastening themselves to her cart as the sixth-floor number dinged. "You have a lovely evening, Miss Ruby." The housekeeper shuffled out the open doors.

Cassandra jabbed the lobby button even though it was already lit up, and quickly tucked the necklace under her sweater, checking her reflection in the mirrored wall to make sure it was fully concealed. Frustratingly, the elevator made several more stops on its way down, picking up passengers each time, including a woman in a wheelchair. Cassandra attracted a few odd looks in her costume, even as she slunk to the back of the elevator and did her best to avoid eye contact.

When they reached the ground floor she was the last to exit, which was fortunate, because just as she was about to step out she caught sight of a large man in a dark suit scurrying toward the front entrance, followed by a bunch of similarly dressed men. The lead man called out to his team: "You three stand by the front door and keep your eyes peeled for anyone in a cat burglar costume, or any young women with long red or brown hair. And you two get over to the service entrance and do the same!" Cassandra backed up into the relative safety of the elevator and after a moment's hesitation she pushed the button for the top floor. A trickle of sweat ran down her back. There had to be another way out of this hotel. In the meantime she would be safer up on the roof where she could lose herself in a crowd full of cat burglar decoys. And if worse came to worst she could always ditch the jewels in a planter and feign innocence.

60. WILFREDO:
A VILLAIN UNMASKED

Back on the roof the DJ was still blasting tunes for a lively dance contingent that included about a dozen costumed cat burglars. Wilfredo's gaze skipped from one to the next, making sure none of them were the real deal. Ruby peeled off to grab Annie from the bar, wanting to enlist her personal assistant's help to track down her missing agent. And Wilfredo wandered over to the far end of the roof, stationing himself close to where the narrow ladder looped over the edge of the building. He craned his head over the side and found himself gazing down on an empty rooftop twenty feet below. The glistening silver roof had a hutch with a rusty door, and beyond that the rickety old water tower, silhouetted in the late afternoon light.

The Captain's voice whispered in his ear: *Looks like you struck out again, Freddy. That Cat Burglar lass has already jumped ship. She's slippery as an eel!*

"I have a hunch she's still around here somewhere," Wilfredo insisted stubbornly.

This is turning into a regular obsession for you, Freddy. Better be careful or you'll wind up like my pal Ahab. And let's just say things didn't end well for him. Unless you consider getting dragged to your death by a giant albino whale to be a fun time!

Wilfredo turned and scrutinized the rooftop partiers one

more time. And there, in a far corner, removed from everyone else, he spotted a redheaded cat burglar skulking about on her cell phone. She was facing away from him, so he couldn't see her face, but judging from her hair, her height, and her figure it had to be her. He took off in her direction, cutting right through a cluster of inebriated dancers, not daring to take his eyes off his target for a second. Creeping up behind her he put his hand firmly on her shoulder. The redheaded figure spun around, and he found himself staring into Ruby's startled face.

"Seriously, Wilfredo? What the heck? You scared the bejesus out of me! I'm busy doing damage control, and I don't need you sneaking up behind me and giving me the Vulcan death grip."

"Sorry, Ruby. I thought you were her. Weren't you headed over to the bar?"

"My agent called me back and I ducked over here for some privacy. Now if you don't mind, I have a major fire to put out, remember?" Annoyed, she turned away and resumed her phone conversation. Wilfredo wandered off dejectedly, taking the long way around the dance floor as he made his way back in the direction of the ladder. That stupid croc was probably right and the Cat Burglar must have already made her escape.

He happened to be facing the entrance at that moment, with the elevators directly in his line of sight, and he could scarcely believe his eyes when another Cat Burglar stepped out of the sliding elevator doors. He stopped short and peered intently at her profile. She was about fifty feet away, but his gut told him that this time there could be no mistake. She had a furtive look about her as she glanced left and right, her long hair swishing from side to side. Wilfredo ducked behind a planter to avoid being seen. Finally he'd caught a break! He figured that with her escape blocked off in the lobby she must have come back up to the roof to hide. Using other guests to shield himself from view he set out to intercept her. Too late he realized she was heading straight toward the back of the roof where the black ladder could be found. His longboard was still tucked under his arm, so when he reached a relatively clear stretch of roof he threw it down and hopped on, giving up on the stealth approach as he rolled across terracotta tiles. He snaked around a waiter in his path as he picked up speed. Sensing his presence she glanced back, surprise registering in her eyes when she saw him. Then she looked straight ahead and her eyes locked on the rails of the ladder. She broke into a sprint.

He drew close just as she threw a leg over the ledge. He jumped off his board and yelled, "Where do you think you're going?!"

"I'll settle for anywhere but here." She took a couple steps down and disappeared over the edge. Wilfredo tucked his board under his arm, grabbed hold of the curved railing, and climbed up on the ledge. He reached down with his foot until he felt it connect with a metal rung, and bit by bit he descended the ladder, peering down occasionally at the masked woman below him.

She reached the rooftop about ten seconds before him and dashed away, making it all the way across the roof to the hutch by the time he'd hopped down from the bottom rung. He sprang onto his board and set off in pursuit, watching as she tugged futilely at the locked door. It would seem her luck had run out.

He skidded to a stop in front of her. He wouldn't underestimate her agility this time. He hesitated as he tried to figure out what would be the best way to tackle her. Grappling with people was well outside his comfort zone, doubly so if it his opponent was a member of the opposite sex. This was going to be tricky. She spun to face him, her back against the wall, a defiant look in her green eyes. "Every time I turn around, there you are. I'm beginning to think maybe you have a thing for me."

He spread out his arms in case she tried to run past him. "Don't flatter yourself. I just don't like people taking things that aren't theirs!"

"Personal property seems to mean a lot to you."

"It does. Especially if it belongs to a friend of mine. Now, give me back the pearl necklace. You should know the police are on their way."

"That's probably them coming down the ladder now."

Wilfredo was sure she was bluffing but he risked a quick glance over his shoulder. Sure enough two figures were descending the ladder from the hotel roof, a bald man in a brown suit, and a younger, stern-faced woman with short brown hair. They both looked vaguely familiar.

"Freeze! This is the police!" yelled the bald man. "Put your hands where we can see them!" At the sound of his baritone voice Wilfredo remembered where he knew them from. These guys were the same two donut-munching detectives who had interviewed him about his stolen wallet.

The two officers of the law soon reached the roof, the

older one huffing and puffing. The woman drew a yellow taser from a holster attached to her belt and Wilfredo's hands shot up of their own accord. "Easy now, I'm on your side. I was just making sure she didn't get away!"

The bald detective let out a snort. "I think you'll find the law takes a dim view of vigilantes. Both of you turn around and put your hands on your heads!"

Wilfredo did as he was told, but as the Cat Burglar spun around her drawstring bag swung in an arc, slipping out of her grasp, and went flying right over the nearby edge of the rooftop. Seconds later they heard it clatter to the ground about seven floors down.

"Whoops." The Cat Burglar said with a hint of a smile.

"You did that on purpose!" The female cop was incensed. "Any more funny business and things will go badly for you."

The bald detective stuck his head over the ledge. "I see the bag down in a basement stairwell. I'd better go and grab it before anyone else picks it up."

"Do we really care about the bag?" asked his partner.

"We can't let her just ditch the evidence. Without the jewels we have nothing to hold them on! We can't arrest them just for being in costume!"

"Damn. I guess you're right."

The bald detective tried the rooftop door without success, then turned around and ran back across the roof to the ladder. "Just cuff 'em and sit tight until I get back! We should have some backup rolling in soon."

"Don't worry. I got this!" the brunette detective assured him.

The bald cop disappeared back up the ladder.

"Okay, listen up. I've had it with you two clowns. Here's how we're going to do this. If you don't want to get zapped, I want both of you to walk back toward this ladder, nice and slow, that's it." With her left hand she undid a small case at her waist, then she crouched down and slid a pair of handcuffs along the ground toward them. "You! In the fox costume. Put one end around her wrist, slide the chain through the railing of the ladder, and then put the other on your own wrist. Nice and tight!" Wilfredo did as he was instructed, clicking the metal rings firmly into place.

"Maybe now you could stop pointing that thing at us?" he suggested.

The detective obligingly holstered her weapon. She stared at them with a smug expression. "You led us on quite the chase, but in the end we caught up with you. And guess what? It's time to find out who's behind the mask. Kitten girl, you're up first! Let's see who you really are!"

The Cat Burglar glanced at Wilfredo and seemed to hesitate. Then she reached up with her free hand and pulled her mask down around her neck, untucking her hair in the back. Wilfred's mouth fell open. Standing there right next to him was Cassandra. His mind reeled as he tried to make sense of the image his eyes were sending him.

The detective seemed as confused as he was. "Wait. You're not Ruby!"

"I was wondering if you might have me confused with someone else. There are a lot of Cat Burglars around tonight."

The detective looked flustered. Grabbing the walkie-talkie from her belt she held it to her mouth and pushed the button: "Molina, you there?"

Her radio crackled. "I'm here. Reading you loud and clear."

"This Cat Burglar isn't Ruby! I think we bagged the decoy!"

"I was worried something like that would happen. It's impossible to keep the two of them straight. And I got some more bad news. I just retrieved the bag, and there are no pearls in it."

"Crap. What do we do?"

"We need to find those jewels!"

The brunette detective was becoming agitated. "My guess is that Ruby Greenwood still has them. Or she stashed them somewhere. I'm gonna go back up to the party and track her down. We need answers!"

"What about those two suspects?"

"Don't worry. I've got them cuffed to the ladder—they aren't going anywhere. We'll swing around and pick them up later. Over and out." The detective clipped her walkie-talkie back on her belt. "You two sit tight. I'll be right back." Then she put a foot on a rung and began to climb.

Wilfredo watched her disappear up the ladder. Then he turned to the Cat Burglar standing silently beside him, staring at her in disbelief.

Cassandra smiled coyly. "You okay, Foxman? You look like you've seen a ghost." Now that she was only a foot away he wondered how he could ever have been fooled by a mask and a wig. Those fiery green eyes of hers were unmistakable. He had no idea whatsoever what to say to her. He'd been wanting to bring the Cat Burglar down all these months, but now she turned out to be the same girl he was nuts about. He felt like his mind was glitching. Cassandra was the Cat Burglar. Cassandra was a thief. An internal battle raged inside him as he attempted to reconcile this unexpected revelation with how he felt about her.

Captain Pete was laughing raucously. *Why don't you pull off your mask, Freddy, then we can have a proper reunion! She's gonna blow her cap when she finds out you were the Foxman all along. She hates that guy!*

Wilfredo considered that an excellent reason not to take his mask off if he could help it. "So what did you have planned for the necklace?" He asked her, his voice a little shaky.

"My plan is to give it to the New York Food Bank."

"That's nice of you. Too bad we're handcuffed to this stupid ladder, and you don't have it anymore. What did you do with it?"

She winked at Wilfredo and tugged down the neckline of her sweater, revealing lustrous black pearl strands tucked beneath it.

He goggled at her. "You were wearing them this whole time! That was risky."

"Hey, it's just a necklace, and I only borrowed it for a good cause, after all. Who knows how many families you could feed with this trinket. Now, as to the handcuffed-to-a-ladder problem . . ." He watched her as she plucked a bobby pin from the fringe of her red wig. "I watched a web video the other day that showed how to pick a handcuff with one of these. It didn't seem that hard."

"I guess that's how professional criminals spend their downtime. Brushing up on their skills."

"I've always considered my Cat Burglar exploits to be more of a hobby. In fact I've been thinking about hanging up my tail. You probably won't believe me, but if I get away tonight I'm calling it quits." She separated the two prongs of the hairpin, and bent a tip first one way and then the other, into a little zigzag shape. Then she poked the end of the pin into the handcuff keyhole. "These babies are double lock, so we gotta turn it counterclockwise first." There was a scraping sound followed by a soft *click*. "And now we turn it the other way." There was another *click*, and she tugged the ratchet teeth out and the cuff fell open. "Voilà!" she grinned. Before he could pull the handcuff free of the ladder she closed the other half on the railing, leaving him chained. She took a step back and regarded him quizzically.

"That was fair play," Wilfredo said. "You wriggled out of that one well enough. I think you'd better get out of here as quickly as you can!"

"And leave you hanging?"

"Don't worry about me."

"Nonsense. Where would I be without my Foxman?" She stepped closer and worked the tip of the bobby pin into his side of the handcuffs.

"Aren't you worried I might tackle you and wrestle the necklace away from you?"

"Do whatever you need to do. If that's how it has to go down, then so be it." Two clicks later his hand was also free, and the handcuffs were left dangling from the ladder.

"Thank you." He massaged his wrist. "What do we do now?"

She snapped her mask back into place. "I take it you aren't performing any citizen arrests?"

"Nope. I've decided it would be wrong of me to do the

NYPD's work for them. I wouldn't want to put anyone out of a job."

"That's very thoughtful of you."

"And, like you said—it's for a good cause."

"Well, what are we standing around for then? Let's get the heck off this roof. I bet we can get over that wall behind the water tower if we work together." Wilfredo grabbed his longboard and they ran over to where the building next door abutted the one they were on. The wall was about ten feet tall, too high up for one person to reach on their own. "Here, I'll give you a boost!" she said. "Try and grab onto the ledge." She interlocked her fingers and when he stepped on her hands she heaved upward.

His fingers snuck over the edge and gripped the slate-gray stonework. With a huge effort, and with Cassandra pushing on his foot from below, he managed to pull himself over the top. Lying facedown he anchored himself by wrapping a leg around the ledge, and extended an arm downward. She handed him his longboard first and he flipped it up onto the roof behind him. Then she grabbed his hand and he heaved upward. She scrambled up and over him nimbly, and they both rolled over the edge and collapsed in a pile on a third rooftop, breathing heavily. A surprised-looking cable guy in a blue polo shirt stared at them in amazement. They smiled and waved, then leaped to their feet and made a mad dash for the rooftop doorway, which the cable guy had helpfully left propped open.

They ran down the stairwell of the residential building, and moments later slipped out onto a murky sidewalk.

Down the street a couple squad cars were parked in front of the hotel, red and white lights flashing. They walked slowly in the opposite direction, sticking to the shadows, until they turned a corner and the hotel disappeared from view.

Captain Pete was incensed. *I can't believe you've thrown your lot in with this crook! She's just gonna lead you down a path of crime that'll land all three of us behind bars! Don't you know I look terrible in stripes?*

Detective Molina hurried back to the hotel entrance and was startled to see Lieutenant Kopski talking to the chief of hotel security. Holding his breath, Molina snuck right past his superior, who had his back turned, and went into the lobby of the hotel. He didn't have much time. Kopski would surely find his way to the roof.

There had been no trace of the pearl necklace in the black bag. All he'd found was a rain slicker, a smashed-up makeup kit, and a handful of genuine-looking Cat Burglar calling cards. Detective Molina had a sinking feeling in the pit of his stomach. They simply couldn't afford another impasse, and right now they weren't even sure who the real Cat Burglar was, since the two women looked so much alike. Having two possible suspects at this stage of the investigation was almost as bad as having none.

Molina hopped into an open elevator, dread beginning to eat away at him. That young woman had just sent him on a wild goose chase ten floors down and back up again. He had underestimated his opponents from day one. He needed to start thinking about dodging the blame if they came up empty yet again. If throwing Detective Garcia under the bus was the only way to save his own neck, then so be it. The whole thing had been her idea after all.

His radio crackled. "I'm back on the roof," said Garcia. "I finally located Ruby Greenwood. She's sitting at the bar drinking white wine with Noah Brogans, looking like she doesn't have a care in the world."

"I'm in the elevator—wait for me. We'll question her together. Kopski is downstairs by the way."

"That's not good," his partner replied.

"We need to wrap up this case and make an arrest. Otherwise we are both toast."

Detective Molina exited the elevator and turned in the direction of the bar. His partner converged with him, notebook in hand, a determined look on her face. They approached the redheaded actress and Molina held up his badge. "Excuse me. Miss Greenwood?" She was still dressed in costume, with her mask on.

She glanced up at him doubtfully, then a look of recognition passed across her face. "Lord love a duck, not you two again! I remember you two from the spa. I hope we're not relying on your investigative skills to find my missing necklace."

"If you don't mind, my partner and I would like to have a word with you. Would you please step over to the side with us."

"Oh we can talk here at the bar. I just told Noah all about the theft!"

Detective Garcia looked piqued. "We have a few questions about that missing pearl necklace. I understand the robbery took place down in your room?"

"Yes. That Cat Burglar swiped it right out from under our noses."

"So you were in the room at the time it went missing."

"Yes. I mean we were out on the terrace."

Molina stared at Ruby blankly. "Who's we? Did you have a friend there with you?" They already knew the answer to this, thanks to their listening device, but asking questions you already knew the answer to was a great way to trip up liars.

"Yes, my friend Wilfredo was with me. He came to the party dressed as Foxman. He's around here somewhere."

Noah Brogans's face lit up. "Great guy that Wilfredo! And an amazing costume. I wonder where he ran off to."

Detective Molina gave the actor a stern look. "If you don't mind, sir, this is official police business."

"Oh, sorry, sorry. My bad. I'll keep my trap shut. Just pretend I'm not here!"

Ruby looked annoyed. "I already told hotel security everything. So why are the two of you standing here harassing me, instead of searching for the thief?"

Garcia tapped her pen on her notebook. "Just answer our questions, Miss Greenwood. Did either you or your friend see the thief?"

"No, we heard the room door click shut, and when we went back inside to investigate the necklace was gone"

Garcia's eyes narrowed. "So for all you know it could have been housekeeping that took it?"

"She left a card!" Ruby fished the card out of her purse and handed it to Detective Molina, who stared at it. It was identical to the cards he'd found in the bag. So either the other Cat Burglar *was* the real one, or the two women were working together.

Garcia pressed on. "Assuming this card is genuine, how do you suppose the thief gained access to your room?"

"I think she stole my room key from my bag."

"How convenient." Detective Garcia scribbled furiously in her notebook. "And you saw no sign of her when you were in your room?"

"No. She was probably hiding somewhere." Ruby's eyes shot out sparks. "Do you make a habit of harassing the victim? What are you guys? The world's worst detectives?" Garcia stiffened, and gave the actress a poisoned look.

Detective Molina jumped in again: "May I ask *why* you decided to go down to your room in the middle of the party with your *friend*?"

"I don't care for your tone," Ruby replied indignantly. "We went down there because someone spilled wine on me and I needed to change."

The bald detective looked thoughtful. In hindsight, considering the location of the burglary, Miss Greenwood's exit from the party seemed suspect. "And who exactly spilled this wine on you?"

"It was my clumsy assistant, Annie." Ruby pointed to a petite young lady in a cat burglar costume standing close by with her hands clasped in front of her and an anxious look on her face.

Detective Molina beckoned her over with a curled finger. "Is this true? You accidentally spilled wine on Miss Greenwood?"

Annie bit her lip as she looked apologetically at her boss. "Sorry, Ruby. I can't lie to the police!" Turning to face the detectives she said: "Ruby asked me to spill wine on her and make it look like an accident."

Detective Molina raised a stiff eyebrow. "I see. So the wine spilling was just a ruse. How peculiar, Miss Greenwood. Fake fainting spells. Faked wine spills. One never quite knows where they stand with you."

Noah Brogans regarded his new costar with curiosity.

Ruby was fuming. "Who cares if the wine-spilling was a ploy. What does that have to do with anything?"

Detective Molina's tone grew severe. "Miss Greenwood, things will go a lot better for you if you just come clean with us about the whole scheme. Was your necklace really stolen? Or was that another *ruse* you arranged?"

"Why would I steal my own necklace?"

"Maybe to drum up publicity for your movie?" Garcia blurted out.

"That's crazy!" protested the actress.

"But kind of genius," Noah Brogans chimed in, before catching himself and making a lip-zipping gesture.

Molina could sense the starlet's patience growing thin. If they could just goad her a bit further there was a chance she might admit to something incriminating in a fit of anger. "So why did your friend accompany you to your room? Was it to help you out of your wet clothes?"

"How dare you!" Ruby jumped to her feet and slapped Detective Molina across the face. Smarting and shocked, Molina put a hand to his burning cheek. Maybe provoking her had been a bad idea after all.

Noah Brogans managed to look both astonished and

gleeful at the same time. "I'm not a lawyer or anything, but you probably shouldn't've done that, Ruby."

"Your friend is correct." Detective Garcia stepped forward, pulling her second set of handcuffs from her belt. Detective Molina was uneasy, and he debated stepping in and stopping his partner. Technically, striking a police officer was an automatic arrest, but when it came to celebrities you sometimes let them get away with things that you would otherwise come down hard on. But Garcia wasted no time, twisting Ruby's arms behind her back, and snapping the handcuffs closed around her wrists. "Ruby Greenwood, we are placing you under arrest for assaulting an officer of the law."

"You can't do this to me! Don't you know who I am?" Ruby looked horror-struck as a lurking press photographer lit up the bar with a sudden burst of flash strobes.

"Anything you say can and will be used against you," Garcia droned.

Detective Molina sucked air through his teeth. "Hey, Garcia, don't forget about those other two jokers. I guess we'll take all three of them back to the thirteenth for questioning."

"Already on it! Babysit this perp for me and I'll be right back with the other two. And lend me some handcuffs—I'm fresh out."

A nervous Detective Molina stood silently next to a flustered Ruby. This was madness. If Ruby clammed up at the station they would be in real trouble. He had half a mind to remove the handcuffs and let her off with a warning. But if he did that they would never get the answers they were looking for, and the police department would probably be looking at a big fat lawsuit. Besides, the press already had photos of her in handcuffs. They were way out on a limb, and Molina could only hope the branch would hold their weight.

His radio crackled. "Molina?"

"Reading you loud and clear."

"They're gone!"

"What do you mean they're gone?" Detective Molina paled. "Didn't you say you handcuffed them?"

"I did! They must have picked the locks or something! The cuffs are hanging from the ladder, but the suspects are nowhere to be seen."

Detective Molina closed his eyes and counted to twenty. His head was beginning to throb, and he pinched the bridge of his nose with his fingers. He had given his partner one simple task, and she had bungled it. *"Infinitus est numerus stultorum,"* he muttered out loud.

He didn't think anybody had heard him, but Noah Brogans, still sitting at the bar, looked up. "That was Latin, right? I played a Latin teacher on a television show once. Had to memorize a bunch of phrases like that one. What does it mean?"

Detective Molina stared at the sunny faced actor. "It means infinite is the number of fools."

"Right on. I'm with you on that one all the way!"

62. WILFREDO:
A WATERY GRAVE BECKONS

Wilfredo trudged up the stairs to his building, exhausted after a long day. As the first understudy his job was less stressful now. With opening night coming up all the pressure was on Sebastian Estrada and Cassandra. But he hated watching Estrada put his own macho stamp on the character of the knight. On top of that, seeing Cassandra rehearsing onstage with that jerk was nauseating. Still he was so happy for her success, and proud of the part he had played in discovering her talent.

Wilfredo had been doing a lot of soul searching these past few days. Now that he knew Cassandra was the Cat Burglar his only option was to come clean with her about his own secret life as a costumed vigilante. But before he did that there was one other bit of business that needed taking care of. A difficult task that was weighing heavily on him.

Wilfredo unlocked the door of his empty apartment, and it swung open before him. All he wanted to do was grab a beer and plop down in front of the TV, but he knew it would be a mistake to put things off any longer. He needed his sanity back. He reached out with his left hand and toggled the hall light. The dummy was sitting in its usual spot on the shelf. Its frozen eyes met his own.

Why the long face, Freddy? Grab a beer or two and put your feet up. That'll fix you. We all have our vices! Yours is cheap suds straight from the bottle, mine is dunking my head in a barrel of rum!

"Actually, Captain, I'm thinking it's a good night for a swim."

What? But I can't swim! And I'm allergic to water! I'm made out of wood, remember? Soak me in brine and I'll start to rot!

"All the same, I'm putting a dip in the East River on the to-do list for tonight. You can't say you didn't have it coming. Constantly undermining me with your little whisper routine. Giving me nothing but lousy advice. And you did your best to sabotage my chances with Cassandra."

So we have different tastes in babes! That's not a crime. And maybe I do stick my oar in when I shouldn't, but I mean well, Freddy. Let me sit here on this shelf and I promise you won't hear a peep out of me all week.

Wilfredo wasted no time digging his duffel bag out of the coat closet. Steeling himself, he walked over to the shelf, grabbed the croc, and stuffed him inside, zipping it closed. "Sorry, Captain, but we're way overdue for this little field trip."

It's dark in here, Freddy! If you're trying to put a scare in me then job done! Why not drop me off at Goodwill? We're not savages, Freddy!

Wilfredo trudged out the door and back down the stairs. Out on the street he unlocked the chain that was wrapped around Toby's rusty old bike and strapped the duffel bag onto the rack over the rear wheel. Hopping on, he rode south along Clinton Street, made a right on Delancey, and then turned left on Chrystie. The sun had long since set, but the city retained a peculiar glow that lit up the streets and the buildings around him.

He soon made it to the entrance of the Manhattan Bridge, which he'd picked because its bike lane ran right along the edge over the water. The narrow path had a smattering of kamikaze cyclists speeding across in both directions. Wilfredo took it slow. It was an uphill climb, and by the time he reached the center of the bridge he had worked up a sweat, in spite of the cool weather. Pulling over to the side he propped the bike up against a concrete pylon. A railing separated the bike path from the river, with a tall chain-link fence projecting upward from it. Wilfredo gazed through the fence at the inky water below, its treacherous currents rippling under the bridge. With shaking hands he unzipped the bag and pulled out the croc. The dummy's eyes rolled open.

Freddy, old pal, You're taking this little joke way too far. Is this really the sort of thing you want on your conscience?

"Sorry, Captain, but this is the end of the road." He held the wooden dummy in his hands and Captain Pete stared up at him with pleading eyes. Wilfredo resisted the temptation to put his hand inside and work the levers one last time.

Wilfredo swung his arm in an arc, lobbing the dummy up and over the fence. Captain Pete spun end over end as he fell silently into the yawning void. It felt like ages before he hit the water, the splash drowned out by the noise from the bridge traffic. Straining his eyes in the dim light, Wilfredo could barely make out a green dot that bobbed to the surface, floating slowly out of sight as it was carried under the bridge. Wilfredo blinked repeatedly, as the significance of what he'd just done finally hit home. He braced himself for an angry verbal onslaught, but for the first time in many months, the only sound in his head was blissful silence.

63. DETECTIVE MOLINA: A KNIFE IN THE BACK

Detectives Molina and Garcia were both called into Lieutenant Kopski's office. They found him sitting silently at his desk, his chair turned to face the window, his steepled fingers tapping silently. Detective Molina cleared his throat. "You wanted to see us, sir?"

Kopski swiveled around, menacing eyes boring into them. "I just finished talking to the captain." Kopski paused to let the significance of this remark sink in. Then, almost yelling, he continued: "And the captain just got off the phone with the chief!" The lieutenant paused again, raising his eyebrows meaningfully. Then his voice reached a thunderous crescendo: "And the chief just got off the phone with the mayor! Miss Greenwood's lawyer has kindly agreed not to sue us for criminal incompetence if we dismiss all the charges immediately and issue a public apology!"

Detective Molina unfolded his handkerchief and used it to mop his brow. He exchanged a worried glance with Garcia. This was their worst nightmare. Celebrities always used their connections to bring political pressure on what might otherwise be a clear-cut case.

Kopski leaned forward on his desk, putting his weight on his beefy fists. "So let me get this straight. You two were on the scene when this high-priced pearl necklace was stolen, and you not only failed to prevent the theft, or recover the stolen item, but you then arrested the victim of the crime, who happens to be a famous actress?"

Detective Garcia looked hurt by this characterization of events. "But, sir, she struck Detective Molina."

"She slapped him. And the way I heard it Molina had just called her a slut! That practically qualifies as entrapment when dealing with a temperamental Hollywood actress."

Detective Molina grimaced. "We are still convinced she's involved with the robberies in some way. That she's trying to drum up publicity for this movie of hers."

Kopski pointed a fat finger at him. "I remember you telling me all about this crazy theory of yours, Molina. But you're forgetting a little thing we in the police business like to call *proof*! You can't run around the city arresting high-profile individuals without proof!" Kopski emphasized this last remark by pounding on his desk with a closed fist. "The real Cat Burglar probably found out about this party and showed up looking for an easy score. Your report says that you captured and handcuffed two likely suspects, but that they managed to escape? Can one of you please explain to me how *that* happened?"

Detective Molina realized he urgently needed to start deflecting blame for this botched investigation onto his partner. He felt a key point was that he hadn't been involved in the two perps' escape. "Well, sir, I initially assisted in apprehending them, but one of the suspects threw her bag off the roof and I went to retrieve it because we thought it might contain the missing necklace."

Lieutenant Kopski's nostrils flared. "But it didn't. So in

other words, you fell for a cheap trick! How does that help your case? And what about you Detective Garcia? How the hell did you manage to lose track of those two suspects?"

The corners of Detective Molina's mouth twitched. Now *she* was in the hot seat. "Well, sir, Detective Molina abandoned me on the roof with the two suspects to go retrieve this irrelevant bag, so I was forced to cuff them both myself, which I did. Then he radioed me that I needed to locate Ruby Greenwood back at the event, since he was convinced she was the ringleader. So I was forced to divert my attention there. And by the time we returned they had picked the lock on the handcuffs."

"Is that accurate, Detective Molina?"

Detective Molina was astounded by his partner's audacity. "I did radio her, that's true, and we did suspect Miss Greenwood at the time, but—"

"But nothing!" Kopski interrupted him.

"I was just following my senior partner's lead the whole time," Garcia insisted. "I figured he had more experience, and that he must have some good reason for suspecting Miss Greenwood. I had no idea it was all based on some wild conjecture."

Detective Molina felt his jaw drop. He stared at Garcia incredulously. Did she think she could get away with pinning it all on him? "Now hold on a minute!"

Kopski sliced the air with his hand. "Zip it, Molina. I think we've heard enough from you. In all my years in the force I've never witnessed this level of incompetence. You are both an embarrassment to the NYPD. But Detective Garcia is right, you were the senior officer, and you took the lead on this investigation, so as far as I'm concerned most of the blame for this fiasco falls on you!" He leaned back in his chair and put his feet up on his desk. "Detective Molina, I'm advising the chief that you be suspended for thirty days without pay. All your open cases will be reassigned to other teams. When you return from suspension, I am going to recommend to the captain that you be demoted to junior detective. The two of you will still be a team but Garcia will take over the senior role, and hopefully keep *you* out of trouble. You're both dismissed."

Detective Molina walked out of the lieutenant's office in a daze. Garcia patted him on the shoulder. "Cheer up, Molina. Just think of it as an overdue vacation. That could've gone a lot worse for both of us. At least we still get to work together. I'll go grab the box of donuts from the break room. A Boston cream will help lift your spirits!"

The bald detective let out a heavy sigh. "*Splendide mendax*," he muttered. Because that's what his young partner was—splendidly false.

"You know, Molina, I've really learned a lot from you these past few months! This could be one of those the-student-has-become-the-master type situations. But as the senior partner going forward, I'm going to have to put the kibosh on all these classical references of yours. We need to find you some new lingo that isn't based on a language that's been dead for the past six hundred years."

64. RUBY:
BIRDS OF A FEATHER

It was nearing 6 p.m. when Ruby Greenwood tottered out of the thirteenth precinct with as much dignity as she could muster. Oversized sunglasses hid her anxious eyes from the world. She was still wearing the black miniskirt from her costume, but Annie and her lawyer had procured her a red sweater so that she didn't have to sit behind bars looking ridiculous in black-and-white stripes.

In the silver lining department there were no paparazzi staking her out. Thank goodness for that, because she had caught a look at herself in the restroom mirror and knew she looked frightful. She would book a session at the spa in the morning, and hopefully they could work their magic to undo the damage done to her complexion from spending five hours locked in a holding cell with a bunch of actual prostitutes. But right now what she needed most was a stiff drink. Something to help settle her frazzled nerves.

She walked west along the south side of Nineteenth Street, the famed gated park on her right, and soon stumbled across a small bar just past the intersection with Irving Place. It had a red awning poking out into the street, a fake elephant head above the door, and a sign that read GRAMERCY PARK SALOON. Her feet marched her through the door of their own accord.

Inside it was dark and narrow, with a long bar running along the left-hand side of the room. There were various other fake animal heads adorning the walls, giving the place a faux explorers club vibe that somehow worked. She parked herself on a barstool at the far end, where it was less crowded, and ordered a whiskey sour from a stocky bow-tied bartender.

When it arrived she drained half of it in one go. Only then did she take off her sunglasses and tuck them into the outside pocket of her purse. Fortunately, no one in the dimly lit bar seemed to have recognized her, as the people around her were all caught up in their own conversations. Or maybe they had recognized her but they simply didn't care? And why would they? She was a fallen star after all. A disgraced television actress who had been arrested like a common criminal, her ghastly mugshot already blanketing the internet. But perhaps that meant they would let her drink quietly by herself.

But to her dismay, a man seated two barstools to her left turned and spoke to her. "Hey, I know you," he said. Her face contorted into an uncomfortable smile as she looked over, bracing herself for the possibility of public derision, only to discover a handsome young man with friendly eyes, sitting there in a spiffy blue suit, drinking a similar cocktail to her own. Her sense of alarm faded a little. He had a pleasant, lopsided smile. "You're the actress from the play at the Cornelius?" he said. "Ruby Greenwood, Wilfredo's friend?"

Hmm. Did she know this man? "Oh, I'm sorry, have we met?"

"We were introduced briefly at that art gallery showing. I'm Cassandra's ex, Gregory. You know Cassandra, right?"

"Of course I do. And I remember you now, Gregory. It's

nice to see you again. But, you'll have to excuse me. I confess I'm not really feeling my best at the moment, and . . ." How could she put this without offending him?

"You just need to be alone with your thoughts. Say no more. I understand completely. I saw what happened to you in the news. Sounds like quite an ordeal. I'm guessing they just let you out of the thirteenth precinct and you wandered down the street."

"That's a good guess, Gregory." She hung her head, her hair draping over her glass.

"Don't feel bad. This bar picks up a lot of clientele that way. I drifted down here from the precinct myself the other day, when they let *me* out. I've been coming back since then. There's a certain camaraderie among the regulars here. Enjoy your drink, Miss Greenwood." He turned away.

She peered at him. "You don't look like the criminal type. Aren't you supposed to be a lawyer or something?"

He faced her once more, seeming surprised that she had chosen to extend their conversation. "I am a corporate lawyer, that's right. And very much an upstanding, law-abiding citizen. I just happened to get caught up in a mess that had nothing to do with me, with incompetent detectives chasing mirages left and right!"

"Exactly the same thing happened to me! I had my necklace stolen, and for some reason they got it in their heads that it had to be an inside job. It was complete garbage!"

"The detectives in that precinct are a bunch of imbeciles."

"Imbeciles! That's precisely what they are." Ruby felt herself warming to her barroom neighbor. She studied him more closely. He certainly knew how to wear a suit, and she was sure his tortoiseshell glasses were designer. He had a sculptured jaw, neatly trimmed sideburns, and a well-defined part in his hair. She couldn't believe Cassandra had blithely tossed away a catch like him. "Gregory, I could do with another whiskey sour. Do you mind doing the honors?"

"It would be my pleasure. Barkeep! Two whiskey sours!"

She patted the stool next to hers. "And on second thought, I think I could use some company after all."

"I'd be delighted. I've seen you on television by the way. I think you're simply marvelously talented, Miss Greenwood." He scooted over one stool so that they were sitting side by side.

"Thank you, Gregory. And you must call me Ruby."

"Of course—*Ruby.*" He pushed his glasses back on his nose.

"So, tell me, if you don't mind. What happened with you and Cassandra?"

"Oh, Cassandra is a great girl," he replied, "but I've come to the conclusion she was right about us. We were never really compatible long-term. She has these wild romantic notions about life, while I prefer a more dignified lifestyle, preferably filled with the finer things in life."

"Like what exactly?"

"Oh, the usual." He waved an arm over the bar. "French wines, Italian truffles, Kobe beef. And I confess to a weakness for dive watches."

"Just for show? Or do you like to scuba?"

"Mostly for show," he chuckled. "Although I've been diving a couple times down in St. Barts. I'm really more of a skier though."

"Where do you like to ski? Colorado?"

"The Alps."

"Oh. Have you been to Chamonix? I just love it there."

"Many times. My dad has a house on Lake Geneva so when I go visit him in the winter I'll spend as much time as I can up on the slopes."

Ruby leaned in a little closer. Close enough for the subtle ocean scent of his cologne to reach her. It was so nice to have a man's full attention. Gregory really knew how to make a woman feel appreciated. The whiskey was beginning to take effect and she felt a little woozy. Wild thoughts were flitting through her head, and she did her best to resist them. She barely knew this man, and a dalliance with an acquaintance was a big no-no in her business. Only, after the day she'd had she wasn't sure she cared anymore. And for some reason, the fact that he was Cassandra's ex made him that much more enticing. She took another sip of her drink, then she placed her hand on his arm and gave it a squeeze. "Gregory, you seem like the kind of man who understands discretion."

"Discretion?" His eyes locked on hers. "Discretion is practically my middle name. I assure you that I am completely reliable when it comes to personal confidences."

"Well then, how about we continue our conversation someplace a little more private? Like my hotel room terrace?"

He arched an eyebrow at her, his face breaking into another lopsided smile. "I think that's a capital idea." Digging a couple twenties from his wallet, he tucked them under his empty glass.

65. WILFREDO:
HUM DUM DINGER

Wilfredo trudged through the East Village, his gloved hands shoved in the pockets of his barn jacket. The early morning light was slowly brightening the city landscape around him, and the windless morning had robbed the cold air of its bite. He hung a left on Sixth Street, walking west, on his way to meet Cassandra for breakfast at the Empress Café, a place she talked up all the time. Apparently, she had been a regular there since she first arrived in the city ten years ago. Part coffee shop, part psychic parlor, it had a loyal following among Alphabet City locals.

Wilfredo had called Cassandra late last night and told her that he needed to see her. That he had something important to tell her. And since breakfast was her only free time of the day, they had agreed to meet early at her favorite spot. He'd woken up at dawn, and spent the early hours of the morning pacing nervously in his apartment, wondering how she would react when he fessed up about his alter ego.

Of course he was a man with two secrets, and part of him wanted to get them both off his chest in one go, but he was leaning toward saving the second for another day. He didn't have high hopes that Cassandra might feel the same way about him. She was probably still smarting from her broken engagement, and even if she was ready to move on it seemed obvious to him that a heart-stoppingly beautiful girl like her was way out of reach. It would be better not to risk their friendship twice in one day.

Crossing Avenue A he saw her up ahead standing outside the café. His heart skipped a beat. She spotted him too and gave a friendly wave, followed moments later by a hug. "I don't think I've ever seen you up this early before, Wilfredo. Wait until you try their hot chocolate. It's out of this world!"

"I hope I'm not late. When do you have to be at the theater?"

"Call time is ten a.m. sharp. But don't worry, we have plenty of time to enjoy our breakfast."

"Feels like they're really running you ragged."

"Ugh. It's nonstop. Weekends, holidays, it's never-ending. But I wouldn't trade it for the world. C'mon, let's go in. This place draws early birds from all over."

They stepped into the café, and Wilfredo found himself standing in a whimsical room with beaded ceilings, the walls covered from floor to ceiling with framed tarot-themed prints. Filtered light coming in through sheer purple curtains gave the room a pinkish glow. "Sweet!"

"Pretty cool, right?" Cassandra looked over at the row of booths along the right-hand wall, and she frowned when she saw that they were all taken. The place was already bustling with a modish young crowd.

"Hey, why don't we get our breakfast to go?" Wilfredo suggested, not relishing the prospect of an audience for his big disclosure.

"Sure. Why not?" Cassandra nodded agreeably. They took their place at the back of the register line, and when they got to the front they ordered hot chocolate and cinnamon twist pastries on Cassandra's recommendation.

Minutes later they were back outside with their breakfast. Wilfredo was clutching a hot chocolate in a paper cup in one hand and a brown paper bag in the other, while Cassandra cupped her hot chocolate in both hands, blowing on the steamy surface.

They wandered down the block, crossing over to the south side of the street, and soon found an empty stoop lit up by a patch of early-morning light. Making himself comfortable on the rust-colored step, Wilfredo took a sip of the hot chocolate. "Wow! You weren't kidding about this cocoa. It's creamy, but not so thick you feel like you're drinking melted chocolate."

"Yep. Try dipping the cinnamon twist in it."

He did as she suggested and his eyebrows shot up with surprise. "So good."

A smiling Cassandra took a few bites of her own pastry, warily eyeing a pigeon that landed on the stoop railing. The bird regarded them with interest, plotting the best way to move in on their crumbs. Cassandra took another sip of her hot chocolate and looked over at Wilfredo questioningly. "So what did you want to talk about?"

Wilfredo stared down at his work boots. "I need to tell you something, but you have to promise me you won't freak out."

"Ooh. This sounds like it's going to be good. Let's hear it!"

Wilfredo hoped he wasn't about to ruin her day. Setting his cup down on the step beside him, he put his hands together and let out a long breath. "You know my Foxman costume at the launch party the other day?"

"And how would I know that?"

"Oh. Right. Right. Right. I see. Jeez, this is going to be more complicated than I thought." Wilfredo unzipped his jacket, feeling suddenly warm. "Okay, so here's the thing. I know you were there, because I saw you there."

"You did?"

"Yes, you were wearing a Cat Burglar costume. Or should I say you were wearing *the* Cat Burglar costume. And you had a stolen necklace around your neck."

"What an extraordinary allegation. Are you accusing me of being the real Cat Burglar?"

"Yes." He looked at her pointedly. "I know your secret."

"You do? Well then. You got me! I confess, I am the Cat Burglar." She grinned, a hint of laughter visible in her eyes.

"I'm being serious, Cassandra."

"Me too. But you know, there were only two people who saw me with my mask off. A female cop and Foxman himself."

"Well that brings me to the other thing I needed to tell you. That was me. I am Foxman."

"You are?"

"Yes. It was me the whole time."

"You're saying you ride around town on a skateboard, dressed as a fox, on the lookout for petty criminals to bust?"

"That's right. I mean, I did. My crime-fighting days are behind me. But I was the guy in those videos. And I'm the one who tackled you on Halloween."

"The one I threw over my shoulder like a sack of potatoes?"

"Me."

"Well, Wilfredo. I have a confession of my own." She took another sip of her drink. "I already knew you were Foxman."

"Wait? What?" Wilfredo felt upended. "How?"

"I peaked in your backpack at the pool hall the other day and saw your costume there. It was the alien face sticker on your longboard that tipped me off."

Wilfredo stared at her, stunned. "I can't believe you already knew! But that means that the other day, when we were handcuffed to the ladder, you knew it was me the whole time?"

"Yep. When I first found out, I admit it knocked me back, and I needed a day or two to wrap my head around it. But eventually I saw the humor in the situation."

"So *that's* why you got so weird at the pool hall."

"Yeah. I was worried you would hate me once you found out I was the Cat Burglar. It seemed to me that Foxman was a guy gripped by a powerful loathing for criminals."

"I could never hate you, Cassandra."

"Well that's settled then. We won't let a little thing like being each other's nemesis ruin our friendship."

"You're enjoying this, aren't you?"

She took another bite of her cinnamon twist. "Sorry, but the look on your face was priceless. But I'm glad you finally decided to tell me."

"I'm done with secrets."

"Me too. But it was rather fun while it lasted."

"We're lucky we didn't end up sitting in neighboring jail cells," Wilfredo pointed out.

"The situation got a little fraught, I admit."

Suddenly, Wilfredo was struck by an alarming thought. "Hold on a minute. Were you in the hotel room the other day when I was alone with Ruby?"

"When you went down to help her change out of her wet

clothes? Yeah. I was there the whole time, hiding on top of the closet dresser. I had a front-row seat for when she whipped off her sweater and threw herself at you!"

"That was something, wasn't it?"

"But rumor has it you're crazy about someone else?" She dipped the last bit of her twist in the hot chocolate and popped it in her mouth. "I can't imagine who that might be?"

Caught off guard, Wilfredo fidgeted with the paper sleeve of his cup. He realized it was no use playing games since his opponent had already gotten a peek at all his cards. "There is this one girl I just can't get out of my head. Not since the first time I met her. I'm crazy about her, even though she likes to run around the city pinching people's wallets for fun."

"That's funny, because there's this amazing guy who I can't stop thinking about. His only failing is that he likes to dress up in a fuzzy orange costume and skateboard around the city chasing crooks."

Wilfredo looked deep into her fiery green eyes. He couldn't bring himself to believe it. "So, does that mean . . ."

Cassandra leaned in and kissed him, soft and slow on the lips. She tasted like chocolate and sugar. "There. Does that answer your question?" she whispered.

Wilfredo felt breathless and dizzy. He couldn't think of what to say, so he just took another sip of his hot chocolate, feeling the warm rays of the sun on his skin, and stealing a glance at the beautiful girl sitting expectantly beside him. Could he really be this lucky? Then it occurred to him that he didn't have to use words to answer her. Reaching out he took her face in his hands, pulled her close, and poured his whole heart into a kiss.

66. THE CAPTAIN: A BAD PENNY

The sun was still low in the winter sky when a mother and her six-year-old boy appeared on the rocky Dumbo beach. A tan miniature poodle trotted contentedly ahead of them, relishing its early-morning walk. The mom parked herself on a wooden beam that was wedged on the rocks and gazed out at a green tugboat steaming up the river with the Manhattan skyline in the background. Her son amused himself by throwing rocks into the water, while the little dog alternated between barking excitedly at the boy and running around in circles, never wandering too far.

Every so often her son would demand that she watch him complete a record-setting throw, and she would conjure up a dose of feigned parental amazement. The beach was peaceful at this early hour when they had it all to themselves. A few other dog walkers and joggers were up and about, but the tourists and day-trippers wouldn't arrive for hours. The only interruption to the morning's quiet was the occasional train rumbling across the Manhattan Bridge.

"Hey look, Mommy. What's this?" He was pointing at an object washed up on the shore, half buried in the line of seaweed. The boy turned it over with a stick and a green crocodile snout poked up out of the muck. "It's some kind of doll!" he yelled. Intrigued, the mother stood up and wandered over to take a closer look. The dog joined them, sniffing warily at the peculiar flotsam.

"He's got a hat. He looks like a sailor." There was an edge of excitement in the boy's voice.

"It's more like a captain's hat, and look at those brass buttons on his coat," replied the mom. "I don't think he's a doll, I think he's a dummy." She could see the line where the jaw hinged.

"Ms. Anna says we're not supposed to use that word."

"I mean, he's a ventriloquist dummy. The kind you put your hand in, and pretend like they talk."

"Oh. I've seen those!" The boy used his stick to pull strands of seaweed off the dummy. "Can we take him home with us, Mommy? Please!"

"I don't know, Owen, he's in pretty bad shape. He's probably rotten from being in the water. And there could be all sorts of crabs and mites burrowed in his clothes. I think we're going to have to just leave him here."

"But, Mommy, he's like treasure! I bet Daddy can clean him up and fix him. We could get him working again!"

She bent down and inspected the dummy. His paint work was still holding up well, and she could tell that real craftsmanship had gone into the making of it. Her husband *was* handy, and it could be a good father-son project. The poodle let out an uncharacteristic growl aimed at the half-buried crocodile, and the boy shooed the dog away. With a sigh, the mom dug out her reusable shopping bag from her tote. She wouldn't be using this bag for groceries again.

Gingerly, she grabbed hold of the wooden head and pulled him out from under the stones and the seaweed.

She gave him a shake, and clumps of sand and algae rained down to the ground. Upright, the doll's painted eyes blinked open and it stared at her with a toothy white smile. There was something distinctly creepy about this thing, and for a second she was tempted to toss him back on the beach. But then her eyes dropped to little Owen, who was gazing up at her hopefully, his little hands holding open the bag. With a sigh she dropped the croc into it. She was going to regret this, she was sure of it.

"What should we call him?" Owen asked.

"You guys will come up with a good name. Captain something or other I imagine."

"He's the Captain! Three cheers for the Captain!" The young boy twisted his face into a sneer and exclaimed: "*Welcome aboard, mateys!*" in a cheerful, raspy voice.